CHAPTER 1
SAFE HOUSE

Focus, Seb. This really isn't that hard.

It really isn't. But all the noise from outside Sebastian's window is making it impossible to concentrate. He sighs heavily, frustrated as he sits by the desk in his cluttered dorm room.

He doesn't mind college, he really doesn't. He actually rather *likes* the studying, the lectures and the assignments. He has always been rather brainy, and he loves learning new things. The *other* part of college life, though, the parties, the noise, the obnoxiously loud students who never actually seem to study at all... Those things, he can do without.

Sadly, though, he doesn't have much of a choice than to simply put up with all of it. His dorm is smack in the middle of a particularly rowdy part of campus, and right now, just weeks before some major exams, everyone seems to have chosen to simply deny the whole thing. That is, denying the fact that they actually have work to do, and instead throwing all that out the window and party, instead. It makes Seb sigh irritably, in his solitude. The one upside of it all is that he doesn't have a roommate, so when he's here in his room, he is generally never directly disturbed.

He stares down at the book in front of him. Normally, he's not really the best at math; he's maybe a bit above average, at best, and he's only taking this course for some extra credit. Literature is his thing, writing and creating, poetry and novels. But still, he has never been so bad with math that all the numbers seem to flow together and glare at him mockingly from the pages, like they're doing right now.

Seb glances at the clock on his wall; it's just past one a.m. No wonder he isn't getting anything done.

He sighs heavily and gets up from his desk, abandoning the notes and books and numbers. Instead, he makes his way over to the window, which is just slightly open. He peers down from his third floor room, at all the people running around on the lawn and in and out of the dormitory buildings. He figures he could just close the window; that would drown out at least *some* of the noise. But it's just so hot outside, unusually hot, and his room has no air conditioning besides an old fan, sitting on his bedside table. It's currently turned on and buzzing away, but not accomplishing much else than simply moving around and directing the already warm air, rather than cooling it down.

Seb is already stripped down to a pair of worn jeans and an old t-shirt, his feet bare and his short, dark brown hair messed up and ruffled from all the times he has pulled his fingers through it in the last few hours, either from frustration, fatigue or heat exhaustion. Closing the window would make it slightly worse. But at least he might be able to get some peace and quiet.

As soon as he closes the window, Seb realizes how little difference it actually makes, but it's worth it. He can't wait for everyone to just shut up and stop keeping him up all night. It's in the middle of the week, for god's sake!

His dorm room is small, but it does have its own bathroom, and he goes into it to splash some water on his face. It helps a bit, clearing his head for a moment, and it leaves part of his hair dripping water onto his face. His hair isn't exactly too long, just long enough to make it look pretty messy all the time, kind of like he has just gotten out of bed.

He just leaves it, though, and doesn't dry off. It's actually cool and nice, and he closes his eyes, leaning with his hands against the sink, exhaling slowly. It's amazing how tired he feels.

It's the sudden sound of someone banging on the door that makes him snap his eyes open again, startled.

"Jake!" a voice calls from out in the hallway, and Seb flicks his gaze to the closed door, his eyes narrowed and a frown on his face. "Come on, man, open up!"

Seb hesitates, hoping the guy outside will just realize that he has the wrong room, and leave, but he just keeps at it.

"Jake," he calls, drawing out the one syllable in a sing-song voice, his banging on the door changing into rhythmic knocking instead. It's almost like he's drumming on the surface with his knuckles. "Come on. If you don't open up, I'm just gonna stand here all night. You know I will!"

Seb sighs in exasperation as the guy keeps knocking. So he *isn't* going to leave anytime soon. Seb might as well let him know that Jake doesn't live here, whoever the hell that is.

The knocking keeps going even as Seb unlocks the door and pulls it open, leaving the guy outside standing with his hands practically frozen in mid-air, before dropping them. He flashes a cocky, slightly triumphant smile.

"Hey, bro—" he says, before cutting off. His smile falters and he just looks at Seb for a few moments, his expression changing into one of almost amusing suspicion. His eyes narrow as he pulls back to scrutinize the guy in front of him, who clearly isn't Jake. Then, finally, he points at Seb.

"You're not Jake," he says, and Seb raises one eyebrow.

"No shit," he says. "I just thought I'd let you know that, so you'd stop breaking down my door."

The guy nods slowly, as though letting this new information sink in, and Seb realizes that he is rather drunk. Or *very* drunk, actually.

"You wouldn't happen to know where my little brother *is*, would you?" he asks, and Seb frowns at him incredulously.

"Dude, I don't even know *who* your brother is," he says, a slightly annoyed edge to his voice. "Go bang on someone else's door, you'll find him eventually."

"I *should* do that," the guy says, cocking his eyebrows and nodding, as though Seb just proved a most excellent point. "I need someplace to hide. He usually helps me out."

At these words, he looks around him, up and down the currently abandoned corridor. He furrows his brow in confusion, and Seb follows his line of sight. Well, he supposes that all these identical doors *would* be confusing to someone who is completely plastered.

The guy sighs heavily and turns back to Seb.

"Alright," he says, slurring slightly. "Well, thanks, I'll just—"

He whips his head to the left at the sudden sound of approaching footsteps, his eyes actually widening the slightest bit. Then he turns back to Seb.

"Dude, let me hide in here," he says, his words rushed, and Seb gives him the best *are you fucking kidding me*-look he can muster.

"Dude, no!" he says, but the guy doesn't relent.

"Please," he says, his expression actually pleading. "Just for a few minutes, I swear."

"You can't just—"

"Awesome, thanks."

Seb definitely isn't skinny (he has always preferred the term *wiry*), but he is still whisked aside with astounding ease by the larger, well-built guy who simply just slips in through the door and into his room. Seb barely has time to make a shocked, disbelieving face, before the other guy snaps him out of it.

"Close the door, man!" he says, his voice hushed, and Seb does as he's told, in lack of anything else. He locks the door out of habit, and just seconds later hears the distinct sound of high heels on the floor of the hallway outside. The steps sound rushed, not really angry, tapping loudly, and Seb hears a frustrated sigh from outside his door. Then the steps fade away again, making their way down the hall and off this floor.

Silence lingers for a few seconds—not counting the muffled noise from outside his window—before Seb turns around at the sound of the other guy sighing with relief.

"Whoa," he says with a chuckle, and Seb just looks at him. He's standing in the middle of the cluttered, dimly lit room, intoxicated relief and light-heartedness all over his face. "That was a close one."

Seb frowns, just utterly confused.

"What the hell was that?" he asks, and the other guy just raises his eyebrows innocently.

"Hm?" he says, and Seb actually rolls his eyes.

"Why did you have to hide from *that*?" he says, jabbing his thumb over his shoulder, referring to the high-heeled girl that just left, and the guy makes a sheepish face.

"Yeah," he says. "I may have hooked up with her a couple of times. And then I may have hooked up with her friend tonight. Not a good idea."

Seb raises his eyebrows in a bored expression.

"So, you're basically hiding from a girl, because you're an asshole?" he says, and the other guy cocks his head slightly, as though deliberating whether or not that is an accurate description.

"More or less," he finally says, shrugging, with a drunk smile on his face. He seems so carefree. Seb can't help but wonder if he's always like that or if it's just when he's drunk.

"Yeah, whatever," he says with sigh. He really doesn't have time for this. "You should go."

The guy looks honestly surprised.

"Dude, come on," he says, throwing his hands up in an almost pleading gesture. "Just give me five minutes. She might not be gone yet."

Seb deliberates for a few seconds, before sighing.

"Fine," he says. "Five minutes."

"Awesome," the guy says, looking pleased. Then he hesitates for a second or so, before stepping forward and holding out his hand. "I'm Evan, by the way. Evan Matthews"

Seb glances down at the extended hand, before taking it.

"Sebastian," he says slowly, as they shake hands, before looking up at Evan's face.

"Sebastian," Evan says. Seb's name slowly rolls off his tongue as though he's sampling it, an almost intrigued expression on his face, and for just a split second, Seb feels weirdly exposed. "Good name."

Seb blinks. He hasn't heard that one before, but he makes nothing of it. Instead, he just shrugs lamely.

"Most people just call me Seb," he says, and Evan nods.

"Seb," he says. "I can work with that."

Seb frowns at that, but Evan just smiles. Even in the dim light, Seb can see the way just a simple smile seems to light up his face, how his eyes are a pleasant green, his short, light brown hair messy and ruffled. He's good-looking, no doubt about that. It doesn't take a genius to figure out why he has to literally hide from girls who want him.

"You don't happen to have any beer, do you?" Evan asks, and Seb blinks.

"Beer?" he asks dumbly. Truth be told, he doesn't really drink much, so beer isn't something he generally has around. "Sorry, no."

He releases Evan's hand, realizing that they still haven't let go of each other, and Evan looks at his own hand with an amused *well, what do you know*-look that only ever seems to show up on drunk people's faces.

"But I've got water," Seb adds, a note of sarcasm in his voice, and Evan chuckles.

"Water's good," he says. "I'll have some of that."

Seb feels a stab of surprise, but doesn't mention it.

"Coming right up," he mutters instead, making his way over to the bathroom. He does have some glasses and cups lying around, and he doesn't think Evan will notice or mind if he just picks a random one. So he ends up choosing the blue TARDIS mug he got for his birthday a few years ago.

"Nice place," he hears Evan say, and he looks over his shoulder. Evan is wandering around the small room, examining the trinkets and books and discarded clothes that litter the floor, the desk chair, the bed and—well, pretty much everything.

"Thanks," Seb says, a bit awkwardly. He's not used to having visitors, and especially not drunk visitors he has never even met before, who are only there simply because they barged in through the door in the middle of the night.

Seb rinses out the mug before filling it up with cold water, and flicks off the light switch in the bathroom on his way out. Evan is standing with his back to him, apparently looking at the black poster on the wall above his bed. It has a long passage of text all over it, and as Seb slides up beside Evan, he notices how the guy is mouthing something. He wonders if he's actually reading the poster or just mumbling to himself.

"Here you go," he says, handing over the mug, but Evan doesn't take it right away.

"*And the raven, never flitting...*" he mumbles, before exhaling slowly. Then he takes the mug held out to him and looks up at Seb, only to be met by a pair of wide open, incredulous blue eyes. Evan chuckles self-consciously.

"*The Raven,*" he explains, gesturing toward the poster, and Seb just blinks.

"You know Poe?" he asks dumbly, as Evan takes a sip of water. The poster on Seb's wall has the entire poem written all over it, but people generally don't really notice it, let alone read it.

"You kidding?" Evan exclaims, his eyes slightly glazed with intoxication. "Buried alive, cutting out hearts, freaky-ass cats and shit... Son of a bitch's crazy."

Seb processes that for a moment, before deciding that that is a pretty good description of Edgar Allan Poe, and he cocks his head.

"Fair enough," he says, as Evan looks around for a place to sit. Seb quickly bends down and shoves some discarded clothes out of the way, and Evan sits down on the edge of the bed, with a tired sigh.

11

"Crazy in a good way," he adds suddenly, and Seb looks at him. "My mom read me *Tell-tale heart* when I was a kid."

He makes a low whistling noise.

"Scared the shit outta me."

Seb makes a face and hesitantly sits down beside him.

"Yeah, I can imagine," he says. "Sounds like a cool mom, though."

Evan chuckles and looks at the mug in his hands.

"Yeah," he says, smiling. "She was."

And just like that, the whole atmosphere changes, suddenly somber, and Seb swallows hard.

Was. She *was.* Is he supposed to ask about it? Offer his condolences or something? Or maybe not say anything at all? He has only known this guy for roughly five minutes, after all.

The silence drags on for a few more seconds, before Evan suddenly clears his throat.

"Whoa," he says, as though realizing the change in atmosphere. "That's, uh..."

He clears his throat again and looks up, looks around the room.

"I should go," he finally says, handing his mug to Seb. "Thanks for the water. And the safe house."

He flashes a crooked grin and Seb takes the mug from him. Evan nods slightly, before getting up from the bed. Seb looks down; he barely touched the water.

"Uh, yeah," he says, getting up as well. Evan is already over by the door. "No worries."

Evan unlocks the door and opens it, peering out into the hallway. It's empty.

"Alright," he says, pulling back and turning to Seb. "The coast is clear."

He seems to hesitate for a moment, before he claps his hand on Seb's lean shoulder. Seb just looks at him, TARDIS mug clutched in his hands, and Evan lets his hand linger for a while, before pulling away. He flashes another grin, and Seb weakly smiles back, as Evan backs out of the room.

"See you around, Seb," he says. And just like that, he's gone, closing the door behind him and walking down the hallway outside. Seb can hear his steps disappear as he leaves the floor, and for several seconds, he just stands there, staring. Then, he reanimates and looked around his room. It looks exactly the same as five minutes ago, cluttered and dimly lit, clothes scattered all over the place and school books open on the desk.

He clutches his mug a bit tighter. Everything looks exactly the same.

So why does something feel different?

CHAPTER 2
HEAT WAVE

It's still unbelievably hot outside. No one around here is really used to this kind of heat, Seb included, and as he makes his way to a lecture on English 19th century literature, he actually huffs in pure annoyance.

It's in the middle of the day, and it seems that most students are completely exhausted, either from the heat or from partying too hard. Because seriously, several of them have been partying for the last three days. Seb thought that everyone might settle down after that first night, but they haven't. And that night was bad enough.

Although, maybe not all bad. It was interesting, at least.

Seb hasn't seen Evan since then. He hasn't seen that random guy again since he barged into his dorm room in the middle of the night, not once.

Then again, he's probably busy sleeping it off or hooking up with some girl. Or both. Seb doesn't really care. It's mostly the fact that, well, he doesn't have that many friends, and so a new person is kind of a big deal, at least for a little while. Not that he's sure he'd want to be friends with Evan, anyway. He didn't really strike Seb as the brainy type.

Although, he apparently *is* a fan of Edgar Allan Poe; Seb has barely met anyone outside the courses he takes that's even properly familiar with him.

It's a rather big campus, and Seb's lecture is to be held on the opposite side of it, from his dorm. Which means that he has to cross pretty much the entire college to get there, and which means that he has to be out in this heat for most of the way.

He's taking the route around another dorm building near his, hands in his pockets and a worn, brown messenger bag slung over his right shoulder. He feels uncharacteristically tired, both due to his lack of sleep, studying for exams, and the weather, and he pulls his fingers through his messy hair, eyes directed at the ground.

He's wearing his headphones around his neck, because it's frankly too warm to bear the synthetic material of them pressing against his ears and head at the moment, and he rubs the bridge of his nose tiredly. That's when he glances at the watch on his wrist and realizes that he's running late.

"Shit, really?" he mutters to himself angrily, before hurrying his steps into a half-run. As he goes, he hears something behind him and looks over his shoulder, but it turns out to be nothing, and he turns to look straight ahead again.

He doesn't have time to stop before literally running straight into another person.

The impact is surprisingly startling, and the other guy actually almost falls over, Seb straightening and trying to stay on his feet.

"Oh, shit! Sorry!" Seb exclaims. He manages to remain standing, even though he practically slammed into this guy, and he adjusts the shoulder strap of his bag. He picks up a bundle the guy dropped on the ground, and straightens. "My bad, I just—"

"I'll take that," the guy says, and Seb looks up from the bundle in his hands—and right into the eyes of none other than Evan Matthews.

"Wha—" he sputters, thoroughly surprised, and Evan just looks at him for a few moments, as though trying to remember where he has seen him before. And then, his entire face becomes more animated.

"Oh! Seb, right?" he says, sounding almost excited, and Seb just nods lamely, mouth half-open. "Man, great timing!"

Seb just keeps standing there, staring.

"Why?" he finally asks, and Evan takes the bundle from his hands. Seb sees now that it's a worn, dark brown leather jacket, and Evan holds something else out to Seb and presses it into his hands.

"Here, hold this," he says, putting on his jacket, and Seb just stares. *What the hell is happening?*

"I don't—" he starts, but is cut off by the sound of something breaking. He looks up; it sounded like it came from the open window Evan apparently just climbed out of. And sure enough, it's followed by an angry cry that is undoubtedly female.

"Evan!" she shouts, and Evan gets the same look on his face that a child gets when getting caught doing something hilarious but forbidden, a mischievous, wide smile on his face. "I swear to god!"

"What the hell's that about?" Seb asks, turning to Evan, who keeps his eyes on the window.

"Nah, it's fine," he says dismissively. "It's just—"

His voice cuts off when he hears the sound of another voice from the window, a male one this time, and his expression changes from amused mischief to slightly amused panic. The voice quickly rises into a shout, and Evan starts.

"Shit," he says, backing away. "We gotta go."

"What?" Seb exclaims. "We? *We* don't *gotta* do anything!"

"Dude, just run!" Evan says, and Seb gapes at him.

"I've got class!" he retorts, but Evan just keeps backing away, before turning around and breaking into a run.

"Your funeral!" he yells over his shoulder, and Seb looks up when he hears the angry voice of the other guy, whom he assumes is the girl's boyfriend, in the open window. He pokes his head out, and his gaze immediately falls on Seb.

"Hey!" he shouts, and that's enough for Seb to curse under his breath and start running, Evan already having a bit of a head start.

They both run and run, and it's not until they've rounded the corner of the building and reached part of the green area that spreads across campus that they actually stop running. Seb nearly falls over from the exhaustion, leaning against a maple tree for support., and for shade, because it really is annoyingly hot outside.

"Shit, man," Evan says, panting, leaning over with his hands on his knees. "Shit. That was close."

Seb actually rolls his eyes.

"Why does that sound familiar," he mutters, and Evan glances at him.

"What?" he asks, but Seb just shakes his head.

"Nothing," he says. "I'm just trying to catch my breath."

He's leaning over now, too, his head spinning. It's so hot outside, and he has never been much of a runner, anyway. He doesn't even notice he's falling over until Evan catches him by the arm to keep him standing.

"Whoa, dude," he says, and Seb blinks. "You okay?"

"Yeah," Seb mutters, vaguely embarrassed. "It's just... really hot."

"I hear ya," Evan says, releasing Seb when he's sure he can stand on his own, and shrugging out of his undoubtedly too warm leather jacket. He lets out a deep huff, before turning to Seb again, who is still leaning against the tree for support. "You sure you're okay?"

Seb nods and straightens, uncomfortably aware of how his shirt is sticking slightly to his back, all of a sudden. He looks up at Evan, whose eyes are shining, despite his clear exhaustion, and forehead sweaty from the heat and exertion. He looks at Seb, and smiles.

"Come on," he says, cocking his head. "I'll buy you a beer."

Seb processes that for a moment, before frowning.

"I've got class," he says, but Evan just shrugs.

"So?" he says, and Seb just looks at him.

"It's in the middle of the day," he tries instead, and Evan shrugs again. Seb looks at him for a while longer, and Evan finally exhales.

"Fine, if you don't want a beer, I'll get you something else," he says, and Seb sighs, his breath finally evening out. *That's not really the issue,* he wants to say, but he refrains.

"Why?" he asks instead, and Evan quirks a smile.

"You kidding?" he says. "That's twice now you've helped me out. I owe you."

Seb just keeps looking at him, unsure how to act.

"You helped me," Evan repeats, clearly amused at Seb's reaction. "I appreciate that. Speaking of which."

He holds out his hand and nods toward Seb's closed fist, and it takes a few moments before Seb realizes that he's still clutching whatever Evan handed to him earlier. He holds it out; it's a cell phone, and he puts it in Evan's hand. Evan gives him another nod.

"Thanks," he says, pocketing it. "Now, come on."

This time, Seb doesn't question it. Instead, he just forgets all about his lecture and goes along with Evan, and he has no idea why.

An hour or so later, Seb and Evan are sitting in a pub on the edge of campus, by the bar. Evan stayed true to his word and bought Seb a beer, which Seb was actually in the mood for, even though he really doesn't drink that often, and they have both finished about half of their bottles by now.

"So, wait," Evan says, holding a hand up. "You just basically study old stories and poetry?"

Seb resists the urge to roll his eyes and sigh.

"When you put it that way, it sounds lame," he says instead, taking a sip from his beer. "But I suppose that is one way to put it."

Evan nods slowly.

"Right," he says, mirroring Seb and lifting his own bottle to his lips, drinking from it. "Sounds way smarter than what I do, though."

"And what do you do?"

"Music."

Seb feels his eyebrows rise in slight surprise. Then again, he's not sure why he would be surprised. What was he expecting Evan to be studying, anyway?

"Really?" he says, and Evan nods.

"Yeah," he says, looking down at his bottle and fiddling with label a bit with his thumb. "It's pretty useless, I guess, but... I don't know. It makes me happy."

"Then it's not useless."

Evan looks at Seb then, sincere surprise in his eyes, as though he's not used to people actually backing up his career choice.

"I guess," he says. "But I'm not the only ass with a guitar, trying to make it. I guess I could have just skipped the whole college thing and kept trying, but I wanted to do more, you know. Like, I wanted to do *only* that, and I wanted to do it *professionally*. So I applied here, and by some miracle, I got in. The music program here is really damn good, I can't believe they picked me."

A small smile spreads across his face, as he looks down at his bottle again. Seb can't help but smile, himself, when he sees it. Something about Evan's smile is just... He barely even knows the guy, but seeing him smile like that makes him feel weirdly content.

Maybe some people just have that effect on you, he thinks.

"What about you?" Evan asks, looking up at him. "Why do you study literature?"

Seb opens his mouth to come up with a good reply, but just ends up half-shrugging.

"For pretty much the exact same reasons you just said," he explains. "Only, I want to be a writer. And, apart from writing, it helps to study what other people have written. Basically."

Evan smiles crookedly at that.

"I get it," he says. And it looks as though he really does.

Neither of them says a word for a little while then. The bar is pretty much empty apart from them, the bartender, and a few lone drinkers, mellow music drifting smoothly from the speakers.

Seb wonders for a second why the place is so empty, before realizing that it's three o'clock in the afternoon. And here he is, ditching class, having a beer with Evan Matthews, a guy he didn't even know existed a few days ago. *Normal* isn't exactly the first word that comes to mind.

"Hey," Evan says, nudging Seb softly with his elbow. "Big party tonight, on campus. Some friends of mine are throwing it, the whole dorm. You coming?"

Seb groans inwardly, but exhibits nothing but a small shrug.

"I don't think so," he says. "Not really my thing."

"Come on, their parties are always off the hook," Evan says. "Trust me."

"If you say so," Seb murmurs, taking a sip of his beer, but Evan catches his words.

"What, you've never been?" he asks, his tone slightly joking. Until he realizes that Seb, in fact, hasn't been. "Seriously?"

Seb just gives him a non-committal eyebrow raise, and Evan exhales pointedly, as though disbelieving.

"Alright, well that settles it," he says. "You're going."

"No, Evan, really," Seb starts, but is interrupted.

"Yes, Seb, really," Evan mimics. "If you haven't been to a party like that, you're missing out on the whole college deal."

He looks at him pointedly, eyebrows raised.

"Don't make me drag you there," he warns, and Seb sighs. He can't believe the words that come out of his mouth.

"Fine," he says. "Alright."

Evan smiles then, in that cocky way of his, and Seb gets the feeling that he's used to getting what he wants. Then again, judging from the seemingly constant trail of girls he leaves behind, this isn't surprising.

"I'll come get you," he then adds, to Seb's surprise. "Can't have you getting lost, now can we?"

Seb smiles weakly, taking another sip of his beer, wondering what the hell he just got himself into.

CHAPTER 3
PARTY

Seb didn't think that his room could possibly be more littered with clothes than it already is.

He was wrong.

His mother has always claimed that his disorganized nature is the result of the *organized chaos in his head* that comes with being a writer and a creative person, but Seb isn't too sure he likes it much anyway. Especially not now, when he's tearing through all his clothes to find something good to wear for tonight.

After spending the better part of two hours at that bar, Evan and Seb parted ways, Evan making Seb promise once again that he would come to that stupid party tonight. And Seb promised. Kind of against his better judgment, sure, but there's just something about Evan that makes him hard to say no to. And besides, it can't hurt. Seb really needs to get out of his comfort zone.

At least, that was his logic then. Now, he's just a little bit frantic.

It's almost nine p.m. when he finally finds a shirt that isn't *too* geeky—his shirts all tend to have prints like *Vote NO on Daleks,* or *Space—the final frontier,* and other moderately embarrassing pop culture references. It's a simple t-shirt, dark grey and deliberately worn-looking, with lighter grey, widely spaced stripes.

About as interesting as my personality, Seb thinks to himself as he pulls it on, but it will do. He has never been much for vanity, anyway, and he's not sure why he's bothering with it now. His dark hair is a lost cause, as usual, all messy and unkempt, kind of like he just got out of bed.

He's just buttoning up his jeans, when there is a knock at the door.

Seb freezes, before taking a deep breath. *Relax,* he tells himself. *It's not a big deal. It's just a party.*

Then again, being rather socially awkward in larger groups of people, there is no such thing as *just* a party.

He makes his way over to the door and opens it, half-expecting to see Evan. Instead, he's met by a ridiculously tall guy with chestnut brown hair that's just long enough to fall into his eyes and touch his shoulders, and Seb vaguely wonders if he's the type to do that hair-flippy thing to get it out of the way.

24

"Hey," the guy says, with just a little hesitation. "You're Sebastian, right?"

Seb nods.

"Seb," he says. "Yeah."

"Seb, right." The guy smiles sincerely. "I'm Jake."

He holds out his hand and Seb takes it. *Jake.* That name rings a bell. Jake seems to notice Seb's confusion and elaborates.

"I'm Evan's brother," he explains. "He's running a bit late and asked me to come get you for the party, seeing as how we live in the same dorm."

Seb's eyes widen slightly in realization. Right, Jake is the one Evan was looking for that night, when he showed up here, banging on the door, completely wasted.

"Right," Seb says hesitantly, shaking Jake's hand. "Great."

Jake's smile widens slightly as he releases his grip, a sincere smile that's difficult not to trust. Seb remembers Evan referring to Jake as his *little* brother, though. He finds that hard to believe, considering how damn big he is.

A door closes somewhere further down the hall, and within moments, someone else shows up at Jake's side. The pretty blonde kisses him on the cheek, before turning to Seb.

"Hi," she says. "I'm Sophie."

Seb gives her a small, awkward wave, and she smiles at him. Her smile is sincere, too, and it's obvious from the way she takes Jake's hand and from the way he looks at her adoringly, that they're a couple.

"Seb," Seb says. "Hi."

Jake glances at them both, before clearing his throat slightly.

"So," he says. "You good to go?"

"Uh, yeah," Seb says, reanimating. "I'll just..."

He trails off and goes back inside, quickly putting on his worn Converse sneakers and double-checking that he has his cell phone and keys with him, before exiting the room and closing the door behind him. Jake and Sophie are waiting patiently, and the three of them set off down the hallway and out through the building's front door.

This was a bad idea. The thought grows stronger and stronger in Seb's head, the further away they get from the dorm. *A fucking terrible idea.*

Why the hell did he agree to this? He doesn't like parties. Hell, he barely even likes *people.* So why is he currently on his way to a place where the two intersect in the most horrible way, with two strangers, no less? On his way to meet up with *another* stranger. Because that's what Evan is, really. They really don't know each other.

Jake and Sophie are easy to talk to, though. They are both really nice, and seem to be doing their best to make Seb feel at ease. They don't even ask how Seb knows Evan, which he's kind of grateful for. He's not even sure how he would have answered that, anyway.

Jake is studying to be a lawyer, Sophie is studying to be a nurse, and all the way to the dorm where the party is, Seb is content with listening to them talk about their respective courses and such. Especially considering that *writer* feels kind of tame in comparison to such ambitious and/or noble careers.

Eventually, they reach their destination, and if nothing else, they would have heard it from miles away. The entire building in front of them seems to be crawling with people, just like the lawn outside, and Seb swallows hard. What is he *doing* here?

It's when the sound of a loud whistle penetrates the rest of the noise that Jake turns around, and after a few moments of scanning the area with his eyes, he smiles and raises his hand in a wave. Seb follows his line of sight, and there he is; Evan. He's making his way toward them, and as soon as he reaches them, he smiles and pulls Jake into a hug.

"Jakey," he says, patting his much taller brother's back, before pulling away. Then he turns to Sophie, who smiles at him in the way family does with a particularly charming and obnoxious member. He kisses her on the cheek. "Hi, Sophie."

"Glad you could make it," she says with some sarcasm, but Evan just shrugs. And then he turns to Seb, who's just standing there, suddenly petrified. He saw Evan just a few hours ago, and they had beers together and talked and hung out, and Evan was so weirdly nice to him, simply because he *helped him out.* And here he is, and suddenly, Seb just wants to run away from all this anxiety and awkwardness. It is surreal.

"Hey, Seb," Evan says, grinning, but before Seb can respond, he has pulled him into a hug and patted him on the back. Seb is so surprised that he doesn't really know what to do, and he barely has time to hug him back before Evan pulls away.

"I was worried you might not show," Evan says, cocking his eyebrows pointedly, and Seb opens his mouth to say something, but nothing comes out. Then Evan just throws his arm over his shoulders and tugs him to his side.

"This guy," he says to Jake and Sophie, pointing at the very startled and uncomfortable Seb, "saved my ass. Twice."

"Well, not really," Seb mutters. "I mean, I—"

"Don't be modest, Seb," Evan says, before releasing him and stepping away. He starts moving toward the house, backwards, arms stretched wide. "Alright, I'm here. Let's do this."

The whole experience turns out to be about as unpleasant as Seb expected.

There are people *everywhere*, drunk people, noisy people, and they keep shoving and shouting, as Seb makes his way through the house. Jake and Sophie immediately spot someone they know and go off to talk to them, but Evan, surprisingly, sticks by Seb's side pretty much the whole time. He introduces him to people, gets him drinks, and is just generally nice to him. He's pretty much the only reason Seb hasn't left yet.

He actually likes Evan. He's a bit loud and boisterous, and yes, maybe a bit obnoxious, but he seems like a good guy. And Seb is glad to have made a new friend.

It's a few hours after they arrive that Seb emerges from the bathroom only to find that Evan has vanished. Jake and Sophie left a little while ago, already. He looks up and down the hall, which is, if possible, even more crowded than before, and sighs.

Great. Maybe Evan has finally gotten sick of him and his awkwardness and actually abandoned him. He supposes he can't blame him. Still, though, it makes him feel rather disappointed, and he tries not to think about it.

It's the sound of approaching voices that makes Seb look up again.

"Come on," some guy says, coming closer. "Why not?"

"Because I said so," comes the reply. It's a girl speaking, this time, and she's making her way past Seb, when she catches his eye. The eye-contact is brief, before she suddenly grabs him and kisses him on the mouth.

Seb doesn't even have time to react, doesn't even manage to widen his eyes in surprise, before the girl has pulled away again.

"There you are," she says, smiling. "I've been looking everywhere for you."

She gives Seb a pointed look that begs him to play along, but he can't muster a single word. She keeps talking, though, saving him the trouble.

"Would you mind telling this asshole that it's not okay to hit on your girlfriend?" she asks, nodding toward the guy that just stopped dead right next to them, but Seb still can't say anything. He doesn't have to, though, because the guy just shakes his head, giving up.

"Whatever," he mutters and walks away. And Seb relaxes as the girl exhales with relief, pulling her hands off of him.

"Sorry about that," she says. "I improvised."

Seb blinks. The girl is pretty, with long, auburn hair and big, blue eyes, and she smiles at his vacant expression.

29

"Hey, do I know you?" she says, and Seb frowns, racking his brain. Yes. He recognizes her. He has seen her at a couple of lectures, always sitting in the back of the hall.

"Maybe," he says. "I'm Seb."

Her face lights up as she remembers.

"Seb, right!" she says. "I knew I'd seen you before. I'm Clara."

Seb laughs nervously, seeing as how they have already crossed whatever personal space line that would normally be there.

"Hey," he says, and she smiles. She has a really nice smile.

"Well, nice meeting you," she says. "Thanks for the help. I'll see you around."

She gives him a small wave and walks off, leaving Seb just standing there, dumbstruck.

Well, that's new. He doesn't have much time to think about it, though, before he hears a surprisingly familiar chuckle right next to him.

"Dude," Evan says, sounding impressed and drawing out the one syllable of the word. "Not bad."

Seb looks up at him, absently noticing how Evan is a couple of inches taller than him. He's smiling, making small crinkles appear at the corners of his eyes.

"I really didn't do anything," Seb says self-consciously, but Evan doesn't seem to care.

"Sure you didn't," he says, draping a heavy arm over Seb's shoulders. "Well, maybe you don't have to, with a face like yours."

Seb glances down, shocked to find that he's suddenly actually *blushing. Shit.* He doesn't blush. He never blushes.

And if nothing else, shouldn't a kiss from a random girl make him blush harder than a compliment from Evan?

"Thanks?" he says, hesitance and sarcasm lacing the word, and Evan laughs.

"It's true, man," he says, and Seb looks up at him again, hoping the flush has faded from his face. Evan is wearing the sincere, open expression of a happy drunk. "Have you looked in the mirror?"

Seb really doesn't know how to respond to that. As far as he knows, he's average-looking, at best, and if nothing else, he wasn't aware that guys could say things like that to each other. And he really doesn't know what to make of the warm, fuzzy feeling he gets as Evan says it.

Evan just looks at him for a few moments, before shaking his head.

"I need some air," he practically slurs, his eyes suddenly a bit glazed over, and he removes his arm from Seb's shoulders.

Seb doesn't move for a second, as Evan brushes past him, but then he finds himself following him.

The house has a rather big yard, and it's crawling with people. A lot of them seem to have stripped down to their underwear, actually running through a sprinkler, laughing with drunk amusement. Seb supposes he can't really blame them; even though it's in the middle of the night by now, it's still pretty hot outside, and the sprinkler probably provides a nice way of cooling off. But still, it's borderline ridiculous.

He follows after the suddenly stumbling Evan as he makes his way past all the people, all the way to the corner of the yard, where Evan actually falls to his knees. And where he proceeds to throw up in the bushes.

Seb stops dead, unsure of how to act. He isn't used to this, he *really* isn't, and he suddenly feels kind of stupid for following Evan out here in the first place.

"Evan?" Seb turns around at the sound of girl's voice, and a lightly dressed, high-heeled blonde struts up to them. "Oh my god, are you okay?"

She doesn't even seem to notice Seb, who's standing right next to Evan, and Seb rolls his eyes, despite the whole situation. He can't help it; he's sarcastic and exasperated by nature. At least when it comes to people.

Evan is still on his knees, palms to the ground, where he's holding himself up, and he doesn't answer the girl. Instead, he just shakes his head, in a way that Seb interprets as frustrated and tired. And he can't help himself.

"He's fine," he says, turning to the girl, who suddenly eyes him up and down as though he just appeared out of thin air. "He just needs some air, that's all."

The girl looks at him, as though a bit confused, then back at Evan, then back at Seb.

"Oh," she says. "Okay. Well, when he snaps out of it, give him this, would you?"

She hands Seb a small piece of paper, before smiling and walking away. Seb shakes his head as she struts off, before he looks down at the note she gave him.

Come see me. xoxo —- Jenny. There's a phone number written below the message, and Seb rolls his eyes again. Seriously.

Evan coughs loudly and Seb turns to him, quickly dropping into a crouch.

"You okay?" he asks, and Evan groans uncomfortably.

"Shit," he mumbles. "Better now."

"Great," Seb says, glancing at the note in his hand. "'Cause Jenny apparently wants you to come see her, reinforced by x's and o's."

Evan looks up then, his attention seized, and Seb holds out the note to him. Evan takes it, sits up properly and looks over at the house. Then he looks back at the note, clearly deliberating. It's obvious that he's itching to find this Jenny, and Seb feels the oddest, sinking sensation in his stomach at the thought of it. But then, to his surprise, Evan actually crumples up the note and tosses it away somewhere in the bushes. Seb raises his eyebrows.

"You're not gonna call her?" he asks, weirdly hopeful, and Evan shakes his head.

"Nah," he says, sounding drunk and exhausted. He looks around, and sighs. "I wanna go."

Seb frowns.

"Go?" he asks, and Evan groans again.

"Yeah," he says. "Where's Jake?"

"Uh," Seb replies, looking around, "I think he and Sophie left about half-an-hour ago."

Evan makes a face. He looks oddly displeased and tired, and Seb sighs heavily.

"Come on," he says, placing his hand on Evan's shoulder. "Let's go."

Evan looks up at him, oddly surprised.

"What?" he says, and Seb gets up from the ground, holding out his hand.

"I'll take you home," he says, and Evan looks at his hand for a moment, before taking it and pulling himself up.

His hand is warm and calloused, and Seb grips it firmly until Evan is standing up properly. He's still swaying a bit, but Seb figures it's good enough, and lets go of him.

"You good?" he asks, and Evan nods lamely, before they both start making their way across the yard.

Along the way, several girls—*Jenny* included—try to get Evan's attention, but it's as though they're nothing more than annoying flies, and he barely even spares them a glance.

The girls, as well as a few other people, are visibly surprised at his lack of enthusiasm, but still let him and Seb pass them by, Seb feeling weirdly self-conscious. It seems that when he's with Evan, he attracts attention in a way he isn't used to; people generally don't even look twice at him, after all.

They make their way out of the house and across the front lawn, and soon enough, they're walking along the paved walkway that zigzags across the entire campus. Seb has his hands in his pockets, Evan half-stumbling along next to him. Seb hasn't had that much to drink, and is stone cold sober compared to Evan, so he can't help but watch Evan struggle to stay focused, as they walk.

Then, he realizes something.

"Hey," he says. "Where do you live?"

Evan exhales with a huff and looks around. It's dark, except for the streetlights that are evenly placed along the walkway.

"There," he says, half-pointing in a seemingly random direction, and Seb follows his gaze.

"I'm pretty sure that's a tree, Evan," he says, and Evan narrows his eyes.

.

"So it is," he says, and Seb sighs.

"I'm gonna need more to work with, here," he says, but Evan isn't being very cooperative. Instead, he almost falls over, and Seb catches him, placing one hand firmly against his chest and the other on his shoulder. He sighs. This isn't going very well. At this rate, Evan is just going to end up passed out on the ground somewhere.

Seb looks over at his own dorm building; it's pretty close by, and he supposes that it's better than leaving his new friend out here.

"Come on," he says, supporting Evan as they start walking again, towards his dorm, this time. "Let's get you inside."

Supporting him is a bit harder than he thought, because *damn*, this guy is heavy. He's all muscle, though, at least judging from the firmness of his chest, back and shoulders, where Seb has strategically placed his hands. He's trying not to find it too weird just how acutely he notices that.

The dorm building is surprisingly quiet when they enter it, and Seb supposes that everyone is either at that party, or asleep. Either way, he's annoyed at the fact that the elevator is still broken (he can't really remember the last time it was actually working), because it means they have to take the stairs—and practically dragging a drunk Evan up three flights is a challenge.

"Alright," Seb mutters to himself as they reach his room. "Here we go."

He manages to unlock and open the door rather smoothly, and help Evan inside, and after a brief look around the room, Evan's face actually lights up a bit.

"Hey, I know this place," he slurs, smiling weakly. "I've been here."

"Yeah," Seb says tiredly. "Safe house, remember?"

Evan snaps his fingers and points at him.

"Right," he says. "The one with the poster."

Seb frowns, before realizing that he's referring to his *The Raven*-poster. And then he frowns incredulously instead, because how the *hell* would Evan remember that? Especially considering the fact that he wasn't exactly sober that night, either.

"Yeah," Seb says, as he drops his keys onto his desk, Evan still leaning against him. "That's the one."

The door is closed now, leaving them in darkness, and in lack of anything else, Seb hauls Evan over to his bed, where he practically dumps him on top of the covers. He feels incredibly light as the weight is lifted off of him, and he flicks on the lamp on his bedside table. He sees Evan's face right next to it, resting against his pillows.

"Thanks, man," Evan mutters, and Seb just looks at him.

"It's fine," he says, making a move to leave, but is surprised to feel Evan grabbing his wrist. Seb looks down at it; the grip is surprisingly soft.

"No," Evan says, looking up at Seb, green eyes glazed over. "No one's ever looked after me like this. Thank you. I mean it."

Seb is taken aback by the sincere and utter honesty in his expression, and freezes for a moment, before nodding.

"You're welcome," he musters, and Evan smiles weakly and gives his wrist a gentle squeeze, before releasing it. Then he sighs deeply, happily, and closes his eyes.

For a moment, Seb just stands there, but then the distinct sound of soft snoring and heavy breathing comes from Evan, and he rolls his eyes. But then he looks back at him. And he actually smiles.

CHAPTER 4

TELL-TALE HEART

It's a combination of being poked in the arm repeatedly, and sunlight on his face, that wakes Seb up the next morning.

He shifts, annoyed at the poking, and he groans tiredly in protest. But the poking continues, and he raises his hand to swat away whatever it is, only to be startled by the sudden feel of a hand against his fingers. His eyes fly open and he looks to his right.

"Hey, man," Evan mumbles almost incoherently, slowly retrieving his hand. "You got any painkillers?"

Seb just stares at him for several seconds. *What the hell?*

"Uh..." he says, before looking around, trying to get his bearings.

He's in his dorm room, but for some reason, Evan is lying in his bed, and Seb is slumped in the armchair nearby, right next to the nightstand. It's just close enough to the bed for Evan to reach him and poke him in the arm, so at least he knows what woke him up. And then it hits him.

Evan is in his bed.

"Dude," Evan says tiredly. "You okay?"

In his *bed*.

"Yeah," Seb says, clearing his throat.

Evan Matthews is *in his bed*.

"I'm good," he continues. "Guess I'm just not really awake yet."

He exhales tiredly and rubs his eyes, before looking at the watch that's still on his wrist; it's just past eleven a.m.. He hasn't even changed clothes since last night. He vaguely remembers sitting down after Evan fell asleep, with the intention of getting up again five minutes later and get a glass of water or something. So much for that.

"Hey," Evan says, poking him in the arm again, and Seb looks at him.

"Don't poke me," he says with tired humor, and Evan quirks an equally tired smile.

"Why not?" he says, poking him again, this time prodding all over his arm. "How else am I supposed to get your attention?"

"Dude, I'm serious," Seb warns, but his growing smile says otherwise, and Evan keeps poking, until he hits a spot by Seb's ribs that makes him squirm. *Damn it*. He hopes Evan didn't notice, but he did.

"Oh," he says, eyebrows raised conspiringly. "Ticklish, are we?"

Seb doesn't have time to deny it, before Evan makes another experimental prod against his ribs and stomach, and Seb flinches again. Evan's face stretches in a triumphant grin.

"What do you know," he says, and suddenly, Seb is a flailing mess, trying to shield himself from Evan's persistent, tickling prods.

"No, no, no," he says, an involuntary laugh bubbling up in his throat, as he tries to shy away from the touch. "Seriously, stop it."

"I can't hear you," Evan says calmly, a smile on his face. "A painkiller might help."

Seb grabs Evan's hand and tries to pry it away, but it's pretty much hopeless.

"Alright," he says, relenting. "Fine!"

Evan pulls his hand away and raises it in a disarming gesture of surrender, while Seb finds himself frozen with his hands up defensively, in some hilarious imitation of a ninja.

"Just hang on a second," he says, unfreezing, his eyes narrowed and focused on Evan as he slowly gets up from the chair. He points at him. "No shenanigans."

Evan chuckles, his eyes hooded from sleep and exhaustion. And a monster of a hangover, most likely.

"Shenanigans?" he says. "Who says that?"

Seb shrugs, and Evan sighs.

"Fine," he says. "No *shenanigans*."

Seb nods, satisfied, and makes his way over to the bathroom. He gets a painkiller from the cupboard and pours some water into a random glass he has standing there, before bringing it out to Evan. He has barely moved, happily sprawled all over Seb's bed.

My bed.

Seb swallows.

"Here you go," he says, setting the glass and the pill down on the bedside table. "Enjoy."

Evan puts the pill in his mouth and swallows it down with a big gulp of water. Then he closes his eyes and makes a pleased sound.

"Mmm," he hums. "Tastes like blackmail."

Seb scoffs, but can't help but smile, and Evan opens his eyes again and looks up at him. And he smiles right back.

"Thanks," he says, and Seb sits down in the armchair again.

"Don't mention it," he says, rubbing his eyes with one hand. He's vaguely reminded of how Evan thanked him last night. When he grabbed his wrist and looked at him like that, so sincere.

"No one's ever looked after me like this. Thank you. I mean it."

Shit, Seb almost forgot about that for a moment. At the time, it didn't feel that weird. But now, in the light of day and lack of alcohol, he suddenly realizes how weird it actually was. He doesn't know Evan that well at all, but he has a feeling that it was out of character for him, all the same.

It makes him slightly uncomfortable. But he also can't help but remember how it felt when Evan squeezed his wrist gently like that, that tired, grateful smile on his face.

"Question," Evan says, and Seb looks at him. He's lying on his back now. "How did I get here?"

Seb is honestly surprised at the sudden, sinking sensation in the pit of his stomach. Evan doesn't remember. Well, of course he doesn't. He was way too drunk for that. Still, though; why does it bother Seb that he doesn't remember?

"Well," Seb says, not showing how he suddenly feels. "You got shitfaced, and it was either bring you here or leave you on the ground somewhere to sleep it off."

Evan looks at him then, surprised.

"Thanks," he says, before the surprised expression falters. Then he frowns a bit, thinking. "Why didn't you take me to my place?"

"Because you seemed to think you lived in a tree," Seb explains, earning an amused smile from Evan. "And I don't know where you actually do live."

"Oh," Evan says, glancing away, as though he hadn't considered that. Then he looks back at Seb. "You should come over sometime."

Seb notices how he actually clenches his fist then, but Evan doesn't seem to.

"I mean," Evan elaborates, "I've been here twice, already. Seems fair."

Seb nods slowly.

"Yeah," he says. "Sure."

Neither of them says anything for a few moments, they just look at each other, and Seb feels oddly frozen. It's like he can't look away, like Evan's eyes are keeping him in place. Keeping him anchored.

The stare is broken, though, when Evan clears his throat and sits up heavily. He flinches, as though someone just hit him in the head.

"Fuck, this hangover's gonna kill me," he mutters, and Seb looks at him as he squeezes his eyes shut.

"You'll be fine," he says, surprised to hear that his own voice is devoid of any sarcasm or awkwardness, and Evan looks over at him. He looks like he's about to say something, but instead, he just smiles. Then he gets up and makes his way over to the bathroom, locking the door behind him as he enters. And Seb exhales slowly, as though relaxing from a kind of tension he wasn't aware of. He can't imagine why.

The knock that's suddenly heard from his door surprises him, and Seb frowns. Who the hell could that be? Still, he gets up from the chair and makes his way over to the door, and pulls it open. He's surprised to find Jake standing there in the hallway.

"Hey," he says, smiling. "Hope I'm not interrupting anything."

"What?" Seb says, before managing to be more articulate. "No, not at all. What's up?"

Jake looks a bit uncomfortable.

"You haven't seen Evan, have you?" he asks. "I haven't seen him since last night, and he won't answer his phone."

Seb's eyes widen slightly, inexplicably uncomfortable.

"Actually, he's—" he starts, but is cut off by the sound of his bathroom door opening, and Jake frowns. Seb glances back at Evan, who comes shuffling out of the bathroom, only to stop dead when he sees his brother. Then he smiles, in a typical, mischievous, big brother kind of way.

"Hey, Jake," he says, giving his brother an upward nod, and Seb slowly looks back at Jake. He's still frowning, as

43

though confused, before he forms his mouth in an attempt to speak.

"Oh," he finally settles on, raising his eyebrows slightly, still confused. "Okay. Great."

He clears his throat, and Evan walks over to the door and places himself next to Seb.

"What?" Evan says, his tone one of joking accusation.

"Nothing," Jake replies. "It's just... Well, I can't remember the last time you *didn't* end up in some random girl's room."

Evan shrugs, and Seb stares downward, at a spot somewhere behind Jake's waist. Suddenly, he feels very uncomfortable and awkward, like he doesn't want to be part of this conversation. If nothing else, it makes him uncomfortable how simultaneously relieved and bothered he feels when Jake says that, about Evan for once *not* hooking up with a girl.

"Anyway," Jake continues, frowning again, suddenly a bit annoyed. "I called you like five times. Why didn't you pick up?"

Evan cocks his head in thought.

"I didn't hear anything," he says, digging through his pockets to find his phone. He pulls it out and checks the screen, before raising his eyebrows. "Look at that."

He looks up at Jake again.

"Sorry, man," he says, shrugging. "Heavy sleeper."

Jake sighs, clearly tired of his brother's behavior.

"Did you hear anything?" Evan asks, nudging Seb, who practically jumps from surprise at being addressed directly.

"What?" he blurts, looking up. "No, nothing."

It's true; he didn't hear Evan's phone ring once during the night.

Evan cocks his head pointedly at Seb, looking at Jake, as though presenting undeniable proof of his own innocence, but Jake just shakes his head.

"Whatever," he says. "I just wanted to see you were okay."

Evan nods.

"Thanks, Jakey," he says, using that ridiculous version of a nickname that Seb has already heard a couple of times, by now. "I'm good."

Jake just looks at him for a moment, concern apparent beneath the annoyance, and he nods.

"Okay," he says. Then he looks at Seb. "Thanks."

Seb doesn't ask him what he means; clearly, Jake understands that he's the one who made sure Evan got home safe. Well, sort of home. Seb can't find the words to respond, though—the concern and gratitude in Jake's expression is a bit much.

"See you around," Jake says then, slapping his hand against Evan's shoulder, and Evan quirks a cocky smile.

"Yeah," he says. "See ya."

And with those words, Jake leaves, and Seb slowly closes the door behind him. He turns to Evan, who just cocks his eyebrows.

"He worries too much," he says, before making his way back into Seb's room, and Seb hesitates for a moment.

"Well," he tries, "you didn't answer your phone. I'd be worried about my big brother, too."

Evan doesn't answer him. Instead, he gets a weirdly tense expression, like he's clenching his jaw. Seb decides not to mention the matter again.

"And, by the way," he says, frowning. "Were you planning on just staying here? 'Cause you're making yourself awful comfortable."

As soon as the words are out of his mouth, he regrets saying them. He meant to sound joking, but like always, his attempt falls flat and he just comes off as rude. At least, that's what he has been told, and that's how most people seem to perceive him.

And if nothing else, as he says it, he realizes that he doesn't *want* Evan to leave. He *really* doesn't want him to.

But whatever other people hear when Seb talks like that, it seems lost on Evan, who just smiles. He's over by the bookcase at the foot of Seb's bed, skimming over the spines of the many books he has there, trailing his finger along some of them.

"I *was* planning on leaving," he says lightly, and Seb's heart stops. "But with that attitude, I think I *should* stay for a bit."

And Seb's heart starts beating again, albeit a bit faster than a moment ago. He watches as Evan keeps trailing along the books with his fingers.

"Nice collection you've got here," he mutters, and Seb finally unfreezes and makes his way over there.

"Thanks," he says, watching Evan as he looks at the books. His eyes are lit up, focused and moving as he quickly reads the titles, and Seb realizes that he's standing rather close. Seb is standing almost right next to him, close enough to smell the worn leather of the jacket Evan was wearing last night. It smells nice.

"Here," Evan says, straightening, and Seb blinks, as though coming out of some trance. Evan uses his finger to pull out one of the books, which he hands to Seb. "This one."

Seb looks at him, confused, before looking down at the book. It's a collection of stories by Edgar Allan Poe, and he can't help but smile a little.

"What about it?" he asks, looking up at Evan, who is wearing an expression of complete comfort and ease.

"Read it," he says, and presses the book into Seb's hand, before turning around and making his way to the bed. Seb just stands there, confused.

"I have," he says, frowning. "Quite a few times."

"So read it again," Evan says plainly, and sits down on Seb's bed. Then, he actually lies down on his back, placing one arm under his head and draping the other over his stomach. He looks at Seb pointedly.

"What, *now*?" Seb says, and Evan nods, eyebrows raised as if saying *obviously,* and Seb hesitantly walks over to him. "Out loud?"

"Yeah," Evan says. "Read me something."

Seb just stares at him, a look of suspicion on his face, but Evan only chuckles.

"Dude," he says, "This hangover's gonna stick around for a while. Might as well lie down and relax."

Then he looks at Seb with just the tiniest, unexpected hint of anxiety in his eyes.

"If you don't mind?" There's a trace of that anxiety in his voice too, all of a sudden, an emotion that Seb never would have imagined could come from Evan. And he sighs, moving to sit in the armchair, but Evan stops him with a motion of his hand.

"I don't bite," he says, not even a trace of humor or sarcasm or flirtation in his voice, as he motions to the bed. Seb is almost entirely sure his heart is suddenly beating really loud, but he still manages to sit down on the bed with his back against the wall, unsure what to do with his legs. Evan is lying with his head on the pillows, as Seb sits down on the lower half of the bed, so the choices are to either put his legs over Evan's, or have Evan's legs draped over his.

He ends up sitting with his legs crossed, folded underneath him.

"What do you want to hear?" Seb asks, trying not to think about how odd the whole situation is, and he glances at Evan. Evan is looking at the ceiling, with a frown on his face, thinking.

"I do like *Tell-tale Heart*," he admits after a few moments, getting a weirdly somber look on his face. "A bit cliché, maybe."

"It's one of my favorites, actually," Seb admits and looks at Evan pointedly. "It's a classic, not a cliché."

Evan looks over at him, and then smiles crookedly. It's the best kind of smile.

"Then I want that one," he says, and he watches Seb intently for a few moments, before Seb shapes up and turns to the book. He checks the table of contents and flips open to the right page. He can practically feel Evan's gaze on him, and he clears his throat, before starting to read.

He makes it through the first few sentences, before he pauses, feeling the absence of Evan's gaze, and he slowly glances over at him. His eyes are closed, and for a moment, Seb just looks at him, assuming he's suddenly asleep.

There is something so relaxing about watching him as he lies there, chest heaving, the fabric of his t-shirt tightening over his body just the tiniest bit with every breath. With his eyes closed and mouth relaxed, there are no crinkles around his eyes, but Seb can still see them. He can still see the traces of them, and he can still imagine them, can imagine Evan's face as it lights up with a smile.

Then, Evan opens his eyes and looks at Seb sleepily, and Seb tries not to jump.

"Go on," Evan says pointedly, and Seb clears his throat again unnecessarily and turns back to the book. He can't believe Evan just caught him looking at him. It's unbelievable how awkward he suddenly feels.

But reading helps. It always helps calm him down, and he finds himself easing into it, easing into the idea of sitting here, reading to Evan, while he lies stretched out on Seb's bed.

On my bed.

That part is a bit harder to ease into. But he licks his lips, and continues reading, Evan's presence warm and heavy beside him

CHAPTER 5
GUITAR

The hard surface of the bench is surprisingly comfortable against Seb's back, as he lies there, the sun on his face. His eyes are closed, and his headphones are on, flooding him with the sweetest mix of music and relaxation. It isn't really like him to relax, like this. He tends to worry so much about studying and work that needs to be done, that he very rarely just sits down, or in this case, lies down, and simply breathes.

The worst of the heat wave has passed by now, and after a rather boring lecture on analyzing poetry, as opposed to literature, which is more of Seb's thing, Seb has taken the time to find a bench in a quieter part of campus, rather than going straight back to his dorm. There, he started out sitting up, reading his lecture notes, but he quickly succumbed to laziness and put the notes away. Instead, he elected to put on his headphones and lie down on his back, feet up on the armrest, messenger bag under his head in place of a pillow. It was a good choice. Just chilling out here in the afternoon sun is something he hasn't done in a very long time.

He's almost half-sleeping, one arm under his head and the other dangling over the edge of the bench, when he's interrupted. It's the feeling of fingers brushing against his neck, with surprising softness, as someone gently lifts one of the headphones from his ear, that does it.

"Hey," someone says softly, and Seb opens his eyes, startled by someone being there. The moment he sees Evan's face though, hovering above him, framed and backlit by sunlight, it goes against every fiber in his being to not jump up in surprise and nervousness. Instead, he remains still, looking up at Evan's smiling face. The light around him gives him the impression of a halo. It's *beautiful*, in lack of a better word.

Seb hopes Evan can't see him blush. He has no idea why he would be blushing in the first place.

"Hey," he replies, raising his hands to take off his headphones and pull them down so that they end up around his neck. Evan is wearing that crooked smile of his, the one that makes Seb feel oddly warm inside.

"Nice peach fuzz," he says, actually touching Seb's cheek with his finger, making Seb freeze up and melt simultaneously. Evan is touching *his face*.

51

"Thanks," he says, awkwardly pulling himself up into sitting position. He hasn't shaved in a couple of days, for no real reason, and it has resulted in dark stubble that now covers his face. He hasn't seen Evan in about as many days, not since they hung out in Seb's dorm.

You know, Seb thinks, after Evan spent the night there, and when the two of them were in Seb's bed, Seb reading out loud to him. He even got to finish the whole story.

Seb still finds the whole scenario a bit hard to believe, even though it happened, and even though his pillows now carry that specific Evan-scent to prove it.

They have texted a bit since then, though, actually exchanging phone numbers on that occasion. Evan will every now and then send a text saying something like *Who do you think would win, Captain America or Batman? This keeps me up at night*; or *I sometimes almost forget how awesome Tyrion Lannister is. Almost.* Or Seb's personal favorite; *Dude, tacos. Yes.*

Evan waits until Seb has sit up properly, before sitting down next to him.

"What you listening to?" Evan asks, gesturing to the headphones around Seb's neck, and Seb glances down at them, before taking them off and handing them to Evan. Evan apprehensively takes them and puts them on, his expression changing into one of gentle concentration, as he listens, and Seb suddenly feels oddly nervous that he might not like it. That Evan might not like the music Seb listens to. There is no need, though, because Evan soon raises his eyebrows in surprised appreciation, before taking off the headphones and handing them back to Seb.

"It's good," he says. "I like it."

Seb half-smiles.

"Yeah," he says, putting the headphones back around his neck out of habit, and pausing the music on his phone, which the headphones are plugged into. "It's a favorite of mine."

Evan nods, and they just sit there for a few moments.

"You done for the day?" Evan suddenly asks, and Seb vaguely realizes how often he's kind of startled by Evan's questions and behavior, for no apparent reason.

"Yeah," he says. "Just had my only lecture for the day. You?"

"Same," Evan says, nodding. And another few moments pass in silence.

"You wanna hang out?" Evan finally asks, and Seb looks up at the odd tone in his voice. He sounds confident, cocky even. He sounds like Evan. But there is something else there, too, something he can't quite put his finger on.

"Sure, I—" he starts, but then cuts himself off. He sighs heavily.

"Shit," he says. "I can't. I've got a paper due, Friday."

The amount of sheer disappointment he feels is overwhelming—not to mention shocking. It's shocking, how badly he suddenly wants to just blow everything off and hang out with Evan. But most shocking of all, is Evan's reaction.

"Oh," he says, an overly carefree expression on his face, one that thinly veils something that looks an awful lot like... is that *shyness*? Disappointment? *Nervousness,* even?

No, Seb immediately thinks, shaking it off. Not Evan. Evan doesn't get *shy*. He doesn't get *nervous*. And Seb seriously doubts that he's even nearly as disappointed as Seb at missing out on spending time together.

"I get it," Evan says, nodding. "Working hard, and all that. Some other time, then."

Seb watches Evan as he turns away and directs his eyes straight ahead, watches that profile, that hair, those freckles, those lips... It's unbelievable how appealing it all suddenly looks. He chews his bottom lip, thinking, oddly terrified.

"But after Friday," he hears himself say. "I mean, Friday night. Or something. Maybe."

Evan looks at him, his expression unreadable, and Seb elaborates, already worried that he has said something too weird or just *too much*.

"Paper's due Friday," he says. "So I'll have the rest of Friday off."

And then, unbelievably, Evan smiles. And it's the weirdest thing.

Seb has seen Evan smile so many times by now—he seems to just be the kind of person who generally smiles. Seb has seen the half-smiles, the cocky grins, the joking smiles, the one where Evan just quirks the corner of his mouth. And best of all, the crooked smile, the one Seb barely ever sees him use, because he only seems to use it when he's genuinely happy or impressed.

But this one—this smile is new, and it makes Evan's face look oddly soft and kind, giving it all a kind of innocence about it, those crinkles showing when the smile reaches his eyes. Seb is too stunned to even smile back.

"Sounds good," Evan says, and Seb swallows.

"Good," he replies lamely, and Evan looks at him for another moment, before chuckling.

"Alright," he says, moving to get up. "You work hard, and I'll see you then."

Seb nods as Evan gets up and turns to him. He seems to hesitate for a moment, before he puts his hand on Seb's shoulder and squeezes it gently.

"Have fun," he says, replacing the new smile with the cocky one, and Seb laughs humorlessly as Evan lets go of his shoulder.

"I'll try," he says, and Evan winks at him, before walking away. And Seb just sits there for a moment, staring into space. Then, he finally reanimates and gathers up his things, getting up from the bench, putting on his headphones as he goes. There is an unfamiliar lightness to his steps as he turns the music back on, making his way home.

◆

Seb is efficient. When it comes to studying, writing, creating, he has pretty much always been efficient. He isn't sure how much of that has to do with talent, and how much has to do with his pretty much lifelong, general lack of friends, but it doesn't really matter. What matters is that it's something he is good at.

This time around, it's different. He isn't being *in*efficient or anything, but he is erratic. On one occasion, he'll get a whole portion of the paper together, suddenly very motivated, and on another, he'll just sit there, completely unable to focus. And he doesn't even have to wonder why this is happening.

Evan. It's all his fault. It's all *Evan.*

When they talked briefly on that bench, Friday was two days away, and Seb realizes that he's rather happy about seeing Evan tomorrow—he is deliberately avoiding the word *excited*. He's looking forward to it, more than he wants to admit, and one minute, this will spur him to work harder and get his paper done faster, and the next, it will distract him so much that he can't get anything done. Basically.

But despite it all, Seb is good at this, so when Thursday night comes along, he's about 95% finished with the whole assignment, and he rubs his eyes as he sits at his desk. He glances at the clock on his wall; it's almost eleven p.m. Good thing he has a late afternoon lecture tomorrow, when he's going to hand in the paper. At least he'll get to sleep properly. As long as he doesn't get too distracted again, that is.

Said distraction comes only moments later, with a knock on the door.

It's Sophie, and Seb finds himself almost frowning, like he so often does, when he opens the door. Especially seeing as how he has only ever spoken to Sophie once, and she has never come over here before.

"Hi." She smiles, her entire face and being radiating kindness. It's unbelievable really, how some people pull that off so well. *She and Jake really are perfect for each other,* Seb thinks to himself. "I was hoping you might be up."

Seb rubs his eyes as he leans slightly against the open door. He's more tired than he realized, and the light in the hallway is harsh compared to the dimness of his room.

"I'm up," he says, smiling weakly, pulling his fingers through his messed-up hair, and Sophie seems relieved.

"Good," she says. "I just need a favor. I'm at Jake's, and the remote died."

Seb then notices that she is indeed holding a remote control for a TV, and he raises his eyebrows at her. She rolls her eyes self-consciously, still smiling.

"Don't judge," she says, a trace of a laugh in her voice. "It's movie night. And it's hard to cuddle up properly when you have to get up and fix the volume all the time."

She looks at Seb pointedly with a pleading expression, wiggling the remote in front of her.

"You don't happen to have any batteries, do you?" she asks sweetly, with a tone that says she knows how weird the request is. But Seb just scoffs, with a smile.

"I'll check," he says, making his way back into his room. He knows there should be a pack of batteries lying around, and he has to dig through only two desk drawers before he finds it. He takes out two batteries and closes the drawer, before walking over to Sophie, who's patiently waiting in the doorway. He hands them to her.

"Great," she says, with a sigh of relief. "Thanks."

"No problem," Seb says, and she turns to leave. But then, she stops. She seems to deliberate for a moment, before hesitantly turning back to him.

"You're Evan's friend, right?" she asks softly, as though worried he might say no, and Seb blinks at the unexpected question.

"Yeah," he says, actually kind of stunned that this is the first time he has confirmed that out loud. "I'd say I am. Why?"

Sophie worries at her bottom lip for a moment.

"That's good," she finally says, sincere thoughtfulness written on her face. "He needs more friends like you."

Seb doesn't know what to say to that. So instead, he just gives Sophie a weak smile as she smiles at him, before she leaves and makes her way down the hall to Jake's room. Seb slowly closes the door behind her.

Yeah, he thinks. *I'm his friend.*

♦

Seb would say that he's uncharacteristically nervous, as he knocks on the door, but that wouldn't be entirely true. Nervousness really is part of his character, after all.

But he still finds himself fidgeting a bit, pulling on his black, deliberately washed out t-shirt that has the vaguest outline of Darth Vader on the front. Smoothing down his hair unnecessarily, shoving his hands in the pockets of his jeans because he suddenly doesn't know where else to put them.

Yeah, not out of character at all.

It's Friday, *finally*, and Seb has just come straight from his lecture. Evan texted him where he lives, and now, Seb is standing in the hallway of his dorm, right outside his door. The building looks pretty much the same as the one where both Seb and Jake live, albeit with a slightly darker coat of paint on the walls. As if any of this is on Seb's mind right now, as he waits for something to happen, his knock lingering in the air.

It's only a matter of seconds, before the door is pulled open, and Seb finds himself taking a deep, steadying breath. And then there he is, Evan, smiling at him.

"You made it," he says, pulling Seb into a surprising hug. Seb isn't used to hugging so casually, so he's a bit taken aback for a moment. But it's worth it; Evan smells so good, warm and rough, with a hint of leather and some kind of spice. And it feels really good to hug him, to be hugged by him, his arms wrapped hard around Seb for just a moment.

"Was worried you might be lost," Evan says as he releases Seb, a jokingly patronizing look on his face, and he steps back so Seb can enter his room.

"Your confidence in my sense of direction is overwhelming," Seb mutters sarcastically, as he looks around the room. And he hears, with a weird sense of satisfaction, how Evan chuckles quietly as he closes the door.

The room is no bigger than Seb's, only a little less cluttered and with a different overall theme. Just like it's rather obvious from Seb's room that he is a writer, it's obvious from Evan's room that he is a musician.

There is an acoustic guitar standing against the wall, and another up on the wall, next to an electric guitar and what looks like a bass, an amplifier standing in the corner. There are guitar picks littered all over the place, and a desk that doesn't look nearly as cluttered as Seb's, and a modest bed in the corner. Somehow, it looks exactly like Seb would have imagined Evan's room to look. And it smells like him. Exactly like him, wrapping Seb up in a blanket of calm that he's barely even aware of.

"How'd it go?" Evan asks as he makes his way past Seb, who drops his messenger bag to the floor. Seb looks at him quizzically.

"The paper," Evan clarifies, and Seb feels the smallest sense of surprise that he remembers, and that it's the first thing he asks.

"Good," he says. "Hopefully. Just turned it in."

He lingers in that one spot for a moment, before hesitantly making his way across the room. There is a couch against the other wall, two-seated, and he vaguely wonders how it can fit in here. Then he remembers that in his own room, he has opted for a bookcase instead, as well as an armchair.

In lack of anything else, Seb slumps down on the couch, feeling too awkward about just standing there, and he glances over at Evan, who is standing by his desk. He's leaning over his laptop, apparently scrolling through his music selection, and Seb notices how music is indeed playing, but he didn't really pay attention to it before. Now that he does, he likes it. The volume is rather low, the tones rather mellow and subdued; perfect for playing in the background.

"Are all the guitars really necessary?" Seb finds himself asking, half-joking, and Evan looks up at him, straightening.

"Excuse you?" he says, eyebrows raised, as he starts making his way over to the couch. "Are all the *books* really necessary?"

Seb cocks his head.

"Touché," he says, and looks up at Evan as he nudges Seb's leg with his own, so he'll move. Seb scoots over on the couch and watches as Evan sits down next to him, his throat suddenly dry.

Why would he react this way? Why is the prospect of Evan sitting so close to him suddenly so terrifying and calming at the same time?

God, he can still smell him; the scent of Evan is all over the couch, all over the room, and Evan himself, as he sits so close that Seb could touch him without barely even reaching. He swallows hard.

"Alright," he says, his voice not betraying his sudden nervousness. "Play."

Evan looks at him, before realizing what he means.

"What, *now*?" he asks, unconsciously mimicking Seb's words from days earlier, and Seb half-smiles.

"Yes," he says, falling back into the corner of the sofa, in a comfortable slouch. "Play me something."

Evan just looks at him for a few moments, before he scoffs, smiling.

"Fine," he says, getting up and picking up the acoustic guitar he's got leaning against the wall. "What do you want to hear?"

This time, he gives Seb a pointed look, well aware of how this conversation is turning into basically a replica of the one they had at Seb's place that time, and Seb smiles.

"You choose," he says, turning the mirror conversation in a new direction, and Evan pauses the music on his laptop before sitting down on the couch again, adjusting the guitar in his lap.

"No pressure," he mutters, and Seb lets out a small laugh, making Evan look up at him from under his eyelashes. He smiles. "So what, anything?"

"Anything," Seb confirms, and Evan exhales, as though wishing Seb would give him more to work with. But then, after a few seconds, he starts playing.

The sound of the guitar is smooth and comforting, Evan's fingers sliding over the strings in practiced, fluid motions, as his whole body seems to relax into it. Seb watches him as he plays, and Evan glances up at him, before he starts singing. And Seb swears his eyes actually widen as he hears it.

Evan's voice is soft, like velvet, flowing through the air and wrapping itself around Seb in a beautiful mist of relaxed satisfaction, leaving him feeling completely content and safe.

He leans back against the softness of the worn leather couch, resisting the urge to close his eyes, wanting to look at Evan, at the way he seems to feel so at home while playing, while singing. Those green eyes are half-closed, barely even looking up, which Seb is grateful for; it means he can look at Evan without getting caught. And the music keeps flowing, intertwining perfectly with Evan's voice. It's beautiful.

When the song is over, the air seems to vibrate slightly with the lingering feel of it, and for a few moments, Seb just sits there, half-lying in the corner of the couch. Evan looks up at him, a bit self-conscious—an expression Seb had never imagined seeing on his face—as though waiting for some kind of feedback. But Seb can't say anything. Instead, he just lies there, looking at Evan, frozen.

His entire body suddenly feels as though it wants to move closer to Evan, to touch him and feel his skin. So Seb doesn't move, because he's afraid he won't be able to help himself, if he does.

"Well?" Evan finally says, clearly a bit uncomfortable at Seb's silence, so Seb forces himself to speak.

"It was beautiful," he says. And a moment later, he panics. Those are *not* the words he meant to say out loud. He did *not* mean to say that it was beautiful. That's a word he has reserved for himself, a way to describe Evan and everything he is, inside his own mind. He can't believe he just said it out loud.

But Evan doesn't seem to mind. Sure, he looks a bit taken aback, and his gaze flicks around for a little bit, as though unsure how to respond, but he doesn't look at Seb like it's the weirdest thing he has ever heard. Instead, he clears his throat a bit.

"Thank you," he says, clearly a bit awkward. But the emotion behind the thanks is real, and it makes Seb feel a little bit better.

"I've never had the patience for that," Seb says then, breaking the tension with a small smile, nodding at the guitar. "Would be awesome to know how to play, though."

Evan glances down at the guitar, before holding it out to Seb.

"Here," he says. "I'll teach you."

Seb's eyes widen, and he shakes his head.

"Oh no," he says. "It's really not my thing, trust me."

"Just the basics," Evan insists. "I'll be nice, I promise."

Seb looks at him suspiciously, and Evan gives him a crooked grin. And just like that, Seb gives in, sitting up properly with a sigh. Evan hands him the guitar.

They are both sitting on opposite ends of the couch, but pretty close together, almost facing each other, and Seb takes the guitar and awkwardly positions it in his lap.

"I just know I'm gonna regret this," he mutters, and Evan chuckles.

"We'll see," he says. "Now, start by putting your fingers like this."

He gestures with his hand, and Seb tries to copy it, wrapping his hand around the neck of the guitar. The strings are made of metal, and he experimentally presses down on them, frowning slightly.

"Alright," Evan says. "Let's start with the A-chord."

He points out the right points to press down on the strings, and Seb makes an attempt, failing rather miserably.

"No, like this," Evan says, and actually takes Seb's hand, guiding his fingers to the right places. Seb tries to ignore how his throat suddenly constricts, and how his face heats up. Evan's hand is warm against his, firm in its instruction, and Seb glances up at Evan's face. He is so close.

"You gotta press down harder," Evan tells him, as Seb makes a swipe at the strings with his other hand, trying to get some reasonably good sound out of the instrument.

"It hurts," he says with annoyed humor, and Evan smiles.

"You get used to it," he says, and Seb knows what he means; as Evan's left hand touches his, he can feel the roughness of his fingertips, hardened from pressing down on guitar strings countless times.

"You sure about that?" he asks with a small, nervous laugh, and Evan chuckles.

"I'm sure," he says. "Practice makes perfect."

And then, Seb dares to look at him again, dares to look up and watch his face—only to see Evan looking up at him at the same time. And for a few, agonizingly long seconds, they both just sit there, frozen, Seb's hands on the guitar and Evan's hands on his.

Their faces are inches apart. Seb can see every little variation of green in those eyes. His heart is beating fast, loudly.

And then, he breaks the spell.

"Maybe I should stick to writing," he says with a small laugh, hoping he isn't being too obvious about the sudden attempt to change the atmosphere. But if Evan notices, he doesn't show it, and he pulls back an inch or so, pulling his hands away from Seb's.

"Here," Seb says, handing over the guitar, and Evan smiles, as he takes it.

"I'm not giving up on you," he says jokingly, and positions the guitar in his lap, as Seb lies back in the corner of the couch, like he did earlier. Evan licks his lips.

"So, something else?" he asks, the slightest hint of anxiety in his voice, like Seb heard before.

"Sure," Seb says, smiling, and Evan seems to hesitate this time, before he starts playing.

It's a happier tune this time, and as Evan starts singing, Seb frowns.

"Hey, I know this song," he says, a hint of suspicion in his voice, and Evan stops playing, a sheepish look on his face.

"I may have heard it the other day," he says pointedly. "And I may have peeked at your phone, to get the title."

Seb feels a blush creep up his neck, as he realizes what Evan is talking about. The other day, when they were sitting on that bench. Evan is playing the same song that Seb was listening to, and suddenly, he gets a weird, fluttering sensation in his stomach.

"So you learned it?" he asks, honestly shocked, and Evan shrugs.

"I was bored," he says. "And I liked the song."

He gives Seb a small smile, one that looks a lot like the one he had that day, the new smile. The one that makes his entire face soften and his eyes shine.

"Go on, then," Seb says over-nonchalantly, and Evan isn't lost on it. He scoffs, smiling, before turning back to his guitar. And as he starts playing, his voice carrying through the air, Seb actually does close his eyes, and just listens.

CHAPTER 6
THE NOTE

Seb's head is buzzing. He's in the middle of a lecture on syntax and grammar (*essential* to writing, according to the lecturer), and he can't remember the last time he felt so restless.

He alternates between sitting upright and slouching in his seat, between fiddling a pen between his fingers and folding his hands on the desk in front of him. He glances up and down the row he's on, fold-up seats occupied by several students, on a row identical to the ones behind him, higher up, and the ones in front of him, descending down to floor level. He glances at the clock above the door; its hands are moving at an agonizingly slow pace.

He can't wait to get out of here, can't wait to pack up his notes and books and hurry out through that door. Can't wait to get out of this stuffy lecture hall and get some fresh air.

He can't wait to see Evan.

It's not as though he hasn't seen Evan recently; after spending Friday night together and just hanging out, they hung out a lot during the weekend, too. They watched movies, played videogames, ate pizza, alternating between Seb's dorm and Evan's. And now, it's Tuesday. Which means it has already been almost two days since Seb last saw him. *Two days.* He can't believe he went for longer than that without really even thinking about Evan, before. How can he not think about him?

It's late afternoon, and almost an hour of the lecture left. Seb is busy scribbling random doodles in his notepad, when he hears a small tap behind him, followed by a very hushed *shit*. He turns around, noticing that someone behind him has dropped their pen, and he picks it up. It's only when he looks up and reaches up to hand it back to them, that he half-freezes.

"Thanks," the girl says, before pausing. Then she remembers. "Hey, Seb."

Seb doesn't reply, only half-smiles. It's Clara, her auburn hair pulled up in a messy knot at the back of her head, and Seb tries not to feel too awkward about the fact that last time he saw her, she kissed him. She smiles, seemingly not at all bothered, herself.

"Haven't seen you in a while," she says, dropping her voice to a whisper. "How are you?"

"I'm good," Seb whispers back, and she nods. He hesitates for a moment, wondering if he should ask something back, turn back around or just sit there and stare. Clara saves him the trouble of deciding.

"How did your assignment go?" she asks, and Seb remembers that they have more than this class together.

"I think it went pretty well," he says, even though he has no way of knowing. "You?"

She makes a face.

"Not the most inspiring stuff," she admits. "But I think I passed."

Seb nods slowly, again wondering what the hell he's supposed to say, when the lecturer clears his throat.

"No talking, please," he says, and Seb turns back in his seat, facing the board. He doesn't reply, only gives a sheepish look, while Clara says *sorry* in a low voice behind him. The lecturer seems content with that, and keeps going.

The rest of the lecture doesn't move much faster and is very uneventful, but eventually, it finally finishes, and Seb gathers up his things as everyone gets up to leave. He's just about to stand up and sling his bag over his shoulder, when a slender, pale hand slaps something down on the desk in front of him, and he looks up. Clara is already hurrying down the stairs from her seat, her back turned to him, and Seb looks down.

She left him a note, and he picks it up and opens it. There is a phone number written on there, signed by Clara, and Seb just stares at it for a moment. And then its hit him;

a girl just gave him her number. He's pretty sure that has only happened once or twice in his entire life, before.

He swallows down the weird sense of satisfaction he feels at it, before folding up the note again and shoving it in his pocket, and leaving the lecture hall.

Despite only having been at Evan's place a couple of times, Seb's feet seem to know exactly where to go, all on their own, and before long, he's standing in front of Evan's dorm room, knocking.

"It's open!" Evan calls from inside, and Seb lets himself in. Evan is seated on the couch, eyes fixed on the TV that usually stands lined up against the wall to save space, but which he occasionally pulls out into the room when he needs to. He's holding a Playstation 3 controller, but as soon as he sees Seb, he throws up his hands.

"Dude," he exclaims. "Finally! Do you have any idea how boring it is to play this game by yourself?"

"Actually, I do," Seb says, dumping his bag on the floor and making his way over to the couch. He pats Evan's shoulder in a jokingly condescending manner. "I'm here to rescue you."

Evan doesn't say anything, only makes a noise of sarcastic gratitude, as if saying *yeah right,* and Seb smiles as he slumps onto the couch next to him.

"*Tekken* or *SoulCalibur*?" he asks, but it's an unnecessary question; it's obvious from the screen and the characters Evan is currently using which game it is.

"*SoulCalibur,*" Evan replies, eyes on the screen, resuming the match he's in the middle of. "*Tekken* blows."

"It really doesn't," Seb says unenthusiastically. They've had this conversation before. "You wanna keep playing by yourself?"

Evan shoots him a glance, and Seb smiles smugly at him.

"Just let me finish this one," Evan mutters, turning back to the game, and Seb keeps his smile, even though Evan can't see it.

"Fair enough."

"There's pizza, by the way," Evan says absently, nodding toward his bedside table, and Seb glances at it. He is hungry, he realizes; he hasn't eaten since lunch.

"Don't mind if I do," he replies and gets up from the couch, making his way over to the small table, where a big, flat box is sitting. He has just picked it up and started moving back to the couch, when he notices Evan stop and pick something up off the floor. It's a piece of paper, and Evan unfolds it.

"What's this?" he asks, holding it up, and Seb realizes that it's the note from Clara.

"Clara's number," he says, sitting back down on the couch, pizza box in his hands. "You know, from the party? The brunette?"

Evan nods slowly as he remembers.

"The one who kissed you," he mutters, looking at the note, almost as though he didn't really mean to say that out loud.

"Apparently," Seb continues, unaware, while Evan looks up, "we've got some classes together, and she handed me that today."

He nods toward the note in Evan's hand, and Evan looks at it again.

"You gonna call her?" he eventually asks, looking up at Seb, who takes a bite out of a pizza slice; it's very cheesy, lukewarm and delicious.

He doesn't know what to answer, at first. He hasn't really thought about it, hasn't really deliberated what he thinks of Clara at all. So he shrugs.

"I don't know," he says, chewing, and Evan looks at him, as though waiting for him to elaborate, but he doesn't. So Evan just looks back at the note and hands it to Seb, who, surprised, takes it and puts it back in his pocket. Silence falls for a few moments, before Evan straightens.

"Alright," he says, handing a controller to Seb. "Time to kick your ass."

Seb is still there by the time it's dark outside. In that time, he and Evan have been through a small tournament of video game violence, watched an episode of *Game of Thrones*, and now, Seb is lying on the couch, legs over the other end's armrest. Evan is sitting on the floor, back against the couch, an acoustic guitar in his hands, and the whole atmosphere is just generally relaxed.

Evan isn't really playing anything. There is music on in the background, and he seems to just be fiddling with the guitar strings, finding comfort in simply holding the instrument. Seb watches him from his vantage point, watching his profile, as Evan seems so utterly relaxed and at peace.

"Did you always want to make music?" Seb asks, and Evan glances up at him.

"Yeah," he says. "For as long as I can remember."

He fiddles with the guitar strings.

"How about you?" he asks. "Always wanted to be a writer?"

"For as long as I can remember," Seb echoes, and smiles when Evan glances up at him again, Evan smiling back.

"I've always made up stories," Seb says, as Evan turns back to his guitar. "Always liked making people feel things, expressing myself with words, telling someone else's story, fictional or not."

"Sounds like me," Evan says, and Seb looks at him. Evan pauses for a split second, as though he meant to word that differently. Then he resumes his fiddling. "Except with music."

Seb doesn't answer him, only watches as Evan picks up the beer can on the floor next to him, lifting it to his lips. He takes a swig, apparently emptying it, because he then sets it down again and reaches for a new one. There is a six pack standing on the floor nearby, and he has already had two cans of beer, Seb only one. Actually, Seb hasn't even really finished his yet.

Seb feels weirdly apprehensive as he watches Evan open his third can in two hours and take a swig.

"Maybe you should slow down a bit," he says, trying to sound light, rather than reprimanding. He has slowly started realizing that Evan gets drunk pretty often. If nothing else, he *drinks* pretty often. The first time they met, going out for beers in the middle of the day after that, then the party... Half the time Seb has spent with Evan, he seems to have been drinking, and he honestly isn't sure how he feels about that.

Suddenly, he can't really blame Jake for worrying about his big brother, and Sophie's words come to him.

"He needs more friends like you."

But Evan only shrugs, setting the beer can down to fiddle with his guitar, and Seb decides that now probably isn't the time to talk about it. If it ever is, if he even has the right to talk to Evan about something like that. He just really cares, he realizes. He *really* cares about Evan, and he wants him to be okay.

"So how'd your parents feel about it," Evan asks, and Seb blinks, refocusing. It's obvious from the way Evan is talking that he's getting pretty drunk, at this point. "Wanting to be a writer."

Seb sighs.

"Not much," he says tiredly. "My dad didn't like it, still doesn't. My mom thinks it's 'too bad' that that's what I want to do, but she also says that I 'have a gift'. And this school is a pretty good one, so at least their son is getting a nice, fancy college education."

Evan smiles at that, and Seb finds himself smiling at the sight of it.

"What about you?" he asks. "What do your parents have to say about your career choice?"

It's almost as though he can feel the sudden tension emit from Evan in waves, and he actually stiffens, waiting for a reply. He can see Evan's jaw working, and for a moment, Seb feels as though he has intruded.

"You don't—" he starts, but Evan cuts him off.

"It's fine," he says, sounding subdued and intoxicated. "It's a valid question."

Seb waits, and Evan seems to deliberate for a few moments.

"My mom doesn't think anything about it," he finally says. "She died when I was a kid. But I like to think she would have supported me."

Seb feels surprised, but at the same time not. He suddenly remembers that first night in his room, when Evan came barging in through the door.

"Yeah, she was."

He had a distinct feeling then that this was what Evan referred to, but he never mentioned it.

"I'm sorry," he says gently. Evan smiles bitterly.

"It's okay," he says. "It was years ago."

He fiddles with his guitar some more, before he swallows hard.

"My dad," he says. "He's not too happy about it. Then again, he's never happy about anything. He's just angry."

Seb doesn't say anything, as Evan picks up his beer can and swallows deeply, emptying at least a fourth of it in one go. Seb doesn't like that. He doesn't like that Evan seems to have such an easy time getting drunk, that he does it on a Tuesday night, while hanging out with a friend, as though it's the most natural, routine thing in the world.

Then again, Evan hasn't done that these past few days, when they hung out this weekend. Seb can't help but wonder if there is something bothering him, this time.

"He's a bit of an asshole, actually," Evan continues, and Seb can tell that he wouldn't be sharing this much if he hadn't been drinking. It feels really personal. "Going to college, moving away from home... It's the best thing I've ever done. That, and getting Jake out of there."

Seb swallows. He knows that Evan and Jake are close, but there seems to be more to the story. Whatever it is, though, Evan doesn't seem to want to talk about it, because he suddenly changes the subject.

"So," he says, his tone considerably lighter, albeit still drunk. That third beer is starting to have quite the effect on him, especially as he swallows down a whole lot more it as he pauses. "You gonna call that girl? Clara?"

Seb raises his eyebrows in pure surprise.

"What?" he says, and Evan half-shrugs.

"Just asking," he says. "She seems into you. Kissing you and giving you her number. Doesn't get much more obvious than that."

Seb doesn't answer him right away. Evan's words are making him oddly uncomfortable.

"I don't know," he says, but as he says it, he knows he's lying. He isn't going to call her. He doesn't even want to. It's so far from his mind that he forgot about it until Evan brought it up.

Seb slowly sits up properly, swinging his legs over the couch's edge, so that he's sitting pretty much next to Evan, except higher up, while Evan stays on the floor.

"Who are you to tell me that, anyway?" he says jokingly. "When was the last time you hooked up with anyone?"

It was meant as a joke, seeing as how Evan constantly seems to hook up with girls—that's even how Seb first met him, after all, even the second time around. But Evan just becomes weirdly quiet. Seb frowns, but doesn't push it.

"Fine," he says. "If you think I should call her, I guess I should."

"I don't," Evan mutters, and Seb looks down at him.

"What?" he says, and Evan glances up at him, his eyes getting that glazed look they get when he's been drinking.

"I don't," he repeats, some odd kind of conviction in his voice, and Seb just stares at him.

"Why not?" he asks, somehow scared of the answer. Why should Evan even care if he hooks up with Clara, or with anyone, for that matter? Hell, when Clara kissed him at that party, Evan practically gave him a high five.

But Evan doesn't answer right away. Instead, he looks a bit lost for a moment, as though thinking and trying to come up with an answer. He puts the guitar down on the floor next to him.

"Maybe she's not good for you," he says, getting up on his knees and swallowing down the last of his beer. He's swaying a bit now, and Seb watches him apprehensively.

"Not good for me?" he repeats, confused at Evan's odd choice of words. "What's that supposed to mean?"

Evan sighs, as he moves over so that he's sitting right in front of Seb, on the floor.

"Just so," he says. Seb frowns.

"You're not making any sense," he says, suddenly uncomfortably aware of how his heart is speeding up. This is very out of character for Evan, all of it. It doesn't help to know that it's probably almost entirely due to his alcohol intake.

"Evan?" Seb says, but Evan doesn't answer. Instead, he just moves closer, until he's sitting really close to the couch's edge. The thing is, he moves so that he's sitting between Seb's knees, to get there, and Seb swallows hard.

This isn't happening. This *can't* be happening.

Seb has the intention of saying something, anything, but he feels as though he's completely frozen. He wonders if he looks as terrified as he suddenly feels, and he watches Evan's eyes as they scan his face. While standing on his knees like that, and with Seb slouching slightly as he sits, Evan reaches roughly up to Seb's chin, and he keeps their gazes locked as he places one hand on Seb's leg. He doesn't seem to have done it consciously, but all the same, it makes a hot shiver run through Seb's entire body, heart thumping violently against his ribcage, and he practically flinches.

Evan is so close, so very close. He's right there. Seb can smell him, can feel how that touch burns hot through his jeans... And how he's suddenly getting the most embarrassing and unexpected hard-on, because of it.

"Evan," he breathes, as though that might stop the whole thing and get him away from this terrifying, exhilarating situation. But it doesn't. Instead, he just lets out a quiet gasp as Evan reaches up and kisses him.

Seb has never kissed a guy. Girls, yes, several times, despite his socially awkward nature. After all. girls tend to find that *adorable*, he has realized, at least on the surface. But guys? Boys? Never. And honestly, it has never really occurred to him that he might want to.

Evan is the exception.

Seb feels the most wonderful shiver run through his entire body, as he feels Evan's lips against his own, their touch so soft he feels as though they might disappear forever if he moves just a fraction of an inch.

It's amazing how he has never really thought about this happening, not consciously, has never really imagined it or dreamt about it, but it can still feel like this. It can still feel

as though it's something he has always wanted, *always*
wished for, and for a moment, he just sits there, marveling
at the whole thing.

And then, he kisses Evan back.

The kiss hasn't lasted longer than a second, but it feels
like longer. Long enough for Seb to feel suspended in time,
and long enough for him to feel, for just a moment, as
though he can't really remember what life was like *before* he
kissed Evan Matthews.

And what a kiss it is. So soft, so tentative, but with a
kind of restrained greed that makes his whole body shiver,
and Seb closes his eyes. He can feel Evan's fingers moving
up to lightly trace the outline of his jaw, can feel how their
noses brush against each other the slightest bit, how his
own hand trails down along Evan's chest and lightly grips
the fabric of his button-up shirt between his fingers. He
can't breathe. He doesn't want to. If he breathes, all of this
might disappear, like a fleeting puff of smoke.

He's surprised to feel Evan moving even closer, his
hand moving up along Seb's leg, over his hips and to his
waist, where Evan stops to press his palm against him,
through the thin fabric of his t-shirt. Seb inhales sharply,
gripping Evan's shirt tighter. He's really hoping Evan hasn't
noticed how he's getting hard, really hoping that his jeans
are decent enough to keep that down enough to go unseen.

It feels so good, though, all of it. Evan's lips are soft and
sweet, unbelievably so, and it doesn't even matter that he
tastes of beer.

Evan's hands on him, Seb feeling the muscles
underneath Evan's clothes as he touches his chest and
shoulders... It just feels so *good*. So much so, that Seb can't

help but emit the smallest moan against Evan's lips. And just like that, Evan freezes up.

Slowly, very slowly, he pulls his mouth away from Seb's, his eyes opening and suddenly looking oddly confused, and Seb doesn't move.

What's happening? Why is he stopping? What's wrong?

Evan doesn't say anything for several seconds, just looks at him, as he slowly moves his hands away from Seb, as well. Then, suddenly, he stands up, leaving Seb sitting there, feeling flustered and hot and confused and disappointed, his mouth half-open as he stares into space. Then he looks up at Evan, who is wearing an expression of confused shock, and for some reason, it breaks Seb's heart, makes it stop beating entirely for what feels like several moments.

"I..." Evan murmurs, clearing his throat and looking anywhere but at Seb. He still has those glazed-over eyes, still drunk, but apparently starting to come back to his senses. He just realized he was kissing Seb. *Kissing* him. And Seb is suddenly acutely aware of an oddly physical, intense pain in his chest.

"I should..." Evan says, trailing off, and he glances at Seb, before moving away. He then walks into the bathroom and locks the door behind him.

Seb just sits there for several seconds, before letting out a deep, shaky breath. What the hell just happened?

Evan kissed him, out of nowhere. And then Evan pulled away. He pulled away from him, with that look on his face.

Seb has never been much of a crier, but this lump in his throat and sudden burning in his eyes is impossible to misinterpret, and he swallows hard. He looks over at the closed bathroom door, before deciding that this is too much. He just can't.

He gets up from the couch, managing to stand on his shaky legs, picks up his messenger bag from the floor, and exits the room without a word, closing the door behind him.

CHAPTER 7
JAKE

Seb has never before in his life felt this gnawing, aching feeling inside, at least not with nearly this much force. It makes it difficult to breathe, makes it feel as though the muscles in his chest are in a near constant state of constriction. It's unbearable.

He hasn't spoken to Evan in days, not since that night. Not since Evan literally pulled away to run and hide, after giving Seb the best kiss of his life. Not since he broke Seb's heart into a thousand pieces, with just a look.

Seb squeezes his eyes shut, rubbing the bridge of his nose. He has to stop thinking about it. He has to stop letting that look ruin everything. It was so painful, that he can't understand why it's etched into his mind like this. He doesn't want to remember it, doesn't want to be reminded of it. But it's hopeless, because he has come to realize that *everything* reminds him of Evan.

The memory of that night is bittersweet. One moment, Seb will relish how Evan's lips felt against his, that rush of quiet excitement as he realized Evan was actually kissing him, actually touching him and making him melt against him.

And the next, he will inevitably be reminded of the seconds that followed, Evan getting up and looking so shocked and confused, and Seb just sitting there, feeling so utterly unwanted and abandoned and *rejected*. It seems that he can't have one without the other.

He's honestly a bit surprised that he hasn't heard from Evan, not a single word. Not a single text. He's certain of this, because he has, pathetically, taken to checking his phone every five minutes or so. Not a single glimpse of him on campus. Nothing.

Seb is surprised, because he kind of hoped that despite everything, Evan was at least his friend, and would want to keep him around. But it seems that he was wrong. And the harsh realization of that is more difficult to deal with than he expected.

Seb is sitting at his desk, trying desperately to focus on his lecture notes. But it's impossible. He feels as though he's reading them through a haze, leaving him feeling numb and subdued. He feels like he isn't even sad anymore; he's just tired.

He actually cried that night, after holding on to that lump in his throat until he was safely within the walls of his own room. He actually cried. Not much, mind you, seeing as how Seb has never been big on crying, but still. It seemed like the only possible outlet for what he was feeling, the only possible way of getting it out of his system. And it helped, at least for a little while. He hasn't cried again since then. He can't bring himself to.

The sun is setting outside, casting a pleasant, golden glow on the walls of his cluttered room, but Seb is completely lost on the beauty. It just isn't relevant.

He isn't lost on the knock on his door, though, and he slowly turns his gaze over to it, complete and utter disinterest on his face. It's amazing how often he's been getting visitors these past few weeks, ever since he first met Evan.

And *ouch*. There is that pain again.

Seb slowly gets up from his desk and shuffles over to the door, his bare feet not making much noise, and he opens the door to let his gaze fall on the person standing outside. It's Jake. And as he sees Seb, he actually looks a bit concerned.

"Hey, Seb," he says, not voicing said concern. It's obvious by his expression, though, that Seb clearly looks worse than he thought. "What's up?"

Seb shrugs lamely. *Hell*, he feels like saying. *I've barely slept, and all food tastes like cardboard. I haven't had a proper emotion in the last two days. I feel like there's a festering wound in my chest that I can't stop poking at, because it hurts when I do, and at least that's something.*

"Not much," he says, his voice flat and devoid of its usual sarcasm and dry humor. He's sure Jake notices, because he sets his brow in a concerned frown, pressing his lips together.

"Can I come in?" he says after a few moments, to Seb's surprise, and the spontaneous reaction is *no*. But there is just something about Jake, something so pure and kind, as though he just radiates helpfulness and concern and comfort. And Seb finds himself opening the door wider and stepping away, making his way back into his room. Jake follows, closing the door behind him, and for a few seconds, there is nothing but silence.

"How you doing, Seb?" Jake asks, but Seb doesn't answer him right away. Instead, he starts fiddling with a pen that's lying on his desk. He doesn't look at Jake, just stands there, keeping his eyes down, and a few more seconds of silence follow.

"Look, I don't know what's up with you and Evan," Jake finally says, straight to the point, and Seb actually clenches his fist. Of course Jake has noticed that something is wrong. "But he's been acting... weird."

"Weird, how?" Seb hears himself ask, completely against his will.

"He's... angry," Jake says, sounding strangely old and sad, like the word holds more meaning that Seb knows. "But he won't say why. He'll barely talk to me. Won't even talk to Sophie."

He pauses, as though waiting for Seb to say something, but he doesn't. He just starts organizing the pen he's fiddling with together with his other pens, instead.

"Did something happen?" Jake asks, and Seb swallows. *Did* something happen? How much does Jake know, if anything? Seb feels certain that Evan hasn't told him anything. And so, Jake is coming to Seb.

"Why are you asking me?" Seb says, putting the first pen into the empty cup he uses to hold pens and scissors and such. It's got *the Avengers* plastered all over it; he got in when he went to see the movie in the theater, when it first came out.

"Because when I ask him about you," Jake says, softly but pointedly, "he bites my head off."

Seb feels his fingers tighten uncomfortably around the pen he's holding, and he has a feeling that Jake notices; he really isn't wearing the best poker face right now. And he is usually so good at it, too.

It's quiet for several more seconds, and Seb can tell from the way Jake says his next words that he's standing with his eyes averted slightly, as though unsure.

"Seb," Jake finally says, hesitantly. "Can I ask you something?"

Seb doesn't answer him. He doesn't want Jake to ask him something, doesn't want him to ask *any*thing. Because whatever it is, it can't possibly help the way he's feeling right now. But Jake takes his silence as permission.

"You like Evan, right?" he asks, and Seb glances at him. It's a perfectly reasonable, innocent question, if you ignore the fact that it makes Seb emotionally double over in pain. It sounds a lot like the one Sophie asked him that one time.

"Sure," he says flatly. "I tend to not hang out with people I don't like."

He doesn't mention how he and Evan haven't hung out in days. But of course, Jake already knows that.

Jake's expression doesn't change, as though Seb didn't answer his question, but Seb just goes back to what he was doing. It's silent for a few moments, before he hears Jake take a deep, steadying breath.

"Seb, are you in love with my brother?"

And there it is.

A blow to the head would have been easier to deal with, a giant punch in the gut, even. Because even though Seb feared this question, in some form or other, he's so incredibly, *wildly* unprepared for it. And so, he just stands there, frozen, staring into thin air, his brain working manically to think of something, *anything*, to say, his face suddenly cold as though all the blood has drained from it. But then he realizes that there is no use.

"Don't ask me that, Jake," he finds himself saying, his voice oddly sad, heavier and more flat than he's used to hearing, and he's surprised at his own honesty. Or rather, his avoidance of the question instead of flat-out denial.

Jake seems surprised, but at the same time not. Seb can feel it, even without looking at him. He keeps his dark blue eyes focused on his hands, instead, trying very hard not to simply fall over. His fingers suddenly feel stiff and cold. Then Jake clears his throat a little bit.

"Okay," he says, but it's clear that he caught Seb's real, underlying answer; *Yes, I am.*

Neither of them speaks for a few seconds, just standing there in complete silence, on opposite sides of the room.

"Have you told him?" Jake finally says, softly, and Seb sighs.

"Not exactly," he says, relieved and terrified at the same time, that someone finally knows about this. Hell, he didn't even really know, himself, until just a few days ago. He didn't get it. *Idiot.*

"What do you mean?"

"I mean that I haven't told him," Seb clarifies. "But..."

The sudden image of Evan's face shows up in his mind's eye, his eyes green and glazed over, scanning across Seb's face, his lips, moving closer. The feel of those calloused fingers against his face, that warm touch against his leg, his waist. Those lips, tentatively pressing against his own, with such soft urgency that it makes Seb shiver just thinking about it.

"But, what?" Jake asks, and Seb glances at him briefly, suddenly very uneasy about this whole thing.

"He—" he starts, trying to think of way of phrasing it that won't sound ridiculous and unbelievable, but failing miserably. He swallows hard, face actually heating up, all that drained blood rushing back. "He may have kissed me."

The shock is complete and obvious this time, in Jake's expression.

"May have?" he finally asks, and Seb sighs quietly.

"As in, he did." He can't look at Jake. "The other night."

Jake doesn't say a word for several seconds. He's probably trying to wrap his head around it, Seb figures. Trying to wrap his head around the concept of his rather butch, womanizing big brother kissing another guy, instead of some hot girl he would usually go for. And then, finally, Jake speaks.

"But..." he says, hesitantly. "Isn't that a good thing?"

Seb looks at him, a bit incredulously.

"I mean," Jake elaborates, when he sees Seb's face. "If you have feelings for him, and he... kissed you."

It's obvious that he's a bit uncomfortable talking about it, but he tries. Bless him.

"Doesn't that mean something?"

Seb laughs bitterly, an equally bitter smile on his face.

"Yeah," he says. "But he was wasted at the time, so I hardly think it counts. Not to mention the fact that he pulled away and looked like he had made the biggest mistake of his life."

He looks at Jake pointedly, and immediately sees the sadness in his eyes. Seb knows Evan—and Jake—well enough by now to understand that Evan has a bit of a drinking problem, among other things. It's something that clearly bothers Jake, and something that makes him nearly constantly worry about his brother, even on top of whatever other issues he may have. And so, he understands what Seb means.

"Still, though," he tries. "You should talk to him."

Seb utters another bitter laugh.

"Have you *met* Evan?" he asks. "Jake, he's not exactly the type."

Jake cocks his head in agreement, but has more to say.

"He's also not the type to kiss other guys." His words sound somehow harsh, but the pointed, sympathetic look he gives Seb softens them, and Seb looks away. Jake exhales.

"And speaking of," he says, hesitantly, trying to pick the right words. "I didn't know you were—"

"I'm not," Seb exclaims, a bit too quickly, as he looks up at Jake. Then he slows down. "I'm not. I mean, I've never..."

He thinks about it, trying to think of a good way of putting it.

"I've never really been into guys," he finally says. "I've maybe had the occasional crush, at most, but nothing serious. I've just never seen myself that way."

He looks down at his desk. It's true; he has never felt this way about a guy, never been with a guy. Hell, he has never even kissed a guy. Evan was his first, drunk or not. And he supposes that if you take away all the circumstances and bullshit that followed, it was a very good first kiss.

But still, he has always seen himself as straight, maybe slightly curious, at most. He supposes that that's why it took him so long to actually realize how he really felt about Evan. That he's more than just a friend to Seb, even if Evan doesn't feel that way about him. Because Evan really is as straight as they come, he thinks bitterly, with that seemingly never-ending parade of girls he has been with.

But then why did you kiss me, Evan? The thought comes unbidden and suddenly, ripping up that wound all over again. *Why would you do that to me?*

"Either way," Seb says after a few moments. "I really don't think he sees me like that."

Jake actually raises his eyebrows then.

"He kissed you, Seb," he says plainly, and Seb tries not to wince. "*Kissed* you."

"He kisses a lot of people," Seb says bitterly. Girls, granted, but still.

"Only girls," Jake points out again, and Seb sighs, a little annoyed.

"So I'm not a girl," he says, some of his trademark sarcasm and cynicism creeping back into his voice. Jake notices, because he smiles briefly. "Considering everything else, how is that relevant here?"

Jake thinks about it for a moment, before he cocks his head.

"Fair enough," he says, taking a few steps closer to Seb. "If you want to see it that way."

He approaches the desk and leans against its edge, folding his arms.

"But let me point out something else, then," he says, and Seb watches him. "I've never seen him act like this before. I don't care if you're a guy or a girl, or whether or not either of you normally does this kind of thing. He's never been like this before."

Seb frowns, reluctantly curious.

"Been like this?" he asks, and Jake sighs, thinking, before he looks up at Seb.

"Heartbroken," he says, and the single word gives Seb the strangest feeling in his stomach. "He's heartbroken, Seb."

"I find that hard to believe," Seb mutters, and Jake actually smiles a bit.

"He may be a bit of an asshole, sometimes," he admits, the affection he holds for his brother clear in his voice. "But it's not like he doesn't have feelings. Trust me."

Seb glances at him, and the suspicion must be written all over his face, because Jake actually chuckles as he sees it.

"What's so funny?" Seb says, and Jake shakes his head. He doesn't look amused; he looks content.

"Nothing," he says. He's swerving around Seb's injured feelings and pride very well.

Several seconds of silence follow, as Seb thinks about what Jake just said. Evan is heartbroken? Out of all the scenarios Seb could think of to apply to this situation, that's the least likely one, in his mind.

"So," Jake says. "You gonna talk to him?"

Seb gives him his expertly executed *are you kidding me-* look.

"He's the one who won't talk to me," he says. "He clearly regrets what he did and now he won't see me. I really can't see how it would help if I tried talking to him, when he's so obviously avoiding me."

Jake nods, as though considering it all.

"Maybe," he says diplomatically. "Or maybe he thinks you freaked out about what he did, and won't talk to *him*."

Seb just stares at him. He hadn't even thought of that. Mostly because it seems so ridiculously unlikely, but still.

"So," he says slowly, "let me get this straight. You think he's under the impression that I won't talk to *him*, when he's the one who acted like he did?"

Jake shrugs.

"I'm saying it's worth a shot," he replies, and when Seb looks uncomfortable, he straightens.

"Look," he says. "I don't know how you guys feel about each other. I don't know the details of what happened, or why he won't talk to you, or why he kissed you."

He looks Seb right in the eyes, sincere concern and something like pleading written all over his face.

"But I do know," he continues, "that I've never seen my brother like this before. I've never seen him broken up like this, never seen him look so... lonely."

He looks sad as he says it, and Seb just stares at him. Somehow, it hurts him to imagine Evan feeling any of that.

"And before this happened," Jake adds. "Before he fucked up... I've never seen him like that, either."

Seb frowns.

"Like what?" he asks.

"Happy," Jake says, simply. "He talked about you a lot, smiled more than I've seen him do in a while. He was even writing music again, and I know for a fact that he's been creatively blocked for some time."

Jake quirks a smile at his own choice of words, but Seb barely notices. He's too busy trying not to fall over. Jake seems to notice that, and he smiles sympathetically.

"Like I said," he continues. "I don't know how he feels, or why he did what he did, or why he's acting this way. But I know my brother, and I'm just reading the signs. And I think it's worth a shot."

He looks at Seb pointedly, with that soft authority Seb has noticed him possess. And finally, Seb sighs.

"What should I do?" he says, surprising himself with his own surrender, and Jake smiles sagely.

"Talk to him," he says. "Or try, at least. What have you got to lose?"

Seb reluctantly realizes that Jake has a point; he feels like he has already lost Evan. Talking to him can't possibly make it worse. Apart from the fact that he hates talking about stuff like that, and really isn't a fan of confrontation.

Seb sighs heavily, and raises his eyebrows at Jake.

"You're gonna make an awesome lawyer."

CHAPTER 8
THE DOOR

What is he doing here? Seriously, what the *hell* is he doing here?

Never before has a door looked so daunting. It's nothing special; plain, a darker shade, made of wood. No, it's what was *behind* the door that makes Seb feel as though there is a heavy stone in his stomach.

He decided to take Jake's advice. He decided to try and talk to Evan, mostly because both he and Jake feel that Evan would never actually do it himself, regardless of how he feels. Yesterday, Seb even went so far as to write down what he wanted to say, but decided against actually bringing the piece of paper along with him when coming here.

Now, though, he's kind of regretting that decision. Even though he would have felt ridiculous and pathetic, reading from some kind of script, he would at least have been able to get out what he wanted to say.

Now, as he stands outside Evan's door, everything he feels, every ounce of articulate skill he has, seems to completely evaporate. All of a sudden, he's nothing but nervous. And not in a good way.

Seb supposes that he could have called Evan, or texted him, even, instead of doing the drastic thing and showing up at his door. But he knows, on some level, that this is the best approach. Despite how much he hates confrontation and actually discussing his feelings with another person, he knows that this is the only way he could actually go through with it. And, hopefully, talking face to face will force Evan into actually having some kind of conversation about this.

Seb takes a deep breath, willing himself to stay put and not run away, as he raises his hand and knocks on the door.

There is no response, at first, so Seb knocks again. And this time, he actually hears a very loud, frustrated sigh from inside the room, followed by the shuffling sound of someone moving about. His heart beats faster.

"Dammit, Jake, I don't—"

The moment Evan pulls open the door and sees Seb, he completely freezes, cutting off the gruff reprimand intended for his brother.

The only adjectives that Seb can think of when he sees Evan's face are *shocked* and *terrified*. Because that's how Evan is looking at him, swallowing hard, eyes wide.

But somehow, it makes Seb feel better to know that he's having at least some kind of effect on him.

"Hey," Seb says after a few moments of tense silence. And Evan just keeps staring at him, the shock and fear dissipating slightly, although not yet entirely gone.

"Hey," he eventually replies, his voice low. He's holding the door open with one hand, as though using it as a barrier between himself and Seb, and Seb can't help but eye him up and down very quickly.

He looks tired, he thinks, with those dark shadows under his eyes. He's wearing jeans that are torn here and there, and a black t-shirt with a dark green, short sleeved button-up shirt open over it. There's light stubble on his face, from days of not shaving. It matches his light brown hair, which looks unusually ruffled. Seb stifles the urge to run his fingers through it.

"Do you mind?" Seb asks, deducing that Evan isn't going to invite him inside, himself. And he's honestly surprised when Evan almost immediately steps aside so he can enter.

Seb hesitantly steps into the room, Evan slowly closing the door behind him. It's funny, how he was almost worried that Evan wouldn't actually think there was a problem, that he would just laugh off the whole thing that happened between the two of them, and the way they have ignored each other ever since then. But he doesn't. It's obvious from his body language and manner that he knows exactly why Seb was here, and that there indeed is a problem.

Seb glances at Evan as he passes him, as he makes his way further into the room. Jake's choice of words come to mind, as he sees Evan's face and the way he carries himself.

Heartbroken.

It's oddly satisfying, and it makes him feel just the slightest bit hopeful.

"So," Evan says, shockingly being the first to speak. He turns around, but doesn't look at Seb. They are standing pretty much in the middle of the room, the afternoon sun giving the space a sort of golden haze. It lights Evan from behind, giving that halo-impression that reminds Seb of the time when Evan found him lying on that bench.

Beautiful.

"So," Seb repeats, in lack of anything else. *Shit.* How had he planned on doing this, again? He racks his brain, but can't find a smooth way of easing into it. So he just gets straight to the point, in his usual, awkward, but blunt manner.

"What the fuck?"

Okay, so maybe not straight to the point, per se. But Evan seems to get the idea, because he looks up at Seb then, the expression on his face saying that he knows exactly what Seb is referring to. He doesn't immediately answer, though. Instead, he shoves his hands in his pockets and glances away, clearly uncomfortable.

"I don't know," he says lamely, half-shrugging, and suddenly, Seb feels rather brave.

"That's not good enough," he finds himself saying, making Evan look up at him again, this time with a different, more pleading expression in his eyes; *Come on man, cut me some slack.* Seb can practically hear the words coming out of his mouth, just from that look.

"Well, I don't," Evan says, looking oddly lost for a moment. "I don't know."

Seb was feeling rather sympathetic towards Evan up until now, but he's quickly realizing that that sympathy is gradually being replaced by annoyance and frustration.

"You don't know?" he says, a hint of cynicism in his voice. "You kiss me, out of nowhere, and when I ask you about it, *you don't know?*"

Wow. He did *not* expect to be so blunt about it. Just saying out loud that Evan *kissed* him, to Evan's *face*, is something he really hadn't thought he was ready for. His discomfort is nothing compared to how Evan looks, though.

"Dude, I—" he starts, as though scrambling to explain, and Seb feels the frustration bubble up again.

"Don't *dude* me," he says, frowning. "It doesn't cover it. It doesn't even begin to cover it."

Where the hell is this coming from? How could he have been so scared a moment ago, and now, he's suddenly speaking his mind?

"Well, what do you want me to say?" Evan says, almost matching his frustration, a frown on his face. "I *don't know.* I'm not saying that to be an asshole, I'm saying it because it's true!"

Seb is a bit taken aback by that.

"Don't know what?" he asks. He's actually getting a bit angry now. "Why you did it? Why you've been avoiding me? Dude, you won't even talk to me."

Evan grits his teeth, and for a moment, Seb thinks he sees something like hurt in those green eyes.

Maybe Jake was right, he finds himself thinking, vaguely. Maybe it *was* the other way around. Maybe Evan does think that Seb was the one avoiding *him*.

"Last time I checked," Evan says bitterly, "you weren't talking to me, either."

And there. It seems that Jake was right, after all. But it doesn't matter.

"Seriously?" Seb says incredulously. "You can say that to me? After what you did? After you literally ran away to hide, and just left me there?"

The hurt is more obvious in Evan's eyes this time, and Seb realizes he hit a nerve. Well, if nothing else, it seems that Evan is at least fully aware of how shitty that behavior was.

"I'm sorry," he mutters, to Seb's surprise. "I panicked."

Seb just looks at him.

"Why?" he asks, and Evan glances away, his body language gradually changing, now. He's slowly looking less lost and more hard, as though replacing his hurt with anger.

"It was a bad idea," he says, his voice low, and Seb almost flinches. "That's all."

His words could have just as well been a sledgehammer, the way they make Seb mentally stagger.

"What?" he hears himself say, his voice weaker than he would like.

"What?" Evan repeats, his tone now annoyed and slightly pissed, rather than hurt and confused.

"I can't believe you just said that," Seb mumbles, saying his thoughts out loud, not really caring that it wasn't on purpose. Evan is frowning now.

"Why not?" he says, and Seb fumbles for the words.

"I just..." he says, unable to find any. "I—"

"Why do you even care?" Evan suddenly says, sounding angry and defensive, all of a sudden. "Why does it matter?"

"Because I like you!" Seb exclaims, shocked at the words coming out of his mouth.

It seems that he found some words, after all. And they hang there, suspended in the air between the them, and he hates it, regrets it immensely. But it's too late now. The words are out there, and they're true. Seb might as well make the best of it.

"I really like you," he continues, angry exasperation in his voice, mixed up with hurt. "In... that way. And you *know* that. You *must* know that."

He pauses for a moment, letting out a deep, shaky breath. The words are coming to him easily now, flowing out of his mouth as he expresses these feelings for the first time.

"And that's what kills me," he says, his voice more subdued and softer. "You must know how I feel, and you still keep doing this to me."

He's not entirely sure what he means Evan is doing to him, exactly. Maybe this. Maybe standing there, looking all adorable and lost and beautiful. Maybe making Seb feel this way, making him fall for him more and more ever since they first met. He doesn't know.

He pauses long enough then to see the reaction on Evan's face. It's a rather stiff one, as though Evan is suddenly having some inner battle about whether or not he should actually talk, or just push Seb away, both literally and figuratively. It's unbearable.

"Say something," Seb says, surprised at how his voice sounds almost desperate, rather than weak. But Evan doesn't move, and he doesn't say a word. So Seb's frustration and panic finally gets the better of him.

Seb only has time to think, *fuck it*, before he suddenly covers the distance between them and grabs the scruff of Evan's shirt to pull him closer. It's more a matter of pulling him*self* closer, perhaps, seeing as how Evan has turned into some immovable rock, but it doesn't matter. It brings him close enough to plant a hard, deliberate kiss on Evan's mouth, one that only lasts a moment, before he pulls away again.

"Tell me you don't want that," he hears himself say, with a kind of courage he has never really felt before, trying to keep himself from kissing Evan again, longer and harder this time. "Tell me, to my face, that you don't want me, and I'll go. And I promise I'll never bother you again."

He's shocked at the words coming out of his mouth. Seb has never really been much for confrontation, but somehow, this feels important. This is *really* important, and he needs to swallow down his own insecurities for just a moment. He needs to know, he needs the closure. He needs to know if he should just walk away right now, before the whole thing gets even more painful. Although, he doubts that it could get more painful.

He's wrong.

The hard expression on Evan's face looks almost like anger, and he doesn't say a word. So Seb deliberately hides the way it feels as though a cold knife has just been shoved into his stomach, and especially how it feels as though someone is slowly twisting it around. It's a pain that's unbelievably physical, and he swallows hard, slowly letting go of Evan's shirt.

Seb exhales slowly, in something like a sigh, one that shakes more than he wants it to. He doesn't want Evan to see him like this, doesn't want *anyone* to see him like this. He just wants to run and hide away and never have to see Evan again. Even though that sounds like the most horrible, most painful thing he can think of.

But Seb isn't an idiot. And he isn't about to stand here and act like one.

"Right," he musters, barely even looking at Evan, who still hasn't said a word and who still hasn't moved a muscle. He's taller than Seb, but Seb has never felt so small compared to him. "I get it."

Seb looks down at the floor, a very uncomfortable lump in his throat. He doesn't trust himself to speak, so he doesn't. Instead, he just turns around and makes his way toward the door. It's a small room, and he covers the distance more quickly than he would have wanted; this is going to be his last time in Evan's room, and he wants to have more time to savor it, to breathe in the scent of him, one last time.

But he can't. Not this time.

Seb slowly moves his hand to open the door, fully focused on not falling apart, when he finally hears Evan speak.

"I don't—" he tries, before sighing, annoyed. For once, it seems that Evan Matthews doesn't know what to say.

But Seb doesn't turn around, even though his hand has frozen, resting on the door's handle. Just the fact that Evan is saying anything at all right now is more than he could have hoped for.

"I'm not—"

Seb can picture it, can picture that frustrated frown on Evan's face, as he searches for the right words. Then comes another frustrated sigh, and a few hesitant, shuffling steps.

"I'm not good at this," Evan mutters gruffly. He has started moving towards Seb, toward the door, very slowly. "The whole... feelings-thing."

Seb resists the urge to glance over his shoulder.

"And this hasn't happened before," Evan continues. "This... thing."

Seb does look over his shoulder then, only to see Evan gesturing vaguely and awkwardly between them. He's standing rather close now, right behind Seb, really. He's frowning, as though this whole thing is just very difficult and bothersome. But he's still trying.

"What?" Seb asks carefully, trying to tone down the defensiveness in his voice. Evan sighs in frustration, again.

"This," he says, nodding at the space between them. Seb bitterly thinks of how Evan has never been more eloquent, as Evan shoves his hands in his pockets. "Whatever this is. It's never happened before. I don't know what to do with it."

Seb blinks. Evan looks so unbelievably uncomfortable. And then Seb catches what he said.

"Never?" he asks hesitantly, frowning, and Evan glances away.

"This," he repeats, as though annoyed that Seb doesn't get exactly what he means with that one, single word. "Feeling like this. It's never happened before."

Seb feels happy for a split second, but then gets the weirdest sinking sensation in his stomach, as though somehow disappointed.

"With a guy, you mean?" he asks, terrified of the answer, hoping that Evan is talking about reciprocated feelings, rather than being on the receiving end of unrequited ones. Seb doesn't know what to expect, and he's terrified.

But Evan surprises him, like he so often does, by shaking his head ever so little.

"No," he mutters, looking as though he's trying to avoid Seb's eyes and focus on them, at the same time. "Not just that. I mean *ever. Never.*"

And just like that, Seb's heart surges into a double beat that's weirdly uncomfortable, and he turns around completely, his eyes on Evan. Evan is still avoiding looking at him, swallowing nervously, hands in his pockets, a frown on his face. Seb has never seen him like this before. He has never seen him so... discomposed.

Is Evan saying what he thinks he's saying? Is he, by some miracle, *not* pushing Seb away? Maybe even doing the opposite? And more than that, is he saying that he has never felt this way about anyone else? At all?

It makes Seb feel uncomfortable and scared and excited, and he clears his throat slightly, for no real reason at all.

"I'm gonna need more to go on," he says, in an awkward attempt at his usual, sarcastic self, failing miserably. He looks down at the floor. "I just need you to be straight with me."

Normally, he would have rolled his eyes at his particular choice of words, or at least seen the irony in them, but not right now. Right now, Seb is too scared to do anything, really, apart from breathing. He looks up at Evan.

"I just need to know," he says.

He watches Evan for several, long seconds, but gets no reply. At least Evan is looking at him, though, but just barely, clearly trying not to. And that sinking feeling comes over Seb again, as Evan says nothing.

But this time, there is frustration there, too. Frustration at Evan's apparent inability to speak his mind and say what he actually feels.

And so Seb follows his impulse after all, the one that is such a fundamental part of his behavior; he doesn't say a word, just shakes his head slightly, and rolls his eyes.

And Evan makes a sound that resembles a muffled groan, as he covers the distance between them.

The sudden kiss is brief, but intense, and Seb barely has time to register what's happening, before Evan pulls away again. He places his forehead against Seb's, moving his hand up to hold his chin firmly between his fingers, and Seb realizes that they're both breathing rather heavily, despite the very short time the kiss lasted. His head is spinning from the sheer intensity of it, not to mention utter shock.

"If you roll your eyes at me again," Evan says huskily, his eyes closed, "I swear to god."

Seb takes a deep breath, mouth half-open, Evan's fingers still gripping his chin, eyes open in pure shock. He watches as Evan pulls away just far enough to open his eyes

and lock their gazes. Those eyes are suddenly fierce.
Unsure, scared even, but fierce.

"Okay," Seb breathes, at loss for words, and Evan keeps
his unusually piercing gaze on him for a few more
moments. And then he forces up Seb's chin with his
fingers, lowering his mouth so that it can crash into his.

The effect is immediate. Seb vaguely thinks of their first
kiss, how soft and sweet it was, relatively innocent. This
one isn't like that.

It doesn't even take a second for Seb to reciprocate the
kiss, closing his eyes and melting into it, and he hears Evan
sigh against him as he moves his body closer, dropping his
hand from Seb's chin to move it to his waist. Seb feels their
chests pressing together, Evan's stubble against his face, as
he suddenly pushes against Seb with such force that Seb
backs into the closed door behind him, leaving him caught
between it and Evan. And he feels trapped. But it's the
sweetest feeling in the world.

It is odd how, even though Seb has never been with a
guy before, this doesn't feel the slightest bit weird. Maybe
it's because Evan isn't just a guy, not just a person Seb
normally never would have seen that way. No, this is *Evan*.
And *Evan* is another thing entirely.

It's also odd, how they were fighting just moments ago,
Seb's heart broken and bleeding. And now this is
happening. Seb would have been confused if he weren't so
distracted.

Seb feels an overwhelming need to touch Evan, *all* of
Evan, to feel his hands on his body—but he's hesitant.
What if Evan changes his mind again? What if he pulls
away again and runs, just like he did last time?

Whatever doubts Seb has, though, are whisked away when he feels Evan practically press him up against the closed door, hands moving down along his body and settling on his hips, one hand moving down to his ass. This time, Seb figures that his hard-on is less embarrassing, especially when he feels how Evan is having the same reaction. And the way Evan pushes his tongue into his mouth isn't helping, reducing Seb to a shivering mess.

But it gives him the push he needs.

Evan's hair is soft against his fingers, as he cards them through it, settling at the back of his head and gripping his hair tightly, giving in to the impulse he had earlier, when Evan opened the door. He earns a groan of surprised pleasure from Evan, who uses his hands to pull Seb even closer, slowly starting to grind against him, making Seb's skin catch fire, as he stays firmly trapped between Evan and the door behind him. He can't believe this is happening. Somewhere in the back of his mind, he can't help but feel as though he's going to wake up from some dream any moment, only to find that he never even met Evan in the first place.

But he did. And this really *is* happening.

Seb moans absently, sliding his free hand down Evan's body and slipping it in underneath his shirt, where he *finally* gets to touch his skin. It's burning hot, and he feels Evan tense up as he touches him, feels his grip tighten on Seb's body, as he groans against his lips. It's all too much, and it's not nearly enough.

Seb isn't entirely sure how long they've been at it—it could be seconds or minutes or hours, for all he cares—when there is a knock at the door. It makes them both jump, pausing for a moment, pulling apart.

Seb glances at the door which he's currently pressed up against, then glances up at Evan, who frowns a bit. Seb raises his eyebrows at him, but he just shakes his head, as though saying that if they don't make a sound, maybe whoever is knocking will leave. But the knock comes again, and even though they don't move a muscle, their plan seems futile.

"Evan," comes Jake's voice from the other side. "I know you're in there. Come on."

Evan makes a face, as though cursing inside his head.

"Not a good time, Jake," he says, and Seb glances between him and the door.

"Come on, man," Jake says. "I need to talk to you."

Evan looks very uncomfortable, and Seb waits, his entire body practically vibrating with impatience. His hand is still underneath Evan's t-shirt, and he absently moves it downwards, slowly. The reaction from Evan is immediate, as he tenses up.

"Can't it wait?" he gets out, and Seb leans in an plants a soft kiss by his throat, making Evan grit his teeth. He actually closes his eyes as Seb slowly kisses up along his neck, squeezing them shut, as though trying to focus.

"Not really," Jake says, oblivious to what he's interrupting, and Seb feels his impatience grow, his hand slipping underneath the hem of Evan's jeans, down over his ass, feeling the soft fabric of his boxers against his fingers. Evan's grip on Seb tightens, as he leans his forehead against the door, exhaling slowly, heavily. Seb's kisses aren't as soft anymore, eagerly tasting Evan's skin.

"Look, I just—" Jake says, and suddenly, it's just too much.

"Really not a good time, Jake," Seb exclaims without thinking, and several seconds of stunned silence follow, from Seb and Evan, as well as Jake. Then, finally, Jake speaks from the other side of the door.

"Never mind," he says shortly, as though suddenly awkward, and Seb relaxes as he hears his hurried steps disappear down the hall outside. Evan chuckles.

"Shit," he says. "Timing, man."

Seb murmurs in agreement, as Evan's hands press against him firmly.

"Maybe it's for the best, though," he says after a few moments, making Evan pull back and look at him.

"What do you mean?" he asks, looking oddly anxious. Seb can't help but quirk his mouth in a smile.

"It's a bit much, don't you think?" he says, glancing down at the general closeness of their bodies, and Evan cocks his head.

"Maybe," he says, before looking at Seb pointedly. "Not that I mind."

"I'm gonna agree with you, there," Seb says, and Evan smiles crookedly at him.

"But...?" he says, and Seb fidgets a bit. He can't believe he's saying this, especially seeing as how he's vibrating with impatient want and suppressed emotion, at this point. But still. He feels like he wants to slow this down, make it last.

"But," he says, honestly feeling a bit silly, "maybe we should take it down a notch. Don't want to rush into anything."

They look at each other for a few moments, and suddenly, the heat of what they were just doing is slightly punctuated by some kind of awkwardness.

"I mean," Seb continues, trying not to blush with embarrassment. "I've never... You know. With a guy, I mean."

Evan swallows, nodding. He looks oddly shy.

"Yeah," he says gruffly. "Me neither."

Seb finds himself smiling a little at that; it makes him feel a bit better to know that Evan is as new as he is, when it comes to that particular matter. And just like that, it's as though they both decide to just stop, or at least slow down. At least for now. Because there is no way in hell they aren't going to do this again, but right now isn't the time.

"So..." Seb says, after several moments of silence. "*SoulCalibur*?"

He curses in his head at this stupid, utterly ridiculous and lame suggestion, but Evan just smiles; it's that new smile, the happy, soft one, that suddenly makes Seb feel somehow adorable.

Evan leans in and places the softest kiss imaginable on Seb's mouth, before pulling away just a little bit.

"Sound like a plan."

CHAPTER 9
DRUGS

Seb taps his notepad with his pen, quickly and erratically, trying to focus. He's sitting at his desk, lecture notes and books spread out in front of him, but his mind just keeps wandering. He knew it was a bad idea to study with Evan nearby; it takes all he has not to turn around and just watch him, as he lies there, sprawled on Seb's bed.

"Do you always do that?" Evan asks, and Seb glances over his shoulder, consciously not lingering. Seeing Evan on his bed does things to him, after all.

"What?" he asks.

"That," Evan clarifies. "The tapping thing. It's distracting."

"*You're* distracting," Seb mutters, marveling in his own, biting comeback, and Evan chuckles.

"It can't be that bad," he says, and Seb sighs, turning a page of his book.

"Drugs *aren't* that bad, I suppose," he says lightly, and he can practically *sense* Evan smiling, from across the room.

"Did you just compare me to drugs?" he says, sounding amused, and Seb feels a tug at the corner of his mouth.

"So what if I did?" he says, and Evan pauses.

"Good drugs or bad drugs?" he asks, and Seb frowns.

"What?" he says, and Evan clarifies.

"Well," he says, "drugs, as in awesome happy-time drugs? Or drugs, as in hair-falling-out, losing-weight kind of drugs?"

Seb is lost for words at Evan's question, at least for a moment. He looks over his shoulder, catching a glimpse of Evan's almost childishly pleased expression and ruffled hair. *Damn*, he's hot.

"The good kind," Seb says, a small smile on his face, as he turns back to his schoolwork. "Although, the hair-falling-out and losing-weight part wouldn't surprise me, considering how little sleep I've been getting lately."

Evan doesn't reply to that, and Seb takes the opportunity to refocus his attention, at least for a couple of minutes. It's a completely futile attempt, though, because suddenly, he feels Evan's hands settling on his shoulders, from behind, before slowly smoothing down over his chest.

"I don't remember you complaining before," Evan says, his voice low, just by Seb's ear, and Seb's body reacts so intensely that he's kind of surprised he's still in solid form and didn't just melt into liquid under Evan's touch.

He takes a deep breath, half-closing his eyes.

"I'm not," he says, aware of how breathless he sounds. "I'm just saying."

Evan kisses his neck, and Seb closes his eyes completely this time. *Oh god.* It's unbelievable what one touch from Evan can do to him, how one kiss can make him completely fall to pieces.

"So you don't mind not getting any sleep?" Evan asks, practically purring against Seb's skin, making all the signals in his brain go haywire.

I should mind, Seb thinks. God knows, he has been constantly tired and unable to focus during lectures, ever since a few days ago, when Evan suddenly, unbelievably, made his move. Ever since then, they've spent pretty much every waking moment together. And the *non*-waking moments, as it were, either at Seb's place or Evan's.

At first, they honestly did try to take things slow, to ease into this shift in their relationship; it's a pretty big deal, after all. Even ignoring the fact that neither of them has fallen for, or even been with, a guy before, they did become really good friends before all this happened, and just switching over to another dynamic was a bit daunting.

Or, at least they thought it would be. It took about forty minutes of video gaming that first day, before Seb accidentally looked at Evan for too long, and Evan basically attacked him. They spent pretty much the rest of that day just making out on Evan's couch. Not that Seb minded. He *really* didn't.

"It is hugely impractical," Seb mutters, losing himself in the way Evan smells, the way his lips feel against his skin, the way his hands burn through his t-shirt. "How am I supposed to get anything done?"

Evan ignores him; he seems to be too focused on just brushing his lips against Seb's neck, inhaling slowly, as though taking in his scent. His hands are moving downward, along Seb's chest, down over his stomach, slowly moving down to his thigh. Seb keeps his eyes closed.

"Evan," he murmurs, almost warningly, as though about to say something else, and Evan makes a sound of acknowledgement against his skin. But Seb doesn't say anything else—his brain is suddenly wrapped up in a thick haze.

He has stopped tapping with his pen, and he leans back in his chair, Evan standing behind him.

Evan seems to take Seb's silence as encouragement, and while one hand stays on Seb's stomach, the other moves down over his thigh, making its way along the inside of his leg. Seb is sitting rather lazily, legs slightly spread, and he's fully aware of how Evan's hand feels through his jeans. It makes him tense up, it makes his heart pound. It makes him squirm, and it makes him hard.

He's too distracted by the whole sensation of it to notice, but Evan notices, because he slowly, hesitantly even, moves his hand closer to Seb's crotch. Closer to the bulge that the jeans are doing a half-assed job at keeping down. And the closer Evan gets, the heavier Seb breathes, until Evan slowly starts massaging him there, making Seb actually gasp through gritted teeth. This is new.

Alright, not exactly *new* new, but new enough. Even though Seb has had his share of sexual experience, as well as Evan (because he most *definitely* has), this is whole new territory to both of them, and it makes the whole thing unsure and hesitant, while simultaneously being insanely hot.

And they haven't actually gone very far, yet. Despite spending so much time together these past few days, not much like this has happened, so far. Sure, there has been some heavy making out, actually sleeping together in the same bed, some heavy groping. But that's mostly it; sleeping. They've held each other, kissed each other sleepily, nuzzled against the warm comfort of each other's skin. But hardly anything like this. Seb isn't even sure if it's because they're both new to it, or because whatever they have together feels... pure.

Seb is startled as the word comes to him, but it feels oddly in place. And why shouldn't it? Seb has never been in love before. Not like this, not like he is with Evan. Somehow, he feels like he wants to get it right. He doesn't want to rush anything. He wants it slow and hot, so that he can savor every moment of it and draw it out for as long as humanly possible.

But that is suddenly very difficult to do, as he feels Evan's hand against him, massaging, using just the right amount of pressure. Seb breathes heavily. He drops the pen from his hand, making it hit the desk surface with a clatter.

"Evan," he breathes, but Evan just kisses his neck, his shoulder, the outline of his jaw, the sensitive skin just below his ear.

"You work too hard," Evan says, his voice low and hoarse, purring into Seb's ear. Seb barely pays attention to his words, as that hand between his legs slowly slips in underneath the hem of his jeans. "You need to relax."

Seb lets out a sharp breath, as Evan touches him again, but this time only with a thin barrier of cotton between his hand and Seb's erection. And he starts massaging again, making Seb tilt his head back, eyes closed, one hand absently curling into a fist. He's breathing a bit faster now, heavier.

Evan's lips are right by his ear, and Seb can hear how he's breathing heavier, too, brushing his lips against Seb's skin. He kisses Seb's neck, but more intensely now, eagerly, smoothing over certain points with the slightest sweep of his tongue. Seb swallows hard, licks his lips, his mouth falling half-open.

"Oh god," he hears himself breathe, and it seems to spur Evan on, because he moans against Seb's skin, his touch intensifying. Seb suddenly notices how Evan's other hand is pinning his hips down against the chair; Seb has started gyrating slightly against Evan's teasing touch, wanting more. He feels like he's getting closer to the edge, agonizingly close.

"Evan," Seb breathes again, more urgently this time, intending to ask him to stop, before this goes too far. But Evan either doesn't want to listen, or he misinterprets Seb's plea, because instead of stopping, he leans down and covers Seb's mouth with his own. And whatever thoughts Seb just had about maybe stopping, immediately vanish.

Evan's tongue is suddenly in his mouth, his lips soft and firm against his, and Seb feels his breath catch. Shit. This feels too good, too unbelievably good. *Shit.*

But just as Seb braces himself for the inevitable outcome of this whole thing, it's as though Evan just *knows*, because he suddenly stops, leaving Seb hanging on the edge.

Evan pulls his mouth away with just a fraction of an inch, and Seb opens his eyes. Evan glances down at his hand, which is still in Seb's pants, and then he smiles, in the most smug, amused way. Seb narrows his eyes at him, and Evan chuckles.

"What?" he asks, amused. "I don't see a problem."

Seb squeezes his eyes shut with a sigh, before looking up at him.

"I hate you," he says. "So much."

Evan can tell he doesn't mean it; the way his annoyance thinly veils such utter affection is a dead giveaway.

"Sure you do," Evan replies, kissing him. It's a lingering kiss, the soft kind. "I can tell."

He adds that last part with a suggestive eyebrow-raise, and Seb groans.

"Get your hand out of my pants," he says, and Evan chuckles again.

"I think you like my hand in your pants," he retorts, and Seb grits his teeth slightly, as he's reminded of it. Evan's hand does feel really good against him, even though his hard-on is actually getting uncomfortable now, and very distracting.

"Yeah," he says. "A bit too much, evidently."

Evan smiles at him, looking down at him, half-upside down from Seb's point of view. Then he slowly does pull his hand out of Seb's pants, and Seb exhales.

"What?" he said snappily, as he sees Evan's expression; he's looking way too smug.

"Nothing," Evan says innocently, planting a kiss on Seb's lips. "Nothing at all."

He straightens and moves away from the chair, clapping Seb on the shoulder casually.

"Now, get back to work," he says, and Seb just gapes at thin air, frowning.

"I'm sorry, what?" he says. Evan makes his way back over to Seb's bed, throwing himself down onto it with a pleased exhale.

"Nothing," he says, folding his arms behind his head, and Seb slowly spins around in his chair, so that he faces him.

As though Evan moving away from him was some kind of trigger, he's suddenly acutely aware of how his whole body seems to be vibrating, aching for release, wanting Evan to finish what he started. And Seb just stares at him suspiciously for a few moments, taking in the sight of him.

How was he ever able to not *always* pay attention to just how fucking *hot* Evan is?

Seb gets up from his chair then and makes his way over to the bed, Evan looking at him, half-expectant and half-surprised. He looks very comfortable, lying there.

"You're so full of shit," Seb says, before joining him, and Evan laughs.

"I like to think of it as part of my charm," he says, scooting over so that Seb can lie down beside him. "And it worked, didn't it?"

Seb frowns.

"What did?" he asks, and Evan turns to him pointedly. They're both lying on their backs.

"I got your attention," he says with a suggestive smile, and Seb can't help but surrender a smile back.

"You did," he says.

Speaking of, he thinks, he is an amazing testament to discipline, lying here next to Evan, with a very distracting boner. He could just attack him. God knows, he wants to. But he doesn't, and he sighs inwardly. For some reason, he feels like such a *virgin*, when it comes to this guy.

It's silent for a few moments, and Seb closes his eyes. It feels good, just lying here, just having Evan right next to him. He doesn't think he has ever really liked that as much before, with anyone, just lying there. But with Evan, it feels natural, soft and easy.

"Can I ask you something?"

Seb murmurs in acknowledgement as Evan speaks.

"What's up with that?" Evan asks, and Seb opens his eyes. Evan nods at the poster on the wall above the bed.

"What?" Seb says, confused, and Evan half-shrugs, which looks funny, seeing as how he's currently lying down on his back.

"Poe," Evan clarifies. "Why do you like him so much?"

Seb flicks his blue gaze over to the poster, the one Evan read and quoted from the night they first met. The memory makes Seb feel all warm inside.

"I don't know," he says. "Why?"

"He's just so depressing," Evan says, and Seb frowns.

"Not all the time," he retorts. "And his writing's not depressing, it's... hauntingly beautiful."

Evan snorts.

"Dude, you're so emo," he says, smiling, and Seb raises an eyebrow at him.

"Don't you dare," he says. "No one even says that anymore."

He smiles to himself a little, though, while refusing to admit how cheesy he did in fact sound, just now.

"And you're the emo one," he says. "With your guitar and your torn jeans and your singing."

Seb doesn't mention how he loves all those things about Evan, but it doesn't need saying.

"No, I'm *brooding*," Evan clarifies, before looking at Seb with a mischievous smile on his face. "Way hotter."

"Are you saying I'm not hot?" Seb says in mock hurt, and Evan raises his eyebrows.

"That's not even close to what I'm saying," he says, smiling. "I'm just saying that as a musician, I have the right to be brooding. It's like a prerequisite."

Seb raises his eyebrows and cocks his head, turning his gaze to the ceiling.

"Clearly you don't know what being a writer means," he says, and Evan smiles.

"Fair enough," he admits. "What else do you like?"

Seb turns to look at him, surprised. They are lying right next to each other, here on Seb's bed. Evan is so close that Seb could have counted every tiny freckle on his face.

"What do you mean?" he asks.

121

"Writing-wise," Evan clarifies. "What else do you like? Any fun stuff, or is it all death and sad and *haunting beauty*?"

He says the last few words mockingly, and Seb narrows his eyes at him.

"I do like other stuff," he says. Then he frowns. "Why do you ask?"

"Because I want to know you," Evan says simply, as though it's the most obvious thing in the world. "I want to know what you like, what you don't like."

Seb just looks at him. It's so weird how he loves hearing Evan say that.

"Well," he says, thinking. "I like Robert Frost, too."

Evan frowns.

"Name rings a bell," he says.

"It should," Seb says, as though personally offended by the lack of literature education among people, as he rolls over onto his side, still facing Evan. "He's amazing."

"If you say so," Evan smiles. He seems to like it when Seb gets passionate about something, even at such a small degree. "What's he done?"

Seb hesitates.

"*The woods are lovely,*" he recites, "'*dark and deep. But I have promises to keep. And miles to go before I sleep.*'"

He's a bit startled at his own words, but he can't help it. Apart from skipping the repeated last line, those are some of his favorite lines of anything ever, and he has the entire poem memorized.

Evan just looks at him for a moment.

"I like it," he says. "Very emo."

Seb actually punches him in the arm lightly, and Evan laughs.

"Sorry," he says. "I'm being an ass, I'm sorry."

Seb settles down again, his elbow under his head, and Evan rolls over onto his side, too. They are facing each other properly, now.

"It was nice, though," Evan says, seriously. "I see the appeal."

"Yeah," Seb says, forgiving him. "What about you?"

Evan makes a face.

"What about me?" he says, and Seb *almost* rolls his eyes. "What do you like?"

Evan thinks about it, his eyes wandering.

"Lots of things," he says. "Can't think of anything right now."

Seb frowns.

"Nothing?" he asks, and Evan shrugs. "There must be something you like."

Evan looks at him.

"Nothing that immediately comes to mind," he says, before moving closer. "Or maybe I could think of a few things."

Seb notices the slight drop in his voice, and he scans Evan's face with his eyes.

"Like what?" he says, and Evan moves his hand to Seb's waist, eyes fixed on his, before looking at his mouth.

"You," Evan says, making Seb's heart skip a beat, both from surprise and joy. "I really like you."

It's funny how Seb seems to de-age about five years when he hears that; suddenly, he feels like a fumbling, shy sixteen-year-old, shocked at being the object of someone's affections. But he isn't sixteen anymore, and he isn't that shy, fumbling guy anymore (well, not nearly as much, anyway), and it doesn't render him speechless for more than two seconds.

"That's good," he says, his own voice dropping slightly. "Nice to know we're on the same page."

Evan moves even closer, his hand slipping in underneath Seb's t-shirt. And just like that, whatever spark Seb managed to douse in the past few minutes just flares back to life, and Evan is sure to have noticed. At least, judging from the way his green eyes suddenly seem to light up, focused and hungry.

Seb swallows, a hint of nervousness creeping up on him. But why is he nervous? He has nothing to be nervous about. He has been in situations like this before, even if never with a guy—the basics are pretty simple and pretty much the same.

But this is Evan. *Evan*. And Evan makes him nervous.

Seb tries to breathe evenly as Evan smoothes his hand over his back, underneath his t-shirt, tries to stay calm. But then Evan kisses him, and Seb closes his eyes, surrendering. He grips Evan's button-up shirt with his fingers, as the two of them press closer together.

Seb inhales deeply, as Evan moves his lips down along his neck. He kisses his throat, his collarbone, his jaw line, tasting his skin and smoothing over those kisses with his tongue, just like before. And Seb grits his teeth, his eyes closed. Then Evan's fingers start undoing the fly of his jeans, and he tenses up.

For some reason, Seb's automatic response is to ask him to stop, but he immediately decides that the idea is stupid, and he therefore elects to ignore it. Instead, he lets out a moan, as Evan's hand slips in underneath his jeans, picking up where he left off just minutes ago. And there is no ramp-up this time; Seb is already hard, as though no time has passed at all between then and now.

Evan is taking it slow though, massaging him through his boxers, and Seb squeezes his eyes shut, his hand pressing against Evan's back, against the hard muscles that move beneath his skin and shirt. Those lips are still trailing over his neck and throat, planting one searing kiss after another, and just as Seb is too wrapped up in it all to notice anything else, Evan decides to slip his hand in underneath his boxers, as well.

Seb exhales loudly in surprise, as those fingers wrap around him, and it doesn't take more than a few seconds, before he simply digs his fingers into Evan's hair and pulls his mouth up to his own. He kisses him hungrily, earning a deep, rumbling moan from Evan, whose hand is doing a thorough job of bringing him closer and closer to the edge.

In fact, Seb realizes, as he loses himself in Evan and everything about him, that edge is right there, staring him in the face. And there is nothing stopping him, this time.

As though Evan can tell, he begins moving his hand at a faster pace, with an amount of pressure that's just right, and Seb grips his hair tightly, his breath heavy and fast.

"Seb." Evan rasps his name against his lips, slightly breathless, in between kisses. "Sebastian."

And that's it. In a sudden, blinding surge, Seb's entire body tenses up. He swears everything just stops for a moment, swears that Evan breathes his name again, as that amazing, blissful release finally comes. When he relaxes again, every muscle in his body has been reduced to jelly, and he feels his fingers loosen their grip on Evan's hair. He's breathing heavily, a slight ringing in his ears.

Evan is breathing heavily, too, and he watches Seb's face.

"Shit," Seb murmurs under his breath, closing his eyes. "*Shit.*"

"Good or bad shit?" Evan asks, and Seb frowns, even without opening his eyes.

"What do you think?" he says, and Evan chuckles, planting a kiss between his eyebrows, where the frown is.

"I think you're beautiful."

CHAPTER 10

IMPERFECT

There are so many cliché ways of describing love. Being *in love*. Seb has always found them to be just that—cliché. He has always kind of wondered why there seems to be only a limited variation when it comes to describing it in literature, in music, why it seems to be the same everywhere, in every era. Now he understands why; the feeling itself is universal and overwhelming, and nearly impossible to describe.

If he had seen his present self only a month or so ago, he would have been annoyed, to say the least. Because lately, Seb is constantly finding himself lost in thought, smiling to himself for no reason. Even in the middle of a lecture, eating lunch, standing in line somewhere, falling asleep... He suddenly always seems to have a reason to smile. And it doesn't take more than the slightest reminder of Evan for that to happen.

There was no need to tell Jake about what happened, about just how Seb's and Evan's relationship changed; he seemed to be fully aware of just what he interrupted that time, when he knocked on Evan's door. And the first time he actually saw Seb and Evan together after that, he was just the slightest bit awkward. But it passed quickly. Sophie was there too, and even though there wasn't exactly an announcement, it was pretty obvious that the dynamic between Evan and Seb had changed, and how. Seb remembers Sophie turning to Jake and nudging him pointedly, with a dimpled smile.

"Sophie is convinced that she called it from the start," Jake explained tiredly.

"I did!" Sophie exclaimed, still smiling, turning to Seb. "I'm just glad you finally did something about it."

Seb just shrugged, a bit uncomfortable at being the direct focus of someone's attention like that. But then Evan looked at Seb and squeezed his hand, and every ounce of discomfort completely vanished.

It has been almost two weeks since they became a couple; the word still sounds weird to Seb, as he's still trying to wrap his head around the concept of Evan being his boyfriend. Even though they haven't exactly gone official about it, it feels natural, comfortable, almost like they have always been together, and as the two of them hang out at Jake's place one day, it doesn't even feel weird.

Evan and Seb are sitting on the couch, watching a movie that held Sophie's and Jake's attention for about twenty minutes, before they started packing again. They are moving in together, seeing as how Jake's dorm room is no bigger than Seb's, and Sophie already practically lives there, anyway. So they're packing for their planned move to an apartment not too far away, just on the edge of campus, and watching a movie was meant to distract them from that for a while. It seems to be doing nothing whatsoever, though, and Seb glances up at them.

"You're missing the best part," he says, and Jake gave him a look.

"Dude," he says, "I'm not missing anything, trust me. Evan's made me watch it about a thousand times, already."

"Because it's a classic," Evan says defensively, stuffing popcorn in his mouth.

"There's nothing classic about *The Crow*, Evan," Jake says, earning an outraged look from his brother.

"Isn't there, though?" Seb says sagely, raising his eyebrows, and Evan cocks his head at him, eyes on Jake, as though saying *see?* Jake shakes his head.

"You gotta to stop backing him up on these things," he says, pointing at Seb.

"I shall stop nothing," Seb says, taking a handful of popcorn, using the hand that isn't currently locked together with Evan's. "Especially not when it comes to movies and truth."

Evan smiles proudly, giving Jake a smug look. And Jake just shakes his head again, while Sophie stands there, just smiling at the whole thing.

Seb munches on some popcorn, watching Eric Draven kick some ass on the TV, while Jake and Sophie keep packing. Evan is sitting in the corner of the couch, one leg up on the cushions and the other over the edge, and Seb is half-lying in the V of his legs, leaning with his back against Evan's chest. Their right hands are resting on Seb's stomach, fingers entwined, popcorn bowl precariously placed on the edge of the tiny coffee table, not too far away.

"Oh, I had almost forgotten about this," Sophie suddenly says, and Seb glances over at her. She's going through one of Jake's dresser drawers—*her* drawer, Seb guesses—and she has found a scarf, which she holds up in front of her. "Not sure if I should keep it or not."

"Well," Jake says diplomatically, but with a certain edge to his voice that sounds very relationship-y. "If you actually forgot that you had it, maybe you won't miss it."

"I said *almost*," Sophie points out, and Jake gives her a look which Seb has very aptly come to call his *bitchface*. "And it's really cute."

She puts on the scarf, a sheer, pastel pink, and looks in the mirror.

"I used to wear it a lot with this dress, actually," she says, putting her hands on her hips. Her dress is a different pastel shade, and it ends just above her knees. "Although..."

She scrunches up her face in thought, before turning around.

"What do you think?" she asks. "With or without?"

She twirls experimentally, and Jake and Seb both shrug uninterestingly. Seb has never been much for stuff like that, anyway, and he senses that Jake isn't, either. Evan glances up at her briefly, though, before flicking his eyes back to the TV.

"Looks better without," he says, mouth full of popcorn, making everyone, including Seb, just stop and stare at him. It takes Evan several seconds to realize why.

"Oh god," he says, sounding appalled. "I can't believe I just said that."

Jake smiles, in a way that's equal parts smug and amused.

"Evan, giving fashion advice," he says. "How gay of you."

"I'm not gay," Evan automatically responds, though not the least bit defensive, and Seb raises his eyebrows at him.

"Really, Evan?" he says, sounding incredibly doubtful as he pointedly looks down at their entwined fingers and the way Seb is practically lying in Evan's lap. Then he looks up at Evan again, cocking his eyebrows. "*Really?*"

Sure, the closest definition of Evan's sexuality would probably be bisexual, just like with Seb, but that's besides the point, right now. Seb just needs to tease.

He sounds almost serious for a moment, but he smiles when Evan glares at him, the slightest flush on his cheeks.

"You're the exception," Evan mumbles, as though a bit awkward about Jake being there to hear him say something like that. But he still plants a soft kiss on Seb's lips, and Jake chuckles.

"Aww," he teases. "That's adorable."

"Shut your hole, Jake," Evan says, shooting him a look. But he says it softly enough for Jake to simply shake it off and keep that smug, amused smile on his face, and the way

Evan is slightly blushing all of a sudden does make his words much less intimidating.

"Jake," Sophie scolds with a smile, slapping her boyfriend's upper arm with her hand. "Be nice to your brother."

Jake just gives her a look that says *what did I do?*, and Sophie shakes her head, turning to the mirror. She angles herself to get a good look, before taking off the scarf around her neck. She tilts her head.

"He's right, though," she says. "It does look better without."

"No, it doesn't," Evan says, a bit frantically, as Jake turns to him with a big smile on his face, the kind he has reserved for teasing his big brother. "I'm not right. Stop it."

But Jake just laughs quietly, and Seb can't help but smile. Then Evan nudges him.

"Aren't you supposed to be on my side?" he says, accusing, but Seb just raises his eyebrows at him.

"I am," he says. "She just happens to be right. And you're really fun to mess with."

He says it matter-of-factly, and Evan glares at him, making Jake laugh harder.

"I hate you," Evan mutters, and Seb smiles.

"I know," he says, lifting up Evan's hand to kiss it, still keeping their hands locked together. And that's all it takes for those green eyes to soften, and to make Seb feel completely at ease.

"So," Evan says, turning to his brother. "You guys need a hand with moving your stuff?"

Jake gets a weird look on his face, but covers it up quickly.

"No, we're good," he says, and Evan frowns.

"Really?" he says. "'Cause you can use my baby if you want."

Seb rolls his eyes, but smiles simultaneously; Evan's irrational affection for his car is both ridiculous and adorable.

"No, really," Jake assures him. "We've got it covered."

Evan looks at him suspiciously.

"How?" he says, and Jake glances at Sophie. They both look a bit uncomfortable, but Jake is worse.

"Well," he says after a few moments, turning back to Evan. He seems reluctant to tell him. "I talked to dad, and... he offered to help."

Seb can feel Evan tense up, can feel every muscle in his body suddenly go rigid. Even his grip on Seb's hand tightens a bit.

"What?" he says, and Jake looks even more uncomfortable.

"Look," he says. "I know it doesn't make a difference. But he wanted to help, so... I figured we'd let him."

Evan doesn't say anything for a few seconds.

"Dad's coming here?" he finally says, sounding oddly tense. Jake half-shrugs in confirmation.

"Yeah," he says. Seb can't really tell if he's more uncomfortable about their father coming, or Evan's reaction to it. "This weekend."

Silence follows, only broken by the sound of theatrical punches and '90s rock on the TV. Finally, Seb can't take the tension anymore.

"Meeting the parents, then," he says, but no one replies. Jake just has that sad, concerned look on his face, and Evan is gritting his teeth. Sophie watches them both with apprehension, like an outsider, like Seb, except with a look that says she knows very well why they're reacting this way.

Seb hesitates for a moment, caught in the tension.

"Wow," he says. "Don't get too excited."

He wishes he hadn't said anything the moment he does. But his sarcasm is his defense, his shield, and he uses it when he's uncomfortable. Thankfully, though, everyone here knows that, so no one takes his comment as rude or insensitive.

"It's nothing personal, Seb," Jake explains sadly, glancing at Evan. "It's just... Maybe not such a good idea."

Sophie looks at Jake with sadness written all over her face, as though she knows what he's talking about, and she most likely does. Jake, on the other hand, looks at Evan, who still hasn't said anything. His eyes are directed straight ahead, and Seb looks up at him. It hurts him to see Evan like this, like he's biting down on something hard to keep himself from expressing anything. It hurts him, because he knows it means Evan is in pain.

Seb squeezes his hand gently, and Evan seems to snap out of it. He turns to Seb, who looks at him with a kind of concern and anxiousness that he knows he hides so well, that only Evan can see it, and only because he has learned to. And Evan smiles tiredly, but sincerely.

"We'll talk about it later, okay?" he says quietly, and Seb gives him a small nod.

And with that, they don't mention it again. Instead, they return to watching *The Crow*, while Jake and Sophie keep discussing what and what not to bring along for the move.

It's amazing how much stuff can be crammed into such a small room, really.

When the movie is over, Evan and Seb say goodbye and retreat to Seb's room, which is only a few doors down the hall, and Evan unceremoniously sits down on Seb's bed. Seb goes over to his laptop to put on some music, as Evan exhales heavily.

"That was weird," Evan says after a few moments, and Seb frowns, turning around to face him.

"Why?" he says, and Evan looks up at him, before glancing away again, a small, almost embarrassed smile on his face.

"Never hung out with my brother and Sophie like that before," he says, and Seb looks at him, confused.

"What do you mean?" he asks, and Evan looks a bit uncomfortable.

"I've never hung out with them," he tries, "*with* someone else."

It takes a few moments for his awkward explanation to sink in, and Seb raises his eyebrows.

"What," he says. "You never brought a girlfriend home?"

Evan shakes his head.

"Not really," he says, and Seb gets the weirdest, happy feeling in his stomach. "This is a first."

He looks up at Seb, a bit alarmed, as though catching himself.

"I mean," he fumbles, "you're not a girlfriend. Obviously. But... you know."

"I'm not?" Seb says dramatically, hand to his chest. "I'm so confused."

"Shut up," Evan mutters, but with a smile on his face, which Seb returns. "You know what I mean."

"I do," Seb confirms, making his way over to sit beside his boyfriend. "And I guess it's a nice ego boost, in a weird way."

Evan glances at him suspiciously, as he sits down.

"What about you?" he asks, and Seb makes a face.

"Girlfriend," he explains. "High school. Didn't last long, though. But my parents liked her."

Evan nods, and Seb finds himself wishing that he hadn't brought a girlfriend home, ever. He wishes that Evan could have been his first relationship like that, the first one to show off as his own to the people closest to him. Somehow, he envies Evan for having that.

"So," he says, nudging Evan gently. "Does that make me special?"

Evan glances at him again. It's unbelievable how *shy* he manages look sometimes.

"I guess," he says gruffly. "Maybe."

Seb smiles.

"Good to know," he says, and Evan smiles crookedly at him. "Next step, family dinners."

He meant it as a joke, but the way Evan's expression changes suddenly reminds him of what they talked about at Jake's place earlier. And suddenly, he feels so stupid.

"I'm sorry," he says. "I know you don't wanna talk about it."

"No, it's fine," Evan says, sounding oddly tired. "It's just as well."

Seb looks at him, waiting, trying to read his expression. It's rather blank, but with something underneath that he can't quite identify.

"Remember what I told you," Evan starts, "about my dad? That he's angry?"

Seb nods; Evan told him that the same night he kissed him for the first time, and Seb remembers everything about that night.

"Yeah, well," Evan says. "*Angry* might be an understatement."

He sighs.

"When me and Jake were kids," he says, "dad used to drink a lot. Especially after mom died. He would get angry, and sometimes violent. Not too bad, though."

He hurries to add that last part when he sees Seb's tense expression.

"It's not like he beat us, or anything." Evan looks lost in thought for a moment, staring into space. "But he wasn't really a dad. Not a good one, at least. He didn't really look after us, so I had to look after Jake. And when dad *did* get angry and violent... I had to make sure he didn't take it out on him."

Seb waits, listens. He's not sure which is affecting him more; what Evan is telling him, or the protective look Evan gets when he talks about his little brother.

"Anyway," Evan continues. "I've never really gotten along with my dad. Neither has Jake. But I think Jake tries to give him second chances, you know? He doesn't really remember it like I do, I guess. He was too young, and I kind of always put myself between them, so he wouldn't have to deal with it. But lately, ever since we left for college, dad's been trying to turn his life around. I think it finally hit him that he might lose us for good, and he's trying to make up for all the bullshit he's done."

Evan looks at Seb.

"I'm just not sure it's that easy," he says. "I just don't think I can unlearn a lifetime of his bullshit, just like that. Even if he *does* want to help his son move in with his girlfriend."

He adds that last part with some sarcasm, and Seb gives him a small smile of approval, one which Evan returns.

"And," he says with a tired sigh, "I know for a fact that he has a hard time dealing with this kind of thing."

He gestures vaguely between the two of them, and Seb nods slowly.

"So," he says carefully. "I'm guessing he wouldn't approve?"

Evan smiles bitterly.

"Not even a little bit," he says. "He's not exactly what you would call open-minded, and especially not about stuff like that."

He looks up at Seb.

"What about your parents?" he asks, changing the subject. Seb lets him, and thinks about the question.

"Honestly," he says, "I don't think they'd care that much. I mean, at worst, they would probably just think it's a thing that'll pass."

He glances down and smiles humorlessly.

"Although," he says, "maybe not taking it seriously would be worse than disapproving."

Evan frowns.

"How so?" he says, and Seb looks up at him.

"Because how I feel isn't just some passing thing," he says, with such determination that he surprises himself. "I know it isn't. I'd rather have them hate me than think that I don't really lo—"

He stops, snapping his mouth shut, and Evan just looks at him.

"Don't really what?" he says, and Seb suddenly feels his heart pounding.

Don't ask me that, Evan, he thinks frantically. *Please. I'm not ready for that.*

"Care about you," Seb finally says, the words sounding oddly stiff, as though he meant to say something else. He looks down as he says it, suddenly feeling very exposed. "I wouldn't want them to think that I don't. Because I do."

He looks up again, wondering if he looks as shy as he suddenly feels.

"I really care about you," he says weakly, as though the words might get less scary to say if he says them quietly. And Evan just looks at him for a few moments. He looks somehow surprised, but at the same time... shy. Again. He looks almost the same as Seb feels.

"I really care about you, too," he finally says, the same hesitation in his voice that Seb just had. They just look at each other for a while, and then, Evan chuckles.

"What?" Seb says, smiling slightly, because he can tell that Evan's laugh is a genuinely happy one.

"You're a bad influence on me, man," Evan says, and Seb raises his eyebrows at him, as Evan moves to lie down on the bed.

"What?" Seb says. "How?"

"You're making me sappy," Evan replies, looking at the ceiling and shaking his head, as he lies down comfortably on his back. "Shit. Never thought I'd be like that."

Seb scoffs.

"You kidding?" he says. "Past me never would have hung with present me. My sarcasm levels have become dangerously low, I hope you realize."

"Really?" Evan says, looking at him and quirking an eyebrow. "I hadn't noticed."

"Oh, yes," Seb says seriously. "You were probably just too busy brooding."

Evan narrows his eyes at him then, a small smile on his face.

"Your sarcasm levels seem just fine to me," he says, and Seb cocks his head.

"Not entirely sure that counts as sarcasm," he points out, and Evan rolls his eyes, still smiling.

"You're such an ass," he says, affection in every layer of his voice, and Seb smiles as he moves closer, leans down, and plants a kiss on his cheek.

"And yet, you still keep me around," he says, and Evan turns to him. He smiles softly and puts his hand by Seb's face, so he can pull him close enough to kiss him. It's a soft kiss, one full of adoration and tenderness, and when they pull apart, Seb lies down and lowers his head to Evan's chest. He places his ear right over Evan's heart, and closes his eyes as Evan automatically starts stroking his dark hair, twirling it between his fingers absent-mindedly. His heartbeat is steady and strong and comforting, stealing Seb's focus away from the music in the background.

"I love this song," Evan says, and Seb smiles.

"I know you do," he murmurs, and he can practically sense Evan smiling, too. It's the main reason he added the song to his playlist, after all.

It's silent between them for a few moments, Seb completely focused on Evan's heartbeat, and the way his chest vibrates as he hums along with the bridge of the song.

"You're missing the good part," Evan says, nudging Seb slightly, and Seb smiles, eyes still closed. Evan's voice rumbles through his chest as he speaks, and Seb moves his hand to place it over Evan's stomach, slipping it in underneath his t-shirt to touch his skin. Evan sighs contentedly as he does, and kisses the top of his head. And Seb curls up a bit closer, hearing the song in the background but not opening his eyes, and not really listening to it. His voice is soft and completely content, when he speaks.

"No, I'm not."

CHAPTER 11
BLUE

It's the sound of the phone ringing that wakes Seb up.

For a moment, he just blinks sleepily, looking around, before automatically fumbling over his bed, groping the sheets. He has become so used to Evan's presence beside him by now, that the absence of it makes him open his eyes properly and actually sit up in his bed. Evan isn't there, and Seb looks around his room. It's empty, apart from him.

His phone is still ringing though, oddly piercing, considering that the song he uses as his ringtone is a rather soft one, and Seb groans. He picks up the phone from his bedside table and flops back down on the bed, checking the screen. The contact picture is one he hasn't seen in a while, and he finds himself frowning, as he answers.

"Hello," he says, putting the phone to his ear. His voice sounds gravelly and sleep-drunk.

"Sebastian?" a familiar voice says on the other end, and Seb closes his eyes.

"Yeah, mom," he says, rubbing the bridge of his nose with his fingers. "It's me."

"You sound awful," his mother says, with the kind of reprimand in her voice that only a mother could pull off. Seb sighs.

"Yeah," he says. "You woke me up."

"Well, it's about time," his mom says. "It's ten a.m."

Seb cracks open one blue eye and glances at the clock on his wall; she's right.

"Yeah, whatever," he mutters, closing his eyes again. "What's up?"

His mother, Eleanor, is a kind woman. She isn't a pushover, but she isn't too stern, either, and Seb has always found that he can talk to her pretty easily about anything. But she's still his mother, and she can still get annoyed about him not calling.

"I haven't heard from you in weeks," she says, slight accusation in her voice, and Seb makes a sound of disbelief.

"What?" he says. "I texted you the other day."

"That was over a week ago, Sebastian," she says. "And anyway, a text isn't the same. You need to call your mother, once in a while."

Seb opens his eyes, a bit surprised. Over a week ago? He hadn't realized.

"Fine, I'm sorry," he says. "I've just been... preoccupied."

Eleanor sighs.

"You work too hard, you know," she says. "Especially considering the career path you've chosen."

Seb frowns into the phone.

"What's that supposed to mean?"

"Well," his mother says diplomatically. "The writer-thing."

Seb makes a bitchface that could have rivaled Jake's.

"*The writer-thing?*" he asks. "You're saying a writer doesn't need to work hard?"

"You know what I mean," Eleanor says, sounding as though they've had this discussion before. Which they have. Many times. "I'm just saying. You should relax a bit."

Seb sighs.

"Don't worry," he hears himself mutter. "I have."

He kind of wishes he hadn't said anything; he mostly just said his thoughts out loud, in his sleepy state. But his mother, of course, catches it.

"What?" she says, as though she isn't quite sure she heard him right. "What do you mean?"

"Nothing," Seb says, a bit too quickly.

"Sebastian—"

"Really, mom," he says. "It's nothing."

She seems to hesitate for a moment.

"Relaxed, as in non-school related?" she asks carefully, with the typical air of a curious mother, and Seb sighs.

"Mom," he tries, but he doesn't stand a chance.

"Is it a girl?"

144

And there it is. Those four words that leave Seb speechless. His mother, though, interprets his silence in her own way.

"I knew it," she says. He can hear her smiling conspiringly. "About time. Who is she?"

Seb doesn't answer her. How is he supposed to answer that, anyway? This isn't exactly how he planned on coming out to his mother, but he can't lie to her, either.

"It is a girl, right?" his mother says after a few moments, and Seb swallows hard. "Not drugs, or anything?"

Seb actually rolls his eyes then.

"No, mom," he says tiredly. "It's not drugs."

Though, it might as well be, he thinks to himself, remembering the conversation he and Evan had the other day. Evan is practically like drugs. The sweetest, very best kind of drugs, that leave Seb completely wrecked and elated, all at the same time.

"So a girl," his mother says. Seb still doesn't answer. And after a few moments of silence, Eleanor sighs, giving in.

"Alright," she says. "If you don't want to talk about it, that's fine. Either way, it's nice to know you're not completely buried in schoolwork anymore."

Seb is vaguely aware of how relieved he suddenly feels, like he just dodged a bullet.

"But you still need to call home more often," his mom reprimands, and Seb nods, even though she can't see him.

"I will," he says. "Promise."

"I'll hold you to that," his mother says, before sounding as though she turns away from the phone for a moment. Then she comes back. "Dad says hi."

Seb swallows, almost nervously.

"Say hi back," he says, and his mother passes on the message on the other end.

"I have to go," she says after a moment. "But you be good, okay?"

"I'll try," Seb says dryly, and he hears his mother smile.

"Alright," she says. "I love you."

"Love you, too."

And with that, they hang up, and Seb takes the phone from his ear. He taps the screen to exit the call, and frowns when he notices how his background has been changed. Instead of the one he usually has, there is now a picture of Evan making a face, and Seb actually laughs. Evan must have changed it, and he shakes his head. Not that he minds, really.

Seb opens up a new text message.

Are you trying to be cute, or just trying to traumatize me? he writes, before attaching the photo Evan has put as his background, and sending the text. Evan's reply comes only a minute or so later.

It's called making an impression, he writes. *You were asleep when I left, I had to leave you with something.*

Seb waits as he receives a photo Evan has attached, and when he opens it, he scoffs. It's a picture of him, sleeping, arms wrapped around the pillow and dark, messy hair sticking out in all directions. He personally feels that the picture makes him look the opposite of attractive.

Touché, Seb replies. *Taking pictures of me while I sleep, though. Creepy.*

Creepy? Or adorable?

Seb smiles.

Both, he writes. *Like a stalker.*

That's what I was going for. I've got class atm, but I'll see you later. Okay?

Can't wait.

They don't add any cute greetings or anything; neither of them are really like that, and Seb isn't sure what he would have written, anyway. Instead, he just smiles to himself, before rolling over and burying his face in the pillow Evan slept on. It smells like him, like warmth and spice and leather and the shampoo he uses. Like home.

A girl. Seb's mom thought Seb had met a girl, a girl special enough to make him relax a bit. Enough to forget about calling his mother.

She's half-right, though. Seb just isn't entirely sure about what she would say if she knew the whole story. He was honest with Evan, after all; his parents would most likely just not take the relationship seriously. It's college, they'd say. Time for experimenting. Nothing serious.

But Seb doesn't want that. He doesn't want them to react like that. He wants them to be just as thrilled about Evan as they would be about a girl, and that they'd want to meet him and talk to him and get to know him. Because Evan isn't just some passing thing, or some experiment, not to Seb. He is so much more than that.

I love him, Seb finds himself thinking, but he immediately pushes the thought away. No. That's dangerous. The moment you think that about something or someone, you put yourself out there enough to get really, really badly hurt, if it goes wrong.

When it goes wrong. *Because it always does,* Seb thinks. Good things don't just happen, and stay that way.

But things are good right now. Really good. And that's good enough for him.

It's a rather slow day; Seb doesn't have any lectures, and no studying to do. So he ends up just lying there for another half-hour or so, drowsing, before rolling out of bed and putting on a pair of pants. He digs through a pile of clothes that litter the armchair in his room, before finding a dark blue t-shirt that someone once told him brings out the color of his eyes. There's a dark silhouette of Batman on the front, and Seb pulls the t-shirt over his head, messing up his already messed-up bed head. He pulls his fingers through it. There is no point in trying to smooth it down.

Seb spends the next hour or so doing nothing in particular, just checking his email, getting some coffee and breakfast from the dorm's common kitchen, going through some old notes and writings. It's calm. And it's so boring.

He misses Evan. Ever since they first met, Seb has either been with him, or been studying, and now, suddenly having a few hours to himself, he can't help but wonder what he usually does with his time off. He didn't always have Evan. What did he do before, when he was by himself? He honestly can't really remember. He's not entirely sure if that's a good or bad thing.

Eventually, though, the restlessness does become too much, and Seb ends up leaving his dorm room, headphones on and music blaring.

He's not sure where he planned on going; he mostly just wants to get out and do something. But the sun is shining, so he decides to go outside, and maybe just wander around for a bit, hands shoved in his pockets and feet shuffling across the pavement. He keeps walking for quite a while, around campus, around the dorm buildings, and it isn't until he realizes where he has eventually ended up that he stops walking and looks around. He knows this place—it's a part of the college he doesn't usually go to. But he knows that Evan does. He takes a course here, and if Seb isn't mistaken, he has a lecture here today.

Well, what do you know. Even without thinking, Seb has found his way to him. Again, he isn't sure if that's a good thing or a bad thing. But he's here, so he figures he might as well go inside.

Seb looks at his watch; Evan's lecture is supposed to be over in about twenty minutes. He looks up and down the hallway, which is mostly empty, and sees that regardless of which lecture hall Evan eventually comes out of, he will see him if he sits somewhere in the middle. So Seb shuffles over to a bench by the wall and sits down, exhaling heavily. The music is still playing in his ears, a rather happy, relaxing song, and he closes his eyes. Maybe he should have slept longer, after all. He's really tired.

It's the sudden sound of a door opening and several footsteps and voices echoing through the hall that makes Seb start, and he opens his eyes. He looks at his watch. Those twenty minutes have passed already. He must have fallen asleep for a bit.

Seb pulls his headphones down so that they end up around his neck, like he usually does, and keeps his eyes peeled for Evan. It doesn't take long; he spots him after only a few seconds, exiting the lecture hall. And then Evan spots him, actually half-freezing, with an openly surprised expression on his face. Seb swallows, suddenly kind of nervous. Maybe this was a bit too much, showing up like this. But then Evan's surprised expression turns into a smile, and he makes his way over to Seb, who gets up from the bench.

"Hey," Evan says, and Seb smiles weakly. It still baffles him, sometimes, how this amazing, gorgeous person is *his*.

"Hey," he replies, taking a step forward so that they end up right in front of each other. He moves to plant a kiss on Evan's lips, but then, Evan does something unexpected. He actually pulls back. Not much, mind you, but enough for Seb to just stand there, frozen, confused. Evan has never done that before, and his suddenly uncomfortable expression tells Seb that he is well aware of that.

Seb just looks at him, not trying to kiss him again. He can take a hint. It hurts, though, more than he wants to admit.

The two of them stand like that for a few seconds, not long enough that an outsider would have noticed something is wrong, but long enough for the hallway to pretty much empty, and Evan looks around.

"Sorry," he mutters, and Seb just frowns slightly. Then Evan gives him a weak smile and actually leans in to kiss him on the mouth. And just like that, Seb forgets for a moment that Evan pulled away when he tried, just seconds ago. For a moment, he's just happy to be kissing him, even if the kiss is brief and chaste.

"It's fine," Seb hears himself say, when they pull apart. His voice sounds oddly stiff and hesitant, and Evan swallows in something that looks a bit like discomfort. But then he smiles again.

"Come on," he says, taking Seb's hand. "I wanna show you something."

Seb doesn't question it, only half-smiles back, as Evan entwines their fingers and leads him down the hallway. But there is suddenly an odd feeling in his chest, something that feels a lot like confusion, like fear. He doesn't like it. And he likes it less when he realizes the real reason he didn't tell his mother about Evan, apart from the whole coming-out thing.

He's afraid that this will end. He's terrified that Evan will suddenly just realize how uninteresting and unimportant Seb really is, and that he'll just snap out of it. He's terrified that Evan isn't sure. Why else would he have pulled away just now?

Seb is afraid to tell his mother, because he feels sure that Evan will eventually, inevitably, go away.

And the pain of that is something he would rather keep to himself, when it happens.

"Nice place," Seb says sarcastically, as he and Evan reach their destination. They're at the edge of campus, and Evan is leading him down along the paved street.

"Shut up," he says fondly, eyes straight ahead, before he suddenly stops walking. "This is it."

Seb looks at Evan, then looks up at the building they just stopped in front of. And his mouth falls open just a little bit.

"Why are we here?" he asks, and Evan looks at him.

"You don't remember?" he asks, and Seb cocks his head.

"No, I remember," he says. He definitely remembers. They're standing outside a bar, the same bar where Evan treated him to that beer, the second time they ever met. It was only a little over a month ago, but it feels like much longer, and Seb smiles fondly at the memory. It was so long ago. He didn't even really know Evan then, didn't know what an amazing person he was.

He didn't know just how hard and how badly he would fall for him.

"Our first date," Evan says, planting a kiss by Seb's temple, and Seb turns to him, eyebrows raised. Evan rolls his eyes, half-smiling. "Fine, maybe not a date. At least, I didn't think so, at the time."

"Well," Seb says, cocking his head. "I *had* just helped you escape the wrath of an angry guy and his cheating girlfriend. If that's not a date, I don't know what is."

He adds the last part with thinly veiled sarcasm, trying not to flinch at the sudden pain he feels at the thought. At the time, he really didn't care. But now, just the thought of Evan being with someone else feels like a punch in the face.

Evan squeezes his hand, as though he can tell.

"Yeah," he says softly. "For what it's worth, though, that was the last one."

Seb looks at him, frowning.

"What do you mean?" he asks, and Evan gets an uncharacteristically nervous look.

"I mean that she was the last one," he explains. "You're the only one I've been with, since then."

Seb just gapes at him.

"Really?" he says, honestly surprised, and Evan half-shrugs.

"Yeah," he says. "After that, after I met you... The idea just didn't seem appealing, anymore."

Seb thinks about it, processing Evan's words. He honestly wasn't expecting that. He was convinced, on some level, that Evan hooked up with girls even after they started hanging out, because why wouldn't he? He didn't see Seb as anything but a friend back then. As far as Seb knew, at least. He has been proven wrong since then, but still.

Seb vaguely remembers how Evan asked him about Clara, the night he kissed him the first time. Seb retorted, asking Evan when he last hooked up with someone, and Evan didn't answer. Now he knows why.

"You're telling me you were crushing on me that whole time?" Seb says, eyes narrowed and a small smile on his face. Evan picks up on the teasing tone, and glances away.

"So what if I was?" he says defensively, but Seb can see the blush creeping up his neck. "Does it matter?"

Seb smiles and plants a soft kiss on Evan's throat, just below his ear. He swears he feels Evan tense up just the slightest bit, tightening his grip on Seb's hand.

"Not really," Seb says. "It's just nice to know it wasn't just me."

Evan squeezes his hand and gives him a small smile, and Seb turns back to the bar.

"So," he says. "Reminiscing aside. What are we doing here?"

Evan's smile widens a bit then, and he drags Seb with him to the bar's entrance, where there are several posters plastered on the wall and the outside of the door. He stops by one of them and points, and Seb looks to see what he's referring to. There is a list of names, not very long, and Seb skims along it, before raising his eyebrows.

"That's you," he says, looking at Evan.

"Yeah," he says. "I'm playing this weekend."

He shrugs self-consciously.

"It's not a big deal," he says. "I'm one out of eight, and I only get to be on stage for, like, five minutes, but..."

He looks at Seb.

"I'd be glad if you came," he says carefully, as though afraid he's asking too much. Seb sucks a breath in through his teeth, as though about to give bad news.

"Oh, I don't know," he says, shaking his head. "You know, exams and stuff..."

He looks at Evan's expression and rolls his eyes.

"Of course I'm coming, you idiot," he says, and he can tell how Evan relaxes a bit, as though honestly a bit surprised that Seb said yes.

"Thanks," he says, and Seb nudges him softly.

"Hey," he says. "Wouldn't miss it."

Evan smiles softly, and kisses him, placing his hand by his cheek. When he pulls away, he just looks at Seb for several seconds, adoringly, until Seb feels uncomfortable.

"What?" he says, but Evan's expression doesn't change.

"I really like your eyes," he says, apparently too caught up in the whole thing to appreciate just how sappy and out of character that is for him to say.

"They're just blue," Seb says self-consciously, feeling a slight blush creep up his neck. *Damn it.* He still hasn't gotten used to how Evan seems to be the only one who can make him actually blush.

But Evan just smiles at him, planting a kiss on his forehead.

"The bluest blue to ever blue."

CHAPTER 12
BRAVE

Seb has never seen Evan this nervous before. Although, maybe *nervous* is the wrong word. He's anxious, rather, pacing and fiddling with the random crap he's got lying around his dorm room, straightening a guitar hanging on the wall, adjusting the one pillow he has on his couch. Seb watches him from the bed, a book propped up on his raised knees.

"I can leave, if you want," he says, but Evan immediately turns to him.

"No," he says, shaking his head. "Please. Stay."

He's scratching the back of his head, like he does when he's worked up and anxious.

"You sure?" Seb asks, and Evan nods.

"Yeah," he says. "If you don't mind."

Seb glances at his book. Truth is, he does have some studying to get done. He needs to read three short-stories (*classics*, apparently) for Monday, and Evan's pacing is really distracting. But Evan wants him to stay, and Evan is anxious. And this book and its short-stories is boring as hell, anyway.

Seb closes the book and just looks at Evan for a moment.

"You sure you're okay?" he asks, and Evan swallows, half-nodding. That's not good enough for Seb.

"Come here," he says, putting the book down on the bedside table, and Evan makes his way over to him. Seb practically holds his arms out, and Evan falls down beside him, curling up against him, burying his face by Seb's neck. Seb settles his arms around him, pulling him close, and Evan sighs heavily against his skin.

"You don't have to see him, you know," Seb says, one hand moving up to pull his fingers through Evan's short, light brown hair. "You really don't."

Evan sighs again.

"I know," he says. His voice sounds slightly muffled, buried in the pillow, against the crook of Seb's neck. His hand trails over Seb's chest, before settling over his stomach, and Seb exhales deeply, content.

"When's he coming, again?" he asks.

"Today," Evan replies. "This afternoon."

Seb nods, unsure if Evan notices.

156

Evan's father is arriving today, to help Jake and Sophie move. Jake said it would be this weekend, but seeing as how it's Thursday, he may have been a bit off about that.

Their dad isn't staying long, apparently, only for a couple of hours, but just the thought of it is making Evan very nervous. And from what Evan has told him about his father, Seb can't really blame him.

"We could just stay here," Seb says lightly, kissing the top of Evan's head. "Stay in bed all day."

He hears Evan chuckle, and it makes him smile.

"Sounds awesome," Evan says, pressing his lips against the pulse of Seb's throat, making Seb close his eyes for a moment. "Really does."

Seb murmurs in agreement, massaging Evan's scalp slightly, as he pulls his fingers through his hair. He feels Evan curl his fingers into a loose fist over his stomach, grasping the fabric of Seb's t-shirt in his hand. He kisses Seb's throat again, and Seb closes his eyes completely. The kiss is warmer this time, lingering, and Seb exhales slowly. He loves this. He loves having Evan close to him like this, just the two of them.

Neither of them says anything for a little while, just lie there, breathing.

"What time is it?" Evan finally asks, and Seb glances at his watch.

"Almost eleven," he says, and Evan murmurs against his skin. Seb spent the night here, and they have just barely gotten up, only putting on some pants and a t-shirt, mostly out of habit. It's an unusually undressed look for Evan; he tends to wear open, button-up shirts over his t-shirts, and seeing him without one is a bit unfamiliar. Not that Seb minds. He likes it.

Evan exhales deeply. He doesn't sound troubled, only tired, and content.

"I'm gonna take a shower," he mumbles against Seb's neck, before moving up to lean on his elbow. Seb just nods, and Evan kisses him warmly. There is something about the kiss, something lingering and hot, that Seb can't quite put his finger on. It makes him shiver, tendrils of warmth spreading through his body. But the kiss doesn't last long, and Evan pulls away, eyes on Seb. He smiles, before getting out of bed and making his way to the bathroom, closing the door behind him as he enters.

Seb just lies there for a few moments, somehow stunned. He waits, thinking, still feeling the effects of that kiss, his body oddly on edge. He hears the shower come on. And then he notices that Evan hasn't locked the bathroom door. He swallows uncertainly, fingers curling into loose fists.

It's amazing how brave Evan can make Seb feel, amazing how much Seb does when it concerns Evan, things he never would have had the balls to do, otherwise.

Like right now, when he gets up from the bed and makes his way over to the bathroom door. He hesitates for a moment, standing in front of it, staring at the handle. He can hear the shower going, can hear the water rushing as Evan steps into it and lets it cover his skin.

Seb squeezes his eyes shut as the image pops into his mind, but mostly from nervousness, and he eventually opens his eyes again. And he exhales.

Seb pulls his t-shirt over his head, dropping it to the floor, before opening the bathroom door and stepping inside. He's sure Evan must have heard it, but if he did, he doesn't let Seb know, and Seb carefully closes the door behind him. The small room is already steamy, and Seb just stares at the opaque, cream-colored shower curtain for a moment, before unbuttoning his jeans and taking them off. Evan's clothes are already in a pile on the floor, and Seb adds to it, taking off his boxers, as well. He takes a deep breath. It's ridiculous how nervous Evan makes him. Nervous and *thrilled*, at the same time.

As soon as Seb pulls the shower curtain aside, he feels his heart suddenly start pounding in his chest. Evan is standing with his back to him, facing the other wall, and Seb swallows hard, taking in the sight of him; his hands as they pull through his wet hair, the way tendrils of water run down his back, where those hard muscles move beneath the skin. The way just looking at him makes Seb hard, and makes him swallow nervously. But again, Evan also makes him brave.

Seb pulls the shower curtain shut and slowly makes his way over to Evan. It's a rather small shower, and covering the distance between them doesn't take more than a second. But even though Evan must know Seb is there, he doesn't turn around. Somehow, Seb appreciates that. It means that he can put himself behind Evan, and place his hands on those strong upper arms, before letting his fingers slide slowly down along that wet skin. Seb feels Evan tense up underneath his hands, and moves even closer, pressing his lips against Evan's shoulder, his hands making their way down along his waist. He hears Evan exhale, slowly and heavily, leaning into Seb's touch, and Seb presses their bodies closer together, feeling Evan's back against his chest. It makes him tighten his grip slightly, hands moving down over Evan's hips.

He feels very brave.

Seb kisses Evan's neck, slowly and hungrily, while one hand moves up along Evan's stomach, tracing the muscles there with his fingers. His other hand is moving further down, agonizingly slow, and Evan lets out a low, deep moan when Seb touches him, wraps his fingers around him. He's already hard, more than Seb expected, and it gives him a ridiculous sense of satisfaction.

He makes Evan *hard*.

It's apparent that Evan is surprised at Seb's behavior; he hasn't done anything like this before, even though Evan has gotten him off a few times, using his hand. But Seb is still taking it slow, making it last—it's just who he is.

Evan has made him shudder and squirm, and now, he wants to return the favor.

Seb has barely gotten started, though, has barely started stroking and making Evan breathe heavily, before Evan suddenly moves. In the blink of an eye, he has turned around, and kissed a rather stunned Seb on the mouth. The kiss is fierce, burning, and Seb automatically reciprocates, melting against him.

"Fuck," Evan rasps between kisses, a small, mischievous smile on his face. "Thought you were never gonna take the hint."

Seb doesn't answer, just groans against his lips, placing his hands on Evan's hips and pushing him backwards, so he ends up with his back against the wall. If Evan was surprised a moment ago, it's nothing compared to how he looks now, eyes wide open as they stare at Seb. Seb looks right into them, and watches as those green irises are slowly eclipsed by dark, lust-blown pupils.

I took the hint, he feels like saying, realizing that Evan really was inviting him to join him in the shower. *Having you like this is all I ever think about.*

But Seb doesn't say it. He can't. Sure, he's acting so much braver than usual, but some things are still too much, and still too unfamiliar and intense for him to admit. And everything he feels about Evan is so different from things he has felt before, nothing like previous relationships or crushes. It makes this feel new.

He looks at Evan, gaze wandering over his face; those eyes, those lips, the way his wet hair looks after he just pulled his fingers through it. Those arms, that chest, the way his hard-on feels against Seb's thigh. And Seb places his forehead against his, inhaling deeply, moving closer, his entire body suddenly aching for him, burning.

"You're so fucking hot," he hears himself say, his voice low and hoarse in a way he definitely isn't used to, and it freaks him out for a moment. He doesn't talk like this, ever. But if Evan finds it odd, he doesn't show it. Instead, that look of surprise on his face blends with something that looks an awful lot like raw, uncompromising *hunger*, and he kisses him again.

"Damn it," he growls against him. "You drive me insane, you know that?"

Seb only hums in response, before he pushes his tongue into Evan's mouth, claiming, possessive, moving his hand down along Evan's stomach to pick up where he left off just moments ago. And Evan moans against his lips as he does, fingers digging into Seb's hair, which is already soaking wet from the shower. Then Seb notices Evan's other hand moving down, as well, and when he feels those fingers wrap around him in a firm grip, he lets out a slow, deep breath. He closes his eyes. He can't believe how good it feels.

Seb leans his forehead against Evan's again, breathing heavily as those fingers start stroking him. It feels good, but somehow, he doesn't want Evan to do anything, this time. This time, he wants to do something for *him*.

Evan seems surprised when Seb gently grabs his wrist and pulls his hand away, but it doesn't last long. Instead, he swallows hard as Seb opens his eyes and looks right at him, just stares as Seb takes them both in his hand, and exhales sharply as Seb slowly starts moving his hips. Seb places his other hand against the wall behind Evan, as he rubs them both together in a lovely sensation of wet friction, thrusting slowly into the tight tunnel of his fingers. He doesn't take his eyes off Evan's for a second, watches with satisfaction as the expression on his face changes, how he grits his teeth and how his eyes glaze over for a moment, how his mouth falls half-open, as he breathes heavily.

Seb starts moving faster when Evan puts his hands on his hips, fingertips digging into his skin. He feels his own heartbeat speed up, as he breathes heavier, faster, inhaling steam and hot air and everything *Evan*, the water from the shower running over his skin, making Evan's hands slip slightly, as they grip him tighter. He wants to close his eyes, wants to savor all of it.

But he wants to see Evan, wants to watch him writhe and moan because of him. He wants to watch him come, because of him.

It's the way Evan practically starts panting that does it, that makes it start building rapidly inside of Seb, and which makes him lean in and kiss Evan with a kind of passion he has never really felt before. Evan moans against his lips, and when Seb pulls away, he can see that his brow is pulled down, eyes squeezed shut.

"No," he hears himself say, to his surprise, and he kisses Evan on the lips. "Look at me."

Evan obeys and opens his eyes. He looks completely wrecked, and it's enough to make Seb speed up just the slightest bit. Enough for him to feel his whole body tense up, and to feel Evan's grip on his hips become painfully tight. He knows he'll have bruises there tomorrow, but it doesn't matter right now. All that matters is the way Evan bites out a deep, guttural moan, as he comes, and the way a second of pure, sheer bliss shoots through Seb's entire body, as he comes almost at the same time.

For several seconds afterwards, they just stand there, the arm Seb uses to lean against the wall shaking slightly, and Evan's fingers loosen their grip. Seb does close his eyes then, moving his head down to lean his forehead against Evan's shoulder. He can hear Evan breathing heavily by his ear, holding onto him as though he might fall over, otherwise.

"Shit," he says, sounding completely exhausted. "Where did that come from?"

Seb shakes his head weakly, trying to even out his breathing.

"I don't know," he says, sounding just as wrecked as Evan. Then Evan chuckles.

"Well, whatever it was," he says. "I like it."

Seb smiles tiredly against Evan's skin.

"I'm glad," he says, and feels a pleased shudder as Evan pulls his fingers through his hair. Seb looks up then, and Evan smiles at him. Seb's wet hair is plastered to his forehead, and Evan pushes it back gently, Seb leaning into his touch.

"You okay there, big guy?" Evan says, almost teasingly, and Seb resists the urge to shake his head at his apparent compulsion to always joke away any tension or awkwardness, but he still can't help but smile.

"Yeah," he says, removing his hand from the wall behind Evan and taking a step back, until he ends up right underneath the showerhead. Evan just looks at him, and Seb holds out his hand and gently grabs Evan's wrist. He pulls him closer, Evan lets him, and Seb put his arms around him, as they stand underneath the running, hot water.

"I'm definitely okay," he says, and Evan smiles, sighing happily as Seb leans in and kisses him.

♦

Evan decides that he doesn't want to see his father. At least, not yet, not now. He doesn't do a very good job of explaining why to Seb, but as far as Seb understands, Evan hasn't seen his dad in months, and he's mad enough as it is about Jake accepting his help. Evan also knows, though, that Jake has a point. It doesn't change anything, doesn't change or excuse the way their father has been their whole lives, but maybe an attempt at making amends is worth some consideration. Seb tries not to have an opinion of his own; he has no right to, and even if he did, he has a feeling that he would have a hard time being objective.

Evan *does* want to see the new apartment, though, where Jake and Sophie have just moved in, so he and Seb are going over to visit later that night. Jake has assured him that their dad will be gone by then, in case Evan doesn't want to see him, and it's almost dark by the time they leave.

Seb is sitting in the passenger seat of the vintage car that Evan worships and adores to the point where it's almost unhealthy, and he glances over at Evan, as he drives. There is music playing at a low volume, and Seb glances at the collection of cassette tapes which he knows lies hidden in the glove compartment.

"You ever thought of updating this thing?" he asks casually, and Evan glances at him.

"What do you mean?" he says, and there is a hint of a warning in his voice. *Don't you dare insult my car*, it says.

"I don't know," Seb says, opening the glove compartment and picking up a random tape. "An iPod, maybe? Or even a CD-player?"

Then Evan actually narrows his eyes a bit, eyes shifting between Seb and the road. It really isn't far at all to Jake and Sophie's new place, but still.

"Don't listen to him, baby," Evan says, actually stroking the dashboard of his car. "You're perfect."

Seb scoffs, but can't help but smile as he shakes his head.

"Dude," he says. "It's getting a bit creepy."

"He's just jealous," Evan says soothingly to the car, and Seb makes a face.

"Yeah," he says. "Not getting any less creepy."

"Don't give me that," Evan says lightly. "I've seen the way you look at that Benjamin guy."

Seb frowns.

"I think you mean Benedict," he says. "And he's Sherlock, which trumps everything."

Evan shakes his head in mock lament.

"I don't know," he says, sounding concerned. "Sherlock is fictional, which makes it creepy."

Seb is unable to come up with a witty response. Instead, he just glares at Evan, who glances at him and gives him a smile that's borderline mischievous.

"You're an asshole," Seb mutters, and Evan laughs.

"I know," he says. "You love it."

"God help me, I do."

They soon reach the apartment building where Jake and Sophie have made their new home, and they get out of the car, Evan locking it behind them.

"This it?" Seb says, and Evan nods as he slides up next to him. Seb looks up at the building, which is only five stories high.

"Yup," he says, and then pulls Seb briefly to his side and kisses his temple, in that affectionate way Seb has come to love. "Let's go."

It's customary to bring along some kind of housewarming gift, but Evan hasn't really gone out of his way to get one. Seb suggested a bottle of wine, because that's what people seem to bring when visiting someone's new home, but he knew as he said it that that isn't really

Evan's style. And Evan knows that too, and ended up bringing a six pack of beer.

They make their way up to the fourth floor, where they find the right apartment and ring the doorbell. Seb is standing rather close to Evan, out of habit, and absently touches his hand. Evan does the same; neither of them really notices when they do that, it's just something they do, for comfort.

After only a few seconds, the door opens, and they're greeted by Jake. He smiles when he sees them, but Seb immediately notices something off about his expression. He looks oddly tense, kind of surprised even, and Seb glances at Evan. He noticed it, too.

"Hey, Jake," he says, his voice not betraying anything. "Wanna invite us in?"

Jake opens his mouth to reply, suddenly looking a bit uncomfortable, and Seb feels himself tense up. None of them has time to react, though, before a voice is heard from inside.

"Jake?" it says. "Who is it?"

Seb has never seen Evan so tense before. His jaw clenches, his eyes actually widen a bit, and his back straightens noticeably. Seb doesn't miss how he even whips his hand away from his, as though wanting to put more distance between the two of them.

Jake's expression changes, as well; he looks tense and uncomfortable, and the look in his eyes when he glances at Evan is an apologetic one. And then, someone shows up behind Jake, making him step away slightly from the door.

Seb can see how Evan swallows hard; he's not sure if anyone else would have noticed. He wants to take his hand

and comfort him, but he has an overwhelming feeling that it would be a bad idea, right now.

"Evan," the stranger says, his expression changing as he spots him. And even without Evan saying anything, Seb knows who this is.

"Hey, dad," Evan says, sounding stiff. His father just looks at him for a few moments, before turning to Seb, something Seb is completely unprepared for. He's so used to going unseen, that he hadn't really thought about Evan's dad actually seeing him.

"Who's this?" Evan's father asks, and Evan glances at Seb.

"This is Seb," he says, sounding oddly young, like he's de-aging in the presence of his father. "He's... he's a friend."

Seb does not expect to feel such a sharp pain in his stomach at Evan's use of the word *friend*, but he contains it, showing nothing on the surface. He has a very good poker face, after all. And he knows that the circumstances here are special. He'll just have to deal with it.

"Seb," Evan says, glancing at him, then at his dad. "This is my father, Peter Matthews."

Seb keeps his eyes on Evan's father—Peter. He looks as though he's actually younger than he looks, prematurely aged by sorrow and bad habits. He's got dark hair and rough stubble to match, and most of all, he looks *tired*. Seb has no trouble imagining him having a drinking problem, and he can see the harder planes in his expression that reinforce what Evan has told him about him. But he can also see the crinkles around his eyes, just like the ones Evan has, and that at least once upon a time, he must have smiled a lot. Just like Evan.

Peter holds out his hand, and Seb shakes it, eyes fixed on Peter's. They resemble Evan's, too, but they are much sadder, and harder.

Peter lets go of his hand and looks at him for a few seconds. Then he gives a half-smile that may have looked awkward, or just generally expressionless.

"A bit scrawny, aren't you?" he says, and Seb resists the overwhelming urge to raise his eyebrows. He has been pretty much neutral concerning this man so far, but at that comment, he suddenly decides that he doesn't like him. He doesn't like him, and he has about a hundred smart-ass comments to throw back at him, not because his feelings are hurt, but because he just can't bear people who are so impolite. Especially not people who don't even know him.

But Seb says nothing; it isn't worth it. Instead, he manages a look that's one he has perfected over the years—the look of silent judgment. He knows it makes his face hard and his normally kind, blue eyes surprisingly condescending, or bored, if nothing else, and for several seconds, no one says anything. Then, finally, Peter clears his throat a bit, and looks at Jake. Seb finds the man's sudden discomfort immensely satisfying.

"Well, I'm gonna go," Peter says. Seb notices that he is indeed fully dressed, as though he really was just about to leave. "Thanks for having me."

"Thanks for the help, dad," Jake says, and reciprocates the one-armed hug his father gives him. Peter throws a glance back into the apartment and smiles warmly, something that looks a bit odd on his haggard face. Seb wonders how often he has reason to smile like that.

"Bye, Sophie," he says, and Seb hears her reply from inside.

Then, finally, Peter turns to Evan, who's still just standing there, stiff as a board.

"Good to see you, son," Peter says. He looks for a moment as though he wants to hug Evan, but decides against it. Instead, he just claps his hand on his shoulder and gives him a tight smile. Evan doesn't say anything, and with that, Peter makes his way past him and into the hallway. A few seconds later, they hear the sound of the elevator doors closing, and Evan visibly relaxes. He looks at Jake.

"Evan, I'm so sorry," his brother says, clearly meaning it. "He stayed longer than we thought, it just sort of happened. I forgot to call you, I'm sorry."

Evan doesn't say anything, just gives Jake a look that says it's alright, and Jake sets his face in a concerned frown, instead of a worried one. Evan looks at Seb then, his expression oddly ashamed.

"Sorry," he says, his voice low, and Seb hesitates for a split second, before taking his hand.

"It's okay," he says, kissing his cheek. The words don't feel entirely true, though.

He realizes that Evan can't just tell his father, just like that, but Seb feels weirdly betrayed, all the same. The selfish, petty part of him does. And he's reminded of the other day, when he went to find Evan outside his lecture hall. He tried to kiss him, and Evan pulled away, only accepting the kiss once everyone else was out of sight. Seb doesn't like it. But right now, it doesn't matter, and he doesn't want to make Evan feel worse.

"Brought you a housewarming gift," Seb says instead, in a lighter tone, as they enter the apartment and Jake closes the door behind them. He turns to Jake, who raises his eyebrows.

"Really?" Jake says, and Evan holds out the six pack of beer.

"Here you go, little brother," he says, his trademark cockiness coming back into his voice. Jake smiles and shakes his head as he accepts the beer, taking it from Evan's hand.

"Isn't wine usually the way to go?" he says, and Seb cocks his head at Evan.

"That's what I said," he points out. "But it's too fancy, apparently."

Sophie shows up then, and she smiles as she sees them.

"Welcome," she says, giving both Evan and Seb a kiss on the cheek. Then she looks at the beer in Jake's hand, before turning to Evan.

"Beer?" she says, still wearing her dimpled smile. "Really?"

"Wine's too fancy," Jake explains, and Seb nods.

"What?" Evan says defensively. "He didn't bring anything!"

He gestures at Seb, who just raises his eyebrows.

"I'm not obligated to," he says, before turning to Jake and Sophie. "Or, you know, I could just give you a man-sized cactus or something, sometime."

Jake laughs then, Sophie joining in.

"I think we're good," he says. "Beer's fine."

He makes his way into the kitchen with Sophie, and Seb turns to Evan, who's lingering a bit by the door.

"You okay?" he says, when Jake and Sophie are out of earshot, and Evan hesitates for a moment, before nodding.

"Yeah," he says. He looks down at their entwined hands. "I'm sorry my dad's such an asshole."

Seb quirks a smile and lifts up their hands to kiss Evan's, and Evan looks at him, green eyes soft.

"Nothing I can't handle," Seb says, and Evan smiles softly. Seb returns the smile, and Evan kisses him gently on the lips.

"You're awesome," he whispers, and Seb squeezes his hand.

"So are you."

CHAPTER 13
SELF-DEFENSE

Evan and Seb both have early lectures the next day, and seeing as how they slept at Evan's place, they go together, making their way toward the school buildings. There's barely anyone around this early in the morning, not at Evan's dorm, but Seb is still uncomfortably aware of how Evan seems to actually look around them, as though making sure the coast is clear, before leaving.

He tries not to think about it, though, and tries not to think about how Evan has done that before. When Seb showed up at the end of his lecture the other day, Evan actually pulled away from a kiss, looking uncomfortable.

And last night, when unexpectedly meeting his dad, he deliberately kept his distance from Seb, referring to him as a *friend*. Seb tries not to think about it, tries not to let it get to him.

That is, until they reach their destination.

They're not much for hand-holding, at least not while walking. Seb assumes it's because they have spent about ninety percent of their time together alone, in Evan's room, or Seb's, or with Jake and Sophie, and therefore simply haven't gotten into the habit of it. And on the walk here, he disregarded Evan's reluctance to hold his hand as something unconscious, something he did without thinking about it, because it's not a habit.

It's when they stop in front of the building where Seb is having his lecture that Seb realizes he was wrong.

"I'll see you later, okay?" he says, and Evan nods, with a small smile. Then Seb moves to kiss him. And Evan pulls away. Just like last time, he jerks away just the tiniest bit, enough for Seb to stop in mid-motion, and he glances around them, looking uncomfortable. Seb just stands there, dumbstruck. He isn't even sure which emotion is more dominant right now; hurt or anger or confusion.

"Yeah," Evan says after a second or so, looking back at Seb. He smiles again, oddly stiff, and then looks at his watch. "I gotta go. But yeah, I'll see you later."

And then, just like that, he turns around and leaves. And Seb watches him go, feeling oddly numb.

It isn't until a group of students rushes past him, no doubt hurrying to the same lecture he's going to, that Seb actually starts moving again. He shuffles inside, finds his lecture hall, and takes his seat. And he feels the strangest, sinking feeling inside, something that feels a lot like shame and hurt. It makes him want to hide.

"Hey." Evan's voice snaps Seb out of his thoughts.

He's standing by a fountain, it's after lunch, and he and Evan decided to meet here. He slowly looks up as Evan slides up next to him, and Evan's smile is so warm and affectionate and genuine that for a moment, Seb forgets all about this morning. But he doesn't kiss him, doesn't even try. He's not quite ready for the rejection he feels certain would follow. And any hope he had of Evan maybe doing it instead is completely snuffed out when Evan just jerks his head.

"Shall we?" he says, and Seb just looks at him.

"You're doing it again," he says, his voice low, and Evan frowns.

"What?" he asks, but Seb just shakes his head.

"Never mind."

They start walking, and Seb can tell that Evan is uncomfortable, all the way to Seb's dorm. They don't really talk, and Seb can't help but wonder if Evan is uncomfortable because Seb is clearly in a weird mood, or because they are around people. Because apparently, Seb has realized, Evan doesn't want to show their relationship to anyone. At least, judging from the way he looks around to see if the coast is clear, before even attempting to kiss Seb or even make the slightest affectionate move.

Seb thinks back to the other day, when Evan first acted like that. It was the first time they were together in public, since becoming a couple, and Seb remembers being so shocked at Evan pulling back like that. But then he checked to see that no one was around, and then he kissed Seb. Then he took Seb's hand, and Seb almost forgot about it. Almost. Even as they were standing outside that bar, Evan was affectionate, kissing him and letting himself be kissed. So Seb hasn't really thought about it. But now, he remembers why. There was pretty much no one else around then, and therefore no one there to see.

It's incredible how painful it is for Seb to think about, to even think about Evan not wanting to touch him, even. Even now, as they walk, any casual bystander would be convinced that they're only friends, walking together. And it hurts Seb so much. More than he wants to admit.

It isn't until they reach Seb's dorm room that Evan actually says something.

"What's wrong?" he asks, as Seb makes his way into the room and dumps his bag on the floor. Seb turns to him.

"What?" he asks, knowing that he's convincing no one. Evan frowns slightly.

"You're acting weird," he says, and Seb grits his teeth.

"Yeah, well," he says lamely. "You tell me."

Evan's frown deepens then, and he moves closer.

"I don't know what you're saying," he says, sounding honestly bewildered. "Did something happen? Did I do something?"

Seb looks right at him, wondering if he looks as hurt and numb as he feels.

"More like the other way around," he says, and he swears that the smallest hint of comprehension shows in those green eyes. "I wasn't aware that being with me was so horrible. You could have said something."

He can't help being sarcastic, as usual, and he kind of hates himself for it. But his words make Evan's expression change.

"Seb, I know, alright?" he says. "It's not you. I just... I'm not—"

"Not what?"

Seb is fully aware, even in this state, that he's probably being unfair. But he can't help it. This has been creeping up on him for some time, this fear, this nagging idea that Evan is simply too good to be true. It's as though he has been waiting for him to realize how bad an idea this is, and that he'll break Seb's heart, when he does. And he doesn't want that.

"It's just a bit new, alright?" Evan tries. "And around people, I freak out a bit."

"I think we both know," Seb says, rather dryly, "that if I'd been a girl, it wouldn't be a problem."

Evan stops talking then. Instead, he just swallows hard, suddenly looking worried, a bit anxious, even. But Seb doesn't relent.

"I know," Evan says. "I know, but it's not you, I promise."

"Really?" Seb says, frowning, sounding doubtful and annoyed. "Are you sure? 'Cause from where I'm standing, it really does look like I'm the fucking problem."

"Seb, it's not you—"

"Well, what does it matter, anyway?" Seb throws his hands up in helpless exasperation. He sounds angrier than he means to. "It's not like you're gonna stay."

Evan frowns at him, confused surprise on his face, replacing the anxious expression he just had.

"What?" he says, disbelieving. But Seb practically ignores him, and just keeps going. His voice has almost risen to yelling, now.

"I have no illusions about what this is," he says, gesturing vaguely between the two of them. "I know that it's fine right now, but that eventually, you're gonna leave. Eventually, you're just gonna realize that this isn't what you want, that it was a bad idea, and you're gonna leave."

Seb is vaguely aware of how he just used the same words Evan used that time, when Seb confronted him about that kiss. *It was a bad idea.*

Evan just stares at him, with an expression as though Seb just punched him in the face.

"What the fuck are you saying?" he says, sounding angry and quietly shocked, at the same time.

"Don't give me that!" Seb is properly angry now. He isn't sure why, but he can't stop himself. "You're the one settling, in this relationship. You're the one who's by some miracle chosen to be with me, but I know that's not gonna last. And if you can't even let other people see it, what we have, then how much could it possibly mean to you, anyway?"

"Seb—"

"You ruined everything, you know that?" Seb can't stop. He's breathing a bit heavier, now. He can't stop spewing this, can't stop hurtling out every ounce of doubt he has ever had about this relationship. He hates himself for it, but he can't stop. "I was fine! Alone, yes, but I was fine. And then you came along, and fucked it all up."

Evan just looks at him. It's unusual to see a guy like him with an expression like that. The confused, surprised hurt in those eyes is enough to break Seb's heart several times over, especially knowing that he's the one who's causing it. But he can't care right now, he doesn't have the energy to. Instead, all he manages to care about is saving himself, protecting himself. And that means pushing Evan away. Evan, who is hurting him.

"That's really how you feel?" Evan's anger has quickly subsided, and instead, his voice sounds oddly subdued and sad. Weak. It's painful to hear.

No, Seb thinks frantically. *I love you. I need you. Please, don't go. Please.*

"Yes. I want you to go."

Seb is shocked at how resolute his own voice sounds, when he's practically screaming in panic on the inside. He doesn't want Evan to go, doesn't want to push him away. But he is so scared. He's so terrified, in a way he has never been before, and he doesn't know what to do. Evan is going to leave anyway. Seb might as well pull away, before he does.

Evan just looks at him for several seconds. It's hard to determine the expression on his face. But then again, he tends to switch over to anger when he doesn't know what to do or how to act, and he's trying to do that right now. But the pain is still there, still horribly present in those eyes, and it makes Seb want to pull him closer and kiss him and make sure he never has to be in pain again.

But Seb is too scared. And he's ashamed of just how scared he is.

Evan takes a deep breath. It shakes slightly, and he swallows hard, before looking down at the floor.

"Right," he says, his voice thick. Then he looks up at Seb again, his eyes pleading, as though waiting for Seb to say something, anything. But Seb says nothing.

Seb doesn't move a muscle as Evan makes his way past him. He doesn't even look when he hears the door open behind him, followed by a few moments of silence, before it closes again. And somehow, he can *feel* the absence of Evan, can feel how he simply isn't there anymore. It feels cold. Hollow.

Seb looks down at his hands. They're starting to shake ever so slightly, and he clenches them into fists. He's surprised when a wet drop lands on his skin, and he sighs. *Damn it.* He's crying. Barely, and quietly, but it's there.

Seb squeezes his eyes shut stubbornly, takes a deep breath. This is for the best. He needs to protect himself. It would only have been a matter of time before this happened, anyway. At least, that's what he keeps telling himself.

He feels a small, annoying sob hitch in his chest, and he presses his lips together.

Fuck.

◆

It doesn't take long before Seb gets a visitor, just the next day. He suspects who it will be, and that's the only reason he forces himself to get up and open his dorm room door, when someone knocks.

"Hi, Seb." Sophie looks so pretty, her face and big eyes so soft and kind, as she waits outside his door when he opens it. She looks so pretty, and so very sad.

"Hey," Seb says. His voice sounds hoarser than usual. He's ashamed to admit that he has actually been crying; he can't remember crying like this before meeting Evan, not really. He thinks about how he felt after Evan kissed him for the first time, about what happened afterwards, and he thought that was the worst thing ever, at the time. He was wrong. This feeling is somehow much worse.

"Can I come in?" Sophie asks, and Seb just steps aside as she makes her way past him. She looks around his room, while Seb closes the door behind her.

"Jake sent you?" Seb says dryly, making his way over to his unmade bed. "Kind of surprised he didn't come, himself, this time."

Seb falls down onto his bed and resumes his activity of staring blankly into space, and he hears Sophie sigh.

"Don't be an ass," she says. It's odd how harsh the words sound, coming from that sweet face with that sweet voice, clashing horribly. It has more impact that way, Seb notices.

Sophie walks over to his bed and stops. Seb looks up at her, and catches that pointed look, making him scoot over just enough for her to sit down on the bed's edge. Seb stays on his back, lying down, staring at the ceiling.

"You okay?" Sophie asks, and Seb almost scoffs. But he doesn't. He's too tired.

"You know," Sophie says, when he doesn't answer. "This is becoming a pattern."

"What is?" Seb says flatly.

"This," Sophie says. "One of you storming out, then both of you ending up in a heap somewhere, feeling sorry for yourselves."

Seb actually glares at her then, but she doesn't flinch.

"It's getting stupid," she says. Seb looks back at the ceiling.

"Can I get Jake instead?" he says. "He sugarcoated it, at least."

"Sorry, no," Sophie says, not taking the least bit offense. "He's busy talking to his brother."

Seb practically feels his heart clench, and he swallows hard. Sophie notices, of course.

"What happened, exactly?" she asks. "I mean, you guys seemed fine the other night. What changed?"

Seb sighs and closes his eyes. He doesn't want to talk about it. He has had time to cool off and think about the whole thing, over and over, and it's painful. And he feels ashamed. He's ashamed of how he acted, ashamed of how he let his own, overwhelming insecurities ruin the best thing that has ever happened to him.

He's not planning on saying anything. He isn't planning on explaining, or defending himself, or anything at all. But still, for some reason, he opens his mouth. And the words he chokes out sum up everything.

"I fucked up."

Seb is almost embarrassed at the thickness of his voice, and he swallows hard, opening his eyes. It sounds stupid, but the words couldn't be more true. He fucked up. So badly.

Sophie sighs sympathetically and gently takes his wrist, conveying so much concern in just one touch.

"Tell me," she says, and Seb exhales heavily. He isn't sure he'll be able to talk without crying.

Fuck. He *hates* this so much, hates feeling tears burn in his eyes. He never cries. It's all Evan's fault.

"I just fucked up," Seb says, slowly sitting up and swinging his legs over the bed's edge. He shakes his head and stares into space. His vision is slightly blurred from threatening tears. "Everything."

"It's okay, Seb," Sophie says softly, stroking his hair, much like a mother or a big sister would. "It's okay."

"No, you don't understand." Seb shakes his head, swallowing hard, trying to get rid of that lump in his throat. "I have no excuse. I just pushed, and... Now he's gone."

He looks down at his knees.

"It's not okay. Trust me."

Sophie seems to deliberate for a moment.

"Why?" she asks, and Seb looks up at her. "What happened?"

Seb hesitates.

"He was gonna leave, anyway," he says weakly. He hears how ridiculous the defense sounds, how irrational. But he doesn't care. "Eventually. They always do. Especially someone like him."

Sophie frowns a bit, confused.

"What do you mean?"

"You know," Seb tries. "Someone like him... Someone like him doesn't waste time with someone like me. I'm... mediocre. And he's..."

Seb just shakes his head, can't even find the words to describe what Evan is. He's amazing. Just *beautiful*, in every sense of the word. And Seb... Well, he isn't. At least, he doesn't really think so.

"He's in love with you, Seb," Sophie says, and her words are like a velvet-clad knife in his chest, soothing and painful, all at once. "He's not wasting his time. I don't think he is, and I know for a fact that he doesn't think so, either."

Seb glances at her.

"How can you be so sure?" he asks.

"I just know," she says, a hint of a jokingly conspiring tone in her voice. "Just trust me. I do. And you know it, too."

Seb looks away again. He does know. At least, he thought he did, he thought he knew.

"I think he's ashamed of me," he hears himself say, and closes his eyes for a moment, frowning. "I mean, maybe not ashamed, but..."

He opens his eyes again.

"I don't know."

Sophie doesn't ask for details. Seb wouldn't be at all surprised if she knew exactly what he's talking about, seeing as how she has known both the Matthews boys much longer than he has. And if nothing else, either Jake or Evan (Jake, most likely) may have told her. Or maybe she just noticed how Evan behaved when confronted with his father, and having to introduce Seb and who he was to him.

Seb suspects that she knows, and her next words confirm it.

"He's not ashamed," she says softly. "He's not ashamed of you, or of what you guys have. I know he's not."

"Then why would he do that?" Seb says sharply, that hurt anger seeping in again. "If he wasn't ashamed, why would he literally pull away from me in public? It's like, as soon as there are people around and someone might see him, he treats me like I'm just a friend, or something. He won't even touch me, just looks around like he's paranoid. I thought I didn't mind, but... I guess I do."

He says the last few words with a certain amount of bitterness, and they are true. Evan doing that was painful, excruciatingly so, and it didn't exactly help the doubts Seb already had about how Evan felt, the doubts he has had since they first met. And as he thinks about it, Seb forgets to feel bad for a moment, to feel guilty. Instead, he remembers that he's angry at Evan, and that Evan has hurt him.

"I know," Sophie says with a sigh. "He can be an asshole."

Seb cocks his head in agreement, and neither of them speaks for a few moments.

"But it's not you," Sophie eventually says, echoing the words Evan used yesterday. "It really isn't. I know he comes off as over-confident, and maybe he is, sometimes. But he does have his own insecurities."

Seb wants to contradict her, but then he thinks about it. She's right. With the drinking and the self-worth issues and the anger, Evan definitely isn't perfect, and he definitely isn't as confident as Seb first thought him to be. But none of that bothers him, not really. Evan isn't perfect, but he is *his*. No matter what. It's just what his insecurities has made him do that's a problem.

"Evan gets scared, too, you know." Seb looks up at Sophie as she says it. "He just isn't so good at communicating that."

She adds that last part with an affectionate smile, and Seb feels himself soften a bit.

"I know," he admits. "But I can't be in this, if he isn't. If he can't even be near me around other people, if he just pulls away from me every time... It makes me feel like he doesn't want me. Like he's ashamed of me."

He looks at Sophie pointedly, knowing that *ashamed* is a rather strong word. But she gets the idea.

"I get that," she says. "I respect it. But he deserves a chance. This whole thing has been hard for him, just like it has been for you. But he's getting there. He just needs time."

Seb hates to admit that she has a point. He hates to admit that it's his own insecurities, rather than Evan's behavior, that has made him act this way. But that still doesn't make Evan's actions okay.

"Fine," he says. "But I'm still mad at him."

Sophie just smiles. Seb shakes his head.

"It's just..." he says, sounding distant and lost in thought. "He's just so amazing, you know? That he even wants to be with me... It feels surreal, sometimes. I feel like I'm just waiting for it to crash, waiting for him to just snap out of it and leave. And when he does stuff like that, it doesn't exactly help."

Sophie nods.

"I know," she says. "And you should be mad at him. But don't let it ruin everything. Just give him some time."

She nudges Seb gently, her hand on his shoulder.

"You guys are so good together," she says. "And he needs you, even if he doesn't say it. Just give him a chance."

Seb looks at her.

"I want to," he says. "I can try."

And for a moment, Seb feels weirdly hopeful, like everything will be okay. But then, he's suddenly reminded of the other part; the part where basically broke up with Evan and sent him away. It doesn't matter if Evan is the reason he acted that way. Seb is still to blame, and he said some incredibly unfair, selfish and shitty things.

"I just don't know how," he hears himself say, and Sophie makes a thinking-noise.

"Well," she says. "You could come with me and Jake tonight."

Seb frowns, before he remembers. Evan is playing tonight, at that bar, and Seb promised to come. He cringes, though, as he thinks about it.

"I don't think so," he says. "I don't think he'll want me there."

"He will." Sophie sounds certain. "It shows you still care."

"You think that'll be enough?" Seb sounds highly doubtful, and Sophie shrugs.

"It's a start," she says. "Baby steps, right?"

Seb thinks about it, before he suddenly laughs.

"What's so funny?" Sophie says, smiling.

"Nothing," Seb says, shaking his head. "It's just that you and Jake... You take care of us. How would we ever manage on our own?"

Sophie smiles wider, planting a kiss on Seb's cheek. She knows he has a point; this is the second time, after all, that either Jake or Sophie has made an intervention and basically turned Seb's and Evan's relationship around. Seb doesn't mind, though. He really doesn't. Jake's advice was incredibly valuable last time, and he knows that he can trust Sophie's judgment as well.

"You'll do fine," Sophie says. "Eventually."

Seb certainly hopes so.

CHAPTER 14

TANGLED

Seb can't quite believe that he actually decided to take Sophie up on her offer.

After she left earlier, Seb considered the idea of going to see Evan play tonight, showing that he still cares, as Sophie put it. It seemed like a good idea, the right thing to do. But he quickly starts freaking out, and actually decides to just stay home, to just stay in his room all night.

That splendid plan quickly falls apart, however, when Jake decides to come by and pick him up.

"Seb," he says, knocking on the locked door. "I know you told Sophie you'd go tonight, but I figured you might wuss out. We're here to get you."

Seb stares at the door, eyes narrowed. It takes another minute of knocking and persuasion from Jake, before he finally opens the door, and Jake smiles at him, a mix of triumph and relief on his face.

"Excellent," he says. "Now come on, let's go."

Seb reluctantly goes with him, to the car waiting outside. It's Jake's car; very ordinary, very clean, and not nearly as personal or impressive as Evan's. But it's just fine. Seb imagines he's probably a bit biased, anyway.

Sophie is waiting in the passenger seat, and she smiles at Seb as he slips in the back. She's kind enough not to tease him, though, or point out the fact that she and Jake actually had to come and get him. She probably knows, just like Jake, that he indeed had wussed out and planned on hiding away all night, rather than facing Evan.

As they start driving, Seb feels himself get oddly nervous. His palms are sweating a bit, and he distractedly drags them against the fabric of his jeans, staring out the window. It's dark outside, and pouring down. He's glad he doesn't have to walk, instead sitting safe and snug inside a car.

Jake and Sophie are talking to each other about when Evan is playing tonight, and about what kind of performances they will see. Seb barely pays attention.

He's nervous, anxious. He wants to make things right with Evan, but even disregarding the fact that he's still angry at him and hurt, he feels guilty about how he acted, himself. He's not sure he can handle seeing Evan. It won't help anything, won't change anything. He doubts that Evan will even change his whole no-proximity-in-public thing; it seems to be simply too hard for him. And that's kind of a deal breaker for Seb, even though he's willing to compromise and let Evan get over his own insecurities about other people's opinions, in his own time. Everyone else knows him as straight (incredibly so, really), and seeing him with a guy would definitely raise more than a few eyebrows, so Seb kind of gets where Evan's apprehension is coming from.

But regardless, Seb doesn't want to be his secret. He doesn't want Evan to feel so insecure about his own sexuality, that he chooses to pretend that Seb means nothing to him, as soon as other people are around.

But Seb still takes Sophie's advice; going tonight can't possibly make things worse. And when they finally reach the bar and park the car, Seb takes a deep breath before stepping out.

It takes about three seconds to get from the car to the bar's entrance, but the persistent rain still manages to get them all quite wet, and they duck inside, Jake cursing to himself.

Seb looks around as they enter the bar, Jake and Sophie right beside him, and he does his best not to tense up.

This is ridiculous; they have been here a total of ten seconds, and he's already doing his very best not to look for Evan, trying not to scan the crowd for his face. But it's impossible not to, of course. Even with all of these people, the place practically full, he can't help himself. Jake and Sophie notice, without a doubt, but they're kind enough not to mention it. They know that Seb is conflicted about coming here, as it is.

Seb reminds himself that he is angry, and that he wanted to stay home. But this night is important to Evan, he realizes, and Seb *did* promise to come. And no matter how angry or hurt he is, no matter how Seb acted and no matter how fucked up it all is, Seb simply can't find it in him to hurt Evan like that. He can't find it in him to hurt him *more*.

Seb, Jake and Sophie sit down at a small, round table near the back, where they have a clear line of sight to the small stage. Seb finds himself fidgeting a bit, as he sits on the high barstool, that leaves him about as high up as he would have been while standing.

What would Evan say if he saw him here? Would he care? What would Seb say? He came here to show some kind of support, but he honestly feels like Evan doesn't deserve it, after how he acted. And he feels like he, himself, doesn't deserve any other response than a glare, either.

"I'm gonna get us something to drink," Jake says, getting up from the table, and Seb sees out of the corner of his eye how Sophie smiles at him, as he leaves. But he doesn't look at her. His blue eyes are sweeping across the room, landing on the bar over by the wall, which Jake makes his way over to. He remembers when Evan took him here, bought him a beer, the second time they ever met. It was nice, fun. They talked and hung out, and Seb remembers being surprised at just how easy it felt, at how much Evan went against his first impressions of him.

"Our first date."

Seb swallows as he thinks about it, and looks away from the bar, looking at the small stage and the crowded audience if front of it, instead. Evan's words echo inside his mind, the tone of them happy and light. His stomach twists.

Seb can practically feel Sophie looking at him.

"You okay?" she says, and Seb tears his gaze away from the audience to look at her. He doesn't reply, and she gives him a kind, sympathetic smile.

"Thank you for coming," she says, reaching out and rubbing his upper arm in a comforting way. "He'll be glad you did, I know it."

Seb still doesn't reply. Instead, he just tries to smile back, before returning to his search for Evan's face. He doesn't know why he bothers. What is he going to say or do if he spots him, anyway?

Jake returns shortly with two beers, and he hands one to Seb, while bringing a coke for Sophie, who is the designated driver. Seb thanks him, but then looks away as Jake gave Sophie a kiss. Somehow, their bliss is painful to him at the moment. He takes a sip of his beer.

There's some guy on stage, wailing into the microphone with a rather nasal voice. Even Seb can hear that his guitar playing is sloppy, and as soon as the song is over, the guy bows out, to the sound of lukewarm and rather unenthusiastic applause.

"That was the fourth one, right?" Sophie asks Jake, and Jake makes a sound of confirmation.

"Yeah," he says. "Evan should be up in a minute."

Seb feels a shudder run through him. Evan is the fifth one on the list of performers tonight, as he heard Jake mention in the car. It's a pity that the performers' time is so short, Seb finds himself thinking; Sophie mentioned that each person only gets to play one song, and a cover, at that. Three or four minutes isn't much, when it comes to making an impression, really.

Then again, Seb remembers Evan definitely making an impression on him during the first few minutes they ever spent together, so maybe it's not so bad.

Seb keeps his eyes on the stage, unable to look away, waiting. The guy who just finished has been off the stage for about a minute or so, when Evan walks on. And when Seb sees him, he feels his grip tighten on his beer bottle.

Evan is wearing those torn jeans that Seb likes, and a short-sleeved, button-up shirt, open over a black t-shirt. The shirt is green, and although Seb can't see properly from where he's sitting, he knows that that shirt must bring out the green of Evan's eyes perfectly.

Evan's light brown hair is ruffled, as though he has just pulled his fingers through it, and if he is nervous, this is probably the case. He sits down in front of the microphone, the strap of his acoustic guitar slung over his shoulder. He scans the crowd and smiles when he catches sight of Sophie and his brother. And then he sees Seb, and his smile falters. Instead, he looks oddly scared, nervous, and Seb doesn't smile, either. He's still angry, he reminds himself. He is still angry.

But Evan just looks *so* beautiful.

Silence falls over the room, as Evan looks down, wrapping his fingers around the neck of the guitar. He raises his other hand to the strings, but then pauses, hesitating. He looks up again, straight at Seb, who feels his heart skip a beat at the expression in those eyes. Evan just watches him intently for a second or so, and then the

194

moment is over, and he turns his attention back to the guitar. Silence for a few more moments, and then he starts playing.

The notes are simple, soft and smooth, as they drift through the silent bar, and Seb finds himself keeping his eyes fixed on Evan. He had almost forgotten how he looks when he plays, how he looks so focused and at peace, and when he starts singing, something warm settles somewhere in Seb's stomach, making his grip on the bottle loosen slightly.

It's the most beautiful sound, Seb thinks, hearing Evan sing. He would have been content just listening. But then Evan looks up, straight at him, and Seb freezes. There is something in those eyes; he can feel it, even from so far away. And Seb isn't sure if it's the look in Evan's eyes that does it, but for once, he finds himself listening to the lyrics of the song, and not just Evan's voice. He pays attention to every word, and as he does, he feels his heart beat a bit faster.

Evan's gaze stays fixed on him, to such an extent that some people in the crowd actually turn to see just who or what he's looking at. But Seb doesn't care. He is focused on Evan, focused on the way his voice sounds, the way he's looking at him, and the words he's singing.

To Seb. He is singing to Seb.

Seb swallows hard as he realizes it, the lyrics of the song suddenly feeling very personal, and very, very honest.

Evan keeps looking at him, his gaze unwavering, and Seb feels the sudden, weirdest urge to cry. He doesn't, though. He hates crying, has had more than enough crying, anyway, and he most definitely won't do it here, in front of other people. But it's the only reaction he can really think of, to how he suddenly feels.

He knows he's supposed to be angry with Evan, he's supposed to feel hurt and vindicated and even guilty. He isn't supposed to sit here and feel himself melt, to feel his anger and guilt slipping away until there is nothing left but pure, warm... He doesn't know what to call it. But whatever it is, it's coming from Evan. It's in every single syllable he sings, every single tone. In every single word, meant for Seb.

Seb doesn't really notice when the song is over. He's only vaguely aware of the applause that follow, which are much more enthusiastic this time. He doesn't applaud, himself. Instead, he just sits there, eyes fixed on Evan, completely paralyzed. He doesn't know what to do. And Evan is still looking at him, unwavering.

Their eye-contact doesn't break for a second, as Evan gets up and steps off the stage. It's a small stage, low enough for him to just lightly jump off the edge. He makes his way between the tables and the people, and when he reaches the table in the back, where Seb, Jake and Sophie are, he stops dead. He takes off his guitar, attached to its shoulder strap, and hands it to Jake. Seb sees in the corner of his eye how Jake takes it, looking completely bewildered, while saying something about how good the performance was. Sophie is smiling. Seb is staring, and doesn't move.

Seb knows he should be surprised when Evan kisses him, here, in front of everyone, hands cupping his face. But he isn't, he doesn't have the focus to be. Instead, he just reciprocates the kiss, every ounce of his anger and hurt completely evaporated, and he feels Evan relax as Seb kisses him back, as though he was afraid that he wouldn't.

Seb is focused on the way Evan's shirt feels against his hands, how he smells, how the kiss is so urgent and hot, yet unbelievably soft, all at the same time. He's vaguely aware of a lot of people actually staring, some of them even gaping at them, freezing in mid-clap, shock written all over their faces. But he doesn't care. All he cares about is Evan, and how it feels to have him so close.

It's only after a few seconds that Evan pulls away the slightest bit, only far enough to smile at Seb and look him in the eyes. It's that soft smile, the one reserved for Seb, and no one else.

Evan doesn't say anything, just takes his hand and laces their fingers together. And Seb doesn't even nod. Instead, he just goes with Evan, as he leads him away from the table and the crowd, and out through the front door. Seb catches a glimpse of Jake just standing there, holding the guitar, exasperation written all over his face, while Sophie just smiles and kisses him on the cheek. And he glimpses the expressions and whispers of everyone else, before simply leaving them behind.

They barely get inside the door of Evan's room, before they're all over each other.

Evan just managed to snatch up his jacket before they left the bar, before they got into Evan's car and drove to his place. The distance between where they parked and the entrance to the dorm building definitely isn't far, but seeing as how Evan actually pulled Seb to him and kissed him against the side of the car, they were outside long enough for them both to get pretty much soaked from the rain. Not that Seb had minds that the least bit.

They managed to make their way up to Evan's room, though, and Evan shoves the door shut as Seb tugs at his brown leather jacket, desperate to get it off of him, not leaving his lips for a second with his own. Evan complies, shrugging the jacket off and dropping it to the floor, while Seb's hands fumble to get his shirt off, too.

"Fucking layers," he mutters between kisses, and Evan smiles, taking off his button-up shirt and throwing it aside.

"Shut up," he murmurs, and Seb does.

There is something so satisfying about pulling his fingers through Evan's rain-wet hair, and Seb moans against Evan's lips, as Evan slips his hands underneath his t-shirt. It's practically plastered to his skin, soaked from the rain as well, but Evan slides it off of him easily, dumping it in a wet pile on the floor. Seb feels a shiver run across his skin. He's cold for a moment, but forgets all about it as soon as Evan puts his hands on him, smoothing down along his back, dragging his nails slightly across his skin, making Seb suck in a sharp breath.

He needs more. It isn't enough.

Seb surprises himself by moving his hands down to Evan's belt, unbuckling it, and Evan breaks the kiss for a split second to glance down. Then he looks up, and Seb catches only a glimpse of the surprised, excited expression in those green eyes, before Evan kisses him again, fiercely and hungrily, hands moving further down along Seb's back. Seb undoes Evan's fly with fumbling fingers, and Evan, taking the hint, pulls away just enough to take off his own t-shirt, before claiming Seb's lips again. Everything seems to be moving in a hazy, intoxicated blur.

Seb is vaguely aware of them moving across the room, kicking off their shoes, and he barely even notices, really, as they practically fall down onto Evan's bed, Evan landing on his back. They move up along the bed, and suddenly Seb finds himself straddling Evan, leaning down to kiss his chest. They haven't even turned the lights on, but even in the dim light from a streetlamp outside the window, Seb can appreciate just how gorgeous Evan is.

"I'm sorry," Evan says, his voice surprisingly thick with emotion, and Seb doesn't have to ask him what he's referring to. Seb was angry with him, hurt and confused, but all of that was forgiven the moment Evan kissed him tonight, in front of everyone, claiming him for his own, for the world to see.

"It doesn't matter," he says, moving up to kiss Evan's lips. "Doesn't matter."

Evan kisses him back with surprising intensity, as though unbelievably relieved at Seb's forgiveness, gripping his dark hair between his fingers. It's the greatest feeling in the world, having him so close again, feeling Evan's skin against his own. It has only been a day, but it somehow felt like an eternity. Seb didn't like being angry with him, sending him away like that; it made him feel as though they would never see each other again, like it was something final and destructive. He's so glad he was so wrong.

"I'm sorry, too," he says against Evan's lips. It doesn't need repeating; he's shocked at the sheer emotion in his own voice, and he's certain that Evan heard it. And Evan doesn't need to reply. The way he kisses Seb speaks louder.

Seb smoothes his hands down over Evan's chest, making his way to his unzipped fly. He feels Evan tense up underneath him, as he pulls those torn jeans down, before Evan shimmies out of them himself and tosses them to the floor. Seb isn't too far behind, managing to pull off his own pants in a fit of awkward acrobatics, leaving Evan smiling, looking much too amused.

"Shut up," Seb says, a bit embarrassed, but he can't help but smile as he leans down to kiss him again. Evan pulls him closer, pulls his body down so that their chests press together, and Seb just relishes at the close proximity, fingers pulling through Evan's hair as he feels his hands against his back. But it isn't enough. He wants more, wants more of Evan, more of this, more of everything. And Evan makes him brave.

Seb is almost surprised to find himself pulling away from Evan's lips and embrace, moving downward, planting searing kisses along Evan's throat and chest and collarbone, moving down along his stomach. Evan tenses up a bit, and Seb keeps trailing kisses down along his skin, until he reaches the hem of Evan's boxers. Seb isn't entirely sure what he's doing, isn't entirely sure what has gotten into him. But it feels right, and he wants it.

Seb ghosts his lips over Evan's underwear, satisfied at the way Evan tenses up and twitches a bit as he does, before he slips his fingers underneath the hem of the boxers, and pulls them down.

The sound Evan makes as Seb takes him into his mouth is deep and guttural, almost a growl, and immensely satisfying to hear. The way he tenses up and gyrates his hips just the slightest bit, as Seb works his tongue and mouth, one hand working over what he can't take, the way he gently pulls his fingers through Seb's dark hair, wordlessly urging for more. It's a huge turn-on, and Seb finds himself moaning quietly, earning more pleased sounds from Evan.

He keeps going for a little while longer, Evan's breathing getting heavier and faster, his fingers gripping Seb's hair tighter.

"I want you, Seb."

Evan says the words breathlessly, as though he can barely articulate, and Seb slows down, before stopping entirely. Slowly, he feels Evan's grip on his hair loosen, and he pulls away, raising his head to look up at Evan. He looks oddly nervous, as though afraid he has said too much. But Seb doesn't say anything. Instead, he just slowly moves up along Evan's body, eyes fixed on his. Then he leans down to kiss his neck.

"Say that again," he murmurs by his ear, letting his tongue sweep across Evan's skin, making him tense up again, exhaling sharply. His hands are moving across Seb's back, slow, but eager and impatient.

"I want you," he breathes, and Seb grits his teeth. God help him, hearing it makes him so unbelievably hot.

"Again," he breathes, closing his eyes.

"I want you," Evan repeats, kissing Seb's neck and nipping the skin with his teeth. He sounds more sure now, more confident. "I wanna be inside you."

Seb makes an odd, strangled sound, and opens his eyes as Evan grips his chin and pulls his face up, so that he can see his eyes. Evan's are open, eager, pupils huge and black. He looks at Seb as though asking for permission. And after only a second of deliberation, Seb gives him the smallest of nods.

Things start moving at a weird pace then. Seb feels a kind of surreal sensation as he moves, ending up on his back instead of Evan, and Evan hovering over him. His heart starts beating faster, and suddenly, he feels nervousness seeping into the unabashed desire that was going on just moments ago. He swallows, looking up at Evan. He swears he sees at least some of his own nervousness reflected in his eyes.

It's with unusual softness that Evan leans down and kisses him, trailing his hand down along Seb's chest and stomach. But there is urgency there, too, so much so that Seb feels like he might be able to push that nervousness away, and he moves his hand up to grip Evan's hair. Evan groans against his lips, and just like that, Seb feels sure again.

Evan has pulled off his boxers completely, and when he starts tugging at Seb's, Seb shimmies out of them and dumps them on the floor beside the bed. Evan presses down against him then, and he tenses up, letting out a moan that sounds lower and hoarser than he expected. Evan seems to approve, though, rutting against him slowly, moving down to kiss his neck. Seb closes his eyes. Evan is still wet where Seb's mouth was just moments earlier, and it creates a hot, slick friction between them that makes Seb tense up all over in the most wonderful way.

Evan's hand wanders down then and wraps his fingers around him, making Seb groan into his hair, his fingertips pressing into Evan's shoulders.

After a little while longer of touching and kissing—Seb feels as though every muscle in his body is taut with anticipation, by now—Evan half-pauses, and Seb opens his eyes. Evan is reaching over the bed's edge and opening a drawer of his nightstand, all the while planting lingering kisses on Seb's chest. Seb glances over, and sees Evan extract a small bottle from the drawer. He swallows, somewhat nervously.

"You've done this before?" he asks, and Evan glances up at him.

"Once," he admits, closing the drawer. He sounds a bit off, and Seb can't blame him; in the heat of passion and in the middle of getting it on, one generally doesn't discuss previous sex partners. And Seb doesn't really want to hear about it, anyway. He knows that he sure as hell isn't keen on talking about girls he has slept with, right now, regardless of if any previous experiences would be helpful in this particular situation.

Evan keeps the bottle of lube in his hand, and sits up slightly on his knees, straddling Seb. He squeezes some lube into his hand.

"But I don't wanna think about that right now," he says, looking up to meet Seb's eyes. He puts the bottle away and leans down, planting a hot kiss against Seb's collarbone. "Let's just say you're my first."

There's something in his voice, in the low, hot hoarseness of it, that makes Seb feel oddly warm and relaxed, even as he huffs a tiny, breathless laugh at the comment. He exhales slowly, deeply, Evan trailing kisses up along his neck.

"How about you?" Evan asks, and Seb probably would have let out another laugh, if he weren't so nervous and turned on and relaxed and excited, all at the same time.

"Definitely my first," he breathes, surprised by how his voice sounds. Evan seems to like it, though, because he has a small smile on his face when he reaches Seb's mouth.

"Okay," he whispers. "We'll take it easy."

Seb nods, eyes on Evan's, and he's very aware of Evan's hand moving further down, their gazes not disconnecting for a second as it does. And then Evan slowly, carefully, slips a finger inside him, and Seb inhales sharply, automatically tightening his grip on Evan's shoulders.

It feels weird at first, uncomfortable even, but then Evan kisses him slowly, soothingly, and Seb relaxes a bit, exhaling.

And eventually, a few minutes later, after adding more fingers and easing into it as slowly and carefully as possible, Seb is moaning against Evan's neck, fingers digging into his back.

"Oh god," he breathes, eyes closed as Evan hits a very sweet spot. He's honestly surprised at just how good it feels, how good it feels to have Evan touching him like this. "Shit."

Evan is breathing heavily, kissing Seb's throat and collarbone and chest, his free hand holding him up so that he can hover over Seb and just look at him. At least, he does until Seb grabs onto him and pulls him down, aching for that sensation of skin on hot skin.

"Evan," he breathes, feeling Evan tense up against him at the way he says his name. "Now."

Evan looks up then, so that their eyes met.

"Yeah?" he asks, sounding breathless and impatient, but concerned, nonetheless, and Seb nods.

"Yeah," he says, planting a hot, lingering kiss on his mouth. "Now."

Evan doesn't need telling twice. Seb can feel how hard he is, can feel it against his thigh, and he watches as Evan leans over to his nightstand again, this time getting a condom. Seb keeps absently touching him, his arms, his chest, his hips, anywhere he can reach. He is impatient now, burning and aching, desperate to get things going again, desperate to feel Evan against him, hot, wet and *moving*.

Evan opens the condom wrapper with his teeth, something that Seb finds unreasonably hot, and then proceeds to put the condom on. Seb is too distracted to be amazed at how Evan manages to do it all one-handed; his fingers are still inside him, still moving and rubbing, making Seb squirm underneath him, and Seb closes his eyes, exhaling slowly, heavily. He's trying to stay calm, trying not to lose control just yet. But *damn*, is it difficult.

It's the feeling of Evan kissing him that makes him open his eyes again, only to see that green gaze above him in the dim light. It looks eager and concerned, all at once. But Seb doesn't say anything. The way he kisses Evan then is permission enough, and Seb exhales sharply in surprised disappointment as he feels those fingers pull out. But then Evan gently pushes his legs apart a bit, and Seb takes the hint, hitching up slightly so that Evan can slide inside.

The lube helps a lot, but Seb still finds himself groaning loudly as Evan enters him, squeezing his eyes shut and digging his nails into Evan's back so hard that he's afraid he might actually draw blood. But if he does, Evan either doesn't notice or doesn't care, because he doesn't react. Instead, he pulls out a bit, breathing heavily, before slowly easing back in, again and again, further each time. And when he bottoms out, Seb groans deeply, and Evan pauses, making Seb open his eyes. He sees Evan's concerned expression, and does some vague kind of half-nod.

"I'm good," he says, barely able to articulate, too wrapped up in the sensation of everything right now to form words; he just wants Evan to fucking *move*. And Evan seems to take the hint, because he starts thrusting then, with slow, deliberate motions. And Seb closes his eyes again, moaning with every thrust, the sound of Evan groaning just by his ear making him shiver and move his hips against Evan's, his hands pressing down against the small of his back, wanting more. It feels so good, so unbelievably good.

Eventually, it finally starts getting *too* good, and Seb feels how he's turning into a squirming, embarrassingly almost whimpering mess. And Evan speeds up, his thrusts becoming deeper and more determined, and Seb clings to him, hitching one leg up to press Evan's hips down against him. He can't take this, can't handle much more of this.

"Evan," he says, practically panting, one hand moving to grip Evan's hair. "Fuck, I'm so close."

Evan groans against his collarbone, planting a hard kiss there, before moving up to kiss his mouth, one hand moving down along Seb's stomach.

The moment Evan wraps his fingers around him and starts stroking, Seb feels as though he might actually choke, overwhelmed by sensation. He clings to Evan, desperately, pushing his tongue into his mouth and claiming, taking what he wants, what he *needs*, making Evan moan against him. He's getting closer, his skin burning, crackling.

"Evan," he breathes against those lips, unable to think of anything else to say. "Evan, please."

"Come with me, Seb," Evan growls, stroking him in unison with his thrusts. "Come on, baby. I got you."

That's all it takes to drive Seb completely over the edge, making him squeeze his eyes shut and utter a noise that sounds like a deep, strangled moan, as he comes over Evan's fingers. And the way he tenses up is the final straw for Evan, who thrusts once, twice, three times, before coming, letting out a low, guttural groan, before practically collapsing on top of Seb.

Neither of them moves for several seconds then, Seb's eyes still closed, as the ringing in his ears subsides. He's breathing heavily, just like Evan, and he swallows, trying to keep himself from passing out. Because he honestly feels like he might. It's like coming down from the most intense high, his head spinning from the overload of sensation.

It's silent for several, long seconds.

"I love you."

Seb hears it, even through all the heavy breathing, through the haze and the ringing in his ears. He opens his eyes, wondering for a second if he imagined it, but as soon as he sees Evan's unsmiling face, he knows he didn't. Those green eyes are shining, unsure and excited and exhausted, so soft and full of pure adoration, that Seb almost forgets to breathe. *Did Evan just say that?*

Evan keeps his expression, even when Seb doesn't answer.

"I love you, Seb," he says, voice low, giving him a quick, soft kiss. "I love you."

And then it really sinks in, and Seb hears the words.

"I love you," he hears himself say, his voice quiet but sure, and Evan pulls back to look at him. His expression is unreadable, but Seb barely notices. It feels so good to say it out loud. It feels so good to finally say what he realizes he has been feeling ever since he first met Evan, that night, so long ago. He knew, even then. He has loved Evan this whole time, completely.

"I love you," Seb repeats, moving his hands up to Evan's face, so that he can pull him down into a kiss. "I love you."

Evan sighs against his lips, relaxing. Then he pulls away to kiss Seb's cheek, then his nose.

"I love you," he murmurs, raining kisses all over Seb's face. "I love you, I love you, I love you."

Seb can't help but smile, suddenly feeling uncharacteristically giddy.

"Don't make it weird," he almost laughs, still a bit breathless, closing his eyes against Evan's onslaught of kisses.

"I'm not making it weird," Evan murmurs, a smile in his voice, as he kisses Seb's closed eyelids. "You're making it weird."

"You've gotten your point across," Seb says, actually laughing now. "I get it, you love me."

Evan stops kissing him then, and Seb opens his eyes. Evan is hovering above him, a big grin on his face.

"Good," he says, and just looks at Seb for the longest time. And Seb loves the way he looks at him, like he's something precious, to be kept and protected.

Then Evan leans down and plants a quick kiss on his lips again, and Seb groans.

"You just had to?" he says, and Evan smiles smugly.

"Yes, I did."

Seb can't help but smile, though. He feels like he will never be able to stop smiling.

It's after a few more seconds of silence that Evan exhales and looks down, and Seb follows his gaze. It's hard not to notice the slight mess they have made, and Seb grimaces slightly.

"Yeah," he says, drawing out the word, and Evan looks up at him again, eyebrows raised. "Sorry about that."

"Don't be sorry," Evan practically laughs, kissing him again. "Comes with the territory, I guess."

Seb has to admit that that attitude makes him feel better, and makes the whole thing less awkward when they eventually clean up, which is a rather quick affair.

Seb just lies there for a few moments afterward, while Evan gets rid of the condom, feeling completely drained and soft and relaxed, and immensely satisfied. Then Evan returns, crawling into bed with him, and Seb pulls the cover up over them both. He automatically fits himself into Evan's arms, as he pulls him closer, Evan placing his head by his shoulder and nuzzling his neck. He exhales heavily.

"So," Evan says sleepily. "How's it feel?"

Seb frowns at the odd question.

"Sore," he says after a moment, and laughs when Evan looks up at him. "But good. Mostly good."

He kisses Evan's forehead, and Evan settles down again.

"Feels very good," Seb says, kissing the top of Evan's head this time. "You?"

"Awesome," Evan murmurs against his skin, and Seb rolls his eyes.

"You can't use that word for everything, Evan," he says, and Evan groans.

"Watch me," he says, and Seb smiles, pulling Evan a bit closer, as if that were possible. Neither of them speaks for a few seconds, and eventually, Seb hears Evan starting to breathe heavier. He glances down; he has fallen asleep. Seb smiles.

"I love you," he whispers, kissing his hair. And to his surprise, Evan replies, in a barely audible, muffled murmur.

"Love you, too."

CHAPTER 15

OUT

Seb wakes to warmth of Evan's breath against his neck.

The two of them are still lying tangled together, like they fell asleep last night, and Seb opens his eyes. He glances down at his boyfriend, eyebrows slightly raised. Evan Matthews may be tough and abrasive a lot of the time, but he is probably the biggest cuddler Seb has ever met, and the way those arms wraps tightly around him makes him smile. Much like last night, he feels like he will never be able to stop smiling, not really.

Seb lets himself lie there and enjoy it for a few more minutes, just watching Evan's sleeping face, before the urge to take a piss becomes a bit too overwhelming, and he gets out of bed. Evan is still soundly asleep, but he seems to instinctively reach for Seb as he gets up, missing his warmth. Seb smoothly evades him, though, and makes his way to the bathroom.

He half-winces as he starts moving, rather startlingly being reminded of what happened last night, what they did. It's not too bad, though, just a bit sore, and it will pass. And if nothing else, it was worth it. He most definitely wants to do it again.

When Seb returns a minute or so later and crawls back into bed, Evan seems to have woken up. At least, judging from the way he immediately grabs Seb and pulls him down, wrapping his arms around him, underneath the covers. Seb just gives a startled laugh, and fits himself into Evan's arms, lying down on his back so that Evan can move closer beside him and nuzzle against his neck, one arm slung over his stomach; it seems to be his very favorite cuddling pose.

"What's gotten into you?" Seb asks, smiling, when Evan plants a few kisses along his throat.

"I missed you," Evan murmurs against his skin, and Seb raises his eyebrows.

"Seriously?" he says, with a light sound of disbelief. "I was gone, like, two seconds."

"That's not what I meant." Evan's voice takes on an oddly somber tone, and Seb looks down at him. And Evan sighs and looks up, resting his chin against Seb's shoulder.

"I'm sorry," he says, unexpectedly, green eyes soft and a bit sad. Seb tugs at his hair gently with his hand.

"Hey," he says chidingly. "We've been over this. It's fine."

"No." Evan shakes his head, propping himself up on his elbows. "No, I never meant to make you feel like that. I never meant to make you feel like I was ashamed of you or that I didn't care. I wasn't thinking, I freaked out, and I'm sorry."

Seb just looks at him, then plants a kiss on his forehead.

"And it's fine," he says. "After what you did at the bar last night, it's kind of hard to stay mad at you."

Evan smiles a bit at that, and Seb can't help but smile back.

"The song helped," Seb adds, and Evan looks a bit sheepish.

"Yeah," he says. "I wasn't gonna do that one, actually."

Seb frowns at him, and Evan cocks his head.

"I mean, I was," he says. "At first. But then all that happened, and... I figured you wouldn't come, anyway. So it seemed pointless."

"All that," Seb repeats, without thinking. "You mean, when I—"

"Broke up with me?" Evan adds helpfully, his voice slightly subdued, and his words hurt so much more than Seb wants to admit.

"Sure," he says, looking away, his voice a bit thick. "If that's what you want to call it."

"That's what it felt like," Evan says, and sighs. "But I get it. I fucked up, I get it."

"I did, too," Seb says, looking back at him. "I never planned to do that, it just sort of happened. I hated myself for it. I guess we both just freaked out."

213

Evan keeps his eyes on him.

"Yeah." The one word is soft, content. Then he moves up a bit, so that his face is closer to Seb's.

"But then you did come to watch me," he says, the smallest hint of a smile on his face; it's mostly in his eyes. "And I guess I thought it must have been a sign, or something. And I figured that since you were there, despite everything, I might as well do the song I'd planned on doing."

"And you just assumed it would work?" Seb says cheekily, and Evan gives him a crooked smile.

"No," he says. "I just wanted you to know. I wanted you to know how I felt. Really."

"And the kiss?"

Evan looks sheepish again.

"That was *not* planned," he says. "Definitely not. I still can't really believe I did that. I was so scared you would just turn me down."

Seb laughs.

"Well, *that* worked," he says. "The whole thing was very romantic."

Evan makes a face, and Seb frowns.

"What?" he asks, and Evan groans softly.

"I don't know if I like being called *romantic*," he says, and Seb gives him a look of disbelief that looks an awful lot like a bitchface.

"Dude, you sang a love song up on stage, with an audience," he says pointedly. "And then you kissed me, with a room full of people watching. What the fuck do you expect to be called?"

Evan narrows his eyes at him, a small smile creeping across his face.

"Fine," he says. "You're right. As usual."

"I know," Seb says matter-of-factly, kissing Evan's forehead. But then Evan steals his lips with his own, and anything he planned on saying just evaporates. Instead, Seb just melts into the kiss, closing his eyes and pulling Evan just a little bit closer. It's difficult to get any closer than this, skin on skin, wrapped up together underneath the covers.

But he still tries. He will keep trying until they somehow merge together into one being, and never have to be apart again.

♦

Seb fights to keep his eyes open. He's in the middle of a lecture on American literature, and even though he normally loves this subject, he's just so damn tired.

He hasn't slept much. Despite him and Evan having been together for several weeks now, they have never been *at it* like this before, not like they have been since that night. Seb isn't sure if it's because something has changed since then, making them feel more secure and certain about the entire relationship, or if it's simply because they finally had sex and just want to keep doing it. Probably both. But the sex definitely isn't bad. Definitely not.

After that first time, about a week ago, and after weeks of baby steps when it comes to the physical aspect of their relationship, it has just become so easy. They can't keep their hands off each other. Then again, Seb supposes that was one of the perks of being in love, still floating around

215

in the euphoria of it all—it makes you really, *really* horny. *Really.* Not that he minds.

They have tried different things, too; after Seb being on the receiving end the first time around, they've switched it up, and that was definitely an experience. Seb isn't sure which part he liked best, to be honest. Feeling Evan inside him like that is amazing, being taken and completely possessed—but then again, making Evan squirm and hearing him moan underneath him is something he feels like he will never get tired of. And that isn't even all they have tried, so far.

So Seb is distracted, to say the least, as he sits there in the lecture hall, trying to stay awake. His mind wanders to the drugs analogy he once used to describe Evan. It's ridiculous how well it fits. But he's also pretty sure Evan sees him the same way.

When the lecture finally ends, Seb makes his way out of the hall. He has just gotten out into the quickly crowding hallway, stuffing his notebook into his bag, when someone speaks to him.

"Hey, Seb." The soft tone of voice makes Seb look up, and he's met with a pair of big, pretty eyes and a head of chestnut brown hair.

"Clara," he says, raising his eyebrows a bit in surprise. He hasn't seen her in a while, or hasn't spoken to her, at least. "Hey."

Clara smiles at him, a bit awkwardly.

"Hi," she says, sounding a bit awkward, too. "How are you?"

"Good," Seb says. "You?"

"I'm good," she replies, nodding. "A bit tired. Exams and all."

Seb nods understandingly, and notices how she looks as though she wants to say something else.

"So, um," she finally says. "Listen. When I gave you my number..."

She makes a face, as though embarrassed.

"I didn't know you were... with him," she says. "I'm sorry."

Seb just stares at her for a moment, before catching on.

"Oh," he says, eyes wide and surprised comprehension on his face. "Oh, no. No, it's fine."

"Really?" Clara says, a bit hopefully, and Seb nods. He had almost forgotten about the very public display of affection Evan made and how pretty much everyone is aware of it, by now, including Clara.

"Yeah," he says. "Yeah, I actually didn't even know, myself, at the time."

He pauses at his own choice of words, and Clara frowns. That was an odd thing to say. But he doesn't bother explaining, and just shakes his head, as though saying *forget it.*

"Right," Clara says, a bit hesitantly. "Well, I feel kind of stupid."

"Don't." Seb shakes his head again. "I mean, who knew, right?"

Clara smiles at his lame attempt at lightening the mood, and she nods.

"Right," she says, clearly more at ease. "Honest mistake, I guess."

Seb smiles back at her, and she just looks at him for a minute.

"I'm happy for you, though," she says, sincerity in her voice. "Even if it a loss for my team."

She adds that last part with a jokingly conspiring tone, and Seb practically blushes, not bothering to explain that he hasn't really left that team entirely, and rather just extended his allegiance to another one.

"Thanks," he gets out instead, trying not to flick his gaze away too much, and trying not to smile in embarrassed discomfort. He really isn't good with compliments. But Clara just laughs lightly, and smiles when he catches her eye again. She squeezes his arm in a friendly gesture.

"I'll see you around, Seb," she says, and Seb nods.

"Yeah," he says. "See ya."

She gives him one last smile, before making her way past him and walking down the hallway. Seb glances over at her; she has practically disappeared into the mass of students crowding in and out of lecture halls, already.

Seb exhales heavily, turning back and starting to walk in the other direction. He has another lecture after lunch, and he can't wait for it to be over. He just wants to get back home, to crawl into bed with Evan and not move for several days.

He has just almost reached the end of the big hallway, where a few restrooms are, when he stops dead.

Speak of the devil. Evan is standing right there, arms folded, leaning against the wall, waiting for him.

"Evan," Seb says, surprise as clear in his voice as it is on his face. "Hey."

"Hey," Evan says, an odd gruffness to his voice. But before Seb has a chance to say anything else, or even ask what he's doing there, Evan has grabbed him and turned him so that his back is pressed against the wall. And Seb doesn't have a chance to say or do anything to react, before Evan suddenly kisses him, with such unexpected fierceness that it makes Seb's head spin. When he pulls away, Seb just stares at him, mouth half-open.

"What?" he breathes, equally shocked at what Evan is doing, as well as him doing it right here, where anyone could see. But Evan doesn't seem to care. Instead, he yanks the nearest restroom door open and pulls Seb inside, locking the door behind them.

"Evan," Seb exclaims, thoroughly confused. "What—"

Evan silences him with a kiss, backing him into the wall again. It's a very small restroom, no bigger than a stall, really, but Evan still manages to cram himself in between Seb and the sink, pressing his whole body against Seb's. And as soon as those lips are on his, Seb forgets everything and anything he planned on saying or asking, like what the hell Evan is doing, or why.

Instead, his entire focus is suddenly centered on Evan, on the way he places his hands on Seb's hips firmly, grinding against him, how his tongue pushes into his mouth and how that light stubble scratches slightly against his face. It elicits a weak moan from Seb, as he just stands there for a moment, too shocked and overwhelmed to do anything but simply close his eyes and try to remember how to breathe.

And that's when Evan's hands suddenly move down to the fly of Seb's jeans and start undoing it, making Seb open his eyes.

"What—" he breathes, confused, looking down, but Evan doesn't seem to notice or care. Instead, he kisses him into silence, and Seb momentarily forgets about where they are, that it's in the middle of the day, and that this whole thing is entirely and thoroughly unexpected. He's almost distracted enough to not notice how Evan tugs his pants down slightly, after unzipping his fly, and how Evan's kisses are now moving down along his neck.

Seb's eyes are closed, his breathing heavy, and it's not until Evan leaves his neck and moves down that he reacts properly.

"Whoa," he says, looking down. Evan is practically on his knees, sliding Seb's shirt up so that he can kiss his stomach, just above the waistline of his boxers. Seb closes his eyes for a moment. "What are you doing?"

He practically breathes the words, unable to speak properly; sudden lust is clouding everything, at the moment.

"Let me know if you want me to stop," Evan says, his voice low and hoarse in a way that makes Seb shiver, and he grit his teeth.

No, he thinks desperately. *Please, don't stop. Don't ever stop.*

But this is *ridiculous*. Anyone could hear them—a main hallway is right outside, constantly occupied by a steady stream of students walking to and from classes and lectures. This is a bad idea, a really bad idea.

But Seb *really* doesn't want Evan to stop. And Evan knows that.

Seb closes his eyes and exhales slowly, as Evan smoothes his hands over Seb's skin, under his shirt, skimming down over the jeans along the inside of his thigh. His lips ghost over the bulge underneath the thin, stretched fabric of Seb's boxers—over the hard-on that Seb felt as soon as Evan pressed him up against this wall. Seb swallows hard.

"This is a bad idea," he murmurs breathlessly, but Evan ignores him. He slips his fingers underneath the hem of the underwear and pulls them down. "I don't—"

Whatever Seb planned on saying next is lost in an odd combination of a surprised gasp and a strangled moan. Suddenly, all that exists, all that Seb can even begin to focus on, is Evan's mouth. That hot, wicked, *sinful* mouth.

Seb doesn't even bother feeling surprised, or awkward, or even the slightest bit uncomfortable. Instead, he just leans his head back against the wall, eyes closed, and parts his lips in a low, breathless moan, his fingers automatically finding their way to the back of Evan's head, where they start pulling through his hair with gentle impatience.

What's happening? Seriously, what the *hell* is happening?

There is something impatient about the way Evan uses his mouth and hands and tongue, something eager and *possessive*, and Seb feels his knees go weak, his fingers gripping Evan's hair absently. He hears himself moan, and he grits his teeth to stifle it; some part of him is still aware of just how public this place is.

Evan doesn't seem to care, though. He just keeps going, keeps teasing and touching and swirling that tongue in the most wonderful way, and when Seb grips his hair tighter, he emits the dirtiest moan imaginable, sending vibrations through Seb's skin.

It takes everything Seb has not to make more noise. He's clenching his jaw, eyes closed, one hand softly pressing against the back of Evan's head, wordlessly begging for more. He's so close, so close... He can feel it.

"Evan," he gets out between heavy breaths. "I'm gonna—"

He chokes on the words, overcome with sensation. He wants to warn Evan, though, out of courtesy, if anything. But instead of stopping or slowing down, Evan seems to take his words as encouragement, moving faster and more intensely, and Seb lets out a strangled moan.

"Evan," he breathes, leaning his head back against the wall, gripping Evan's hair, his other hand clenching into a fist as his side. "Oh shit."

And then it happens, and Seb tenses up, letting out a long, low groan, eyes squeezing shut. It's over quickly, but it's the most intense, blinding few seconds, and Seb eventually relaxes, barely even noticing how his grip loosens on Evan's hair. He keeps his eyes closed, heart pounding, as he leans against the wall, trying to remain standing—his knees are just about to fold underneath him.

Seb breathes heavily, a slight ringing in his ears. He's vaguely aware of Evan pulling his boxers back up and getting to his feet.

"The fuck was that?" Seb finally gets out, eyes still closed. He sounds completely exhausted, and he hears a low chuckle from Evan, who plants a small kiss against his neck.

"Couldn't help myself," Evan murmurs, zipping up Seb's jeans. "I saw you, and I just had to."

Seb opens his eyes then, and finds himself looking into the lust-blown pupils of Evan's.

"Just had to?" he says, still a bit breathless, a small frown on his face.

"I didn't like her talking to you," Evan practically growls, planting another kiss on his neck. "Didn't like how she touched you."

Seb has to think for a few moments, before realizing he means Clara. He's pretty sure that Evan knows it was completely platonic, but he can't blame him. Clara was the trigger that set their relationship in motion, after all.

"Really?" he says, sounding a bit doubtful and surprised, his frown deepening. "That's all it takes?"

Evan pulls back and looks at him, a small smile on his face.

"Not really," he admits. "I've been wanting to do that all day. I *was* gonna wait 'til you got home, but..."

He kisses Seb on the mouth, slowly.

"Then she touched you," he says. "And it couldn't wait."

Seb half-smiles then.

"So," he says, "you were jealous?"

Evan looks away, as though reluctant to admit it.

"Maybe," he says. "Just a bit."

He looks back at Seb.

"What, you mind?"

"God, no," Seb says. "If this is how you handle it, I'm good."

Evan smiles mischievously, leaning in and placing a lingering kiss on Seb's lips.

"I'll see you later," he says, touching Seb's stubbled cheek with his finger in a light stroke, and Seb nods.

"You go ahead," he says, still sounding exhausted. "I'll just... I'm gonna need a minute."

Evan smiles again, before unlocking the door and slipping out into the hallway. Seb locks the door behind him and lets out a deep, heavy breath, feeling immensely satisfied and strangely lethargic. He could get used to this.

♦

Hours later, Seb is sitting in his dorm room, staring at his phone. He's holding it in his hand, screen staring up at him from his palm, and he swallows. He has dialed this number over and over for the past hour or so, trying to pluck up the courage he needs to actually call. And now, finally, he has managed.

He lets out a deep breath, before pressing the call icon and lifting the cell phone to his ear. It only rings four times, before his mother picks up.

"Hello?" she says, and Seb looks up at the ceiling.

"Hi, mom," he says, and he can practically sense her smiling.

"Sebastian," she says, the smile seeping into her voice. "So nice to hear from you. How are you?"

"I'm good," Seb says, nodding to himself. "Working hard, and all that. How are you and dad? How's home?"

"Oh, it's fine," Eleanor says. "Dad's fine, he says hi. Angie and Mark have finally set a date, so that's nice."

Seb nods. Mark is his cousin, and he and his girlfriend Angie got engaged a few months ago, after dating for years. It's about damn time.

"That's good," Seb says. "When's the wedding?"

"In a few months," his mother says. "I don't remember the exact date. Why, you bringing someone?"

She says the last part with the kind of conspiring tone that mothers everywhere seem to have perfected, and Seb swallows.

"Um," he says, hesitating. Then he closes his eyes, exhaling. He might as well get this over with. "Actually, I kind of wanted to talk to you about something like that."

"Really?" his mother says. "You're not engaged, are you?"

"No," Seb says, opening his eyes and hinting a small smile that she can't see. "No, I just... I need to tell you something."

"Alright," his mom says. "Tell me."

And Seb realizes that he doesn't want to. But he has to. He has to tell her, has to explain. If nothing else, for Evan's sake; he owes him that, especially after the way he faced his fears concerning Seb and their relationship. And he doesn't want Evan to be his secret, any more than he wants to be Evan's.

"Remember when we talked, a while back?" Seb finally says, glad that his mother can't see him. "And you asked me about a girl?"

His mother makes a sound of confirmation.

"Yeah, I remember," she says, and Seb swallows.

"Well, you were right," he says. "And not."

225

Eleanor doesn't answer him right away, probably thinking.

"What do you mean?" she eventually says.

"I mean, it's not exactly a girl." Seb tries to find a good way of putting it, struggling. "At all."

Again, his mother doesn't say anything for a few moments.

"Then," she finally says, slowly, as though still confused. "What—"

"His name is Evan," Seb interrupts her, blurting it out. *Well, fuck, that wasn't how I planned it.* But it's too late now.

Eleanor just responds with silence for several seconds, as though trying to think of any other explanation or interpretation of what Seb just said. But there is none.

"Oh," she eventually says, and Seb can practically sense her stiffen slightly, her voice a bit off. "So... A boy..."

"Evan," Seb says. "Yeah."

She makes a *hmm* sound.

"He's..."

"My boyfriend." The word still feels weird to say. Seb isn't even sure he has said it out loud before. But it feels right.

His mother's silence makes him a bit uncomfortable, though.

"Mom?" he asks.

"Alright," she finally says, still sounding a bit off. She seems determined not to freak out. But she clearly isn't completely comfortable with the idea of what Seb is telling her, either. "Okay."

Seb just waits.

"Okay?" he says, raising his eyebrows the slightest bit, even though she can't see him.

"Yeah," she says, in a way that makes him think she's nodding. It's something about the edge to her voice, and he gets the impression that she's nodding a bit too much, in his opinion. "Okay."

Seb feels a slight wave of relief. Maybe he was worried for no reason. Maybe his mom will be okay with this whole thing. He isn't entirely sure about his dad, but that's another matter for another time.

"Good," he says, exhaling with relief. He wasn't quite aware of how tense he'd been up until now, and he relaxes his shoulders slightly. Maybe this is going to be okay.

"I mean, it's college, right?" his mother says. "Nothing's off-limits."

And there it is.

Seb is sure she meant to sound understanding and relaxed about it, but all her words do is make him tense up again. Only, this time, his anxiety is replaced by annoyance.

"And here we go," he mutters.

"What?" his mother says. "I'm just saying that I get it."

"No," Seb says, shaking his head. "You really don't."

"Sebastian—"

"Jesus, mom." He puts his hand over his face, rubbing his eyes. "Would it kill you to take things seriously for just a minute?"

Eleanor just seems stunned at that.

"I do," she says. "I am. But sweetie, I've been to college too. I know what it's like."

"I'm sure you do," Seb says dryly, trying not to think about his mother being in college and doing whatever one is supposed to be doing in college. "But that doesn't mean you automatically get it."

"Look," she says, diplomatically. "I'm sure you feel that you like this boy—"

Seb just looks up at the ceiling and lets out a frustrated, annoyed moan that makes him sound an awful lot like a seventeen-year-old. He can't help it, though. This is his mother, and it's impossible not to fall back into old habits. Even if he feels a bit embarrassed at himself.

"Don't do that, Sebastian," Eleanor snaps, and Seb just looks straight ahead.

"What?" he says. His voice is flat, with just a hint of his trademark sarcasm. "Belittle your argument? Make you feel like I'm not taking you seriously?"

He tilts his head, kind of wishing she *could* see him now, to get the full effect.

"Gee, I wonder what that feels like."

Eleanor sighs; he can imagine her pursing her lips.

"You're young," she says. "And you've always been very passionate. But—"

"Mom," Seb says calmly, and she falls silent. "Let me ask you something."

He takes a deep breath, and takes her silence as permission.

"If it *were* a girl," he says. "If I *had* met a girl. Would you still be saying this to me?"

His mother doesn't answer him, but he can tell from the feeling of her silence that no, she wouldn't.

"I know you like to think that I'm full of ideas that aren't the best," Seb continues. "I know that even though you support me in wanting to be a writer, you deep down

228

think that I'll eventually snap out of it and do something else, and that's the only reason you haven't talked me out of it."

Seb looks down, looking for the right words.

"And I know you think I'm just crushing on some guy for the fun of it," he says. "And no, this hasn't ever happened before."

He looks up again, at nothing.

"But I love him," he says, shocked at his own honesty. He has never admitted that to anyone before, to anyone but Evan, barely even to himself. And he realizes that he really does feel that way, unquestionably.

He's also shocked at just how well he's putting all of this, without getting angry or yelling at his mother.

"And I know you want me to be happy," he says. "And he makes me happy."

His mother doesn't reply for several seconds. Instead, she waits, thoughts and responses clearly moving through her mind. It's as though she wants to contradict her son, wants to talk him out of it, tell him that it's just a phase and that it will pass. And maybe she really does think all those things. But something in the way Seb is talking about it, perhaps, stops her from saying any of it out loud.

"You love him?" she says instead, her voice weak and a bit wary. Seb nods to himself.

"Very much," he says. He didn't mean to add that, but it's true. Eleanor seems to hesitate for a moment.

"And he loves you?" she asks, and Seb nods again. "And he makes you happy?"

"He does."

Eleanor takes a deep breath.

"Then, I guess I'm happy, too," she finally says, and Seb feels an almost irrational relief and joy in his chest. His mother exhales into the phone, and Seb can tell that she's struggling not to contradict him. But this is good enough.

"Thank you," he says, and his mother makes a sound of confirmation. She deliberates for a moment.

"Is he handsome?" she asks, in an attempt to lighten the mood, and Seb smiles, actually blushing a bit.

"He is," he says, knowing she can hear his smile. "He really is. Out of my league."

His mother laughs softly, kindly, and Seb knows that if she had been with him right now, she would have ruffled his hair and kissed his cheek.

"No one is out of my son's league."

"Seb." Evan's voice is soft, and just as the one word reaches Seb's ear, those lips brush against his cheekbone. "Wake up, baby."

Seb blinks tiredly, disoriented for a moment. Then he glances up and sees Evan's face, smiling down at him, those crinkles ever-present around his eyes.

"This is getting out of hand, dude," he says, straightening. He's standing beside Seb, who lifts his head to look around. He's sitting in the chair by his desk; he actually fell asleep with his head against the surface beside his laptop, and he blinks to clear his blurry, sleep-drunk vision.

"What time is it?" he slurs, slowly sitting up properly, and Evan chuckles.

"Not nearly late enough to justify falling asleep like that," he says, and Seb looks up at him. Then Evan's smile widens.

"What?" Seb says, frowning, and Evan shakes his head, actually laughing. The laughter is laced with unyielding affection.

"You got a little something there," he says, reaching down to Seb's face. Seb barely has time to react, before Evan plucks something that has gotten stuck to his cheek, and hands it to Seb. Seb frowns at it; it's a yellow post-it note, with a few scribbled page numbers on it. And he groans tiredly. He remembers writing this down earlier, going through his notes and making sure he knew where to find everything he needed in his books.

"Awesome," he mutters, putting the post-it down on the desk. Then he looks up at Evan again, and they just stare at each other for a few moments, before Evan takes his hand and pulls him to his feet.

"Really?" Seb says crankily. "I just woke up, man."

Evan doesn't answer him. Instead, he just pulls him closer as he stands, and looks at him, pushing back dark hair that has fallen over his forehead. Seb always loves it when he does that. It makes him feel so safe and loved, in some weird way. Evan smiles.

"You're adorable," he says, and Seb narrows his eyes at him.

"Thanks," he says sarcastically. "Because every guy wants to be called *adorable*."

"You called me *romantic*," Evan says, cocking his eyebrows. "It's only fair."

Seb rolls his eyes.

"Fine," he says, giving in. "I guess."

Evan chuckles, and kisses him on the mouth, pulling his fingers softly through his hair, making Seb's knees buckle. Evan always has a way of kissing him, like it's the first and last time, softly and urgently, all at once.

"Come on, sleepyface," Evan says when they part, lacing his fingers with Seb's. He pulls him along over to the bed, where they both lie down and fit together like puzzle pieces, Seb placing his head against Evan's chest, closing his eyes for a moment.

"You ever think that maybe we should do something else, besides just lying in bed all the time?" he says, and Evan makes a small *meh* sound.

"Maybe," he admits. "But I like this, so I can't see why we should."

Seb smiles.

"You make a valid point, my good sir," he says, and Evan's chuckle rumbles through his chest. "And it's not like we just lie here, anyway. Not all the time."

"Now, that's true," Evan says, and Seb can imagine him cocking his eyebrows suggestively. "And the stuff we do, I like as well."

Seb rolls his eyes.

"Are you rolling your eyes at me?" Evan says, and Seb glances up at him.

"You're creeping me out, dude," he says, but can't help but smile to himself, as Evan smiles at him. He settles his head against his chest again.

"I talked to my mom," he says after a moment.

"Really?" Evan says. "About what?"

Seb frowns.

232

"About the weather," he says dryly. "The stock market, the new British royal baby. What do you think, asshole?"

Evan laughs. It's amazing, really, how often they sound like they insult each other, when it's really nothing but sweet talk.

"I told her about you," Seb says. "About us."

Evan hesitates, waiting.

"And?" he finally says, sounding a bit tense. Seb exhales.

"And," he said, "*okay*."

"Okay?"

"Okay." Seb half-shrugs. "I don't think she's completely wrapped her head around it, but she said *okay*. And she seems to still call me her son, so that's nice."

"That's good," Evan says, his tone half-serious and half-joking. Seb doesn't mention Evan's father, or anything about maybe telling him; that's a different matter, and one that will be dealt with in time, when Evan feels ready. He isn't about to push him into anything.

"Yeah," Seb says. "She asked about you."

"Really?" Evan sounds honestly surprised, and just a bit pleased.

"Yeah. She wanted to know if you were handsome, that sort of thing."

"Handsome?" Evan says, a smile in his voice. "And what did you say?"

"I said that you were," Seb sighs. "Obviously. I believe I used the term, *out of my league*."

Evan chuckles.

"I'm flattered," he says, pushing Seb's hair back and combing through it with his fingers. "But I'd say it's the other way around."

233

Seb frowns at that and looks up at him.

"Seriously?" he says, and Evan shrugs, lying on his back. "You're a musician, for god's sake. You're hot, and charming, and just generally cool."

Evan smiles at him.

"True," he says immodestly, in a way he knows is part of said charm. "And you're a writer, an artist. You're gorgeous and sarcastic, and really smart."

"How is sarcasm an attractive trait?" Seb says, frowning in disbelief, but Evan just keeps that smile, the soft one. It makes him look oddly at peace, like Seb is equal parts amusing and adorable and just perfect.

"It is when it's done right," he says, kissing the top of Seb's head. "And you do it right."

Seb doesn't answer him, just looks at him, for several, long seconds.

"I love you, you know," he finally says, and Evan keeps his eyes on his, unwavering.

"And I love you," he replies, reciprocating the kiss Seb moves up to give him. It's a soft kiss, one summing up everything they just said, and when they pull apart, Evan studies Seb's face, pulling his fingers through his hair.

"So," he says lightly. "It's out and official, then."

Seb nods, knowing that he's referring to the conversation Seb had with his mother.

"Guess so," he confirms, and Evan nods slowly. Then he cocks his eyebrows.

"So, when do I get to meet the family?" he says, and Seb smiles at him.

"Well," he says, drawing out the word and glancing up at the ceiling, as though deliberating. "There's this wedding..."

PART TWO

CHAPTER 16
FAMILY

"Would you stop fidgeting?"

Evan puts his hand on Sebastian's shoulder to keep him still, and Seb sighs at him.

"I'm not *fidgeting*," he says, and Evan cocks his head.

"Dude, you're fidgeting," he retorts, directing his eyes at Seb's chest. "And stop pulling at your tie."

Seb sighs again, trying to relax his shoulders, to no avail. He looks down at Evan's hands, which are straightening his dark blue tie and fixing the knot.

"I can't help it," he says defensively. It's true; he has been pulling at the tie and loosening it several times in the past hour, Evan pulling it back into place every time. "I'm nervous."

"Don't be," Evan says simply, pulling the tie knot into place and fixing Seb's white shirt collar. He looks up and meets his eyes. "It'll be fine."

"That's easy for you to say," Seb mutters, and Evan raises his eyebrows at him.

"Really?" he says. "'Cause last time I checked, I was the one meeting your entire family, and not the other way around."

Seb narrows his eyes at him.

"True," he admits. "But last time *I* checked, I was the one about to be shoved into a room full of people silently judging me."

He looks down.

"Or not so silently," he adds, fiddling with his tie. Evan gently slaps his hand away.

"Like I said," he insists. "It'll be fine."

Seb sighs again, looking up at him.

"How can you be so sure?"

"Because," Evan says matter-of-factly, "it's a wedding. And hopefully, people will be too focused on the actual reason for the whole thing, rather than who your date is. As in, they'll probably be too busy silently judging the bride and groom, and everyone else, rather than you."

He watches Seb frown uncomfortably and cracks a small smile.

"And also," he says, planting a quick, soft kiss on his mouth, "we're adorable. Let 'em judge. I dare them."

Seb smiles then, feeling his shoulders relax properly, and Evan moves his hand up to gently stroke his cheekbone with his thumb.

"Well," Seb admits, cocking his head. "We *are* adorable."

"Damn straight."

Evan smiles at him and plants another quick kiss on his lips.

"Now, come on," he says, backing away toward his car. "We've got a wedding to get to."

Seb isn't used to wearing a suit. He has worn one before, obviously, but he still feels a bit awkward, absently tugging at the sleeves and the jacket, smoothing over the black fabric with his hands. He glances over at Evan, who looks impeccable in a suit, right next to him. Then again, he seems to look gorgeous, no matter what. It's a bit annoying, really.

"How do you do that?" Seb asks, frowning, and Evan glances at him.

"Do what?" he says.

"That," Seb says, gesturing at him. "You put on a suit and look like a fucking agent, and I just..."

He picks at his sleeve.

"I feel like I'm playing dress-up, or something."

"Well, technically," Evan says, "I am, too."

He glances at Seb pointedly, and Seb glares at him.

"You know what I mean," he says. "I'm not cut out for this."

Evan sighs and turns to him. They're standing outside the church where the wedding is to be held, next to Evan's vintage car. Evan has just parked and locked it, and slips the keys into his pocket.

"Yes, you are," he says, pulling Seb's hands away from their sleeve-picking. "You're awesome and hot, and seeing you in that suit makes me want to rip it off and fuck you against my car."

Seb blinks. He's used to Evan's blunt way of talking, but they are right outside a church at the moment, and the whole thing just feels ironically blasphemous and hilarious, somehow. Not to mention that there are people around, and someone might hear. Although, Seb really doesn't care enough to take their innocent, smut-sensitive ears into consideration, at least not right now.

Instead, he gives Evan a slow smile.

"Well," he says. "That's some incentive."

Evan doesn't even smile, just gives him a look that's enough to make pretty much Seb's entire being tingle and burn, as those eyes wander up and down along his body.

"Yeah," Evan says hoarsely, moving a bit closer. "I could do that when we get home, if you like."

He plants a slow, burning kiss against the pulse of Seb's throat, and Seb exhales heavily, closing his eyes for a moment.

"Promise?" he says, his voice almost a whisper, and Evan hums against his skin.

"If you behave," he says, and Seb smiles.

"Fine," he says, pulling away just enough for Evan to stop kissing him and look into his eyes, instead. "I'll hold you to that."

He combs through Evan's short hair with his fingers, settling his hand behind his neck, before quirking a smile.

"But at the moment," he says, "we need to get inside. And you need to back off, before I take you up on your offer right now."

Evan smiles mischievously, but obligingly steps away from his boyfriend.

"Fair enough," he says, extending his hand, and Seb laces their fingers together as he takes it. "Shall we?"

Seb only agrees, and they head inside

It's a beautiful ceremony.

Seeing as how Seb has known Mark his whole life, because despite them being cousins, they have basically grown up like brothers, it makes him smile to see him so happy. Jim, Mark's actual brother and best friend, is his best man, standing beside him and teasing him until the very last minute, when Angie starts walking down the aisle. Everyone turns to look at her, but Seb only glances, before turning back to Mark, whose eyes widen at the sight of his bride. Jim glances at his brother and laughs, before leaning over and whispering in his ear. It looks like something along the lines of *you should see your face*, and if Seb knows Jim, that's exactly what he's saying.

Angie really does look beautiful, though, in a rather old-fashioned, cream white dress. Her blonde hair is up in curls, and her soft, kind face shaped into a huge grin that she's clearly trying to tune down, but to no avail. As she passes by, Seb can clearly see her blush, and when she catches his eye for a second, he just raises his eyebrows at her, smiling amusedly. She narrows her eyes at him for a split second, like she tends to do, before turning her gaze back ahead, that smile still on her face, as she makes her way to the altar.

As Mark and Angie say their vows, everyone's eyes are on them, and Seb can't help but smile as he watches their expressions. They look happy. So completely and blissfully happy, and he feels such deep affection for the both of them.

He must be looking rather sappy, though, because he suddenly feels Evan's fingers lace with his, and he looks at him. He's sitting right beside Seb, and he smiles.

"You okay, there?" he whispers, a bit cheekily, and Seb rolls his eyes, but still keeps the smile on his face.

"I'm fine," he whispers back, turning back to the ceremony. Then Evan leans in and kisses him on the cheek, and Seb feels a blush creep up his neck, as he turns back to his boyfriend. He feels embarrassed, but when he sees Evan's half-cocky smile, he can't help but smile back, squeezing his hand.

If a wedding ceremony isn't the right time and place for something like that, when is, after all?

"Seb, I swear, don't make me handcuff you."

Evan is tugging Seb's hands away from his tie for the hundredth time, as Seb nervously pulls at it, loosening it.

"That doesn't sound like a bad idea," Seb says dryly, eyes scanning the crowd that files into the room, where the wedding reception is being held. "Should probably handcuff me to a radiator. Safest that way."

"Easy there, wolf man," Evan says, trying to fix Seb's tie. Then he sighs, throwing his hands up. "Great. Now it's backwards."

Seb looks down; his tie is indeed backwards, having been tugged and loosened a hundred times by now. He groans.

"Just leave it," he says. "It's the least of my problems, anyway."

"Dude, you really need to chill." Evan stubbornly undoes the tie completely and redoes the knot, pulling it into place and fixing Seb's collar. "Getting real tired of your shit."

"Already?" Seb says sarcastically. "That should have happened months ago."

Evan smiles at him then, affection clear on his face.

"Sebastian," he says, taking Seb's hands in his own, Seb suddenly very focused on the way he's saying his name; Evan barely ever uses his full name. But Seb likes it. "You know I love you, but you need to relax. We're here, alright? Might as well make the best of it."

He moves one hand up to cup Seb's face, and kisses him softly.

"And if nothing else," he says, his voice a bit lower, "I keep my promises, and this will be worth your while, once we get home."

Seb tenses up involuntarily, his grip on Evan's hand tightening just the slightest bit. He hasn't exactly forgotten what Evan said before, outside, by the car. And it makes his blood rush to currently inappropriate places of his body.

"Fine," he says, his voice as low as Evan's. "Bribing does work, I suppose."

Evan smiles, mischievously, this time.

"Good," he says. "Now, relax."

Seb tries to, he really does. He barely has time to lower his heart rate, though, before Mark walks up to him.

"Seb," he says, hugging him tightly and slapping his back as he does. "Good to see you."

"You, too," Seb says, as they pull apart.

Mark has a kind face, with kind eyes and a smile that makes him look somehow older than his actual, twenty-six years. His almost black hair is combed down neatly, and he looks as clean-cut and sharp as ever, wedding or no.

"How's college?" Mark asks, and Seb half-shrugs.

"It's alright," he says. "How's marriage?"

Mark smirks at his obvious joke.

"You're hilarious," he says flatly. "But if you must know, it feels pretty damn good."

"Well, that's a relief." Seb smiles, and Mark looks at Evan.

"You must be Evan," he says, extending his hand. "Eleanor told me about you."

Evan looks a little bit surprised, but shakes Mark's hand.

"Great," Seb says to Evan, also half-surprised that Mark knows who Evan is; his tone suggests that he knows who he is to Seb, too. "My mom hasn't even met you yet, and she's already telling everyone."

"Not everyone," Mark points out, putting his hands in the pants pockets of his black suit. "Just me and Angie. So far, at least. I think she just wanted someone else here to know. You know how she feels about keeping secrets."

"Well, it's not like it's an actual secret," Seb points out uncomfortably.

"Still, though," Mark says. "You know how she gets."

Seb just nods, exhaling, and is just about to say something else, when they're interrupted.

"Hey, bro," Jim says, sliding up beside Mark and putting his arm over his shoulder. "Already hiding from the missus, huh?"

Jim doesn't really look like Mark, with his lighter brown hair and completely different facial features. He's shorter, too, by a few inches. But he has the same kindness to his face, and it's hard not to like him.

Mark doesn't dignify his question with an answer, and Jim turns to Seb instead, a smile on his face.

"Seb," he says, and Seb lets out an exasperated breath. "Haven't seen you in forever."

Seb likes Jim just fine; he grew up with him like he grew up with Mark. But where Mark has always been the responsible and rather well-behaved one, Jim has always been quite the opposite, being the rebellious little brother and all. He and Seb have always gotten along, but Seb has never been quite comfortable with Jim's prankster nature, always making other people the butt of his jokes.

"James," Seb says, deliberately forcing a smile which he knows looks sarcastic and fake. "Always the asshole."

Jim laughs and claps a hand against Seb's shoulder.

"Shit, I kind of missed you, kid," he says. And underneath the teasing and general douchey-ness, there is a layer of affection in his voice. Seb allows an equal layer of affection to show in his smile.

Jim turns to Evan, then.

"And who's this?" he asks, with an almost suggestive tone, and Seb clears his throat a bit.

"Evan, this is my cousin, Jim, brother of the groom."
He looks back and forth between the two of them. "And
Jim, this is Evan. My boyfriend."

Seb feels himself tense up slightly as he says it. *There it is.*
That's the first time since they arrived here that he has
introduced Evan as his *boyfriend.* And it feels just about as
nervous as he thought it would. And just like he thought,
Mark doesn't seem surprised.

It's obvious that the news shocks Jim, at least judging
from the way he actually widens his eyes a bit, eyebrows
raised. But then, his expression changes into one of
somehow impressed surprise.

"Well," he says, turning his gaze from Seb to Evan, and
Evan holds out his hand.

"Good to meet you, man," he says, and Jim glances at
his hand, before shaking it.

"Yeah," he says, eyeing Evan up and down. Then he
kind of cocks his head and leans toward Seb conspiringly.

"You did good, little brother," he says in a theatrical
whisper, and Seb rolls his eyes. But the glint in Jim's eyes,
and his use of *little brother*, which he has only ever used a
handful of times with Seb, makes Seb relax. Jim may be
kind of a dick a lot of the time, but he isn't mean, not really.
And he's clearly happy for Seb, and doesn't judge. Even if
he is surprised.

"Thanks," Evan says, chuckling as he lets go of Jim's
hand. "I think I did pretty good, too."

He nudges Seb slightly, and Seb looks up at him.

"Really?" he says, frowning. "And here I thought you
didn't appreciate my dashing good looks and perky
personality."

"Well," Evan replies, cocking his head. "It's grown on me, I guess."

Seb gives him the smallest smile, which is mostly in his eyes, and Evan returns it. They just stand like that for a second, until Jim clears his throat.

"Alright," he says. "Simmer down, you two."

Seb looks at him.

"Jim, don't be a dick." Mark sounds oddly calm and serene, in a way that's positively inhuman, sometimes. Jim just raises his eyebrows at him, though.

"What?" he says defensively. "You gotta admit that there's some serious and inappropriate eye-fucking going on here."

He gestures between Seb and Evan, eyes still on his brother, and Seb actually blushes. Mark laughs.

"And that's our cue to leave," he says, grabbing Jim by the arm and pulling him away. "It's almost time for cake, anyway."

He looks at Seb, then Evan. "Good to see you, Seb. Evan."

Evan nods at him as he pulls Jim away, who gives them both a small salute as he departed. Seb groans.

"I would apologize," he says. "But it doesn't quite cut it."

Evan just chuckles, looking at him.

"It's fine," he says. "How about we—"

Evan cuts himself off as soon as he notices Seb's expression, which is suddenly stiff. Seb tenses up. Shit. *Shit.*

"Seb?" Evan's voice sounds concerned, in a way that anyone else probably wouldn't have noticed. "Seb, what's wrong?"

Seb doesn't look at him, doesn't answer him right away. Instead, he swallows hard. He just spotted someone across the room, and he's keeping his eyes on her, hoping to god that she won't see him.

"Seb."

Seb looks at Evan then, those green eyes alert and concerned.

"I'm good," Seb says. "It's just..."

He glances back at the girl he saw, before turning back to Evan. He lowers his voice a bit, unconsciously.

"That girl over there," he says, seeing Evan glance over in that direction. "Dark hair, short, talking to Angie."

Evan nods, and Seb swallows hard.

"That's Olivia," he says, and as Evan looks back at him, he knows he understands, even before Seb says anything. "My ex."

Evan raises his eyebrows slightly, glancing back at Olivia again.

"That so?" he says absently, and Seb nods. He hasn't told Evan much about Olivia, or about anyone he has been with, for that matter. Evan has extended him the same courtesy. They basically decided that unless it's important, they really don't need to know about each other's past love lives; their relationship is in the present, and doesn't need any baggage.

But he knows who Olivia is. He knows that she is Seb's ex, and that she was his first girlfriend—the one his parents liked, even though the whole relationship didn't really work out. That was a long time ago, though, and Seb hasn't even seen her since after they graduated high school, over three years ago.

But still. Seeing her here is awkward, to say the least, and not something he feels he is quite prepared for.

"Did you know she was coming?" Evan asks, his tone not the least bit accusing, as he looks back at Seb.

"No," Seb exclaims, his voice still lowered. "I had no idea."

Then he cocks his head, thinking about it.

"Although," he admits. "She got pretty close with Angie while we were dating, and I think they kept in touch."

Seb groans, closing his eyes.

"Shit," he says, lowering his head and face-palming himself. "I should have thought about that."

"Hey," Evan says soothingly, taking Seb's hand and removing it from his face. "It's fine. It's all good."

Seb looks up at him, and Evan raises his eyebrows.

"You're here with me," he says, lacing their fingers together at their sides. "Man up."

Seb gives him his best *really?*-look, and Evan's small smile turns into a slightly cocky one, making Seb shake his head. When Evan smiles at him, it's impossible not to smile back, and he feels the corners of his mouth turn up.

"What would I do without you, man?" he says, and Evan just smiles.

"I could ask you the same thing," he says, before he leans in and slowly kisses Seb on the forehead. He moves his free hand up and lets his fingers gently smooth over Seb's jaw and neck, murmuring his next words against his skin. "God knows, I was a mess before I met you."

Seb closes his eyes for a moment, squeezing Evan's hand, entwined with his own.

"Careful, Mr. Matthews," he says. "You're having a chick-flick moment. And in public, no less."

Evan chuckles, moving his lips away from Seb's forehead.

"Fuck, you're right," he says, and their eyes meet. "I'd better go wrestle a bear, or something."

"After," Seb says seriously, nodding, and Evan gives him a curt nod back.

"Of course," he agrees. "Don't wanna ruin the suit."

Seb makes a face, one admitting that Evan has a point, and is just about to kiss him when they are interrupted.

"Seb?"

The sound of that voice alone makes Seb practically freeze. He turns his head, trying not to look too shocked or startled or uncomfortable.

"Olivia," he says. "Hey."

"Hi," Olivia says, her dark, curly hair up in a rather elaborate do, with pins that match her pastel pink dress. She smiles at him. "Thought you might be here. Long time, no see."

Seb just nods, suddenly feeling unbelievably awkward.

"Yeah," he musters, clearing his throat unnecessarily. "You look good."

He isn't really having a good day, conversation-wise, but it feels like a perfectly innocent and polite thing to say. Olivia does look pretty good, her round face as kind-looking as always, her dark eyes sharp.

"You, too," Olivia replies, before glancing at Evan. Seb takes the hint.

"Oh, right," he says to himself, louder than he intended. "Evan, Olivia. Olivia, Evan."

He glances between the two of them, suddenly tongue-tied, and Evan comes to the rescue.

"The boyfriend," he says, to Seb's vague surprise, and extends his hand—the one not locked together with Seb's. Olivia takes it, a bit apprehensively.

"Oh," she says, blatant surprise written all over her face. She shakes Evan's hand slowly, looking back and forth between him and Seb, before making a small thinking noise.

"I guess that explains a few things," she says, in what she probably intended to be a barely audible murmur, as she releases Evan's hand. And Seb resists the urge to put on a Jake-class bitchface.

"Really?" he says, acid seeping into his voice, nonetheless. "And how's that?"

Olivia smiles at him, in that patronizing way he has always hated. Actually, it's more of a smirk, really.

"Oh, Sebastian," she says, tilting her head. "Maybe we remember our time together a little differently."

"Yeah, maybe we do," he says, returning her smile with an icy, sarcastic one of his own. "Good thing that's over, though, huh?"

No one does sarcasm quite like Seb, and at the moment, he's using it almost poisonously. But Olivia doesn't seem very fazed; she's used to it, and she's pretty versed in sarcasm and sardonic attitudes, herself.

"Right," she says, her smile faltering a bit, dark eyes hard. "I guess I'll see you, Seb."

She looks at Evan.

"Nice meeting you, Evan."

Evan doesn't answer her, just nods, and Olivia glances back at Seb, before walking away. And Seb exhales heavily, relaxing his shoulders he didn't even realize he was tensing up.

"I'm guessing *you* broke up with *her*?" Evan ventures, as soon as Olivia is out of earshot.

"Yup."

"Can't imagine why."

Seb sighs with some frustration.

"I had almost forgotten how much of a bitch she is," he mutters, watching Olivia's back as she walks away. "It's weird to think that I actually liked her, once."

Evan makes a sound of agreement.

"So, let me get this straight," he says, and Seb looks up at him. "She's the one you brought home? The one your parents liked?"

Seb shrugs, a sheepish and uncomfortable look on his face.

"Huh," Evan says, eyebrows raised. "So the bar isn't that high, then."

"To be fair, she has a way of manipulating people," Seb says, cocking his head. Then he shakes his head a bit, as though trying to shake something off.

"I don't wanna talk about her," he says resolutely. "I'm here with you, remember?"

Evan smiles.

"That you are," he says, kissing Seb on the lips. "Now, how about meeting your *actual* family?"

Introducing Evan to people at the wedding turns out to be a surprisingly painless affair. After the initial surprise on most people's part, there seems to be a general, if apprehensive, acceptance, and Seb finds himself gradually relaxing. It doesn't exactly hurt to have Evan by his side, squeezing his hand every now and then.

And then they get to his parents.

Eleanor Cohen is a kind woman, and Richard, Seb's father, isn't exactly mean, either. Seb was a little bit worried about how he might react, though, to his son's new relationship. It isn't so much that Seb thinks his father wouldn't accept it, but more a matter of him maybe being too uncomfortable to really face it or talk about it. He's happily surprised, though.

"So, this is Evan," Eleanor says, eyeing Evan up and down in that typical, mother kind of way. "It's so nice to finally meet you."

She shakes Evan's hand.

"Sebastian has told me a lot about you."

"Really?" Evan says neutrally, but glances at Seb with one raised eyebrow. Seb just gives him the smallest shrug.

"Yes," Seb's mother says. "And it's also nice to know he wasn't exaggerating."

Seb groans quietly.

"Mom," he says. "Really?"

"You're the one who said he was handsome," his mother says with a shrug. "Is it so bad of me to agree?"

Evan smiles kindly, and Eleanor smiles back, while Seb looks at the floor.

"Evan," Seb's father says, stepping forward and shaking Evan's hand. "Richard."

"Nice to meet you," Evan says, and Seb looks up. Evan must be at least a bit nervous, he figures, at least judging from the way he's suddenly a bit more tense than before. Meeting all these people is one thing, but these are Seb's parents, and it's bound to make him edgy. But he doesn't show it. Seb is pretty sure he's the only one who would notice, but Evan is nervous, and he's trying to keep Seb from being nervous, so he keeps it to himself.

The sudden surge of pure affection Seb feels for his boyfriend right then is ridiculous.

"So," Seb's father says, as the four of them sit down at one of the tables that surround the dance floor. "Eleanor tells me you're a musician."

Evan clears his throat a bit.

"Well, yeah," he says. "Guitar, mostly. And singing."

Richard nods, and Eleanor chimes in, asking her own questions and trying to get to know this boy their son has brought home (sort of).

Seb sits and listens, eyes darting back and forth between all of them, keeping out of the conversation as much as he can. Evan is doing really well, but Seb can sense his tension, and reaches for his hand under the table. He laces their fingers together and squeezes Evan's hand gently, and he notices how Evan almost immediately relaxes a bit. Seb smiles. This is going really well.

He isn't sure what, exactly, he was worried about.

It's a rather long drive back home.

The wedding was held in Seb's hometown, which is a couple of hours away from his and Evan's shared apartment, but not quite far enough away for them to bother spending the night there. Instead, they left late, and drove all the way back home.

Evan sat in the driver's seat of his car, Seb drowsing in the passenger seat, only half-waking up when Evan draped a jacket over him, like a cover. It made Seb smile to himself, half-awake and half-asleep.

It was a long drive, and it's past two a.m. by the time they finally get home. Needless to say, Evan's promise about what they'd do when they got home is one neither of them has the energy to actually keep, right now.

"I'm so tired," Seb mumbles, after dragging himself out of the car and up to their apartment, Evan half-supporting him all the way. "I'm so tired, it's not even funny."

He slumps down onto their double bed, suit still on, eyes closed, and Evan sighs at him.

"You're hogging the bed," he says, and Seb opens his eyes. Evan has taken off his suit jacket and his tie, and Seb sits up properly on the bed's edge.

"Sorry," he says sleepily. "I'll move."

Evan smiles tiredly.

"Don't worry about it," he says. "You're too cute to stay mad at."

Ten minutes later, the two of them crawl into bed, and Seb lies down flat on his back, closing his eyes. The lights are out, and it's silent for several seconds, before Evan suddenly speaks.

"You ever want to get married?" he says, and Seb frowns in confused surprise, suddenly wide awake.

"Evan," he says. "If this is a proposal, I swear to god."

"No, you dick." Evan laughs in the darkness, and Seb smiles. "I mean, generally. You ever thought about it?"

Seb thinks about it then.

"I don't know," he finally says, truthfully. "Not really. Maybe. I guess it never really occurred to me. Why, you?"

"Me?" Evan says, and makes a thinking noise, before sighing. "I suppose it's every little girl's dream. White dress, string quartet, the whole shebang."

Seb rolls his eyes and groans, as he senses the sarcasm.

"Alright," he says, sinking deeper underneath the covers. "Okay."

"Flowers and a cake," Evan continues, his tone now more obvious in its blatant joking and girly excitement. Seb groans again, pulling the covers up over his face.

"Stop it," he says, but Evan doesn't.

"And there'll be crying," he says, even more obvious still. "And vows and a party."

"I swear to god, Evan," Seb says warningly, his voice muffled underneath the covers.

"There'll be pigeons!" Evan exclaims enthusiastically, rolling over and landing half on top of Seb. "Hundreds of them!"

"Doves." Seb's voice is still muffled, the covers covering even his eyes. He can't see Evan, but he can practically sense him frowning.

"What?" Evan says, and Seb peeks out from underneath the covers. Evan is hovering above him; he can just barely see his expression in the dim darkness.

"Doves," Seb repeats. "Pigeons are gross and shit all over everything."

"And *doves* don't?" Evan says, raising his eyebrows pointedly.

"They do," Seb admits. "They just get away with it, 'cause they're pretty."

Evan smiles.

"Fine," he says. "No doves *or* pigeons at our wedding."

"We're not having a wedding, Evan."

"But then what about all that cake?" Evan says in mock offense, kissing Seb's cheekbone. "And the band, and the dress?"

He kisses Seb's other cheekbone.

"What about *the pigeons?*"

"I will murder you, Evan," Seb practically groans, muffled, his mouth still under the covers. His eyes are closed now.

"Right, *doves*," Evan corrects himself, before kissing Seb's forehead. "Can't have shitty pigeons everywhere."

Seb just groans again as Evan keeps raining kisses all over his face, or at least the part that isn't hidden underneath the covers.

"You're such an ass," Seb says, and this time, Evan actually laughs.

"I know," he says, the joking, girly enthusiasm gone. "But you love me, anyway."

Seb sighs heavily.

"God help me, I do," he says, before opening his eyes. He can see Evan grinning at him in the dark. Then Evan pulls down the covers and kisses him on the mouth.

"Good thing we're on the same page."

Seb rolls his eyes, but he smiles as Evan uses his fingers to push his dark hair back from his forehead, like he always does. Their gazes lock.

"Your family seems nice," Evan says after a few moments of silence, his tone sincere. Seb cocks his head.

"Yeah, I guess," he says. "Sorry about Jim, though. And the whole... Olivia thing."

He adds that last part with some apprehension, and Evan glances away for a moment.

"It's alright," he says. "We all have our baggage."

He looks back at Seb and quirks a smile.

"I kind of like Jim, though," he says. "He's alright. In a douchey, asshole-ish kind of way."

"You'd be surprised how often I hear that," Seb says, and Evan chuckles. Then he kisses Seb softly on the lips, before placing his head against his chest. Seb automatically starts pulling his fingers through that light brown hair, and Evan sighs tiredly.

"He can come to our wedding," he murmurs, and Seb chuckles, but doesn't answer him. Instead, they just lie there, together, slowly drifting off to sleep.

CHAPTER 17
HOME

X

TWO MONTHS AGO

"Have you seen my shirt?" Seb calls, digging through a pile of clothes on Evan's couch.

"Which one?" Evan murmurs sleepily from the bed, and Seb looks over at him.

"The Vader one," he says, and Evan squints, thinking. Then his face breaks into a sleep-drunk smile.

"I remember that one," he says, and Seb frowns.

"What?" he asks.

"You were wearing it the first time you came over here," Evan explains. "I remember. You were so cute."

Seb glances away, actually blushing, a small smile on his face. It has been about four months since that night, but it still makes him giddy to think that Evan thought of him that way, even then.

"Yeah, well," he says. "I need it. Can't go to class like this, now can I?"

He gestures down at his naked torso, and Evan cocks his eyebrows.

"Well, I don't mind," he says, and Seb glares at him. But Evan just smiles.

"You know," Seb says, resuming his rummaging. "It would be a lot easier if I just had a drawer, or something."

"Dude, even *I* don't have a drawer," Evan says. "I've got like one closet. I can barely fit my stuff in there. And it's not like I've got a drawer at your place."

"No," Seb admits. "You've just invaded my place with other stuff."

"Like what?" Evan says defensively, and Seb rolls his eyes.

"Like leather bracelets and guitar picks," he says dryly. "I even found a random bandana under my desk the other day, and I've never even seen you use one."

He straightens and looks at Evan, an incredulous frown on his face.

"And who needs that many guitar picks?" he says, throwing up his hands. "Seriously?"

"What?" Evan half-shrugs under the covers. "I like keeping one on me at all times."

"One is fine," Seb says, holding up his finger. "Fourteen is pushing it."

Evan shrugs again. It looks funny, when he's lying down.

"They might come in handy," he says, and Seb shakes his head.

"Yeah, if you say so," he mutters, turning back to the pile of clothes. He exhales.

"Seriously," he breathes, shaking his head. "Where—"

It's the faint rustling of fabric that makes him turn his head, and he looks over at Evan, who is slowly picking something up from the floor. It's a black t-shirt, that has apparently been hidden underneath a pair of jeans, right next to the bed. Evan slowly pulls the t-shirt up and in underneath the covers, eyes on Seb; the print on the shirt's front is unmistakably the silhouette of Darth Vader.

"Really?" Seb says, narrowing his eyes but unable to help but half-smile. "We're doing this?"

"Doing what?" Evan says innocently, pulling the t-shirt to him so that it disappears completely underneath the covers. "I don't know what you're talking about."

"Is that so?" Seb says, making his way over to the bed. Evan keeps his eyes on his.

"Yes," he says, and Seb leans down over him, placing one knee against the bed's edge for support. He slowly puts one hand on the mattress, so that Evan is looking up at him, as Seb looms over him. Seb tilts his head.

"Give it back, Evan," he says, but Evan just raises his eyebrows.

"Make me," he says, and Seb tenses up a bit at the low hoarseness of his voice. He licks his lips.

"I'm gonna be late," he says, and looks down as he feels Evan grab onto the waistline of his jeans.

"Why?" Evan asks. "I'm not stopping you. Just take the shirt and go."

Seb looks up at him again, up into those green eyes that are currently anything but rejecting. He feels Evan's hand tug at his pants, pulling him down just the slightest bit.

"Just give it back," Seb says, his voice a bit lower, as he finds himself moving down lower, so that he leans with his elbow against the mattress, rather than his hand. Evan's eyes skim over his face.

"Just take it back," he retorts, and Seb looks at him for a few moments. Then he gives a breathy chuckle and shakes his head.

"Fuck," he murmurs, smiling, before leaning down to Evan's mouth and kissing him.

Evan doesn't waste a second. The hand that's gripping Seb's jeans tugs downward roughly, and Seb moves so that he's straddling Evan, leaning down with his lower arms resting on either side of Evan's head. He feels those hands move to his hips, as Evan starts grinding against him through the covers, their lips moving together in the most wonderful way. Seb feels Evan's hair against his fingers, and sighs as one calloused hand starts trailing up along his bare back.

"I really need to go," Seb murmurs between kisses, and Evan groans.

"No, you don't," he says against his lips. "It's a trap."

Seb laughs.

"*This* is a trap," he says. "And a pretty obvious one, at that."

"And yet, you fell for it."

"Maybe I wanted to," Seb says, his voice low, getting the words out in the brief moments their lips are apart from each other. "You're not as cunning as you think, you know."

Now Evan laughs.

"I have no illusions of how cunning I am," he says, one hand moving in underneath Seb's jeans, down over his ass. "I just want to fuck you, that's all."

Seb groans against his lips, deepening the kiss. *Damn it.* He hates it when Evan talks like that, because it means that there is no going back, hooking Seb completely. It pulls him in and makes him forget about anything else he should be doing, and it's dangerous.

"I just wanted my shirt back," he says in mock lament, his hands gripping Evan's hair and smoothing down over the naked skin he can reach under the cover that separates them. "Dammit, man. I need a drawer."

"Or we could just get our own place."

Seb freezes up. He can feel Evan stiffen underneath him as he does, and he slowly pulls back, so that he can look at him.

"What?" he says lamely after a few moments, sounding a bit stunned, and Evan swallows. He suddenly looks a bit nervous.

"I—" he says, opening and closing his mouth like a goldfish. "I didn't—"

He swallows again, closing his mouth. They just stare at each other for several seconds.

"D'you mean that?" Seb finally says, and Evan glances away, clearly uncomfortable.

"I don't know," he mutters. "Maybe. I mean, I've thought about it..."

He looks back at Seb, green eyes a bit wide and a bit scared.

"But if you don't want to," he adds hastily. "I mean, if you—"

"No," Seb says, cutting him off. He feels his own eyes widen just a bit, surprised, scared and excited, all at once. "No, I mean... I've thought about it, too. Sort of."

He swallows, and Evan mirrors him.

"Really?" Evan finally asks, and Seb nods.

"Yeah," he says. "I have. I just..."

He glances away for a moment.

"I just figured you'd think it was too soon," he says. "I mean, we didn't even know each other a few months ago."

"So?" The one word is simple, unwavering, and Seb looks at Evan, sees the utter conviction in those eyes.

"So?" Seb mirrors, and Evan cocks his head a bit.

"Yeah," he says. "I mean, I know it hasn't been that long. I know we haven't even known each other for more than a few months."

He looks down at Seb's chest and shoulders, tracing the bare skin there with his fingers.

"But," he says, "with the risk of sounding really cliché... I feel like I've known you forever. And I wanna be with you. I'm sure of that."

He looks back up and meets Seb's eyes, his expression oddly tentative and scared. It makes Seb's heart skip a beat.

"Me too," he says, in lack of anything else; Evan just said everything he was thinking, after all. And neither of them says anything else for a few seconds, just stare at each other. Then, Evan smiles crookedly, in that nervous, but somehow cocky, way of his.

"So," he says. "You wanna move in together?"

Seb just stares at him for another second or so, before he smiles.

"I'd love to," he says, and Evan's smile widens. He chews at his bottom lip for a moment, as though thinking, trying to contain himself.

"Awesome."

It isn't big, this place, the apartment they have found. It has two rooms, apart from the kitchen and bathroom, and is on the third floor. The building itself is on campus, at the edge, not too far away from where Jake and Sophie made their new home. That wasn't on purpose, though; bigger apartments are just all kind of bunched together, intended for students living together, just like all the dorms are bunched together, intended for students living alone. But it's just fine. It will do.

It didn't take long for Evan and Seb to find a suitable apartment. Just a couple of weeks after their rather impromptu decision to move in together, they found this place, with its reasonable rent and size, and reasonable distance from the school.

Seb is really excited about it. He has never had his own place before, apart from his measly dorm room, and neither has Evan. And now, they are going to have one together, and share a home. It's terrifying, but exciting, at the same time.

Jake and Sophie help them move, carrying boxes and such (thankfully, the elevator in this building is actually working), and Sophie even gets them a cactus as a housewarming gift. It isn't man-sized, but it's a clear jab at Seb's offer to get her and Jake one, back when they moved.

Both Jake and Sophie were surprised, but at the same not, when Seb and Evan announced their plans on moving in together. It seemed that they long ago, even before Seb and Evan were even aware of how they really felt themselves, apparently, accepted that the two of them were anything but conventional, anyway.

So they simply decide to help, both with finding the place and moving all the stuff.

Seb loves all of that, everything from packing up his dorm room and throwing out what he won't need, to picking up the keys to their new place and even carrying the boxes. But the best part is probably shopping for kitchen supplies; as both he and Evan have lived in dorms with shared kitchens, they have never really needed any supplies of their own. Now, however, they have their very own kitchen, and therefore need their very own plates and pots and pans and utensils, which requires a shopping trip or two.

Now, after finally moving in all of their stuff and shopping for most of what they needed, Seb is sitting on the floor of the living room in their new apartment. It's late at night, it's dark outside, and the reason Seb is sitting on the floor is because the couch they brought from Evan's dorm room, and Seb's armchair, are both currently littered with boxes and stuff wrapped up in newspapers. And they are the only pieces of furniture they have in there, so far, so the seating options are rather limited.

But Seb doesn't mind. There is something oddly peaceful about it, about sitting here, back against the wall, just staring out the window from across the room. It's dark, except for a lamp standing on the floor nearby; the lamp in the ceiling needs a new bulb, and they haven't gotten around to changing it yet.

"Hey." Seb looks up at the sound of Evan's voice, and finds him standing next to him, in the doorway. He's holding two bowls in his hands, and gestures at Seb to move over. Seb obliges, and Evan sits down on the floor next to him. He hands a bowl to Seb.

"Dinner," he says, and Seb takes it. It's warm, and he looks down at it.

"Ramen," he says, raising his eyebrows and looking impressed. "Fancy."

"Yeah, well," Evan says, cocking his head, and handing him a pair of chopsticks. "After that shopping spree, ramen is what we'll be eating for the next few years or so."

Seb takes the chopsticks.

"Be that as it may," he says. "That bed is worth a few years of this. Although, I don't see how that mattress was really necessary."

Evan gives him an outraged look, some noodles hanging from his mouth.

"Dude," he says, his words slightly muffled. "Memory foam."

Seb just raises his eyebrows at the hilarious image of Evan looking offended, while trying to keep his dignity in slurping up those noodles.

"Right," Seb says, smiling. "How could I forget."

They bought a new bed, seeing as how their previous beds belong to the dorm rooms they moved out of, and it's now standing unpacked and all prepped in the bedroom. It's a double bed, big and comfy, and Seb has to admit that that stupid memory foam mattress probably was worth the extra money. Although, seeing as how this is their first night in their new apartment, they haven't had the chance to try it out, just yet.

Seb turns back to his food, and used his chopsticks to twirl around and catch some noodles, before gingerly putting them into his mouth. Every now and then, he hears Evan drinking the soup straight from the bowl, but other than that, neither of them makes a sound during the rest of the meal. When they're done, they simply set down the empty bowls onto the floor, and lean back against the wall.

Seb gazes around the empty room, empty apart from several half-unpacked boxes, Evan's worn leather couch, Seb's armchair, and that random-looking cactus Sophie gave them. It's standing almost in the middle of the room, for some reason.

Despite the emptiness, though, and despite the completely chaotic state their new home is currently in, Seb feels at ease, at peace. He smiles softly and leans his head against Evan's shoulder, and Evan automatically puts his arm around him and kisses the top of his head.

"I think I'm gonna like it here," Seb says. "Once we get all our shit together."

Evan grunts in agreement.

"Should we get curtains, or something?" he says, and Seb chuckles.

"I have a very hard time imagining either of us picking out curtains," he says. "Maybe we could make Sophie do it."

Evan chuckles softly.

"Somehow, I don't think she would mind," he says. "I mean, she got us that badass cactus."

He nods toward the plant that's standing practically in the center of the room, on the floor. It's rather small, with long pale thorns and a little flower at the top.

"Why did we put it there?" Seb says, frowning, and Evan shrugs.

"Seemed like a good idea at the time?"

Seb doesn't answer, only gives a shrug of his own, and Evan doesn't push it.

They sit like that for a little while, just being close to each other, staring at their empty, dimly lit living room. Then Seb takes Evan's hand and laces their fingers together, lifting his hand up to kiss it. He meant for it to be just a small kiss, a sweet one, but he ends up moving his lips across the back of Evan's hand and down to his wrist, letting his kisses linger, slowly and warmly.

When Seb looks up at Evan, those green eyes are on him, and the expression in them makes him pause. That is, until Evan takes his face in his hands and kisses him on the mouth, with such surprising urgency that it makes Seb forget how to breathe, for a moment. But only for a moment. Then, he kisses him back.

It's one of those kisses, Seb thinks vaguely, as he leans into Evan, pulling at his t-shirt. The kind that comes out of nowhere, with such heat and such impatience, that it's impossible not to get sucked into it and lose yourself completely.

And lose himself is just what Seb does.

It doesn't take more than a second, before Seb is lying on his back on the hard floor, Evan pressing down against him, grinding their hips together, fingers in his dark hair. Seb groans against Evan's mouth, pulls at his bottom lip gently with his teeth, sliding his hands underneath his t-shirt so he can take it off. Evan lets him, raising his arms so that Seb can pull the shirt over his head, before swooping back down and covering Seb's mouth with his own, claiming, pushing his tongue inside, past his lips.

Seb closes his eyes, as Evan starts moving his mouth down along the skin of his throat, moans as those lips press against his collarbone, his neck, that sensitive spot right below his ear. He doesn't object for a second, as Evan undresses him, throwing his t-shirt away somewhere on the floor, and barely thinks about it as his own fingers fumble to undo Evan's pants.

Within moments, Evan is moaning above him, Seb's hand in his boxers, stroking him, and all the while, Seb keeps his lips pressed against that sweet mouth. In the middle of it all, Evan somehow manages to undo Seb's pants and tug at them, making Seb pause and look up at him.

"Get these off," Evan says, his voice deep and breathy, his face flushed, and Seb pulls his hand out of Evan's underwear to shimmy out of his own jeans and boxers. Evan still has his pants on, and the rough fabric creates an oddly sweet kind of friction against Seb's bare skin.

He has just barely gotten his clothes off, though, before Evan leans to the side, reaching for something.

"What are you doing?" Seb says, and Evan grunts.

"I know I put it in here," he mutters, rummaging through a duffel bag sitting nearby, before finding what he's looking for.

"Move," he says hoarsely, grabbing Seb's hips and rolling them both over, so that Evan ends up on his back, Seb straddling him. Seb doesn't take long to get with the program, but is still a bit surprised when he sees Evan pull his pants down just far enough to put on a condom. Seb leans down to kiss his chest, hands trailing over his bare skin.

"You don't want me to—" he says, glancing down at Evan's very noticeable hard-on, but Evan just shakes his head.

"No," he breathes, sounding completely wrecked. "No time."

Seb smiles amusedly, but doesn't object. Honestly, he agrees; he isn't going to last long enough to draw this out much more. They aren't even going to make it to the bedroom, at this rate.

He moves his lips along Evan's throat, hands smoothing over his chest, his stomach, his hip bones, then back up again, and he closes his eyes as he feels a rumbling moan beneath him. Then he notices Evan's hands busying themselves with a small bottle for a moment, before a finger slowly slides inside him, slick with lube, then another only seconds later.

Seb tenses up, squeezing his eyes shut, as he lets out a groan. He clenches a fist against the hard surface of the floor, as he starts slowly rocking himself against Evan's fingers, trying to be careful about it, as not to come undone too fast.

They only keep at it for barely a minute, though, before Seb gets impatient.

"Now," he breathes against Evan's throat, and Evan swallows hard.

"You sure?" he says, sounding just as wrecked as Seb feels, concern lacing his words. But Seb isn't having it, not this time. He's too impatient, too eager, and he just *needs* this.

"Jesus, Evan," he bites out through gritted teeth. "Just get on me."

Evan doesn't need telling twice. In a matter of seconds, he has pulled his fingers out and grabbed Seb's hips, sitting up and taking Seb with him. He keeps his eyes on his, as he steers himself into place, and Seb slowly sinks down onto him, gripping Evan's shoulders tightly, as he does. He does it carefully, very slowly, a little bit at a time, pulling up and then sliding down again, until Evan is completely inside him, and Seb squeezes his eyes shut. It burns a little bit, considering the lack of preparation this time, but it passes quickly, and he doesn't care. Even the burn feels good.

Evan groans deeply, placing his forehead against Seb's collarbone, his fingers digging into the bare skin of Seb's lower back. And Seb keeps his eyes closed as he slowly starts moving, up and down, breathing heavily. With every move, Evan lets out a deep moan, moving his lips to Seb's chest and throat, placing lingering, searing kisses against his skin.

It doesn't take long before Seb starts moving faster, digging his fingers into Evan's hair and bracing himself against his shoulders, riding him like his life depends on it, his breath coming out in quick, heavy bursts. And Evan's hands grip him tighter, cling to him desperately, Evan very nearly whimpering underneath him; it's a sound Seb has barely ever heard him make before.

"Oh god," Evan breathes, sounding strained, as though speaking is the most difficult thing in the world, right now. "God, Seb, you feel so good."

His hands hold onto Seb's hips so hard that Seb is sure it will leave bruises, but he doesn't care. It's so typically Evan, and he loves it, loves making him come undone like this.

Seb groans as he feels Evan's lips move across his chest, that tongue smoothing over his skin, over his nipples, up along his throat. He's so close. He isn't going to last much longer. But neither is Evan.

And sure enough, it doesn't take long before he feels Evan's entire body tense up, Evan groaning against his neck, pushing Seb's hips down hard against him, keeping him locked in place and unable to move. Seb kisses Evan's temple slowly, soothing him through his orgasm, until Evan finally relaxes and loosens his grip on Seb's hips.

Seb has stopped moving entirely, but they aren't finished just yet. Evan pulls back so that he can lock his green eyes on Seb's blue ones, as he takes him in his hand and starts stroking, slowly at first, but then at a faster and rougher pace. It doesn't take more than a few seconds before Seb comes over his fingers—he was agonizingly close, already, as soon as Evan touched him.

They remain still for several seconds then, as they come down from the high, both of them breathing heavily, skin hot and slick with sweat. Seb leans his forehead against Evan's, and kisses him softly on the mouth. Then, he actually laughs, a breathless, exhausted chuckle, which Evan returns. He's not sure why. Laughing just feels like the best reaction to this feeling, in some weird, ridiculous way.

Then again, Seb feels so completely and incandescently happy at the moment, so maybe laughing isn't such a weird reaction, after all.

"I love you," Seb breathes against Evan's lips, closing his eyes as Evan moves his hand up to pull his fingers through his dark hair.

"I love *you*," Evan says, kissing him on the mouth, slowly and warmly, making Seb feel so completely and utterly safe.

He could get used to this whole living-together-thing. This is their first night here, after all, and it's already off to a very good start.

♦

About a month after moving in together, it isn't so much that Seb will never get used to waking up with Evan every morning; it's rather that he feels like he will never stop enjoying it.

"Morning," Evan murmurs in his ear, as he moves up behind him and slips his arms around his waist. Seb is standing by the stove in their kitchen, in the process of making breakfast.

"Good morning," he says, smiling as Evan's hands lock together over his stomach. "About time."

Evan grunts, planting a kiss against Seb's neck.

"It's practically still nighttime," he says, his voice gravelly with sleep. Seb raises his eyebrows and glances at the clock they moved from his old dorm room to the wall above their kitchen door.

"It's eight a.m.," he says, and he feels Evan shrug.

"Exactly."

Seb scoffs and shakes his head, smiling.

"Yeah, well," he says. "Some of us have places to be, so if you want some bacon, sit down."

Evan tightens his arms around Seb's waist and groans against his neck, kissing the bare skin there, slowly. Seb closes his eyes for a moment, before deciding not to be so easily distracted.

"Evan, sit your ass down," he says, certain that Evan can hear the smile in his voice. And Evan chuckles lightly, planting one last, quick kiss on his neck.

"You're the best," he says.

"I know."

Evan turns on the coffee maker before sitting down at the kitchen table, and Seb glances over at him. Evan has barely gotten dressed, just put on a pair of sweatpants, and he slowly places his head against his folded arms that rest on the table. Seb smiles.

No, he won't be getting tired of this anytime soon.

Evan is pretty much a zombie at the moment, while Seb, on the other hand, has to leave in about half-an-hour, so he's already dressed. He still has time for breakfast, though, and he appreciates Evan getting up to keep him company, if nothing else.

"When are you getting home tonight?" Seb asks, as they both start digging into their food. Evan shrugs as he takes a sip of coffee, practically flinching at the hot temperature of the strong beverage.

"I get off at seven," he says. "So, there-ish."

Seb nods. Evan has gotten a part-time job at a pub on campus, one not too far from the bar where he performed once. Not too far from where he and Seb had their *first date*, as Evan put it, as well as where they reconciled after their first big fight (and sort-of breakup).

The pub where he works is closer to the main school building, though, which means that there is a steady stream of students through there most of the time, and the pub needs a bigger staff, even during the day. Evan's shift doesn't start until two today, which sadly is about an hour before Seb's second lecture ends, so they won't see each other until tonight. This means that Evan has the morning off.

"What are you gonna do all day?" Seb asks. "You know, seeing as how the center of your universe won't be here."

Evan glares at him through sleepy, green eyes, as Seb takes a bite of toast.

"Probably just roll around on the floor," Evan retorts dryly. "Cry into a pillow. Maybe even vacuum."

Seb snorts.

"Now, that I'd like to see," he says, and Evan leans back in his chair.

"Oh, really?" he says, tilting his head. "And what's that supposed to mean?"

"Nothing," Seb says innocently, taking another bite of toast. "You go ahead. Vacuum away."

Evan narrows his eyes at him.

"Maybe I will," he says, actually folding his arms, and Seb raises his eyebrows, as he swallows down his last bite of food.

"Alright," he says, smiling. "Don't get your panties in a bunch."

Evan makes a grumbling noise that Seb finds oddly endearing, and he keeps smiling as he gets up from the table to put his plate and mug in the sink. Then he makes his way over to Evan, who is looking out through the kitchen window, arms still folded over his chest.

"You're adorable, you know that?" Seb says, leaning down and planting a kiss on Evan's temple. And Evan pulls away dramatically.

"I'm not adorable," he says defensively, in a way that Seb just knows not to take too seriously. "I'm a strong, angry man."

"Sure you are." Seb ruffles his hair. "And the best spooner ever."

Evan glares at him then, but Seb expertly backs away out of his reach, a mischievous smile on his face.

"Calm down, now," he says, backing out of the kitchen. "It's too early in the morning to get pissed off."

Evan keeps glaring at him.

"I hate you," he says, and Seb's smile widens as he leaves the kitchen.

"I know you do."

Seb goes into the bathroom to quickly brush his teeth, his dark, messy hair, as usual, being a lost cause, before snatching up his messenger bag and heading for the door. Then, he looks around for a sweater, before making his way back into the kitchen, where he finds one hanging over the back of a chair. Evan is still sitting at the table, and Seb tilts his head at him, picking up his dark teal hoodie from the chair.

"You still hate me?" he asks, and Evan looks up at him.

"Are you still a douche?" Evan responds, and Seb doesn't even flinch.

"Undoubtedly." He looks at Evan for a moment, before leaning down and kissing him on the mouth. It's a kiss that removes any doubt whatsoever about either of them ever actually hating the other, and Seb closes his eyes, savoring it. Then he pulls away again.

"Good luck with the vacuuming," he whispers, and Evan's expression becomes annoyed in the same way it was earlier. But Seb is quick, and jerks away, hoodie in his hand, before hurrying out of the kitchen.

"Okay, love you, bye!" he calls, as he rushes toward the apartment's front door. He catches a glimpse of a smile on Evan's face, one full of exasperated affection, before he leaves and closes the door behind him.

X

CHAPTER 18
BIRTHDAY

"What do you mean, you don't want to celebrate?"

Seb sighs in slight exasperation, his back turned to Evan.

"It's no big deal," he says, digging a t-shirt out of the dresser. "Just drop it."

"No big deal?" Evan sounds confused. "Seb, it's your birthday."

Seb rolls his eyes.

"Yeah," he says, pulling on the t-shirt he found. "And it's no big deal."

He closes the dresser drawer and turns around. Evan is sitting on the edge of their double bed, still in nothing but his boxers.

"So I get a year older," Seb says, shrugging. "Who cares?"

Evan cocks his head.

"Well, I kind of do," he says. "I mean, not that you get a year older. But I wanna celebrate your birthday. How is that weird?"

Seb just looks at him.

"I don't generally celebrate my birthday," he says. "At most, it's a family thing, and mostly just involves a phone call and maybe a late cake with my parents."

"Why?"

Seb glances away, before quirking a slightly bitter smile.

"Don't know if you've noticed," he says, "but I don't exactly have many friends. And I never did."

Evan looks oddly sad when Seb looks back at him, and he regrets saying anything at all.

"Look," he says, moving closer to the bed. "It's not as bad as it sounds. I'm just used to not making a big deal out of it. That's all."

Evan sighs.

"Well, maybe I wanna make a big deal out of it," he says, looking up at Seb, as he comes to a halt in front of him. He takes his hand. "Can't just let your birthday slide."

"Yes, you can." Seb squeezes his hand. "And what would we do, anyway?"

Evan shrugs.

"I don't know," he says. "Party?"

Seb makes a face, and Evan chuckles.

"Not that kind of party," he says, knowing that Seb is a bit apprehensive about the whole getting-shitfaced-and-puking-in-the-bushes-thing. And if nothing else, Evan has dialed back on that quite a bit, himself. He doesn't drink nearly as much as he used to, and doesn't find such parties, or getting drunk, nearly as entertaining as before.

Seb knows that a lot of that—the drinking, the sleeping around, the screwing up—was a coping mechanism for Evan, and that during the eight months or so now, since the two of them first met, he has become much more comfortable in his own skin. He doesn't really need all of that anymore.

That's not to say that he doesn't still get drunk or party once in a while; he has just taken it down about ten notches, which Seb is glad for. He still worries about Evan, sometimes, knowing how easy it is to just fall off the wagon again.

"Then what kind, exactly?" Seb says, and Evan makes a thinking noise.

"A small one," he says. "Nothing too big."

He smiles and tugs at Seb's hand, pulling him down so that he ends up straddling him, and he moves his hands to Seb's hips. He tilts his head slightly, looking at his face.

"I just want to do something," he says, moving one hand up to Seb's face, pulling his fingers back through his dark, mussed hair. "You mean a lot to me. I want to celebrate that."

Seb narrows his eyes.

"Will you stop bitching about it if I say yes?" he asks, tilting his head, mirroring Evan.

"I might," Evan says, smiling. "But only if you want it."

Seb sighs heavily, thinking, as he places his arms around Evan's neck.

"Fine," he says, giving in. "Alright."

He leans in and kisses Evan softly on the mouth.

"But nothing big," he clarifies, and Evan nods.

"Promise."

♦

Evan keeps his promise.

By the time Seb's twenty-second birthday rolls around, a few days later, they do indeed have a party. It's at their place, in their apartment (Seb still loves the sound of that), and only fifteen people or so have been invited. Among them are Jake and Sophie, and Clara, as well as Matt, a guy Evan knows from one of his courses. Matt brought his girlfriend, Em, along too, but that's about as far they go with drawing the line between friends and people they don't know well enough to invite—most people there are friends of Evan's, or Jake's. Persuading Seb to have a party at all seems to have been a big enough victory for Evan, for him not to push it.

Seb finds himself liking this, though. Since he met Evan, he has slowly started becoming a bit more social, having a slightly easier time with meeting new people, and he's actually enjoying himself.

It isn't much; there's mostly just hanging out, drinking, having fun, and there is even gift-opening. Seb dreaded that. He actually asked people *not* to bring gifts, because it makes him feel so awkward, but Jake and Sophie did, anyway.

"You really didn't have to do that," Seb says, a bit awkwardly, as he unwraps the headphones they got him. It isn't that he minds. The headphones are great, and the exact ones he planned on getting, himself, actually—he suspects that Evan had something to do with that. But he has always been a bit awkward about accepting gifts, and especially in such a social setting, so he kind of avoids anyone's gaze.

"Yes, we did," Sophie insists, smiling rather smugly. "You were whining about your old ones glitching, just last week."

Seb looks up at her with a glare, but she just smiles wider. She's right, of course. His trusted headphones have been glitching for a while, and he just hasn't gotten around to buying new ones. He has bitched to Evan about it, though, so much so that he now knows exactly which ones he wanted. Seb shoots a glare at Evan, who just raises his eyebrows in mock innocence.

"Thanks," Seb says with a smile then, turning back to Sophie, who is sitting right next to him. He hugs her tightly. "Really."

Jake is sitting right next to Sophie, but Seb doesn't hug him. Instead, he just gives him a nod and a smile, which Jake returns. They don't really hug much, anyway.

The whole thing is rather mellow and chilled out, and everyone has a really good time. They order pizza, and end up just sitting in the living room, hanging out on the floor, in the couch or in the armchairs. Seb and Evan bought another armchair when they first moved in, one that doesn't even match the one they brought from Seb's old dorm room, but it still works.

They talk, they laugh, get a little bit drunk, and mostly share stories and play a few rounds of *Never have I ever,* music playing in the background. It's all really relaxed, and by the time the night ends, Seb feels that this whole party idea was actually worth it.

Jake and Sophie are the last to leave, and as soon as they do, Seb closes the door behind them, letting out a heavy breath. He locks the door and leans his forehead against it for a few moments, closing his eyes. But then he feels Evan's hands on his hips, and he smiles tiredly, automatically leaning into Evan's chest, as he comes up behind him.

"So," Evan murmurs, kissing him right below his ear, both of them still a bit drunk, by now bordering on just tipsy. "Happy?"

"I'd say so," Seb says, opening his eyes and turning around in Evan's arms, so that he can face him and slide his hands down along his waist. "I had fun."

Evan smiles.

"Good," he says, planting a kiss on Seb's forehead. Then he just looks at him for a moment, before perking up a bit. "Come on. I wanna show you something."

Seb frowns as Evan moves away from him, tugging on his hand slightly. Evan turns around and makes his way into the bedroom, and Seb slowly follows. He doesn't even make it in there, though, before Evan emerges again, something hidden behind his back. He then stops dead in front of Seb, and holds the hidden object out to him.

"Happy birthday," he says, and Seb looks down at what he's holding. It's a small package wrapped in plain, black paper, with string that looks more like twine, wrapped around it. Seb glances up at Evan, before accepting the gift, and he feels the light weight of it in his hand. He frowns, but all he gets from Evan, when he looks up at him again, is an encouraging, albeit slightly nervous, eyebrow-raise. Seb looks back at the present, and starts unwrapping it.

The string is first to go, and he can practically feel Evan's gaze on him the whole time, as the matte paper eventually falls to the floor. And then he turns the object over in his hand, smiling.

It's a book. Not just any book, though; it's one of Seb's all-time favorites. He looks up at Evan.

"Thank you," he says, and Evan gives him a small, slightly nervous smile. Seb will never quite get used to seeing Evan *nervous*.

"Look inside," he says, and Seb does, reading the title page. And he feels the surprise show on his face.

"First edition," he murmurs, before looking up at Evan, eyes widened. "Are you serious?"

Evan cocks his head, and Seb feels the sheer surprise show on his face, even more, as he turns back to the book. He lets his fingers smooth over the cover and the pages, which he now notices are slightly worn and yellowed. He knows the reverence that's probably showing on his face, as he does; he has been told just how he can look at books as though they are sacred, or made of gold.

"Yeah," Evan says, a bit awkwardly. "Don't worry, though, I didn't spend a fortune on it. Just got lucky."

Seb smiles a bit at that, eyes still on the book. He knows that a first edition of anything can reach pretty steep prices, so he's glad that Evan didn't spend a fortune, as he put it. He wouldn't have wanted that.

Seb inhales deeply, looking back up at Evan.

"Thank you," he says again, sounding kind of breathless, and Evan just gives him another uncharacteristically nervous smile.

"Glad you like it," he says. "I was a bit worried."

Seb uses his free hand to cradle Evan's face, and he kisses him, hard.

"I love it," he says, with complete honesty. "I love it."

He kisses him again, and Evan relaxes against him, putting his hands on his waist to pull him closer.

"I love *you*," Seb says, pulling away from Evan's lips for a moment. "Thank you."

Evan smiles against his mouth, a small chuckle emerging from his throat.

"You're welcome," he says, and Seb kisses him again. He closes his eyes, and for several, long seconds, they just stand there, in the hallway between the bedroom and the living room, in each other's arms, kissing as though they don't have a care in the world.

They kind of do, though—the mess the party has left isn't going to clean up itself.

There isn't much of a mess, sure, but there are bottles and pizza boxes all over the place, and Seb picks up a plastic bag and starts cleaning up, in lack of anything else. Evan objects, of course, pointing out that it's Seb's birthday, after all.

"I am *not* cleaning this up tomorrow," Seb protests. "Not when I'm all tired and hungover."

"Still, though," Evan says, but Seb doesn't listen. Instead, he keeps cleaning up, and eventually, Evan just helps him out, instead of wasting his breath trying to convince him not to.

There is still music playing, slow and mellow, and Seb feels happily tired and still slightly intoxicated. It's a nice feeling, one that makes him feel all warm and soft inside, and he honestly doesn't mind cleaning up, at the moment. It's past two a.m., though, and he would probably like to go to bed, soon, the dimmed lights of the room making him drowsy.

It's after a little while, while gathering up the last of the trash in the living room, that Evan clears his throat, and Seb looks up. Evan is holding out his hand to him, a few feet away, garbage bag discarded on the floor nearby. Seb frowns, nodding toward the plastic bag in his hand, but Evan just cocks is head as though saying *leave it*. So Seb slowly puts the bag down and makes his way across to Evan, who is standing pretty much in the middle of the room.

When Seb reaches him, he unceremoniously takes his hand and pulls him to him, steering Seb's hands and placing them against his own waist. And then, slowly, he starts moving, rotating very slowly on the spot.

It takes Seb a moment to realize what's happening.

"Are we slow dancing?" he says, frowning the slightest bit.

"Yeah," Evan says simply, sliding his hands down Seb's waist and settling them somewhere by his lower back. "What about it?"

Seb cocks his head a bit.

"Nothing," he says. "It's just, we haven't really slow danced before."

"Well," Evan says. "There's a first time for everything."

"Yeah, but—"

"Seb," Evan interrupts softly, and Seb looks up at him. Their eyes meet. "It's your birthday. Just let me spoil you a bit, okay?"

Seb just looks at him, before a small smile shapes his lips.

"This is you spoiling me?" he says, a bit teasingly, and Evan glances away almost in an eye-roll, as though a bit self-conscious.

"Well, sorry it's not more impressive," he grumbles, and Seb chuckles quietly.

"No, I'm sorry," he says. The gift alone was more than enough, when it comes to spoiling him. "That's not what I meant."

Evan looks back at him slowly, almost suspiciously, and Seb grips his hands on his waist a bit tighter. Evan is taller than him, but not by more than two inches or so, and Seb barely has to look up to keep eye-contact.

"I'm just not used to it," he explains softly, vaguely aware of how they keep moving slowly with the music. So slowly, on the spot. "I'm still not used to *you*. Just the way you look at me..."

He trails off, glancing down. It's true; even after so many months, he still isn't *quite* used to how Evan looks at him like he's precious, valuable, wanted and loved. He has never been looked at like that before, not like this. And it still feels surreal, at times, to think that someone else actually sees him that way, that someone has *chosen* him, like Evan has. Like he has chosen Evan.

Seb looks up at Evan again, those green eyes soft.

"This is the best birthday ever," he says. "It's perfect."
He plants a soft kiss on Evan's lips.

"And you can spoil me all you want."

Evan smiles then, a smile that Seb returns, before he leans in and kisses Seb properly, a slow kiss that makes Seb close his eyes and exhale softly through his nose. Evan pulls away a bit then and leans their foreheads together. He makes a small, humming sound.

"I might twirl you," he says, and Seb groans, a sound that quickly turns into a soft chuckle.

"Please, don't," he says, smiling, eyes still closed, and Evan laughs.

"Wow, you take the fun out of everything."

"Well, it's *my* birthday, isn't it?" Seb moves his hands up along Evan's back, so that they end up, fingers slightly splayed, over his shoulder blades, elbows tucked against Evan's waist, underneath his arms. It presses the two of them closer together, chest to chest. "And there will be no twirling."

Evan emits a soft grunt and plants a kiss on Seb's forehead.

"Fair enough," he says, and Seb leans his head against his shoulder, nuzzling his neck. Evan kisses his hair then, pulling him closer against him, hands secure against the small of his back. And when he softly starts humming along with the song playing, Seb smiles against his neck, eyes still closed.

Best birthday ever.

CHAPTER 19

DISTANCE

Evan is actually a pretty good cook. You never would have thought it, looking at him, and even Seb doubted it, at first. That is, until Evan actually cooked for him for the first time.

Given that they both lived in dorms before, with shared kitchens, they have never really had the opportunity to cook a nice, proper dinner. Not that Seb really minded; he's more the ramen and microwave-pizzas type of guy, anyway.

Evan minded, though, because apparently, he loves to cook, and is pretty good at it. He explained to Seb that this is most likely due to the fact that he had to do pretty much all of the cooking when he and Jake were kids, and he has taken quite a liking to it, over the years.

Seb still doubted Evan's claimed excellence in the kitchen, but was proven wrong during the first week or so they spent in their new apartment. Evan treated him to a nice, three-course dinner, and it left Seb both surprised and impressed. Not to mention very satisfied—although, he remembers some of that satisfaction taking place after dessert, in the bedroom.

So, seeing as how the two of them have been living together for months, now—and after being together for even longer, still—good food is something Seb has gotten quite used to. Evan has even tried to teach him a few tricks, along the way, almost always ending up with Seb backing away from the stove, swearing loudly, while Evan laughs and pulls him into a kiss, which Seb will pointlessly and grumpily try to fight off, before giving in and forgetting all about what Evan was just trying to teach him.

Tonight is just like any other night, and it's already dark outside the kitchen window, as they clean up after dinner. Seb doesn't like this part; it's all cleaning and dishes and wiping down surfaces, and he find it boring and monotonous. The only good part is doing it together with Evan, who always seems so calm and at peace after cooking and enjoying a nice meal. Sometimes, he'll still comment about how happy he is they have a proper kitchen, and Seb will smile, glad at the way Evan's face lights up as he talks about it.

Evan is busy doing the dishes, and Seb has just finished wiping down the table and the counter. He puts down the dishrag with a sigh and turns to look at Evan; his gaze is on his hands, cleaning and rinsing plates, his face relaxed and a bit tired, the freckles on his skin highlighted by the lamplight from above the counter. Seb just stares at him for a few seconds. He will never quite get over how *beautiful* Evan is.

Seb pauses for another moment, before moving closer to Evan and planting a soft kiss against his temple. He can feel Evan smiling, then, those crinkles around his eyes creasing.

"You're in a good mood," he says, sounding almost jokingly suspicious, and Seb frowns indignantly.

"Why wouldn't I be?" he says, kissing Evan again, on his cheekbone, this time. "Can't really find anything to complain about, right now."

Evan chuckles, not looking up from the dishes, rinsing and placing plates on the dish rack. He visibly reacts, though, softening his posture, when Seb softly skims his fingers along the hem of his jeans. It's something Seb does automatically, just one of the ways the two of them will casually touch each other, whenever they get the chance. Almost as though they occasionally need to remind each other, and themselves, that the other is still there, still real.

"Sometimes, I almost forget how worth it this is," Evan murmurs, and Seb frowns.

"What do you mean?" he asks, and Evan quirks a cocky smile.

"You always get like this," he explains."I cook some nice food, and suddenly you're just the sweetest boyfriend in the world."

Seb snorts.

"I'm not *that* easy," he objects, but Evan just smiles.

"Sure you are," he said, jokingly patronizing. "You just need a treat. Like a puppy."

Seb raises his eyebrows.

"A puppy?"

"Yeah," Evan says, smiling teasingly toward the dishes. "It's cute."

Seb cocks his head.

"Sure," he admits. "But it kind of stops being cute, as soon as you remember that you also fuck me, once in a while."

He plants a slow kiss against Evan's throat, feeling him shiver under his lips.

"Then it's just creepy."

Evan groans.

"Just let me have this one," he says. "Like, just one metaphor. Even a shitty one."

Seb chuckles against his skin, hands sliding around Evan's waist and locking together on the other side. Seb is standing next to him, his body angled so that his chest presses against Evan's shoulder.

"Fine," he murmurs, nuzzling the skin below Evan's ear slightly with his nose. "Your cooking really is amazing, though."

He exhales.

"We should invite our families over for a big dinner party, sometime."

He means it as a joke; just the idea of dinner parties is something that makes him laugh and cringe, at the same time, and Evan knows that. But Evan still tenses up a bit, and Seb frowns, while Evan replies.

"Sometime, maybe," he says unenthusiastically, eyes on the dishes. "When hell freezes over, or something."

Seb gets that Evan is joking, and that he has pretty much the same attitude towards dinner parties as Seb does, anyway. But for some reason, he stiffens, automatically thinking about something else, as he hears it.

Seb just looks at Evan, watches his profile in the light of the lamp above the counter.

"This shouldn't have to be such a big deal, you know," he finally says, to his own surprise. He really isn't in a confrontational mood right now, but he can't help it.

Evan glances at him. Seb immediately knows that Evan knows what he's referring to—this is far from the first time they have talked about that particular subject. Evan's father still does come up every now and then.

"Well, it is," Evan replies, the sudden tension in his voice saying that he wants to drop the subject. But Seb isn't giving in.

"Not if you do something about it," he says, and Evan lets out a short, slightly irritated breath, and Seb slowly loosens his arms around his body, pulling them away entirely.

"And what am I supposed to do, Seb?" Evan asks, a tense question that sounds mostly rhetorical, and Seb cocks his head.

"Oh, I don't know," he says dryly. "Maybe tell him."

Evan looks at him then, frowning, his expression almost angry for a moment.

"You know I can't do that," he says tensely, and Seb resists the overwhelming urge to roll his eyes.

"Yes, you can," he says. "You just won't. You just haven't."

"In my own time," Evan retorts, that almost-anger in his eyes seeping into his voice, as he actually points at Seb. "*You* said that."

Seb sighs, trying not to sound too frustrated.

"I know what I said," he says. "And I meant it. But Evan..."

He pauses, shaking his head, a look of hurt mingling with the frustration.

"It's been almost a year."

Evan doesn't say anything. Instead, he just looks at him, gritting his teeth, jaw working. His gaze falls, as he places his hands against the edge of the counter, leaning against it. He knows Seb has a point, Seb is sure of it. They have talked about this before, after all. Not like this, sure, not with Seb practically forcing Evan to talk about it properly, actually demanding some action.

But it's enough, now. It has been almost a year since the two of them first met, and Evan *still* hasn't told his father about their relationship, and that's becoming increasingly difficult for Seb to accept.

Evan hasn't exactly been lying to his dad; there's no lying, if you barely even talk, in the first place. But Evan has spoken to his father a few times since Seb first met him, and none of the times has he so much as mentioned even being in a relationship. So fine, he hasn't been flat-out lying, and perhaps Seb shouldn't care so much about it.

But seeing as how Evan has actually met Seb's family by now and even gone with him to a wedding, and seeing as how Seb has become so close to Jake and Sophie that they're practically family, not to mention the fact that him and Evan are *living together*, hiding their relationship from his father just feels so stupid. And it's really starting to piss Seb off. He has been patient, he has been understanding. But Evan hiding him like this is really, *really* starting to hurt.

Neither of them says anything for a few moments, Evan still staring at the smooth surface of the kitchen counter. Seb sighs quietly.

"Evan—" he says, but Evan cuts him off.

"I know, Seb," he says, sounding subdued. "I know. And I'm sorry."

He looks up at him, managing to look so small and kind of scared, despite being both bigger and taller than Seb.

"I just..." He sighs. "I know I shouldn't care. I mean, even if he's not okay with it, which I'm pretty sure he won't be, it's not my problem. It just makes him even more of an asshole, and it's got nothing to do with me. And I know that."

Evan looks down again.

"I shouldn't care," he says, his voice lower. "Even if he hates me, I shouldn't care, but..."

His voice breaks, and Seb hesitates, before finishing his sentence.

"But he's your dad," he says, simply, and Evan looks up at him. His eyes are glossy with tears that Seb knows he desperately wants to keep back, and Evan grits his teeth for a moment.

"I don't want him to hate me, Seb," he finally says, his voice breaking, and Seb's arms are around him in a split second, on instinct, pulling him closer.

"Hey," he says soothingly, smoothing over his short hair with his fingers. "Hey, it's okay."

It took some time for Seb to get used to how emotional Evan really is, as a person. He always figured that *he* would be the emotional one, but he has learned, since they first met, that pretty much everything Evan does is fuelled by emotion, one way or another. It doesn't matter if it's anger, happiness, love or fear—it's what makes him tick. It's not so much sensitivity, but rather passion, and it's something that Seb really loves about him.

So Evan turns to Seb, and he clings to him, desperately, gripping the fabric of his t-shirt and pulling him as close as he possibly can. He isn't crying. Even though he actually cries pretty easily, he never likes doing it, not even in front of Seb. It took months before he even let Seb see that side of him, properly.

"It's okay, baby," Seb murmurs soothingly, rubbing circles with his hand into the small of his back. "It's okay."

Evan breathes deeply, face buried against Seb's neck, and for several seconds, they just stand like that, not saying anything.

But Seb wants to say something, he needs to. Even though every fiber of his being instinctively wants to protect Evan and keep him safe, wants to comfort him and not in any way add to his pain, he can't let this go. He can't. They have to talk about this, even if it is hard for Evan.

"Evan," Seb finally says, pulling away just a bit, just enough so that they can look at each other properly. He's pretty sure his dark blue eyes are full of concerned sympathy, right now. He can't hide that when it comes to his boyfriend.

"I know it's difficult for you," he says, one hand still absently stroking the back of his head, fingers pulling through his hair just the slightest bit. "And I know you don't want to think about it."

He sighs, and he can tell from the look in Evan's eyes that he knows Seb is right, and that he knows what he's going to say.

"But you can't just keep putting this off," Seb says softly. "Look, I'm not saying, make a big deal out of it. I'm not even saying, call him up specifically to tell him."

He pauses.

"I'm just saying—" he stops himself and revises. "I'm *asking*, that next time you talk to him, tell him. Just tell him. Get it over with."

Seb realizes that if he weren't speaking so softly right now, with such comforting intent, his words would have sounded kind of harsh. Evan doesn't seem to notice, though, or if he does, he doesn't mind. He knows exactly what Seb means, and that he means well.

Evan sighs heavily, glancing down at the floor. He nods.

"Okay," he says, and Seb blinks. Not that he isn't glad to hear that, but after several months of Evan avoiding this issue entirely, he wasn't expecting him to just roll over so easily.

"Really?" he asks hesitantly, and Evan nods again, looking up at him.

"Yeah," he says. "You're right."

He smiles ruefully, with a small scoff.

"You're always right," he mutters, and Seb can't help but smile smugly, but in a very benevolent way.

"It's getting stupid, anyway," Evan continues, subdued. "I mean, doesn't really seem right, does it? I love you. I don't want to hide you."

Seb doesn't say anything, just looks at him, a small, concerned frown on his face. Then he leans in and plants a soft, chaste kiss on Evan's lips.

"Thank you," he says, and Evan nods. Seb knows that there is probably more to this than Evan is letting on, and that he isn't simply accepting it as easily as he wants to make it seem.

But this is the first time Evan has actually given Seb anything like this, when it comes to this subject, and Seb isn't about to turn it down. Just admitting that the whole thing is something that needed to be done is a huge step for Evan, and Seb really appreciates it.

Evan sighs heavily, and kisses Seb softly on the mouth, moving one hand up to cup his face. He smoothes over his cheekbone with his thumb, in a familiar, adoring gesture that Seb loves.

"How about we finish up here," Evan suggests quietly, "and just go to bed?"

Seb pulls away far enough to be able to look into those green eyes, and all he sees there is pure affection and a look that suggested several, exciting interpretations of *going to bed*. Seb smiles.

"Sounds like a plan."

♦

It takes over a week before anything actually happens, before Seb sees any sign of Evan actually going through with what he promised.

Seb has had a late lecture, and it's early evening by the time he gets home. After the lecture, he, Clara and a few others went out for a beer, and he's tired and comfortably, just very slightly, tipsy by the time he unlocks the front door to the apartment. He steps inside, flicking on the light switch. As soon as he does, though, the lamp above his head flashes, sputters, and then suddenly goes out. Seb flicks the switch again, experimentally. Nothing. The hall is still dark, and the lamp still dead. He sighs.

"The lamp fried again," he calls into the apartment, shrugging off his jacket, but freezes slightly when there is no reply. He glances over his shoulder.

"Evan?" he calls. Still no reply. He takes off his shoes and makes his way into the apartment. "Babe, you home?"

No lights are on, which leaves the place pretty dark, seeing as how the sun is starting to set outside. The hall by the front door leads into a hallway, where Seb flicks on the lights, and he makes his way into the living room. It's empty.

"Evan?" he calls again, but there is still no answer. He checks the kitchen, the bedroom, and even the bathroom, but Evan is nowhere to be seen. Seb frowns. That's odd.

He doesn't make much of it, though. As far as he knows, Evan doesn't have any other plans for tonight, but he sometimes ends up at Jake's place, or just spending a couple of extra hours in the giant music room that the college boasts, and Seb knows he can lose track of time. It's only around seven o'clock, anyway. No rush.

It's nine o'clock by the time Seb starts to wonder. He's sitting in the living room, in the new, three-seated couch he and Evan bought recently, watching *Doctor Who*-reruns and eating ramen, when he takes out his phone.

Where are you? he writes, fully aware of the blunt and paranoid-sounding phrase, but sends the text anyway. Then he waits a few minutes, and writes another one, since there was no reply.

I only ask because there's ramen and low-budget sci-fi, and I know how you'd hate to miss out on that action.

He sends it, and decides to leave it alone for a while.

But at ten o'clock, Evan still hasn't answered, and Seb gets a weird feeling. It isn't like Evan to ignore his texts, especially not when he's already later than usual, in coming home.

So Seb calls him, muting the TV, and after several rings, he gets Evan's voicemail. Seb frowns.

"Hey," he says, after the beep. "So, it's getting pretty late, and you're not home, so... You'd let me know if you'd been abducted by aliens or some shit, right?"

He pauses for a moment.

"Or maybe not, I don't know," he continues, with a tired sigh. "Just call me back, okay? Or come home. Preferably. Just an idea. Okay, love you."

He hangs up, and stares at the screen of his phone, for a moment. It isn't like Evan to ignore his texts, but it's even more unlike him to ignore his calls.

Then again, he rationalizes, *it could just be that Evan can't hear his phone, right now.* It's not like he hung up on Seb, or anything.

It's eleven-thirty by the time Seb turns off the TV and goes to bed. He hasn't for more than a minute stopped wondering about where the hell Evan is, but he resists the urge to text or call him again. Except for one more time.

So I'm going to bed now, he wrote, *and you're still not back. Just let me know you're okay, alright?*

He considers adding something else, or rephrasing it, but he doesn't. Instead, he just sends the text and turns off the lights, and after a little while of anxiously listening for a reply that doesn't come, he finally drifts off to sleep.

The first thing Seb notices the next morning is that the bed is still empty, except for him.

He gropes at the sheets absently, but opens his eyes when he finds nothing there. No warm body, no soft skin. No Evan. He actually sits up in bed, looking around. The cream color of the bedroom walls is illuminated by the sunlight sifting through the blinds over the windows, and it all looks very peaceful and calm. But it's empty. Seb is the only one there. He even checks his phone, but there is nothing from Evan; not a single text, not a missed call.

It's with hesitant confusion that Seb gets up and exits the bedroom, shuffling across the floor, wearing nothing but sweatpants, and he feels a very unsettling sensation in his stomach. Until he walks past the hall, that is, and notices Evan's boots discarded inside the door. Then he frowns, and makes his way into the living room.

He immediately spots him. Evan is lying on the couch, and Seb is absently grateful that they decided to get rid of the old, two-seated one they brought from Evan's dorm.

This one is much bigger, and accommodates Evan's body easily.

Seb can't help but keep his frown, though, as he shuffles over there and stops right beside the couch, looking down at his sleeping boyfriend. Evan looks like he's practically in a coma, snoring lightly, arm under his head as he lies on his side. Then Seb nudges him gently.

"Hey," he says, and Evan twitches. "Come on, wake up."

Evan groans, slowly uncoiling as Seb keeps prodding him gently, until he finally cracks open his eyes and looks around. He almost immediately finds Seb's face, above him. He smiles sleepily.

"Hey," he says, his voice rough and sleep-drunk, and Seb tilts his head.

"What are you doing?" he asks, and Evan deliberates for a moment, as though still trying to wake up and not really understanding Seb's question. Then he get it.

"Oh," he says, glancing down at himself and looking around the room, realizing that he slept on the couch, rather than in their shared bed. "I didn't wanna wake you. Sorry."

Seb frowns.

"When did you get home?" he asks, and Evan rubs his eyes.

"Not sure," he says. "Two-ish, maybe?"

Seb raises his eyebrows, instead.

"What?" he says. "Why?"

Evan lets out a heavy breath.

"I, uh..." He clears his throat. "I went out for a bit."

Seb just looks at him, expression neutral, and as Evan sees it, he exhales.

"I'm sorry," he says, reaching up to take Seb's hand. "I should have called, or something."

"Yeah, you should have." Seb can't help himself. Evan seems to get it, though, because he averts his eyes, clearly ashamed.

"I know." He looks up at Seb again, tugging on his hand gently, and Seb feels himself soften. He can't help it; he'd do anything Evan asked of him, when faced with those gorgeous, green eyes.

Seb slowly sits down on the edge of the couch, and Evan scoots in slightly, to make room. Then he takes Seb's hand properly, laces their fingers together.

"I didn't mean to make you worried," he says, trailing his other hand along the skin of Seb's arm, making small goose bumps appear all over. "Sorry."

Seb sighs.

"It's okay," he says, subdued. "Just let me know next time, okay? Or at least answer your fucking phone."

Evan smiles, and when he tugs on Seb's arm, Seb obliges and leans down to kiss him. As he does, though, he feels his breath, and he blinks.

"What exactly did you do last night?" he asks, and Evan instantly looks a bit sheepish.

"Like I said," he says. "I went out for a bit."

Seb narrows his eyes slightly.

"Out, where?"

Evan seems to hesitate.

"To a bar, okay?" he says, and Seb pulls back just the slightest bit. "I had a few drinks."

So that was alcohol Seb smelled on his breath.

Seb opens his mouth to ask something else, but Evan answers the question, before he has the chance.

"Alone," he clarifies, and Seb knows him well enough to immediately tell if he's lying. He isn't lying.

"Why didn't you call me?" Seb asks, confused, and Evan sighs.

"I don't know," he admits. "I just... I was having a shitty night, okay?"

"What do you mean?" Seb says, suddenly feeling a bit offended. "I tried getting a hold of you."

"I know."

"You know?" Seb raises his eyebrows. "You know, and you didn't—"

He takes a deep breath.

"You were deliberately ignoring me, is that it?"

Evan exhales, clearly bothered by how this is affecting Seb.

"No," he says, shaking his head, voice soft and trying to soothe. "No, I just... I couldn't talk."

"Why not?"

"I just couldn't, okay?"

Neither of them says anything for a few moments, just look at each other, Evan's fingers still stroking Seb's arm.

Then, finally, Evan speaks.

"I talked to my dad," he says, and Seb tenses up.

"What?" he says dumbly. "When?"

"Yesterday."

Evan looks down at their entwined fingers.

"He called," he says. "Apparently, he'd just spoken to Jake, and he sometimes calls me too, after. I don't know, I guess he wants it to be fair, or some shit."

Evan sighs heavily.

"And I told him."

The words hang in the air, and Seb just sits there, stiff, waiting.

"Okay," he finally says, uncertainly, in lack of anything else. The question of how it went is implied, but it still takes Evan a few more seconds to answer.

"He wasn't happy about it," he says, and Seb swallows. "Pretty pissed, actually."

Seb lets out a slow breath. *Shit.*

Evan doesn't really react as Seb leans down and pushes his hair back with his hand, gently, planting a soft kiss against his forehead.

"It's okay," he says. "It'll be fine."

But Evan doesn't react then, either. He doesn't even look up. Instead, he doesn't move for several seconds, before slowly shaking his head.

"No, it's not," he says. "It won't be."

The words feel like punch in the gut, and Seb grits his teeth slightly, trying not to react. And neither of them says anything for several moments; Seb isn't sure what to say, anyway. Neither of them even moves until Evan gets up from the couch, leaving Seb sitting there, as he shuffles off toward the bathroom, the pounding hangover he's most surely enduring blatantly obvious in the way he moves. And Seb doesn't stop him, doesn't say anything, just watches him go.

He doesn't even breathe until he hears the bathroom door shut.

♦

It's weird, how Evan acts after that.

Later that day, he seems off, but Seb figures that's mostly due to his hangover; he tends to become pretty incapacitated during those, after all.

He still tries talking to him, though, but to no avail. He tentatively tries asking about the conversation Evan had with his father, how it went, exactly. Although, Seb is about 95% sure that it really didn't go well, and judging from Evan's reaction and behavior, he's right. He didn't expect Evan to react this way, to take it so hard. And he wants to help, to make it better, especially considering that he's the one who asked Evan to tell his father, in the first place. He just doesn't know how.

When Seb comes home from another late lecture, Evan is drowsing on the couch, watching TV. It's some random hospital show, and he can't help but roll his eyes. Evan can deny his love for shows like that all he wants, but it's obvious that he's a huge fanboy.

Seb tentatively tries talking to Evan for a bit. He was planning on sitting down next to him, but Evan feels so cold and standoffish, that Seb decides against it. Maybe Evan is just feeling down, and needs some space. Seb isn't going to force him into a conversation, exactly. So he leaves him alone, and when it's time for bed, he lets Evan know, but all he receives in return is a grunt and a mumbled *okay*.

Seb wants him to join him, on his own, but doesn't want to push it.

Evan doesn't come to bed. He sleeps on the couch, and by the time Seb gets up the next day, he's gone. He has an early lecture, Seb remembers, so even though it makes him feel unsettled, he doesn't make much of it.

Evan comes home later that day, and Seb once again tries talking to him, but it's no use. Evan just seems so subdued, shut down, and it's making Seb feel increasingly worried. He tries lightening the mood, but it doesn't help. He tries touching him, moving closer, kissing him softly. But it's no good. Evan practically pushes him away, and it hurts so bad that Seb feels an almost physical ache in his chest.

It lasts for three days. For three days, Evan dodges him, avoids him, avoids eye contact, and even considering that they are apart for some of the time by work and school, they barely talk. And it's making Seb increasingly anxious. Evan won't talk to him, won't even tell him about what his father said. And more than once, Evan drinks more than one beer, or glasses of whiskey, and Seb can smell alcohol on his breath, when he comes home. Because Evan still comes home, even though it honestly feels like he doesn't want to be there.

He still comes home, even though he still won't sleep in their bed, and he won't even bother explaining why.

One night, he does sleep in their bed again, but he's so closed-off and cold, that Seb doesn't even dare to touch him. Evan is lying just inches away from him, but he has never felt more distant.

Seb has no idea what's happening. He has no idea why Evan was acting like this. And he has no idea what to do about it.

It's after those three days that Seb finally has enough.

Evan is sitting in front of the TV, absently watching, and Seb is standing in the doorway of the living room, looking at him. He glances at the acoustic guitar standing in the corner. Evan usually plays almost every day, but in the past few days, he hasn't so much as touched the instrument. It's just one of the things on the list of things that makes Seb feel very worried.

"I'm gonna go to bed," Seb says, trying to sound neutral. Evan glances at him, before turning back to the TV.

"Okay," he says, and Seb waits. He swallows.

"You coming, too?" he asks, afraid of the answer, and Evan just exhales.

"In a minute," he says, and Seb sighs. He hesitates.

"I can tell there's something wrong, you know," he says, trying to sound like himself, relaxed and slightly dry. He's afraid that he's pushing it, but he can't help himself. "It's pretty obvious."

Evan doesn't answer him. Instead, he looks determined to keep his attention focused on the television. Seb grits his teeth slightly.

"Would it kill you to talk to me?" he says, and he swears Evan shifts slightly in his seat. "I mean, you've barely said a word to me in days."

And not just that, he feels like saying. *You've barely even touched me, barely even a kiss. Like I'm some kind of leper.*

But he doesn't say that. He has a feeling that Evan really doesn't need to hear that right now, anyway.

311

It's true, though. Even though Evan has been here this whole time, in their home, eating and sleeping and simply being there, he feels so far away. Seb has never before known how much you can miss someone who is already there. Because he misses Evan. He misses him so much, it hurts. And he has no idea how to handle that, since Evan isn't physically missing, in the first place.

Seb waits patiently for any kind of reply, but when none comes, he sighs.

"Evan," he says, voice slightly edged. "Talk to me."

Evan fidgets then, shifts slightly in his seat, but he doesn't look up. And somehow, that's the last straw for Seb, who simply walks over and shuts off the TV.

"For fuck's sake," he says, anger and frustration seeping into his voice, unconsciously, as Evan looks up at him. "What are you doing?"

Evan doesn't answer him at first, and Seb waits, patiently.

"I don't wanna talk about it," Evan finally says, and Seb cocks his head.

"Well, tough," he says. "*I* wanna talk about it. Whatever *it* is."

Evan just looks at him. He's still sitting on the couch, Seb standing nearby, their gazes locked. Evan looks oddly annoyed, but mostly just tired. And somehow, sad. But Seb has had enough of waiting and being nice. He has the right to know what Evan is thinking, what he's doing. He can't take this, anymore.

"Okay," he finally says, since Evan isn't talking. "I'm gonna take a shot in the dark, here."

He can't help but notice how his trademark, dry sarcasm immediately creeps into his voice. He kind of hates that, right now, but he can't help it—it's his defense mechanism, after all, and the only way he knows how to react to something like this.

"Is it about your dad?" he says, and Evan immediately tenses up. Seb doesn't need to say any more than that, because he clearly hit home.

"I don't wanna talk about it," Evan repeats, and Seb resists the urge to sigh irritably.

"So, it is about your dad," he says, and Evan keeps his eyes on him. "Why don't you just tell me? Tell me what happened."

"Seb—"

"Something clearly happened, Evan," Seb insists. "I just don't get why you won't tell me."

"It didn't go well, okay," Evan says, anger seeping into his voice, as he suddenly gets up from the couch. "That's it. And I don't wanna talk about it."

"Yeah, well, that doesn't really matter," Seb finds himself saying. "Because this is bothering you, and that means it's bothering me."

"Seb—"

"You owe me this, Evan." Seb's voice is resolute, and he half-regrets saying that, the moment he does. "You fucking owe me."

But he knows he has a point. They are in a relationship, after all, and Evan really does owe him this. He owes Seb honesty, and he owes him at least the reason for him acting like he has been doing these past few days.

"Even if it went badly," Seb continues, "why won't you talk to me? Why are you mad at me?"

"Don't give me that," Evan says, voice suddenly low with controlled anger. "Not you."

Seb frowns, confused.

"What?" he says, and Evan looks at him.

"This is on you," he says, now suddenly sounding genuinely angry. He actually points at Seb, then, like he sometimes does when he's angry and gets all accusing.

"Me?" Seb says incredulously. "What the fuck's that supposed to mean?"

"You pushed me into this!" Evan says. "He basically disowned me. You pushed me, and that fucking happened!"

Seb just gapes at him for a second, eyes wide and brow furrowed.

"Are you serious?" he says, equal parts confused and pissed off. "You're blaming *me* for this? No offense, but your dad would have reacted the exact same way, no matter what I did or said, or *pushed you into*."

He says the last part with some heavy, disapproving sarcasm, which Evan clearly notices, because Seb can see his jaw working in irritation. And Seb kind of hates himself for saying something like that, for somehow glossing over Evan's use of the word *disowned,* and the fact that that is a *huge* fucking deal, and he knows, deep down, that he's focusing on the wrong thing here. But he can't help it. He's just so *angry* at Evan, over the way he has been acting. Angry and *hurt.*

"You couldn't just let me do it in my own time," Evan says. "Even though you said so."

"A year, Evan!" Seb exclaims. "An entire, fucking year!"

He pauses for a second, surprised at his own anger, somehow.

"For an entire year, you've basically pretended that I don't exist, when it comes to him," he continues. "You even used to do that with strangers, and you have no idea how much that hurt."

"Oh, I think I've got a pretty good idea," Evan bites back, with such scathing, unexpected sarcasm that Seb almost flinches; he isn't used to Evan talking like that. Like him.

Then he remembers, though. He remembers how he basically broke up with Evan, over that exact issue, so long ago now, and he suddenly feels ashamed for bringing it up. Evan has made that up to him a hundred times over, and Seb was such a cowardly asshole about it, at the time.

Seb sighs quietly, glancing away.

"I know," he says, voice significantly more subdued. "I'm sorry."

He looks back at Evan only to see an expression that says *fine, but I'm still pissed at you,* and he relaxes just the slightest bit. At least that isn't an issue anymore.

Though, the whole thing about Evan's dad and how he took the news of his son's relationship, that's still a very big issue. And it isn't one that's going to go away any time soon.

"But Evan," Seb tries, doing his best to sound as understanding as possible. "What was the option, here? Just hiding it forever?"

"I was gonna tell him," Evan exclaims, taking a step closer, eyes blazing. "You know I was! But not like that! And now, he hates me! He didn't exactly take it well."

"And I'm sorry that that happened," Seb retorts, sounding desperate, rather than angry, but matching Evan's intensity, all the same. "But this isn't my fault!"

Silence. For a few seconds of drawn-out silence, they just look at each other.

"I didn't do this, Evan," Seb eventually says, softening his voice just a bit. "It's not my fault, and I'm not gonna apologize for something I didn't do."

The words are risky, he realizes that. But despite his deep-seated instinct to protect Evan and never cause him pain, he knows that this isn't his fault. Because it isn't. Right?

Neither of them says anything for several, agonizingly long seconds, and Seb waits. He waits, waits for Evan to just give in and relax, to admit that this really *isn't* Seb's fault, and that he's angry at the wrong person for the wrong reasons. He knows it's stupid to expect that, but fuck it—he's feeling angry and petty and selfish, and he just wants everything to be okay again, and for Evan talk to him again and smile and kiss him, like everything is normal.

But Evan doesn't do that. Instead, he just looks at Seb, before suddenly making his way past him and walking out into the hall. Seb is stunned for a second, confused, before he turns around.

"Evan," he says, still angry, but scared.

Evan doesn't answer him. Instead, Seb can hear the sound of him putting on his boots and getting his jacket, and panic rises in Seb's chest.

"Where are you going?" he says, fear drowning out the anger, as he makes his way out into the hall. He finds Evan shrugging his jacket on, and he just glances at Seb, before opening the door.

"Out," he says curtly, and Seb takes a step closer. But Evan just holds up his hand, making Seb stop dead in his tracks.

"Don't." The single word is cold, harsh, and it's almost as though the sheer power of it makes Seb unable to move.

He can't move, and he can only watch, helplessly, as Evan throws him one last glance and walks out the door, slamming it shut behind him.

CHAPTER 20

RAIN

Evan won't answer his phone.

Seb just stood there, at first, not moving for what he could have sworn were several minutes, after Evan stormed out. Then, he got angry again, practically shouting at thin air, pacing, restless. He had no outlet, really, no way of venting the sudden anger he felt, which drowned out any hurt or fear he was feeling before.

So he tried to calm down, instead, getting a glass of water. He ended up throwing the glass against the kitchen wall, though, shattering it to pieces, and it felt so satisfying, that he threw another.

But it didn't last long. The satisfaction ebbed away only seconds after the shattering sound of glass shards faded, and Seb just stood there, breathing heavily, before slowly sliding down to the floor. And now, here he sits, back against the cupboards below the counter, staring at the opposite wall. There is broken glass everywhere, water running in droplets down along the wallpaper, and the silence is suddenly deafening. He takes a deep breath.

The clock above the kitchen door is ticking loudly. Funny, Seb has never noticed that before, not even when he had the clock in his own dorm room. He glances up at it. It's almost midnight; it has been almost an hour since Evan left. It's odd how it feels like it just happened, but at the same time, it feels like a lifetime ago.

Seb sits there for a while longer, thinking, going it all over in his head.

What happened? Seriously, what *the hell* happened?

He looks down at his hands, and frowns, surprised at the blood he sees there. It seems that he placed his left hand against the floor, right on some tiny shards of glass, and there are a couple of small cuts on the heel of his palm. They sting, even more so when he slowly pulls out a piece of glass that has wedged itself there. And they keep bleeding.

Seb absently reaches for a towel hanging close by, over the handle of the oven, and twists around so he can reach the sink. He turns on the faucet and gets part of the towel wet, before turning it off again and sinking back down to the floor. He then proceeds to wipe away the blood, as well as he can, before he gingerly wrapped the towel around his hand, trying to stem the flow. All the while, he barely even flinches; it really hurts, but the pain feels oddly good. It's a welcome alternative to the sudden numbness he feels, anyway.

That's when he, for some reason, takes out his phone and dials Evan's number.

He should have known that Evan wouldn't answer. He doesn't even bother letting it ring, this time—Seb hears one ring, before it goes to voicemail, which he knows means that Evan deliberately cut him off. And he chews his bottom lip, hanging up even before the beep. He doesn't leave a message, doesn't know what he would say, anyway.

I'm sorry? Is that what Evan wants to hear? Seb is sorry, sure, but not for the reason Evan will think. He's sorry they fought, sorry he pushed him into talking about something he clearly didn't want to talk about at the moment, sorry for hurting him and making him leave. Sorry for being so selfish, and not for a second thinking about the kind of pain Evan must be in, instead only focusing on how hurt and unfairly treated he felt at Evan's behavior.

He is sorry. He is so very sorry.

Seb tries calling him again, but to no avail. Evan cuts him off again, and again, Seb hangs up before getting the chance to leave a message.

He isn't really aware of how he starts crying. Or maybe crying is the wrong word; there is no sobbing, no hitching in the throat, no anguished sounds. Instead, there's just... well, crying. Just tears, slowly and silently running down his face, more of them than he would like.

He hasn't cried in quite a while. Actually, as he thinks about it, last time he cried was because of Evan, too. It was almost a year ago, when Seb fucked up so badly and basically broke up with him. He remembers talking to Sophie that time, admitting his own fears about Evan leaving him, anyway. It seems that he is doing a pretty good job of making that happen, himself.

It takes another hour of painstakingly picking up all the glass and vacuuming the kitchen floor, as well as more thoroughly cleaning the cuts on his hand, before Seb finally goes to bed. And when he does, he can't sleep. Instead, it's all he can do to just lie there, cold and alone, trying to not so much as look at Evan's empty half of the bed. And *fuck*, he even starts crying again, just as silently as before. Like he's too tired and too numb to cry properly.

He has no idea what to do.

♦

Seb tries calling Evan again the next day, more than once. But there is still no answer. Evan hasn't come back home, and Seb can't help but wonder where he has gone.

He's probably staying with Jake and Sophie, though, he realizes. Seb hasn't talked to either of them for a while, and he's so tempted to call them, right now. They have become really good friends, and apart from Evan, they are really the only people he trusts.

But they have done so much already. Jake and Sophie were both there, every time Evan and Seb fought and fucked up, and Seb can't help but feel that somehow, it's time to man up and handle this, himself. Although, it irks him a bit that Evan somehow has dibs on them, simply because he has known them longer, and Jake is his brother. Seb is certain that neither Sophie nor Jake would have minded in the least if he wanted to talk to either of them, but still—they need to deal with this, him and Evan. *He* needs to deal with this.

It's hard, though. It's hard, because unlike Evan, Seb is stuck here, in their shared home, where *everything* reminds him of Evan, who had the luxury of simply running away. And it's hard, because although Seb wants more than anything to fix this, whatever it was, he has no idea where to start.

What is he supposed to do? Should he keep trying to talk to Evan? Should he give him some space? He isn't even sure what the problem is, only that Evan is angry and hurt about his father, and that he's somehow projecting that onto Seb. And of course, that Seb acted like a complete, selfish child, unable to see the bigger picture.

They have both behaved like assholes, pretty much.

Seb has no lectures today, which is too bad, honestly; he would have welcomed the distraction. Instead, he does his best to study at home, and when that fails, he spends two hours playing *Bioshock*, before realizing that nothing can really distract him, anyway.

He calls Evan again. It's probably the third time today, and he doesn't expect him to pick up. And he doesn't pick up. And Seb hangs up without leaving a message, again.

It isn't until the seventh try, late that afternoon, that he for some reason doesn't hang up. Instead, he's almost startled at the beep that follows Evan's voice, asking the caller to leave a message, and he just sits there for a second. Then he blinks.

"Hi," he says dumbly, realizing how oddly broken and subdued he sounds. That wasn't really his intention. "I, uh... I'm not sure what to say."

He pauses, honestly at a loss for words. He swallows.

"I guess you're still mad at me," he finally says. "Can't blame you."

He chews his bottom lip.

"I just... I'm sorry."

Fuck. Despite however Seb wants to rationalize it, *sorry* really is all he wants to say, all he *can* say.

"I'm sorry we fought," he says. "I'm sorry about what I said. You didn't want to talk about it, and I made you, anyway, and..."

He sighs heavily, leans his forehead against his palm, eyes closed.

"I just want to talk to you," he says. The words come out in a whisper, a breath, and sound so much more broken and sad than he intended. He didn't even really mean to say it out loud—he can't tell what difference it will make, anyway.

Seb feels like he wants to say something else, but he can't think of anything. There is so much he *wants* to say, but nothing would quite cut it, and after the way Evan has been acting the past several days, not to mention the night before, he very much doubts that it would matter. He feels like Evan just isn't coming back. Ever.

So Seb just swallows down the lump in his throat and hangs up the phone, taking a deep, shaky breath.

And he's crying again.

Seb would have gone to bed at a reasonable time that night, if he thought he would have any chance of actually falling asleep. Instead, he stays up, trying to distract himself with books and TV and video games, but it's pretty much pointless. And his stomach rumbles, because he has barely eaten anything all day, seeing as how he doesn't really have much of an appetite, at the moment.

At least he managed to fix up the cuts on his hand properly, though; they stopped bleeding pretty quickly last night, and the cuts are too small to even need a band-aid, at this point.

He's half-surprised, actually, that he hasn't heard anything from Jake, or Sophie. Despite the fact that he decided to deal with this on his own, they have always been there before, checking up on him, trying to mend whatever was broken between him and Evan. They care so much, and Seb is eternally grateful for all the support and help they have provided. Without it, he's almost certain that he and Evan never would have made it, in the first place.

But he hasn't heard from them today, not this time. Not a phone call, nothing. But that's probably a good thing, and if nothing else, maybe they have finally gotten tired of cleaning up his and Evan's messes. Not to mention the fact that if Evan is at their place right now, they're bound to take his side and not talk to Seb about it, especially if Evan is mad at him.

And that makes sense, Seb thinks to himself. Because Evan has the right to be mad at him.

Seb was only half-expecting to hear from Jake or Sophie, considering their track record, but he's still surprised when he hears the doorbell ring. He glances at his phone to check the time; it's just past ten p.m. It isn't that late, but still.

He has the TV on, watching some show that he isn't even paying attention to, and he turns it off as he gets up from the couch, leaving the entire apartment in silence. He can hear that it's raining outside now, though. He hasn't noticed that, before.

Seb shuffles out into the hall, slowly, but the doorbell doesn't ring again. He isn't surprised; Jake and Sophie both know him well enough to give him some time and space, if he needs it, that he will answer in his own time.

So he takes a breath, bracing himself, but when he opens the front door, all the air practically goes out of him.

"Hi." The one word is tense, careful, and it perfectly matches Evan's entire posture, as he stands there, hands in the pockets of his jeans. He looks slightly slumped, as though weighed down, smaller, and Seb isn't used to seeing him like that.

Seb just stands there, eyes actually widened a bit, his hand suddenly gripping the door handle almost painfully tight. Evan looks at him, his entire expression careful and... he looks almost *ashamed*. And it doesn't help that he is completely drenched, Seb notices, wearing only an open, button-up shirt over his t-shirt, the sleeves rolled up to his elbows. His clothes are soaking wet, his skin, his hair, as though someone just dumped a bucket over his head.

Evan seems to notice Seb scrutinizing him, and he looks self-conscious for a moment.

"I, uh..." He glances away, glances downwards, moving one hand up to smooth down over his face and stubble, his skin actually wet from the rain. "I sort of went for a walk, and... it started raining."

He's pretty much mumbling, and those green eyes are oddly scared, when they look back up at Seb. Seb doesn't move, doesn't say anything. Instead, he can't help but simply stare at Evan, as he stands there, outside the door, soaking wet, looking so lost and so small. And Evan looks at him, before shoving his hands back in his pockets.

"Can I come in?" he finally asks hesitantly, very gently, as though expecting Seb to say no.

Of course, Seb wants to say. *Of course, this is your home.*

"Yeah," is all he musters, and steps away from the door to make his way back into the apartment. He hears Evan enter behind him, tentatively closing the door.

Seb's heart is suddenly pounding, for some reason. Just the fact that Evan simply showed up, just like that, is starting to sink in, and he suddenly feels oddly scared.

He came back. He came back, against every expectation, and Seb really doesn't want him to leave again.

Seb is vaguely aware of Evan following slowly behind him, as he makes his way into the living room, in lack of anything else. It's dimly lit, the tall floor lamp in the corner giving the room a nice, warm glow. It's pleasant, and Seb realizes just how flattering that lighting is, as he turns around and sees Evan standing there, by the doorway, hands still in his pockets. He hasn't taken his shoes off, or his soaking wet, button-up shirt, but dear *god*, he looks so beautiful, it hurts.

Neither of them speaks for a few seconds, the silence only broken by the smattering of rain against the window. Then, Seb watches as Evan opens his mouth to speak, but then closes it again. He ends up doing that a few times, as though looking for the right words, before finally just exhaling heavily.

"I'm sorry," he says. He sounds sad, almost ashamed, and Seb swallows dryly.

"Yeah," he says, his voice low and subdued. "Me, too."

Evan's eyes looks just the slightest bit hopeful for a moment, before he shakes his head.

"No," he says. "No, I'm really sorry. I fucked up."

He looks down at the floor, and Seb waits, lets him speak.

"You didn't deserve that," Evan says, shaking his head. "Any of it."

He looks up again, eyes slightly glossy, as he grits his teeth.

"I freaked out about my dad," he says. "It did a real number on my head. And I took it out on you."

He swallows hard, biting down, as though trying to stay in control, and Seb resists the urge to reach out to him. Instead, he just sighs quietly.

"I get it," he says, before pausing, cocking his head. "I mean, I don't *get* it, obviously... But I get why you acted the way you did, I guess."

He glances over at the wall, simply to avoid Evan's gaze.

"I mean, I'm not happy about it," he admits. "But I get it. Just wish you would have told me."

Evan sighs, as though in pain.

"I know," he says softly, and his voice is full of sad regret. "I know. I just... I didn't know what to say."

"You could have said *some*thing," Seb says softly, looking back at him. "Anything. It was like you weren't even here. Felt like you hated me, like I was... like I repelled you."

The words hurt to say, but they're true and have to be said. And Evan just looks at him, clearly fighting tears now, although the silent kind, the kind that only shows in his eyes. He nods.

"I know," he repeats. "And I'm so sorry. I never meant for that to happen. I didn't know what to do, I just shut down. I—"

For a moment, he looks like he's about to move closer to Seb, but decides against it.

"I never meant to hurt you," he says, green eyes sad and pleading. "I never meant to make you feel like that. I never wanted that."

He shakes his head, chewing his bottom lip.

"And the stuff I said to you..." He grimaces, almost as though thinking about it causes him physical pain. "I hated myself for it. Still do. None of it was true, I don't..."

He exhales heavily and looks down at the floor again.

"The minute I left," he continues, "I regretted it. I wished I hadn't left, but I couldn't come back here, not after what I'd said, what I'd done. So I stayed away. I figured, I didn't deserve to come back."

Evan fidgets, where he stands, and Seb doesn't say a thing. Instead, he lets him speak, lets him explain. He knows how hard this kind of thing is for Evan, and he knows how important it is to let him talk, when he so clearly needs to. And after several days of the opposite, Seb is honestly just so glad to hear him talk to him again.

"I couldn't even bring myself to call you," Evan continues. "'Cause I didn't know what to say."

He scoffs bitterly.

"And I couldn't even pick up when you called," he says, "because I didn't know what to say. I couldn't even understand why you called, at all. I was so sure I had ruined everything, that I couldn't come back."

He looks up at Seb then, tentatively.

"Then I got your message," he says, and Seb reacts. So it did come through. And Evan listened to it. "And I thought that maybe, there was still a shot."

He sounds downright scared, beneath that soft pleading, and Seb just looks at him. He can feel the sad concern in own eyes, and he's certain Evan can see it, too.

He wants to do something, wants to put his arms around Evan and pull him as close as he possibly can, and just feel him there. But he is afraid to—after several days of being rejected, both physically and emotionally, he's afraid to even look at Evan for too long.

It's as though Evan can tell what he's thinking, because he looks so sad when he sees Seb's expression, that it's simply heartbreaking.

"I just want to come back," Evan says, when Seb doesn't respond, his voice breaking. "I want to come home."

That does it.

Seb isn't sure if he moves closer to Evan, if it's the other way around, or if they somehow meet halfway, but suddenly, he's holding Evan, arms wrapped tightly around his muscled frame, burrowing his face into the side of his neck. And Evan holds him so tightly that it almost hurts, but even if it does, Seb doesn't care. He is just so relieved, so glad to have Evan close to him again, and he closes his eyes, practically squeezes them shut, as he breathes him in.

Seb can both feel and hear the deep, relieved exhale from Evan, as those arms tighten around him, pulling him as close as possible, and the way Evan murmurs kisses into his hair, one hand softly placed by the back of his head. Seb feels it, and he savors it, without saying a word.

He doesn't have to say anything. Evan has said what needs to be said, and Seb has said what needs to be said, through that voicemail he left what feels like ages ago. It feels as though the whole world has changed since then.

They just stand like that for a pretty long time, just holding each other, clinging to each other, as though they might be ripped apart if they let up for just a second. After a little while, though, they loosen their grip just the slightest bit, and settle slowly against each other, softly, shaping their bodies to fit the other.

"You wanna talk about it?" Seb asks, carefully, and he hears Evan sigh softly.

"Later," he says, voice slightly muffled, as he kisses Seb's hair. "Right now, I just want this."

Seb nods.

"Okay."

They lapse back into silence, and Seb exhales slowly, closing his eyes against the coarse stubble of Evan's cheek. He absently moves one hand up, slowly sliding it up along the side of Evan's neck, fingertips gently pulling through that rain-wet hair the slightest bit, and Evan softens against him.

Suddenly, Seb just feels so acutely aware of it, of how Evan feels, how he smells, how he tenses up underneath his touch. And those warm, calloused hands settle against Seb's waist, before slowly sliding down, to reach underneath Seb's t-shirt and touch his skin.

Seb breathes in deeply, head suddenly almost spinning from the sheer presence of Evan, from the way he touches him, the way he feels. From how his skin tastes against Seb's tongue, as Seb plants a slow, burning kiss against the pulse of his throat.

He isn't sure what he's doing. He just really needs this, and he can tell that Evan does, too.

Evan's hands move further up along Seb's waist, under his shirt, tightening their grip ever so slightly at the pressure of Seb's mouth against his skin.

"I missed you," Evan murmurs, his voice sounding subdued, wrecked and almost sad, all at once, and Seb exhales.

"I know," he says, nearly whispering against the skin just below Evan's ear, making Evan noticeably tense up. He kisses him there, pulling his fingers further up into that short, wet hair. "I'm just glad you're home."

He pulls away the slightest bit then, just enough to be able to look at Evan, to see his face, to savor those beautiful, green eyes and that lightly freckle-dusted skin.

"I missed you so much," he says, his voice low and more emotional than he's used to hearing from himself. But it's true. It doesn't matter that Evan was right here, almost this whole time, because he *wasn't,* not really. He was somewhere else for the past several days, and Seb missed him so much that it turned into an almost physical ache.

Now that he has him here again, he never wants to let him go.

He still misses him. He needs him closer.

There are only a couple of inches between them, and Evan just looks at him, eyes bright, before moving one hand up to gently hold Seb's chin between his fingers. It sends an immediate rush through Seb's body, as he feels it, and for a moment, he can't help but wonder why. But then he remembers.

Another time Evan did that, was about a year ago. It was their first kiss, after admitting how they felt about each other. Granted, not their *first* first kiss, but the first one as a couple. The first kiss they shared without any confusion or doubt, the first time just being with each other simply because they wanted to, because they *needed* to, as proof of what their relationship had just changed into.

Seb remembers it vividly. He remembers the look in Evan's eyes, that terrified, fierce determination, the way it made Seb simply stare, mesmerized, shocked and kind of scared.

There is no such look in Evan's eyes, this time. This time, there is just complete and utter affection, devotion, *love*, as he looks at Seb, whose eyes are focused on his. It feels safe and strong, but at the same time, Seb feels like he will never quite stop being terrified of it, of the way you can simply love someone so much. It still blows his mind, how he can just *love* Evan so much, how he can *need* him like this. And it blows his mind even more, that Evan feels the exact same way.

Evan just looks at him for a few more seconds, as though trying to memorize every inch of his face. Then he leans in slightly, and Seb is sure he's going to kiss him. But he doesn't. Instead, Evan so softly plants a kiss at the corner of his mouth, before brushing his lips along the outline of his jaw, barely hinting at a kiss, and Seb closes his eyes. He inhales deeply, slowly, as Evan moves his lips over his cheekbone, before softly kissing his temple, just below his eyebrow.

Seb lets out his deep breath, his skin suddenly burning, crackling with energy, with heat. He tightens his grip on Evan's hair ever so slightly, patiently letting Evan map out his face with his lips. And Evan's hand against his waist, against his skin, tightens its grip just the slightest bit, Evan exhaling slowly.

Evan's hair is wet, Seb realizes. Wet from the rain. Just like that time, the first time, which feels like forever ago. His shirt is wet too, drenched, and Seb suddenly feels his entire body buzzing.

He remembers that, the first time. He remembers the two of them kissing against the side of Evan's car, kissing like they had been apart for years, both of them getting soaked from the rain. He remembers them eagerly pulling each other's clothes off in the dorm room, awkwardly making their way to Evan's bed and falling down, hands all over each other.

He remembers the oddly satisfying sensation of gripping onto Evan's rain-wet hair, those warm hands sending tendrils of fire all over his skin, and the way it all felt so new and hot and perfect, like Seb hadn't wanted anything more in his entire life, than he wanted that.

He still misses Evan. He needs him closer.

Seb knows what will happen if he kisses Evan, now. He knows that it will be like igniting a gunpowder-keg, and that there will be no stopping them. He knows that the tension between them, the missing each other and the fighting and the reconciliation, will all ignite, and it will send them completely over the edge.

The sheer sensation of knowing that feels like molten heat, slowly moving underneath the surface, ready to explode, and Seb wonders if he has ever felt it so intensely, before. Not that he would remember it right now, if he had. He can't think, too wrapped up in the way his heart is suddenly pounding against his ribcage, his breathing becoming heavier.

He has missed Evan so much. He has missed him more than he ever thought he could miss anyone.

And he still misses him. He needs him closer.

Seb's lips almost fumble as they found Evan's, desperately pressing themselves against them, Seb breathing in deeply, as though he can take in Evan's very essence in just one kiss. And Evan wastes no time, in his response.

In just a second, Evan's hand finds its way to the back of Seb's neck, the other still firmly planted by his waist, pulling him closer and pressing their bodies together as close as he possibly can. And Seb almost loses his breath at the sheer intensity of it, gripping tightly onto Evan's soaking wet hair, crushing his mouth against his own.

It isn't enough. He needs him closer.

Seb finds himself pushing forward, pushing against Evan until he hits the wall that's right behind him, before sliding his hand down along his back and over his ass, grinding against him. The surprise is obvious on Evan's part, but he doesn't object. Instead, he groans against Seb's lips, moving both his hands down to Seb's hips, as Seb keeps a firm grip on his hair, keeping his head in place, his tongue pushing into his mouth.

Seb tries to remember how to breathe. His head is really spinning now, everything starting to blur together. Nothing matters anymore. Only Evan. Only Evan, and the way his body feels against him, the way his tongue feels in his mouth, the way he tastes, the way holds onto Seb so tightly and kisses him like he wants to brand him, for the world to see. Like he wants Seb to remember this for the rest of his life—and Seb is pretty sure that he will.

It's through a mess of incoherent murmurs and heavy breathing that they somehow decide to move out of the living room and into the bedroom, barely pulling apart for a second, Evan kicking off his shoes, on the way.

Seb isn't entirely sure how they manage, but suddenly, he finds himself sliding his hands underneath Evan's soaking wet t-shirt and practically peeling it off his skin, before dumping it on the bedroom floor. He awkwardly tugged off the button-up shirt on the way here, but the t-shirt underneath was just as drenched, and he's glad to have them both off, so he can touch Evan properly.

Evan's skin is hot and wet underneath his eager hands, and Seb plants a hard kiss against Evan's collarbone, moving up along his throat and tasting heat and sweat and rainwater on his skin. Evan groans, roughly tugging at Seb's t-shirt, before Seb takes the hint and pulls away just enough for Evan to take it off of him.

They aren't apart for more than a second, mouths crashing together and hands smoothing over bare skin, leaving heated trails, as they clumsily make their way over to the bed, falling down onto the memory foam mattress, limbs tangled and fingers eagerly unzipping jeans.

Seb ends up on his back, more by accident than by design, and it feels like only a matter of seconds, before they both manage to get their pants off and toss them to the floor, Seb's hands eagerly sliding in underneath Evan's underwear, down over his ass. Evan groans against his lips, as Seb roughly pulls him downwards, grinding against him. He's so hard it was almost painful, at this point, and Evan is having the exact same reaction, gritting his teeth and moving his face away from Seb's, so he can bury it against the crook of Seb's neck.

"Seb," he breathes raggedly, sending shivers up Seb's spine. "Fuck, I've missed you so much."

He sounds wrecked, desperate, and Seb moans as Evan plants slow, burning kisses against his throat, nipping the skin gently with his teeth and smoothing it over with his tongue.

"I love you." Evan still sounds wrecked, almost as though he's in some kind of exquisite pain. "I love you."

Seb grabs onto his hair then, pulling him back up, so that he can kiss him fiercely, deeply, almost as though they're fused together. He needs him closer, *closer*.

"And I love you so much, it's stupid," he musters, not wanting to take his lips away from Evan's for more than a split second.

Evan laughs then, breathlessly, smoothing his hands over Seb's body, kissing him, grinding against him with such slow, sweet urgency that it makes Seb's head start spinning again.

Seb could just stay like that forever, the two of them entwined, wrapped up in the heat and urgency and the exquisite sensation of skin on hot skin. But he wants more. He *needs* more, needs to remedy the ache he has been feeling for the past several days.

He needs *Evan, all* of him.

It's without saying anything that Seb grabs onto Evan and simply rolls them both over, so that Evan ends up on his back, instead. He looks only slightly surprised; this isn't how they usually do things. A lot of the time, Evan is the one in charge, so to speak, Seb only occasionally taking on that role. But tonight, he won't have it any other way, and Evan isn't exactly about to go against him on that.

Seb pauses for a second. It's dark, the light from the hallway just enough to let him see Evan properly, and for a moment, he just stares. He sits there, straddling Evan, chest rising and falling heavily, and just lets his eyes take in the perfect, gorgeous epiphany of the man in front of him, underneath him. Evan is so beautiful, like he always has been. So beautiful.

And he is *his*.

Seb moves down to once again claim Evan's lips with his own, feeling Evan's splayed fingers pushing down against his back, pulling him against him, their chests pressing together. It's the best feeling in the world, urgent and perfect, heightened by the fact that Seb has felt as though he would never get to feel it again, and he maps out Evan's body with his hands, desperate to make sure he's still there, still real.

It's with hands just slightly fumbling from eagerness, that Seb moves down to pull off Evan's boxers, and Evan helps out by arching his hips a bit, so Seb can get them off properly and throw them away, landing them somewhere on the floor. Evan is as hard as he is, that much is obvious, and Seb finds himself moaning absently, as he feels it against his stomach, Evan tensing up and sucking in a sharp breath through his teeth.

"Would you get these off?" Evan breathes, tugging at Seb's underwear, and Seb actually laughs.

"Would you relax?" he says, kissing him, placing his hands against the mattress, on either side of Evan's head. Evan laughs against his lips, slipping his hands underneath the hem of Seb's boxers.

"Just trying to expedite things," he says, smiling, and Seb moans as he feels Evan's hands slowly pulling his underwear down. "Hardly seems fair, does it?"

"Fine," Seb grumbles, and Evan chuckles, as Seb through some quick maneuvering gets his underwear off and throws them away. He doesn't waste a second in reclaiming Evan's mouth, though, and as soon as he presses down against him, it's as though someone just injected fire into his veins. Just the feeling of Evan's hardness against his own is nearly enough to send him over the edge.

They don't say much after that, they don't need to. Instead, Seb keeps his lips practically glued to Evan's, as he leans over to the nightstand and opens the drawer. They generally don't use a condom, only do it when they don't want to make too much of a mess, really, and Seb generally doesn't care. This time, though, he cares. He doesn't want anything between them, this time, not even the thinnest layer of latex, so as he digs through the drawer, it's the lube he's going for.

338

He would draw this out, if he could. Hell, he wants to do so many things to Evan right now, but it's as though his body was screaming at him not to, screaming at him to just go for it. And Evan doesn't seem to mind at all, at least not judging from the way he groans loudly, as Seb pushes a slick finger inside him, hands scrabbling for purchase all over the sheets as well as Seb's body.

"Oh, shit," Evan murmurs, breath hot against Seb's neck. "God, I missed you."

Seb wants to say it back—mostly because he feels the same way so strongly that it's almost painful—but Evan barely gives him a chance to say anything. Instead, he just reclaims his mouth, biting his lip and pushing in his tongue, eager and possessive, making Seb ache with restrained release, as he adds another finger. And the way Evan tenses and arches up against him, is almost enough to make him come, right there. Almost.

"Do it," Evan suddenly breathes, and Seb's eyes fly open at the sheer intensity of his plea. "Now."

Seb swallows dryly.

"Evan—"

"Just fuck me, Seb." Evan pulls him closer, his grip digging into Seb's dark hair, hips arching for more proximity, moving against the pressure of Seb's fingers. "I want to forget about everything but you."

Seb is stunned for a moment. Evan doesn't usually talk like that. Hell, he isn't even usually the one in a position *to say* something like that, and it's simply unusual. Unusual, surprising, and different.

And it makes Seb more turned on than he can remember being in a very long time.

Seb would have maybe preferred to keep going a little bit longer, stretching and scissoring with his fingers; even though he can hardly wait, he doesn't want to risk hurting Evan. But the way Evan practically begs him to move things along, and the way he's practically squirming underneath him, seemingly going crazy from Seb's touch, makes it very difficult to wait. So Seb doesn't.

Just prepping himself with lube is bad enough, the slick sensation so good he has to close his eyes. He has no idea how he's going to last more than a second, at this point.

"Come on, Seb," Evan breathes, skimming his hands all over Seb's skin, as though unable to decide where to apply their pressure, and Seb takes a deep breath. He can barely take it when Evan sounds like that, so desperate and hot and completely wrecked. "Come on, I need you."

Pushing in is effortless. It's hot and tight, but the lube and preparation make it easier, and Seb lets out a loud groan, as he bottoms out.

And Evan is already a mess beneath him, arching his hips and opening his mouth in long, deep moan that sounds like he's balancing somewhere between pleasure and pain. Seb stills for a moment, about to ask if he's okay, but Evan doesn't let him. Instead, he surprises Seb by pulling him closer, fingers digging into his hair, crushing his mouth against his own and using his other hand to press Seb's hips downward, more roughly and with more force than Seb anticipated.

Not that he minds, at all.

Seb had no idea that it could be this good, that it could feel so new and intense, even though they have done this so many times before. He had no idea that it could feel so downright *perfect*, Evan moaning with every thrust that Seb lays into him, gripping his shoulders so tightly it almost hurts, sliding his hands down to his ass, pushing him in even deeper, as though that were possible.

He didn't know how amazing it would feel, to have Evan here again, desperately moving against him, so perfect and gorgeous, hot skin slick with sweat.

He isn't sure how he ever would have been able to survive without this.

It isn't going to last long, though, that much he knew from the start. At this rate, he feels like they're both going to fall apart in a matter of seconds.

"Evan." He doesn't know why he says it, only that it's all he can think of, breathing it, exhaling it. "Evan."

And Evan responds by gripping him tighter, burrowing his face against his shoulder, biting out incoherent moans and sounds, until suddenly, finally, his entire body goes rigid. Seb can feel the warmth of it against his stomach, as Evan lets out a sound that Seb has never really heard him make before, and the way Evan tenses up around him is enough to make Seb shudder and groan, as he comes.

It's the most amazing thing, like the most intense shot of the most intense drug, and it takes several, long seconds, before Seb finally comes back down, shivering, collapsing against Evan's body. And neither of them moves for several more seconds, until Evan moves one hand up to pull his shaking fingers through Seb's damp hair, which is sticking to his forehead and the back of his neck.

"Fuck, that was amazing." Evan's voice sounds broken, cracked, and completely exhausted, and Seb summons the strength to actually lift his head from the crook of Evan's neck, and look at him.

"Not awesome?" he pants, and Evan quirks a smile.

"You've told me not to use that," he says, and Seb cocks his head.

"Fair enough," he says, swallowing dryly. He looks at Evan's smiling face for a moment longer, those fingers still pulling through his hair, before his exhaustion gets the better of him, and he drops his head to Evan's neck again. Evan laughs, the sound rumbling through his body, and Seb closes his eyes.

"But if it helps," Evan says, "it was awesome."

He plants a soft kiss against Seb's hair.

"Just like you."

Seb means to exhale, but it comes out so heavily that it turns into a groan, and he lazily kisses Evan's throat. It's the only spot he can reach without moving, and he feels like he doesn't want to move for weeks.

"God, you're adorable," Evan says, laughing, and Seb groans on purpose, this time.

"Am not," he murmurs, muffled against Evan's neck.

"Yes, you are." Evan nudges him slightly, so that Seb actually lifts his head up again, and Evan takes his face in his hands. He pushes Seb's hair back from his forehead, and Seb closes his eyes for a moment; the gesture feels so safe and so familiar that it feels like he might cry.

"And you're beautiful," Evan says. Seb opens his eyes again. Evan's green ones are looking back at him, utter devotion and adoration in their expression. "And amazing."

He kisses him softly, leaning their foreheads together.

"And so much better than I deserve."

342

Seb exhales slowly, closing his eyes. He moves one hand up so he can touch Evan's face, feeling that familiar stubble beneath his fingertips.

"Just stay," he says, his voice just above a whisper. And Evan kisses his forehead, as Seb puts his head down against his shoulder, and his voice is soft, when he replies.

"Always."

CHAPTER 21
COFFEE

Waking up with Evan by his side is something Seb was honestly afraid he would never get to experience again, and it's simply glorious. That being said, his utter joy at feeling his boyfriend's warm shape against his skin only manages to hold off his worries for about a minute.

They still have a lot to talk about, after all.

Evan is still sleeping, apparently, at least judging from the heavy breathing that borders on snoring, and Seb smiles a bit, as he hears it. Evan doesn't usually snore, but it is, weirdly, something that Seb suddenly appreciates. It means that Evan is really here, in their shared bed, and he is cuddled up against Seb so close that it makes a warm feeling settle somewhere in Seb's stomach.

God, he missed him.

It's with some reluctance that Seb slowly slides out of bed, eyes on Evan, as he does. Evan doesn't wake up, but absently gropes at the sheets as Seb's warm body disappears, seemingly uncomfortable at the sudden absence of it. But he stays asleep, and Seb backs away from the bed.

He's still naked, but doesn't really think about it, as he makes his way out of the bedroom and into the hallway outside. The first thing he spots there is Evan's button-up shirt, rumpled on the floor, only a few feet away from the boots that were discarded somewhere along the way. Seb can't help but smile, and he picks up the shirt. It's still wet, damp from the heavy rain, and he brings it with him as he goes into the bathroom. There, he hangs it over the bar on the wall which is normally for towels, and turns on the shower.

Seb takes his time in the shower, still half-asleep, and he has no idea how long he has been in there by the time he's done. It feels good, though, and he relishes the feeling of soft cotton against his skin, as he wraps a towel around him. He feels warm and soft and clean, and so relaxed, it's ridiculous. He hasn't felt this good in days.

The bathroom door is ajar—neither he nor Evan really have a habit of closing it properly while showering, seeing as how they don't really have any boundaries, living together, and all—and as soon as Seb pushes it open, he feels himself perk up. There is the distinct smell of coffee in the air, and he keeps the towel wrapped around his hips as he pads out into the kitchen. The sight that meets him is enough to make his chest somehow feel like it's bursting with joy, for a moment.

"Hey," Evan says, as he spots him, and smiles. There is something tentative about his smile, though, as though unsure whether or not Seb is happy with him.

But Seb smiles back, and makes his way over to him.

"Good morning," he says, and dares to lean in and kiss his boyfriend on the mouth. And Evan doesn't flinch, not the slightest bit. Instead, he leans into the kiss, and it makes Seb feel oddly relieved.

Evan's slightly tentative look dissipates as they pull apart, but it's still there, and Seb just looks at him.

"Uh, I made coffee," Evan says after a moment, seemingly fumbling slightly, as he looks over at the coffee maker. And Seb can't help but smile a little, amused.

"Thanks," he says, reaching for the cupboard where they keep the mugs, but Evan stops him.

"I got it," he says. "You, sit."

Seb frowns, but doesn't argue. It isn't really like Evan to be so bossy, but he seems to really want to do something nice for Seb, so Seb lets him. And he doesn't mention it, as he makes his way over to the kitchen table. He has just sat down, when Evan makes a humming noise, looking at the cupboard's contents, as he opens it.

"What?" Seb says, and Evan frowns.

"Are we missing some glasses?" he says, as though hesitant, like it might be a stupid question, and Seb frowns for a moment, before he remembers.

"Uh, yeah," he says, a bit sheepishly. "Two, actually. I may have thrown them into a wall."

Evan looks over at him, puzzled and surprised, and Seb cocks his eyebrows, along with a small, half-shrug. He isn't exactly proud of that, the rage-fit he had the other night, and he had almost managed to forget about it.

"You, what?" Evan asks, and Seb sighs.

"After you left," he explains. "I may have... *overreacted* a bit."

He doesn't need to explain further. It takes only a second, before Evan's face falls, and he glances down at the counter. He looks downright ashamed, but he doesn't say anything. Seb doesn't blame him.

Neither of them speaks, as Evan pours two cups of coffee, adding a nice helping of sugar to his own and adding nothing to Seb's; he prefers his coffee black, anyway.

"Here you go," Evan says, sounding slightly subdued, as he hands Seb his mug, and Seb takes it, resisting the urge to wrap his hands around it. It's too hot, so he sets it down on the table in front of him, instead. And Evan sits down across from him, and several seconds of silence follow.

Seb absently glances at the clock above the door, and is a bit startled to see that it's just past nine o'clock. He can't help but wonder how early then, exactly, he woke up, seeing as how he spent quite a while in the shower.

And more to the point, why is Evan up already? It isn't like him, and he usually stays in bed, even if Seb gets up early, on a day off.

Seb blows on his coffee, in lack of anything else, feeling oddly exposed where he sits. He's wearing nothing but a towel, after all, and he can feel Evan's eyes on him, so he looks up. Sure enough, there are those green eyes, practically staring, before they look down at the table, as though Evan is actually afraid of looking for too long. It's almost as though he doesn't want to take any liberties, like he isn't sure what or how much he is allowed to do, after how he has been acting this past week.

It makes Seb feel vindicated and sad, at the same time.

"So," Seb finally says, and he swears Evan almost flinches at the sudden breaking of silence. "I guess we should... talk about this. Or something."

Evan clears his throat slightly and looks up. Those eyes look oddly lost, like they sometimes do, like he honestly isn't sure what to do or say.

"Yeah," he says. "I guess we should."

More silence. It drags on for another few seconds, before Seb decides to finally say something. Something he has honestly been thinking about since he woke up.

"I wish we didn't have to," he says, glancing down at his coffee. "I wish it was all fine, but..."

He sighs heavily, scratching the back of his head, pulling through the shower-wet, messed up hair.

"I mean, I'm glad you came home," he says. "Really glad, you have no idea."

Seb is half-surprised at the sheer emotion in his words, but it seems appropriate; he means them, with every fiber of his being.

"But everything's not fine." He looks up at Evan, wondering vaguely if he looks as sad as he thinks he does. "There's still a lot of shit to work through. And some long overdue, mind-blowing sex isn't gonna change that."

He adds that last part with the slightest hint of joking sarcasm, and Evan quirks a small smile, before relaxing his face again. He looks tense, sad and just slightly anxious, all at once.

"I know," he says, sounding subdued. "Wasn't expecting it to."

He sighs heavily, looking down at his own coffee mug.

"I just don't really know where to start," he admits. "I mean, I know I've been a dick. I know that."

He keeps his eyes on the coffee mug, while Seb cups his own with both hands, waiting.

"I just don't know what to say." Evan's voice is low, and sounds unusually soft.

Seb chews his lip, watching his boyfriend for a few moments.

"How about starting at the beginning," he suggests, and Evan looks up, that tentative look back on his face. "Just tell me what happened."

Evan seems to consider this, for several seconds, in fact, before he takes a breath.

"Okay," he says, looking back down at his coffee mug. "Well, you know how it started. My dad called, and we talked for a little bit. He asked about life, school, the usual. And then, I thought about what you said. About telling him. Just, you know, saying it."

He runs his fingers along the mug's handle, and Seb waits. Then, Evan sighs.

"It didn't go well," he says. "I just figured, fuck it, and I said that there actually was something going on, something I hadn't told him about. He seemed fine, at first. And I asked him if he remembered you, back when he helped Jake and Sophie move, and we came over."

Evan lets out a short, humorless laugh, along with a small, equally humorless smile.

"He did remember you," he says. "*The rude one.*"

Seb bites back the urge to point out that Peter Matthews was the *rude one*, whereas Seb actually didn't even say a word. He knows that Evan is fully aware of that, hence the bitter laugh.

"And I just told him," Evan says, still looking at his coffee mug. Seb suspects that the coffee must have gone a bit cold, by now. "I told him that yeah, that's the one. And he's my boyfriend."

It's silent for a few moments, and then, Evan lets out another, humorless laugh.

"I don't think he saw that coming," he says, absently rubbing the back of his neck with his hand. "I think he expected me to have knocked up some girl, or something. Actually, I think he would have preferred that."

Seb doesn't say anything.

"Anyway," Evan says, exhaling, as though pulling himself together. "He got pissed, obviously. He asked if I was joking, at first, and when I made it clear that I wasn't, he wanted to know how long it had been going on. I told him it had been about a year, and he freaked out, even more. It was kind of like he had been hoping it was just some phase, or something, but that possibility backfired then, I guess. And then I told him we were living together, and shit really hit the fan."

Evan looks up at Seb, looking tired, rather than sad.

"He said he didn't raise me to be a faggot," he says, sounding subdued. "I tried pointing out to him that I still like chicks too, but that didn't seem to matter."

He adds that last part with a different air, as though trying to lighten the mood a bit, and Seb offers him a small smile of support, before Evan continues.

"So he yelled," he says. "And I yelled. I mean, I hadn't expected him to take it well, but he was even more pissed about it than I'd thought he would be. And a whole bunch of shit was said there, in between, but in the end, he basically told me not to talk to him again, until I 'had that guy's dick out of my ass'."

Seb nearly winces, and Evan gives him a sympathetic look.

"His words," he says. "Not mine."

Seb doesn't respond. He doesn't really know what to say. And knowing that Evan's father actually said that to him, doesn't exactly make him feel better.

"So," Evan says with a heavy sigh, as though somehow relieved at getting this off his chest. "That's how it went down. He hung up on me, and... it pretty much went to shit, from there. And I didn't exactly handle it well, as you well know."

He sounds downright ashamed, at that last part, and the past few days don't exactly need repeating; they were both there for it, they know what happened.

"I should have been there." Seb nearly murmurs the words, suddenly realizing how awful he actually feels about it. But Evan just shakes his head, looking somehow desperate for Seb not to think that.

"No," he says, and he looks like wants to reach across the table and take Seb's hand, but decides against it; he still isn't sure about the boundaries. "No, don't say that."

He sounds sad, sad that Seb would somehow put this on himself.

"No, you shouldn't have had to do that alone," Seb insists, suddenly angry with himself, shaking his head. "I should have been there."

"Seb." Evan says the name softly, looking oddly sad. "It was my thing. And don't get me wrong, I wanted to call you, right after, but I knew you were busy. And I didn't want to put that on you."

Seb frowns.

"Well, you should have called anyway," he says.

"Seb, it was my problem," Evan insists, trying to sound caring, despite the harsh words. "It wasn't your business."

"Of course, it was my business!" Seb actually raises his voice a bit, to both his and Evan's surprise. "It *is* my fucking business!"

Somewhat stunned silence follows his little outburst, and Seb takes a deep, slow breath.

"I get that you didn't talk to me," he says, voice much softer than before. "I get that you didn't want to put that on me, and I get that you just wanted to protect me."

He sighs heavily.

"But it's not just *your* business, anymore," he says. "It's not *your* problem. There's no such thing."

Seb looks down at the table, and with a kind of hesitation he hasn't felt in a very long time, especially considering Evan, he moves his hand across the surface. Carefully, he reaches for Evan's hand, and to his immensely surprised relief, Evan doesn't hesitate, as he takes it. When Seb looks up at him, there is such soft relief on his face, a lot like gratitude, and Seb absently smoothes over the back of Evan's hand with his thumb, out of habit.

"It's you and me," he says. "Just us. And that means that if there's a problem, it's *our* problem. Okay?"

Evan swallows, and he nods. Then, he just looks at Seb for a few seconds, before chuckling softly.

"That's what Jake said," he says, with a tone that suggests he's fully aware of the eye-roll inducing effect it will have on Seb. And sure enough, Seb does roll his eyes, albeit with a small smile on his face.

"Oh, joy," he says. "I guess we've finally learned something from them, huh?"

Evan smiles, chuckling, and Seb can't help but smile back.

Sure, Jake and Sophie have by no means the perfect relationship—no one does. But they seem to have a hell of a lot better understanding of the whole thing, than Seb and Evan do.

"I went there," Evan says after a few seconds, his look a bit serious, again. "After I left, the other night."

Seb nods.

"I figured as much," he says, and Evan doesn't look the slightest bit surprised that he reached that conclusion.

"He tore me a new one," Evan says, eyebrows slightly raised, as though reluctantly impressed with his little brother's conviction. "Even Sophie was mad. She mostly stayed out of it, though. But they let me spend the night, mostly because I wouldn't leave, and then they basically ordered me out of the apartment, yesterday."

Evan smiles ruefully.

"They told me that I was welcome there whenever," he says, "but that I really had to deal with this. That you and me had to 'stow our crap' and talk about it."

Seb can't help but smile, and Evan visibly relaxes.

"So, I went for a walk," he says. "Lost track of time, but it was light out, when I left. And then it started raining, and... Well, you know the rest."

He gives Seb a pointed look that's just the slightest bit suggestive, and in the midst of all the emotional talk and confessions, Seb can't help but think of last night.

Shit, that was amazing. He honestly can't remember the last time they went at it like that, so desperately and with such urgency. Evan practically begged for it.

Screw "practically", Seb thinks. He *did* beg for it, begged Seb to just take him, to fuck him right then and there. And Seb did. And it was mind-blowing.

He swallows hard.

Evan is more observant than one might think, and Seb is only half-surprised when he raises his eyebrows slightly at him.

"What are you thinking about?" he asks, in a way that loudly says he knows full well what Seb is most likely thinking about.

But Seb isn't having it, not right now. It's still early in the morning, and he's wearing only a *towel*, for god's sake.

"I'm thinking," he says, pointedly pushing out his chair, "that I should probably put some pants on."

He gets up from the table, ignoring his untouched coffee. Evan immediately notices this, and Seb knows he's screwed. If Seb is ignoring his morning coffee, he's clearly desperate to leave.

Evan eyes him up and down, as he stands, from the edge of the white, fluffy towel, wrapped around his hips, up along his bare stomach and chest, up to the messy, towel-dried hair, where his gaze lingers. And Seb tenses up a bit, because he recognizes that look that's suddenly in Evan's eyes. He recognizes it, and he knows it's capable of making him beg on his knees, if Evan asks him to.

But Seb decides not to give in, not right now. For some reason, sex, and anything in that vicinity, feels somehow inappropriate after the conversation they just had. But then again, the atmosphere is fine now, clear and relaxed, any ounce of tension dissipated. So maybe it's pride that makes Seb resist.

Either way, he feels very exposed, wearing only a towel. A towel that isn't even secured, and could be pulled off with just the slightest little tug.

"Seems unnecessary," Evan says, not releasing Seb's hand. "Pants, I mean."

He eyes Seb up and down again, as Seb moves to stand beside the table.

"Yeah, you would think that," Seb retorts, and Evan smiles slowly. It's an approving smile, one he sometimes has when Seb is acting snarky. Seb will never quite be able to understand how that aspect of his personality can be so appealing to Evan, to the man he loved.

They just look at each other, but then, Evan half-surprises Seb by slowly getting out of his chair. He still hasn't let go of Seb's hand, and for a few seconds, they just stand there, close together, eyes locked. Evan still has that look in his eyes, and Seb actually shivers.

Then, when Evan kisses him, he feels his skin practically catch fire.

It isn't a soft kiss, but it's slow, and the way Evan's tongue pushes into Seb's mouth and simply claims it, is enough to make Seb's knees go weak. He's barely aware of Evan moving his free hand to his waist, the other hand still grasping Seb's, and it's only when Seb feels the edge of the kitchen counter lightly bump into his lower back, that he notices that they have actually moved.

"You're not wearing anything under here," Evan murmurs against his lips, his hand smoothing down over the towel, "are you?"

Seb swallows hard, trying to focus.

"Very observant of you," he says, his words only a breath. Damn it, he's so turned on right now, it's ridiculous. And Evan moving his hand down to his crotch isn't exactly helping.

Evan smiles against his mouth, moving in closer and pressing himself against Seb's body. He's fully dressed, wearing sweatpants and a t-shirt, and it makes Seb feel even more exposed, in contrast.

"Can't help it," Evan murmurs. "It's hard to miss."

Seb lets out something like a low moan, as Evan slips his hand underneath the towel, smoothing up along the bare skin of Seb's thigh. It's close to embarrassing, but Seb is already hard, unexpectedly so, and Evan has definitely noticed.

"You know," Evan murmurs, and Seb closes his eyes, as Evan's mouth ends up somewhere by his ear. "I can't stop thinking about last night."

He kisses Seb's throat, slowly, and Seb shivers.

"You felt so good, baby," Evan continues, voice low and husky. "So good."

Seb can practically feel his heartbeat pounding in his ears—and in other, certain parts of his body—and he absently grabs Evan's t-shirt, gripping it tight. Evan is hard too, he can feel it, can feel it through the layers of cotton that make up the towel and those sweatpants, and he suddenly, desperately, wants them gone.

As though Evan can read his mind, he tugs at the towel, just enough to make it come undone and fall to the kitchen floor. Seb barely notices. Instead, all he notices is Evan's mouth, as it moves together with his, that tongue, as it smoothes along his bottom lip, before sliding into his mouth.

Seb barely has time to react, before Evan slowly pulls away and moves downward, and he has just barely opened his eyes, before he feels Evan suddenly swallow him down.

Seb gasps, and looks down. Evan is on his knees, one hand smoothing over the bare skin of Seb's thighs and stomach and hip bones, while he uses his mouth to make Seb moan and pant and make all kinds of embarrassing sounds.

Seb is vaguely aware, and equally surprised, to find that Evan is still holding his hand. He still hasn't let go, and somehow, Seb likes that. It feels like some kind of anchor, like some out of place, but simultaneously completely perfect thing to do.

It doesn't take long before Seb is moaning loudly, his free hand pulling fingers through Evan's hair, before he reluctantly moves it to the counter's edge, behind him. He can barely stand, at this point, and he needs the support, so he opts for slightly thrusting his hips forward, instead, just enough for Evan to take the hint and keep going with a whole new fervor.

When Seb comes, it's with a shudder that leaves him feeling nearly paralyzed, and he has to physically, very consciously, keep himself from falling over.

Evan is there in a matter of seconds, though, standing up and practically catching him in his arms. He chuckles lightly, as Seb struggles to open his eyes.

"You okay, babe?" he asks, and Seb swallows dryly.

"I hate you," he musters, and Evan smiles as he plants a kiss on his mouth, a kiss that Seb reciprocates without question.

"Well," Evan says, sounding just slightly amused, and he squeezes Seb's hand, which he is still holding in his own. "We're gonna have to work on that, aren't we?"

CHAPTER 22

MOVE

Seb isn't entirely sure what it is, but somehow, he and Evan always seem to find their way back to each other. Despite their fights never really being earth-shatteringly big, it always catches him slightly by surprise, in some weird way, whenever they manage to get over their differences and make up.

This latest fight was pretty huge, though, and Seb really thought that it would be the end. He felt as though it was something that neither of them would ever be able to make it through, despite how much they loved each other.

He has never been happier to be wrong.

Things slowly go back to normal, after Evan's return, as though both of them decided that dwelling on the whole thing was pointless. Instead, they appreciate the fact that they actually talked about it, sorted it out, and effectively chose each other over all the bullshit. And it feels good. It feels safe, and Seb has never really felt so sure and secure about the whole relationship, before. He has always been happy with Evan, but this is different. This is strong, final.

Jake and Sophie seem happy about the whole thing, too (no surprise, there), and Evan actually even relents and lets Seb invite them over for dinner. It's not like they have never been at their place before, but an actual, proper dinner is something that hasn't been done yet. Sophie calls it a double-date, but mostly to tease Evan, who seems to find the whole thing cheesy and unbearably cozy, much to Seb's amusement.

It's all in good fun, though, and Evan even cooks that night, pulling off one of his somewhat surprising, culinary miracles.

"So, what's the plan?" Evan asks, as they all sit at Seb's and Evan's kitchen table. "After graduation."

Sophie is graduating soon, although Jake still has a while left to go with his studies, and Sophie seems to mull over the question, as she sips some red wine from her glass. Seb and Evan never really drink red wine, or wine at all, for that matter, but Sophie and Jake brought some, for the occasion. Seb is vaguely reminded of their housewarming, when Evan brought a six pack, and Seb offered to get the two of them a man-sized cactus.

"Well," Sophie says, swirling the wine around in her glass a bit. "I've got an offer from a free clinic. It doesn't pay that much, but it's for a good cause."

"What," Evan says, raising his eyebrows teasingly, "and leave Jake to fend for himself? Poor guy can barely keep it together, as it is."

Jake glares at him, but with a small smile creeping into his expression.

"Gee, thanks, Evan," he says, eyes narrowed. "That means a lot."

Evan just laughs at him, taking a drink from his own wine glass, a sight that looks somehow odd and simultaneously natural, and Seb can't help but roll his eyes a bit.

"Would you stop it?" Sophie laughs, shoving Jake playfully, as he sits right next to her. "Both of you. I know that a small paycheck isn't exactly ideal, but I'm not exactly becoming a nurse to get rich, either. I want to help people."

"An admirable cause," Evan says in mock, formal seriousness, while raising his glass in a small toast. "Who needs money, anyway?"

Sophie just glares at him affectionately, and Evan winks at her, before taking another sip of wine.

"You're gonna do great," Jake says to his girlfriend, giving her a light kiss. "I know it."

Sophie doesn't reply, simply smiles at him, and Seb can't help but smile, as he sees it. He likes this, likes having them all together, having dinner and talking about completely ordinary, non-heavy things. It feels good, and he discreetly reaches under the table to place his hand on Evan's leg, rubbing his thumb gently against the rough fabric of his jeans. And Evan turns to him, giving him that small, Seb-reserved smile, while covering Seb's hand with his own and lacing their fingers together. And for a night, everything is perfect.

♦

Weeks go by, filled with studies and school, Evan still working part-time at that pub. Seb ends up getting a part-time job at the same place, when someone else quits, which although lands him mostly with shifts that don't coincide with Evan's. They would both leap at the opportunity to get to actually work at the same time, which is both good and bad.

It's undoubtedly more fun, but it also kind of slows down their productivity, sometimes. One night, when both of them are working, Evan spends most of his time blatantly flirting with Seb, winking and smiling at him, leaning in and so-not-at-all-accidentally brushing his lips against his jaw, letting his hand slide down over Seb's ass, whispering things in his ear so discreetly that no one else notices.

It drives Seb completely crazy, and eventually, they end up in the men's room, door locked and hands all over each other. Evan gets Seb off right then and there, with Seb simultaneously returning the favor, their mouths fused together as they touch, to keep them both from moaning too loudly.

It's so wildly, insanely hot, and nearly costs Evan his job. Not that either of them seems to care.

Evan gets a few more gigs, albeit very small ones, gradually building a rather local fan base. And Seb is there, every time, along with Jake and Sophie, who show up to support Evan as often as they can.

Neither Seb nor Evan have brought up Evan's father again. Seb carefully asked Jake about it, and he sadly admitted that their father has talked to him, making it clear how he doesn't want to speak to Evan, anymore. And Jake stood up for his brother, causing a bit of a rift between him and their father. But Peter Matthews seems to have a soft spot for his youngest son; he's still talking to Jake, even if he won't talk to Evan. And Evan doesn't seem to want to talk to him, anyway. So Seb, along with Jake, feels it might be best to just leave it alone, at least for the foreseeable future.

It's almost two months after the big fight, almost two months since their relationship seemed to reach a new level, somehow, that Seb and Evan are just enjoying a night in. It's not like they rarely do this, but especially after the past couple of weeks, with an extra heavy workload from school, and both of them still working part-time at the pub, this is a welcome break.

They're sitting on the couch in the living room, half-empty paper containers of Chinese takeout on the table, and Seb is drowsing to the sounds of *Die Hard*, playing on the TV. He sighs tiredly and leans his head against Evan's shoulder, almost snuggling up against him, and Evan chuckles.

"What?" he says. "John McClane not doing it for you?"

Seb hums in thought.

"Oh, no," he assures him drowsily, closing his eyes and moving Evan's arm so that it rests over his shoulders. "He's a real stud. A beefcake."

Evan laughs, louder this time.

"Beefcake?" he says doubtfully, and Seb hums in confirmation.

"Yeah," he says, feeling himself starting to drift off. "Watch out for that competition."

Evan just chuckles softly, planting a soft kiss in Seb's hair.

"I will," he says. "Can't have you running off with him, now can I?"

"I might," Seb murmured. "Won't make any promises."

He inhales the wonderful scent of Evan—laundry detergent, warmth, faded leather—and he feels Evan's arm tighten around him slightly. For several seconds, neither of them speaks.

Seb has almost fallen asleep, by the time Evan says anything.

"Marry me," he says, and Seb makes a small, tired noise of confirmation.

"Sure thing," he says, eyes still closed. "After the movie."

He expects Evan to chuckle, to reply, anything. But he doesn't make a sound, and Seb slowly opens his eyes. Evan is looking straight ahead, at the TV, and he looks strangely tense, jaw working.

"Evan?" Seb says, quickly waking up, and Evan turns to him. Seb lifts his head properly from his shoulder, so that they can see each other's eyes.

"Marry me," Evan says again. He looks somehow terrified and determined, at the same time. Seb just stares at him.

"You serious?" he finally says, his tone more disbelieving than he intended, and Evan just keeps his eyes on him. He doesn't answer, but his silence is answer enough.

And Seb's throat suddenly goes dry.

"Are you proposing to me?" he asks, his voice oddly weak and unsure, reflecting the awkwardness he suddenly feels.

"Yes, I am." Evan's voice is, by contrast, completely certain, albeit scared. "I'm proposing to you."

Seb just keeps staring at him, his mind completely blank.

Then his defense mechanism kicks in.

"In front of Chinese takeout and *Die Hard*," he says lightly, some sarcasm in his voice. "Quite the romantic, aren't you?"

But then Evan shakes his head.

"No," he says, his tone completely serious. "No, just..."

He looks at Seb, exhales slowly.

"Just for once, Seb," he says. "Just for once. No sarcasm, no smart-ass comments. No bullshit."

He keeps his gaze on Seb's blue eyes, unwavering.

"No dodging," he says. "Just give me a straight answer."

Seb inhales slowly, steadily.

"Evan—"

"How about I phrase it as a question," Evan says. "Will you marry me?"

Seb swallows hard.

"Evan, you can't just—

"Can't what?" Evan just looks at him, the fear still in his eyes, but dissipating slightly. "I want to marry you. So I figured I should just ask."

Seb just looks at him. And for several, long seconds, neither of them says a word.

Then, when Seb finally speaks, it's with weak, wavering uncertainty.

"Evan, you don't want to marry me," he says, shaking his head. He's surprised at how sad he sounds. "No one in their right mind would want that."

"I'm pretty sure I do."

Months ago, Evan would have been exasperated and annoyed at Seb's reply, at his way of voicing his own insecurities, the ones he keeps constantly hidden beneath a hundred layers of sarcasm and cynicism. But now, Evan knows better, and he knows that there is no point in getting annoyed. He has learned that all he can do is to try and convince Seb of his feelings, instead.

And Seb, months ago, would have kept at his sarcasm and cynicism, and refused to give Evan the straight answer he was asking for, too stuck in his own patterns. But now, he has learned that there's no point with Evan, because he will just keep prodding, until Seb finally gives in and drops his defenses. So all Seb can do is to just skip past all that and answer properly and honestly, right away. Even if it isn't the answer Evan wants.

"Why?" Seb finally asks, after several seconds of silence. He's honestly confused.

Being in a relationship is one thing, hell, even living together is. But getting married... That's permanent—at least *semi*-permanent. And even though Seb doesn't doubt for a second that he wants that, he is, as usual, scared that Evan doesn't. Not really.

"That's a stupid-ass question," Evan says flatly. "And you know that."

Seb glances down at the gray fabric of the couch. Evan sighs quietly.

"I love you, you idiot," he says, some of that gruffness seeping into his voice, the kind he unconsciously uses when he's feeling uncomfortable, especially concerning feelings and such. "And when you love someone, you want to spend your life with them. As least, as far as I can tell. And after everything that's happened... I just know."

Seb looks up at him again, then. Evan looks as uncomfortable as he sounds, and Seb is reminded of that first conversation they had about this thing, the way they felt about each other, so long ago, now. When Seb confronted Evan in his dorm room, and Evan just stood there, fumbling, trying to get the words out and explain how he felt and why he had been such an ass about it.

Evan has come a long way since then, but conversations like that still make him uncomfortable, and this is clearly bordering on too emotional.

So right now, Seb is just sitting there, pretty much shocked into silence.

Evan is proposing to him. Just like that. And Seb doesn't know what to say.

"Don't leave me hanging here, man," Evan says after several seconds of silence.

The movie is still on in the background, the sound of gunshots and shouting breaking the silence at a rather low volume. Seb barely notices. He's too focused on Evan, on the way his eyes are starting to look scared again.

Seb swallows.

"I know that," he says tentatively. "I know you love me. And I love you, too."

Just saying those words is somehow more difficult than it should have been, considering how they are so completely and utterly true.

"Then, what's the problem?" Evan says.

"It's pretty permanent," Seb replies, a trace of something like sarcasm seeping back into his voice; he can't help it. "You won't be able to get out of it so easily."

"I don't want to get out of it." Both Evan's tone and expression are completely certain, as he shakes his head the slightest bit. "Why, do you?"

Seb actually widens his eyes a bit then, shocked and terrified that Evan might actually think that, even for a second.

"No," he says, shaking his head. For once, he sounds just as certain as Evan. "Never."

Evan cocks his head.

"Then, marry me," he says. He looks a bit cocky now, almost, like his old self. But Seb can still see some insecurity there, underneath it, as Evan waits for an answer.

And Seb waits. He isn't hesitating; he knew what his answer was the moment Evan asked, even before he knew it was an actual, serious proposal. He knows, and he is sure. But he still waits, as though giving Evan a chance to get out of it.

But he won't try to get out of it. He wants it. And deep down, Seb knows that, too.

"Okay," Seb says, his voice rather low. Evan raises his eyebrows a bit.

"Okay?" he asks, and Seb gives a small nod.

"Yeah," he says, but Evan just keeps looking at him. And finally, Seb sighs and glances away.

"Fine," he says, giving in. "Yes."

"Yes, what?"

Seb sighs again, not looking at Evan.

"Yes, I'll marry you."

He looks back at Evan then, slowly, as though waiting for a reaction. And when he catches Evan's eye, that beautiful, hard mouth smiles.

"You don't sound very convincing," Evan says, cocking his eyebrows, and Seb actually rolls his eyes.

"Why must you do this to me?" he says, his voice low, a smile slowly shaping his lips.

"Do what?" Evan asks, but the smile on his face takes any ounce of seriousness out of the question.

"You can't propose to me," Seb says, stuttering just the tiniest bit on the word *propose*, making Evan's smile widen, "and then be a dick about it. I said yes, didn't I?"

"Did you?" Evan says, leaning in slightly.

"Yes, I did," Seb says stubbornly; he refuses to play along. But the way Evan eyes him up and down and watches his face makes him all warm inside, and it's kind of hard not to.

"You sure?" Evan says, his voice lower, and Seb smiles a bit as Evan's face comes even closer to his.

"Yes," he says, the tone of his voice matching Evan's.

"Didn't quite catch that." Evan's lips are just barely brushing against Seb's, and Seb swallows dryly.

"Yes." It's nearly a whisper, this time, and he feels Evan smile against his lips.

"So you'll marry me?" he says, and Seb exhales.

"Yes."

Evan's lips are on his then, soft and urgent, all at once, and Seb closes his eyes.

If there is one thing he feels like he will never, *ever* get tired of, it's kissing Evan. And it doesn't take long before he's leaning into him, gripping his hair with his fingers, pushing his tongue into his mouth, Evan's fingers tracing his skin. Seb's head is suddenly spinning, his entire body buzzing with excitement and pure joy.

"Yes," he murmurs absently against those wonderful lips, pulling Evan closer and never wanting to let him go, ever again.

"Yes."

CHAPTER 23
AFTERMATH

"You're *what?*"

Jake looks positively shocked, while Sophie just stands there, slowly letting her mouth fall open in surprise. Seb can't help but fidget slightly, suddenly feeling very awkward about the whole thing.

"We're getting married," Evan repeats, clearly half-amused and half-uncomfortable about the reactions from Jake and his girlfriend, at the news. "As in, we're engaged."

Jake just blinks at him, eyes wide, while Sophie reanimates and tries to form words.

"Wow," she says slowly. "That's— *Wow.*"

Her face suddenly breaks out in a smile, then, and she launches herself at Evan, giving him a hug.

"That's amazing!" she says. "Congratulations!"

"Thanks, Sophie," Evan says with a smile, reciprocating the hug, tightly. "Nice that someone's happy for us, at least."

Jake's surprised expression morphs into a bitchface, then, and he gives his brother a look.

"I *am* happy for you," he says, a bit defensively. "I'm just... *surprised*, that's all."

Seb can't help but smile as Sophie turns to hug him, too, and when they pull apart, she just beams at him.

"Tell me everything," she says. "Details. How did this happen?"

Seb gestures vaguely at Evan.

"Well," he says, "Evan proposed, and—"

"Wait, wait, wait," Jake interrupts, holding up his hand, a grin on his face. "You're saying that my *brother*, no-chick-flicks Evan Matthews, proposed to you?"

Evan glares at him, but Seb cocks his head with a small smile, unable to resist teasing Evan.

"That's what I'm saying," he says, and Jake suddenly just bursts out laughing.

"Oh, man," Jake laughs. "That is *priceless*!"

"Yeah, alright, we get it." Evan sounds annoyed and a bit embarrassed, at the same time. "It's hilarious. Can we move on, please?"

"Sorry, that's just not gonna happen anytime soon," Jake says, still laughing. "I mean, I'm happy for you guys, I really am. But come on."

He gestures with his hands, as though pointing out just how funny the whole thing is.

"It is hilarious."

Seb can't help but laugh along with Jake, just a little bit, mostly because what he's saying is completely true. When Evan glares at him, though, he squeezes his hand, before giving him a light kiss.

"Sorry," he says. "Can't help it."

"So, when's the wedding?" Sophie asks, ignoring her boyfriend's teasing reaction.

Seb pulls back a little.

"Uh," he says eloquently. "Haven't gotten quite that far, yet."

Sophie looks a bit disappointed at that.

"Well, anything?" she says hopefully. "Do you have rings? Where's the ceremony gonna be?"

Seb widens his eyes slightly, suddenly a bit intimidated by Sophie's apparent enthusiasm.

"Uh—" he says again, but this time, Jake comes to his rescue.

"How about we deal with that later," he suggests, looking at Sophie pointedly, but she just shrugs, with an innocent look on her face.

"I'm just curious," she says. "They're getting married, I'm excited."

She adds that last part with a smile, before looking at Evan.

"You *are* getting married, right?" she asks. "Not just staying engaged, for the hell of it?"

"No, we're definitely going through with it," Evan says, without an ounce of hesitation, and Seb can't help but glance at him, a sudden burst of happy, blissful warmth building in his chest. He really can't help it; he still finds it oddly surreal that Evan is actually his *fiancé*, although surreal in the very best way.

"But it's only been a few days," Evan continues, half-shrugging. "And we're not exactly rich, so a big-ass ceremony isn't really on the table."

"Not that we really want one," Seb points out, and Evan looks at him.

"Right," he says, looking back at Sophie and Jake. "We just wanna be married, really. Who gives a shit about the ceremony?"

"I kind of do," Sophie says, practically pouting, while Jake just watches the exchange, a teasing, but genuinely happy smile spreading across his face. "Weddings are always the best. And it's a great excuse to dress up and feel pretty, and there's decorations, and food..."

When her tone starts taking on a more dreamy tone, Seb raises his eyebrows a little.

"Who's getting married, here?" he asks. "Us, or you?"

Sophie makes a face, as though admitting his point, before giving her boyfriend a look just full of hints that they've had a conversation about just this, several times, already. Jake gets a look of slight terror.

"Oh, no," he says, shaking his head and holding his palms out in front of him. "Don't drag me into this. This is about them."

He gestures pointedly at Seb and Evan, and Evan cocks his head at him.

"Thanks, Jakey," he says, and Jake gives him a nod back.

"You're welcome," he says, and Sophie rolls her eyes.

"Fine," she says tiredly. "Whatever."

She gives Evan an almost stern look.

"But you'd better set a date," she says. "Or I'll have your head."

Seb pulls back a little, glancing at Evan, before glancing at Jake, who just shrugs, as if to say *isn't she adorable?*

Seb isn't entirely sure he agrees.

What they said to Jake and Sophie is true; neither Seb nor Evan want a big wedding. As Evan put it, they just want to be married, and a huge ceremony is really the last thing on their minds.

It has been about a week since Evan popped the question, and in that time, they both figured that they at least should get rings. Not that Seb really needs one to be reminded of just what kind of relationship he and Evan have just entered into; they already have a deep bond, one that Seb feels that not even marriage could cement any further. But still. The thought of actually being Evan's husband makes him smile stupidly, far more often than he would like to admit.

They are having a day off, for once. For once, there is no work, no classes, and all in that blissful, extremely rare, three-day period that comes along every now and then, where neither of them has any assignments due, or exams to study for. For once, they're actually free to just hang out together and have lazy morning sex, and sleep in until noon, without feeling the weight of responsibilities looming over them like a cloud. The only thing they can think of was the wedding, which doesn't fill either of them with an ounce of dread.

"You think we should have gone all-in?" Evan asks, as he and Seb lie together in their shared bed. Seb is still slightly exhausted from their recent activities, his whole body pleasantly sore from the treatment it just received, and he hums against Evan's skin. His head is resting against Evan's chest, and he opens his eyes, only to see Evan holding up his hand and eyeing the ring on his finger.

"What do you mean?" Seb asks.

"Well," Evan replies. "They're not very extravagant, are they?"

Seb glances at his own ring, the one secured on his left ring finger. It's dark silver, almost grey, identical to Evan's. They got them the other day, on a whim, more than anything, seeing as how they barely planned out this whole engagement-thing, to begin with.

"True," Seb admits. "But I wasn't aware that you wanted gold and diamonds and swirls."

Evan's chest vibrates slightly with laughter.

"I don't," he says. "But still. They're pretty simple."

"*We're* pretty simple," Seb says, planting a lazy kiss against Evan's chest. "In a good way. They're perfect, really."

"Yeah, they are," Evan says, and Seb can hear a smile in his voice.

By the time they actually get out of bed, it's well past noon, and they end up in the shower only minutes later, spending a much longer time in there than necessary. They skip breakfast and lunch, altogether, instead settling for eating cereal, and cuddling in front of the TV. Seb is barely even paying attention to what they're watching, but he doesn't care. He's just too happy, feeling like he will never, *ever* tire of having Evan by his side, like this.

When the doorbell suddenly rings, they both almost jump, and then they glance at each other. Seb knows there is no point, though; they have this unwritten rule that whoever is closest to the door has to get it. And at the moment, Seb is a few inches closer, making Evan raise his eyebrows at him pointedly, and Seb glares back, before rising from the couch, with a huff.

"Please, don't get up," he says sarcastically, shuffling over toward the hall. "I got it."

"Love you," Evan calls, and Seb just grumbles in reply. He's just glad he's actually wearing clothes, having decided to put on a pair of sweatpants and an old, worn-out *Motörhead* t-shirt that belongs to Evan.

The doorbell doesn't ring again, allowing Seb to reach it, and he yawns lazily, as he opens the door.

The first thing he notices is the bright red hair, before his attention is drawn to the slightly stunned expression, and those slightly widened eyes, currently framed by rectangular, black-rimmed glassed. The girl doesn't say anything, just looks at him, and Seb blinks.

"Hi," Seb finally says, just a little bit hesitantly, and the girl smiles.

"Hi," she says, actually giving him a small wave, as though they're already the best of friends. "You must be Sebastian."

Seb can't help but frown incredulously, in a way that he knows Evan tends to find very amusing. And this girl finds it amusing too, apparently, because her smile widens when she sees his expression.

"Yeah," she says, nodding to herself. "You're definitely Sebastian."

She frowns then, eyeing him up and down, before raising her eyebrows and making a face, actually looking kind of impressed.

"And I must say," she says, "Evan did good."

Seb opens his mouth to say something then, trying to gather his thoughts and handle this whole situation, but doesn't have the chance to speak, before he's interrupted.

"Dana?" Evan's voice carries into the hall from the living room, and Seb feels his expression change into incredulous, confused surprise.

Evan hurries out of through kitchen and steps into the hall, and as soon as he sees the girl in the doorway, his face breaks into a huge grin.

"Holy shit," he says, immediately lunging forward and throwing his arms around her. And the girl just laughs and hugged him back tightly, before they pull apart.

"What the hell are you doing here?" Evan asks, blatant, happy surprise on his face. The girl raises her eyebrows at him.

"Excuse you," she says, punching him lightly in the shoulder. "You're getting *married*. Why the hell would I *not* be here?"

Evan just smiles at her, surprise faltering into pure joy.

Then the two of them seem to remember Seb, who is just standing there, confused and slightly annoyed, and Evan turns to him.

"Seb," he says, automatically placing his hand at the small of Seb's back. "This is Dana. She's basically my sister."

Dana gives Seb another small wave, like before, smiling.

"Yo," she says, and Seb finally reanimates. He nods.

"Hey," he says. Then he turns to Evan. "I'm gonna need some more back story, here."

Evan laughs and kisses his temple.

"Sure thing," he says, then looks at Dana. "Come on in."

It's not that Seb has never heard of Dana before; Evan has mentioned her every now and then, with obvious fondness written all over his face. But Seb has never really thought about it, and he never really expected to meet her, seeing as how she apparently moved halfway across the country to become a videogame developer at a different college.

He's glad she's here, though. He's always glad to meet people who are important to Evan, and it's nice to see him so happy—and surprised.

"So," Evan says, as they sit in the living room later, the three of them. "How's life? How's Julie?"

Dana sits curled up in an armchair—the one that used to be in Seb's dorm room, before—legs pulled up underneath her, gripping a cup of tea in her hands. Evan isn't much of a tea-drinker, but Seb occasionally is, so their kitchen is pretty well stocked on the stuff.

"It's good," Dana says, nodding. "Julie's good. Got our two-year anniversary coming up. I might have an internship next summer, over at Blizzard."

She cocks her head, looking smug in a way that Seb simply knows to take as nothing but charming and sweet.

"Things are coming up Dana," she says, smiling. "What about you guys?"

Seb is sitting on the couch, next to Evan, legs crossed and folded underneath him, with a cup of tea cradled in his hands. Evan opted for coffee, and he's sitting pretty spread out on the couch, like he tends to do, being generally more boisterous and taking up more room than Seb does.

"Well," Evan says, cocking his head. "There is the whole engaged-thing."

Seb rolls his eyes, taking sip of his tea, and Dana laughs, as she sees it.

"Wow, you guys are adorable," she says, and Seb raises his eyebrows at her.

"What?" he says, honestly confused. "I didn't say anything."

"You didn't have to," Dana says pointedly, and Seb looks back at his tea, taking another sip. "And don't worry, that's a good thing."

She sighs.

"And speaking of," she says. "What are the wedding plans, exactly?"

Seb looks up then and automatically turns to Evan, who looks at him at the exact same time. And they both half-shrug, not mentioning how Sophie has already badgered them about it so much more than necessary.

"Haven't really gotten that far, yet," Evan says, turning back to Dana. "Haven't really thought about it much."

Dana raises her eyebrows.

"You're kidding," she says; it's more of a statement, than a question. "What do you mean, 'haven't thought about it'?"

"I mean," Evan says, sounding exasperated in a big brother kind of way, "that we've got other stuff to do. And we weren't really planning on making a big deal out of it, anyway."

Seb cocks his head in agreement, and Dana nods.

"Right," she says. "I get that. But anything? A date? Place?"

Evan glances at Seb, who just shrugs.

"We were thinking, soon," Seb says, looking over at Dana. "It's not really a money issue, seeing as how it won't be a big deal, as it is. And as for the place..."

He looks at Evan again, who seems to deliberate for a moment.

"How about we get back to you on that?" he says, looking over at Dana, who rolls her eyes.

"Fine," she says. "You're lucky I can spare being away from school for a bit."

"Hey," Evan says, eyebrows raised. "No one asked you to come here."

Dana scoffs incredulously.

"Ouch," she says. "Dick move, sir."

"You know what I mean." Evan doesn't look too anxious to spare her feelings, and she doesn't seem that offended, anyway. "I would have invited you, you know, to the wedding."

"Yeah, I know." Dana runs her finger along her cup's edge. "But I had some time off, and I kind of missed you."

Evan smiles, and Dana smiles back.

"Speaking of which," she says, straightening up and putting her cup down on the coffee table. "We're going out, all of us. Jake, too, I haven't seen him in ages."

"Sounds fair," Evan says, nodding, and Seb nods, as well. He really likes Dana, actually, despite only having met her about an hour ago.

"Great." Dana gets up from the armchair. "I'm gonna hog your bathroom, and then we'll talk."

She makes her way past the couch and out into the hallway, but on the way, she turns around to say something else.

"And I'll be crashing on your couch, by the way," she says, eyebrows raised, as though daring them to stop her. "Just so you know."

Seb glances at the weekend-bag she dumped on the floor on her way in, and he doesn't even feel surprised. He gets the feeling that this spontaneous kind of behavior is kind of typical for Dana, and he finds that he really doesn't mind at all.

Jake is just as thrilled to see Dana, as Evan was. They aren't quite as close as Evan and her, but they're still basically siblings, and when they all go out together, that night, he won't stop badgering her with questions. He asks about her studies, her life, her girlfriend, while Dana playfully brushes him off, in favor of talking to Sophie. They already know each other, but have apparently only met a handful of times, before.

They're at a bar on campus, the one where Evan usually performs, although he isn't on the stage, tonight. He and Seb have just grown really fond of this place, and when it came to choosing somewhere to go out for drinks, this was it.

"Alright, you guys," Sophie says, slamming her palm down on the table. "Seriously. A date. Place. Come on."

Seb groans in frustration, looking up at the ceiling.

"Yeah, no," Evan helpfully adds, shaking his head.

"But guys—"

"Sophie, I swear to god," Evan says, looking at her pointedly. "Just, no."

Jake cocks his head.

"I don't know," he says, fiddling with the label on his beer bottle. "It's kind of important."

Evan glares at his brother, and Jake smiles in a way that lets him know how he's just agreeing with his girlfriend right now to tease Evan.

"Well, don't you have any ideas?" Dana asks diplomatically.

"Not really," Evan says, while Seb hangs back and glares passively around the table.

"Church?" Dana says, and both Evan and Seb shake their heads, responding a little too quickly.

"No," they both say. They haven't really discussed it, but neither of them is too big on institutionalized religion, and feels no need to tie the knot in a church, anyway.

"Outside?" Dana says, her voice taking on a more sarcastic tone. "On a damn beach? Maybe in the woods, surrounded by fairies?"

Jake and Sophie both laugh then, but Seb rolls his eyes.

"Oh, for god's sake," he says, throwing his hands up slightly. "It's no big deal. Shit, we might as well have it here."

He gestures around the bar lamely, expecting murmurs and the occasional, small laugh. But none of that comes, and he narrows his eyes, as he notices everyone at the table frown a little, in thought.

"What?" he asks, and Sophie tilts her head.

"That's not a bad idea," she says, and Seb's eyebrows go right up.

"Wait, what?" he says, honestly a bit confused.

"Yeah," Jake agrees. "Maybe you should."

Seb just gapes at them, before turning to Evan, expecting some support. But instead, he's met with a surprising look of deliberation, Evan's brow furrowed in thought.

"This place is kind of important to you guys, right?" Sophie asks, and Seb looks over at her.

"Yeah," Jake agrees. "I mean, first date, and your big make-up scene. Hell, Evan even sang to you, here."

Seb shifts a little in his seat.

"Well, yeah," he admits. "But—"

"I kind of like it," Evan says, interrupting him, and Seb turns to him.

"Really?" Seb asks, frowning, and Evan half-shrugs.

"Yeah," he says. "I mean, Jake's right. This place does have some meaning. Why not?"

Seb looks at him, a little incredulously.

"It's a bar," he points out, and Evan shrugs again.

"Exactly," he says. "Sounds kind of perfect for us, don't you think?"

Seb thinks about that for a few moments, really thinks about it.

They are all right, he has to admit that; this bar does hold some meaning to both him and Evan, and for their entire relationship, really. But still. Getting married in a *bar*? Is that really how it's going to go down?

Although, he can't help but think. Evan is right. It really does sound pretty perfect for them—nothing big, just small and simple, in a place with meaning, and with no real, big hassle. Just like their rings, it would be like them, all symbolism, more than anything.

Seb leans back in his chair, looks around the large room, tilting his beer bottle a little. It's definitely doable. Maybe they could rent it out for a day, a night? It's unorthodox, to say the least, but the more he thinks about it, the more sense it makes.

"Yeah," he finally says, and he can practically feel the pleased surprise emanating from his fiancé. "I guess so."

He turns to Evan, whose green eyes are suddenly alight, mirroring the smile that's slowly spreading across his face.

"Awesome," he says, and Seb glimpses Jake, Sophie, and Dana, all of them with dopey smiles, as Evan leans in and kisses him.

After some closer consideration, there is simply nothing about this idea that doesn't feel good.

Dana makes good on her promise to crash on their couch; by the time they get back home, it's past two a.m., and everyone left the bar feeling pleasantly tipsy, and not too drunk.

Dana seems to immediately fall asleep, as soon as her head hits the borrowed pillow that has been placed against the armrest of the couch. Evan rolls his eyes a little as he explains to Seb about Dana's apparent knack for falling asleep on command. He describes the talent as *freaky*, but also admits his great jealousy for it.

Seb is exhausted when he and Evan actually get to bed, but at the same time, he's weirdly excited. It's finally happening, after all. Well, at least the plans are. They agreed tonight that they'll go back to the bar and talk to the owner, some other time, about actually having the wedding there.

"Hey," Evan says, as they lie together in bed, his arms wrapped around Seb, who nuzzles against his throat. "Remember when we went to your cousin's wedding?"

Seb hums in confirmation, eyes closed.

"Uh-huh," he says sleepily. It was quite some time ago, now, but he remembers. "What about it?"

"Remember when we got back home," Evan says, "and I asked if you ever wanted to get married? And you freaked out a bit?"

"I did not freak out," Seb says, his tone tired and defensive. "But yeah, I remember. Why?"

"Well," Evan says, a bit hesitantly. "I know I backed off, but... Honestly, I did kind of wanna ask you."

Seb opens his eyes.

"Wait, what?" he asks, raising his head a little, so he can look at Evan, properly. And Evan gives him a small, crooked smile.

"Yeah," he confirms. "I mean, maybe not full-on *propose*, but... Yeah, I asked because, well... I felt like I wanted to marry you, somewhere down the line."

He huffs a small, rueful laugh.

"Your reaction kind of scared me off, though," he says, and Seb thinks about it. That night was months ago. Months ago, before their huge fight and falling-out, and

Evan actually thought about it, even back then. And suddenly, Seb feels almost a bit guilty.

"Wait, I scared you off?" he asks, a little incredulously, and Evan does an awkward, lying-down shrug.

"Kind of," he admits. "But not forever, obviously. Seeing as how I finally grew a pair, and asked."

Seb just looks at him, slightly stunned, before smiling.

"Well, what do you know," he says, moving one hand up to Evan's face, as he gives him a soft kiss. "I could have married you, ages ago."

Evan smiles.

"You could have," he agrees. "But I suppose now is a good a time, as any."

Seb chuckles, and for a few moments, they just lie there, absently touching each other. Until Seb thinks of something else, that is. He hesitates, though, fully aware of the dangerous subject matter.

"You gonna invite your father?" he asks quietly, and he can practically feel Evan tense up. He shifts slightly, looking away, and for a moment, Seb feels a little worried. But there is no need; when Evan speaks, he sounds sad, more than anything.

"I guess," he says. "Probably. I mean, I don't think he'll show up, but... He's my dad. You know?"

He looks back at Seb, his eyes reflecting the sadness of his tone.

"You think he'd do that?" Seb asks carefully. "Miss his son's wedding?"

Evan sighs tiredly.

"Honestly," he says, shaking his head. "I don't even know anymore, man. At this point, I wouldn't really put it past him."

Seb doesn't answer, just watches Evan, silently, until his fiancé takes a deep breath, in a clear attempt at steering the conversation in a different direction.

"But your cousin is definitely invited," he says, and Seb smiles a little.

"Which one?" he asks, and Evan cocks his head.

"Either," he says. "Both. Especially Jim. I liked that dude."

Seb groans a little, but can't help but smile a bit wider.

"I was afraid of that," he says, but his heart isn't really in it. He likes Jim, after all, and he would love to have him at his wedding.

"Your parents can come, too," Evan continues, and Seb's eyebrows go up.

"Gee, really?" he says sarcastically, and Evan nods.

"Yeah," he says. "And Angie, and Mark."

He moves in a little closer then, giving Seb a slow kiss.

"You sure you don't want any pigeons, though?" he asks against Seb's mouth, and Seb groans and pulls away.

"Doves," he corrects, while Evan just laughs. "And no."

Evan pulls Seb in closer, even as he tries to get away from his embrace, and finally, Seb gives in, settling back against Evan's chest.

"Fine," Evan says, still laughing. "As long as I get to marry you, I'm good."

He kisses Seb's hair.

"So, no fucking pigeons. Deal?"

Seb smiles, closing his eyes as he nuzzles back against Evan's throat.

"Deal."

CHAPTER 24

BEGINNING

The weeks seem to practically fly by, after the announcement of Seb's and Evan's engagement. Dana goes back home, promising to return for the actual wedding, and Sophie gets gradually more excited, having to be reined in by Jake at every turn, lest she go completely over the top.

Seb and Evan are still sticking to their original plan; no big event, with only friends and family, at the bar that has come to achieve such sentimental value to them both, as well as for their relationship. The owner was actually thrilled about the whole thing, offering to rent out the place for an entire night, and for a very reasonable price—there will even be a bartender on shift.

The wedding is to be kept simple, and therefore, there isn't that much to plan. What little planning it requires, Sophie takes care of, to her great joy, and as soon as the date is set, they send out invitations; they invite both Dana and her girlfriend, as well Clara, and Matt and Em, along with most of Seb's family. The only people invited on Evan's side, apart from Jake, are his surrogate uncle, Morgan, Morgan's fiancée, Josie, and Evan's father. But Evan still has doubts about Peter actually showing up; even Jake seems hesitant about it.

It isn't long before the day arrives. In the blink of an eye, it seems, it's time, and Seb wakes up in his and Evan's shared bed, knowing that next time he goes to sleep, he will be married. *Married.* To *Evan.*

Yeah, it's all still a bit surreal.

Evan is already up by the time Seb gets out of bed, and Seb finds him standing in the kitchen, staring at the coffee maker. He doesn't look up as Seb makes his way over to him, and only reacts once Seb reaches out and touches his arm, turning those green eyes in his direction.

"Hey," Seb says, and Evan smiles a little, taking his hand.

"Morning," he says, pulling Seb a little closer. "How you feeling?"

Seb groans quietly, but mostly from some weird kind of fatigue, more than anything.

"I'm fine," he says. "A little nervous. You?"

They didn't really want a big wedding, not a priest, or anything. At first, they asked Jake if he would marry them, but he's going to be Evan's best man, just like Mark is going to be Seb's, which prompted Jim to offer up his services, to everyone's honest surprise. No one really saw a problem with it, though, and so he got ordained, so that he could wed Evan and his younger cousin. Seb never would have guessed that Jim would end up playing such a huge, important part in frankly the most important day of his life.

"Yeah," Seb says, a bit dryly. "I just hope he manages to keep his mouth shut and not tell too many sweet childhood stories."

Evan chuckles, but he knows that Seb probably has a point. Jim has always been more of a big brother than a cousin, after all, and he's bound to know all kinds of embarrassing anecdotes from when he and Seb were kids. And honestly, Seb wouldn't put it past him to tell several of them, especially with a room full of people listening.

"I'm sure he'll behave," Evan says, but Seb just grumbles doubtfully, in response, making Evan plant a fond kiss on his forehead. "And the whole ceremony could be a mess, for all I care. That's not what I'm there for, anyway."

And Seb smiles at him, honestly unable to express just how much he sympathizes with that statement.

Seb is very aware of the fact that last time he wore a suit, was at a wedding. At the time, though, he never expected to be attending *his own* wedding anytime soon, wearing a different suit, and feeling so terribly nervous.

Not that he minds being wrong.

Not that much has been done, in ways of decoration. The several, round tables of the bar have been cleared out of the way, to create a small aisle, leading up to the stage. The chairs have been lined up like pews, while Sophie has apparently taken it upon herself to get some flowers to put all over the place. It makes Seb groan a little, but he isn't about to complain, even if he personally wouldn't have done it this way. Because it doesn't matter. Evan is here, and he is here, and that's all that matters.

The sight of it makes Seb feel oddly nervous, though, and he swallows hard. Evan notices, of course, and squeezes his hand.

"Hey," he says, nudging him gently. "You okay?"

Seb hesitates only for a split second.

"Yeah," he says, nodding, glad that he doesn't sound quite as nervous as he feels. He glances at his fiancé. "Just a bit... weird, I guess."

Evan lets out a small chuckle.

"You'll be fine," he says, and as Seb gives him a somehow affectionate glare, Evan leans in and kisses his temple. "I'm gonna go find Jake."

He gives Seb a jokingly stern look.

"Don't run off on me," he says warningly, and Seb scoffs, but can't help but smile.

"I'll try not to," he says, before nodding in Jake's direction, over by the bar. "You, go ahead."

And Evan gives him another small smile, before making his way into the rather large room, toward his brother.

Meanwhile, Seb stands there, watching. Most of the guests have arrived already; he can see Matt and Em over there, talking to Clara. He remembers them all being introduced at his birthday party, ages ago. Dana has joined them, as easily sociable as always, from what Seb can tell, and Jake, Sophie and Angie are talking to Seb's parents. Morgan has made his way over to the bar, Josie joining in a conversation with Seb's mother, while Jim and Mark seem to be discussing something over by the stage, where Seb and Evan will soon be standing, by a makeshift altar.

And suddenly, Seb just feels overwhelmingly nervous.

He makes his way over to the nearest table, where some of the chairs have been left in place, and he sits down, taking a deep breath.

His hands are actually shaking a bit. He doesn't like big social gatherings much, after all, despite having an easier time with it, since he met Evan. He can actually enjoy it, now.

But these people are all here because of him. Well, him and Evan, but they have still come here to focus their attention on him, in some way or other. And this isn't like his birthday party. He kind of thought it would be, in a way, as far as the social aspect is concerned, but this really is completely different.

He's getting married today. *Married.*

"You okay?" Seb looks up at the sound of Dana's voice, and he half-smiles tiredly.

"Yeah," he says. "Just a bit nervous, I guess."

He's aware of how that reply sounds almost identical to the one he gave Evan, earlier, but Dana just smiles.

"It's your wedding day," she says, sounding a bit jokingly melodramatic, which Seb somehow appreciates. "I would expect there to be all kinds of butterflies."

"Butterflies," Seb mutters. "That's a nice way of putting it. I prefer the term anxiety attack."

It's an exaggeration, but he doesn't care.

Dana chuckles, and nudges him gently in the shoulder. She sits down beside him, at the table.

"You'll do fine," she says, sounding confident, and unconsciously mirroring Evan's reply from earlier. "If it helps, I know for a fact that Evan's nervous, too."

Seb raises an eyebrow at her, and she cocks hers, as if to say *true story*. Seb sighs.

"Yeah, well, he would be," he says, looking out across the room. "He's marrying *me*."

Jesus, the words still sound so weird to say out loud.

"And I don't think I've ever seen him happier." Dana sounds completely confident this time, and Seb looks back at her. She looks calm, and sure. And then, she chuckles.

"Although," she says. "I must admit, I didn't really see this coming."

Seb raises his eyebrows.

"What," he says, "him marrying a dude?"

"Oh no," Dana replies, raising her eyebrows, as well. "*That* I saw coming, like *miles* away."

Seb frowns, and Dana gives him a look.

"I've known him for years, Seb," she says, matter-of-factly, and just a little bit smugly. "And my gay-dar is simply excellent."

She frowns, thinking.

"Or... *bi*-dar, in this case?" she tries, squinting, before shuddering at the weird word.

Seb is surprised for only a split second or so, at what Dana says. He was under the impression that Evan has

397

been pretty much the epitome of a typical, straight guy, and therefore, everyone was surprised when he and Seb ended up together. But then again, he supposes that one maybe doesn't simply change sexual preferences, over night, and it makes sense that Dana saw it coming.

"I mean," Dana continues, "I didn't really expect him to actually own up to it anytime soon, at least not like that. He's always had a preference for girls, like me."

She quirks a small smile and cocks her eyebrows at that, before continuing.

"But he's always had a thing for guys, too," she says, her voice taking on a more serious tone. "He never did anything about it, though, ever. He admitted it to me, once. But he was shitfaced, at the time, and I'm not even sure he remembers."

She looks over at where Evan and Jake are talking, and Seb follows her gaze. She looks relieved, as though she has been concerned for a long time, but that she finally doesn't have a reason to be, anymore.

"I think it was mostly because of his dad," she says, sounding slightly subdued. "He's not exactly okay with stuff like that."

Seb nods, painfully reminded of how Evan's father reacted when his son came out to him. And the fact that he isn't here, today. He knows that pains Evan more than he's letting on.

"But then he met you," Dana says, turning back to Seb, a small, genuinely glad smile on her face. "And now, he looks happier than I've ever seen him."

She pauses, and Seb doesn't reply, unsure what to say to that. So Dana saves him the trouble.

"He went against all that, for you," she says, softly, as though aware how weirdly difficult it is for Seb to hear. "He stood up to his dad, for you. He's gone against every preconceived notion of him, for you."

She smiles.

"So yeah," she says. "He loves you. Definitely."

She makes another pause, while Seb takes it in. He feels like he has just gotten her blessing, somehow, even though he knows she has been supporting his and Evan's relationship from day one.

Dana takes a breath.

"What I *didn't* see coming," she says, sounding lighter, "was the actual wedding."

She smiles at Seb's slightly confused look.

"He's never really been the marrying type," she explains. "Or the long-term type. Or any-kind-of-commitment type."

Seb rolls his eyes, a small smile on his face.

"Right, I get it," he says. "I'm a unique snowflake."

Dana laughs.

"That's one way of putting it," she says. "You're definitely something, that's for sure."

She looks out across the room, at all the guests and decorations. Seb takes a deep breath.

"Well," he says. "I guess I couldn't have foreseen this."

Dana turns to him.

"What?" she asks, and Seb cocks his head.

"If you had told me about a year ago," he says, "that today, I would be marrying a dude, in a bar, I probably wouldn't have believed you."

Dana laughs.

"Well, there's a story in there, I guess." She sounds happy, and Seb is glad that the two of them have hit it off so well, from the start.

It's true, though. He *never* would have seen this coming.

They sit there for another minute or so, before Dana's cell phone makes a sound, and she checks it.

"I gotta go," she says. "Gotta pick Julie up at the airport."

Seb nods, and she sighs.

"Relax," she says, putting her hand on Seb's shoulder. "You love him, he loves you, you both wanna be here. It's gonna be awesome."

Seb smiles weakly, and Dana gives him a quick hug, before getting up and leaving the table. Seb watches as she goes over to Evan, probably to let him know she's leaving, before hurrying out the door. Evan looks over at Seb then, smiles, and Seb swears that his insides turn to warm, squishy liquid.

Evan makes his way over to him then, and the squishiness gets even more intense.

"You're not bailing on me, are you?" Evan says jokingly as he reaches him, and Seb looks around shiftily.

"Well, there goes that plan," he says. "I was gonna sneak out, just before the ceremony, but..."

He shrugs, as though his fiancé has ruined everything, and Evan chuckles, as he sits down beside Seb.

Fiancé. Ceremony. Yeah, Seb definitely hasn't quite processed any of that. It's honestly ridiculous how long it is taking for that to sink in.

"You doing okay?" Evan asks, automatically putting his hand at the back of Seb's neck, softly rubbing circles into his skin with his fingers. Seb sighs, but leans into the touch, all the same.

"Why do people keep asking me that?" he says, and Evan smiles, eyes crinkling.

"Because you're a twenty-two year-old guy," he explains, "who doesn't have a full-time job, who's in college, and you're marrying a guy you've been with for little over a year, today."

Seb narrows his eyes, and glares at Evan with such intensity that it straddles the line between funny and scary.

"Oh, that," he says, voice dripping with sarcasm. "I had forgotten about all that."

Evan laughs, leaning in and planting a kiss on Seb's mouth.

"Sorry," he says. "But if it helps, the situation's pretty much the same, over here."

Seb looks at him, and Evan cocks his head slightly.

"I mean," he says, "I'm twenty-four, I work part-time at a pub, I'm studying *music*, of all things, and I'm a mess, with baggage full of daddy-issues and borderline alcoholism."

He smiles. It's a small smile, but a genuine one, and Seb can't help but smile back, scoffing slightly. He takes Evan's hand and looks down.

"Yeah," he says. "We're a great match, aren't we?"

Evan kisses his temple.

"The best."

It's after another half hour or so of mingling and waiting and slight agonizing (at least on Seb's part), that Dana returns, Julie in tow, and Jim goes up to the makeshift altar. He clears his throat loudly, with huge exaggeration, making everyone turn their heads, and Mark raises his eyebrows a little at him.

"Real subtle," he says, and Jim gives him a look that can only be described as pure *sass*.

"Whatever works," he says, and Mark shakes his head, while Jim straightens a little.

"Alright, everyone settle down," he says, and all the guests sit down in their seats, while Seb tries to resist hiding in a corner. "Let's get these guys married."

Jim catches Seb's eye then and does a small, slightly obnoxious beckoning motion with his hand, making Seb glare at him, his nervousness momentarily replaced by annoyance, as he and Evan make their way up to the altar. By the time they get there and position themselves on either side of Jim, in front of him, Seb finds that nervousness seeping back again. Then he looks at Evan, though, standing in front of him, and any doubt or ounce of hesitation he has, completely melts away.

The ceremony isn't long. Honestly, Seb is only vaguely aware of most of it; he's too busy staring at Evan's face, just marveling at it, marveling at *him*. At some point, Jim says something funny, making everyone laugh, and Seb smiles a little, too. And Mark and Jake hand Seb and Evan the rings, which are slipped on with just slightly shaky fingers, and Seb swears Evan almost cries a little. And that would have been so typically him, of course. Seb, on the other hand, has a lump in his throat that's honestly threatening to turn him into a bawling mess, if he lets it, and he firmly keeps it down; he isn't about to cry in front of a room full of people.

They doesn't say any vows; they both figure that's private, anyway, and none of it needs to be said in front of an audience. Instead, Seb just feels his heart stutter, as Evan says *I do*, and he himself somehow manages to get the same words out, even though his pulse is racing, at that point.

And when Jim finally says they can kiss, Seb can't imagine anything better, anything sweeter, than feeling Evan's lips against his own, as he pulls him closer and feels those warm, calloused hands cradle his face. It's just all kinds of perfect, and when they break apart, it's to the sound of cheers and applause, and although it makes Seb feel a little awkward, to say the least, he's too happy to care, at the moment, anyway.

The night proceeds with music and drinking and what might pass for dancing if you look hard enough, and Jim turns out to be a pretty good entertainer, being the center of attention, while everyone gets gradually more drunk. He does share a few embarrassing childhood stories, but it isn't that bad, and Seb doesn't mind.

As the night wears on, and some of the spotlight is taken off the newlyweds, Seb and Evan make their way outside, where it's considerably more quiet, although the laughter and music from inside the bar can be heard through the ajar door. Evan takes Seb's hand, and Seb looks up at him, Evan's brow slightly furrowed, as he eyes their interlaced hands.

"I feel like I wanna call you something different, now," he says. "Just don't know what. I mean, we're both keeping our last names, so it kind of takes the flavor out of it."

"Well," Seb says, kind of agreeing; they decided that taking the other's name doesn't matter, so there will be no change, there. But still. "I *am* your husband now, though."

He says it pointedly, feeling a small thrill at the word, and Evan looks up at him, with a small smile.

"Yeah, you are," he says. "Aren't you?"

As though this fact is starting to sink in properly then, Evan's expression grows gradually happier, until he looks positively thrilled. He leans in and kisses Seb, slowly, warmly, but with unparalleled enthusiasm.

"You're my husband," he says against his lips, and Seb can't help but smile.

"Yeah, I think we've established that."

"You're mine, now," Evan continues, kissing him again, and Seb kisses him back.

"I've always been yours," he points out, and Evan chuckles.

"Yeah, but it's forever now," he says. "And I'm yours."

He kisses him, the touch oddly chaste, but excited.

"Forever."

And Seb squeezes his hand, hearing the sounds of his friends and family celebrating inside, while the warm evening air sends a pleasant shiver across his skin, as Evan's fingers gently brush against his jaw.

"Yeah," he says, smiling. "I like the sound of that."

Printed in Great Britain
by Amazon.co.uk, Ltd.,
Marston Gate.